A Basket
of
Devils

A Basket of Devils

of

Elves Unwelcome Book 1

J.C. hartcarver

Dorwik Publishing

A Basket of Devils

Copyright 2023 Jesslyn Carver

This is a work of fiction. Names, characters, businesses, places, events, locales, and incidents are either the products of the author's imagination or used in a fictitious manner. Any resemblance to actual persons, living or dead, or actual events is purely coincidental.

This book was written by a human.

Cover art "Arson the Runt" oil on wood panel, and all interior illustrations by Jesslyn Carver. Back cover images are digital works by Jesslyn Carver.

Fan mail can be sent to J.C. Hartcarver via the "contact" page on her website: www.jchartcarver.com.

Publisher's Cataloging-in-Publication data

Names: Hartcarver, J. C., author.
Title: A basket of devils / J.C. Hartcarver.
Series: Elves Unwelcome
Description: Greenbrier, TN: Dorwik Publishing, 2023.
Identifiers: LCCN: 2023918514 | ISBN: 979-8-9874210-5-5 (hardcover) | 979-8-9874210-3-1 (paperback) | 979-8-9874210-4-8 (ebook)
Subjects: LCSH Elves--Fiction. | Assassins--Fiction. | Orphans--Fiction. | Magic--Fiction. | Fantasy fiction. | Love stories. | Adventure fiction. | BISAC FICTION / Fantasy / Romantic | FICTION / Fantasy / Epic | FICTION / Fantasy / Action & Adventure
Classification: LCC PS3608.A787155 B37 2023 | DDC 813.6--dc23

Dorwik Publishing
Greenbrier, TN

Table of Contents

More titles from J.C. hartcarver!

The Sufferborn series:

Sufferborn
Unwilling Deity
Flesh Embodied

A Basket of Devils

Prologue

That sound. What could that high-pitched squalling sound be? It pierced Haus's ears and pinched his heart from over the rolling waves. Haus squinted and strained to hear the bizarre multipart harmony. Haunting. Disturbing.

"There, my lord!"

Haus nearly missed it. A speck rode the waves up and down in the distance. What was that blasted sound? He had to know!

But they were all exhausted after a secret deal with House Perkins went sour this morning. The bastards had thought they could rob Haus on the spot and get away with it. They fought hard and managed to escape with their lives, commandeering a pinnace, which happened to be tied to a lonely dock down a rough trail below the bluff on which the fight had broken out. Even on the water, they weren't safe. The crossbow bolts rained before they could row out of range. One had hit Warren in the hip!

And now the strangest thing was happening…

"Row, you fools!"

His men obeyed. They had been lost out there for hours, trying to find the shore again, when those horrid clouds rumbled in over the horizon to threaten their peace at sea. Warren lay helplessly curled at the stern, holding pressure to his wound. He shouldn't die, but his loss of blood kept him weak and useless. A handful of the other injured were still able to row.

"My lord, we should row away from the storm!"

"Did you not hear me? Go toward the noise or get off the boat!"

The object popped into view again, between the distant swell of waves constantly dipping and rising along the surface. Some sort of raft it was.

"Retrieve that vessel or die!"

The men rowed to exhaustion, fighting against the ferocious waves and wind augmented with stinging raindrops. Muscles popped on their backs and shoulders. Their hair quickly dampened down to their skin with the introduction of the heavy ocean spray. They all began to moan and swear.

Haus dropped to his knees and hugged the boat's only mast. The ominous wailing grew in volume, and he locked his determination on that floating vessel.

Once in its vicinity, he ordered Jiminick and Gilqured to throw out the stolen boat's available fishing net to snag it—a raft packed tightly with a crate roped down to it. That sound. Like crying, but...

The men used the net to tie the raft to the side of their boat, cut the ropes around its cargo, and hauled the bundle over on deck.

"Careful now!" Haus snapped. "Could be breakable valuables."

Jiminick, the youngest on board, struggled under the wind and rain and swaying motions of the boat. He pried the crate open, peeked under the lid, and then peered up with his mouth hanging open.

"What is it?"

"Babies, my lord," Jiminick said.

Against the raucous wind, Haus crawled the short distance over the deck to the boy and their find. The crate was packed thickly with straw with a lidded basket nested inside. Jiminick lifted the lid slightly so Haus could spy four bundled infants, now silent and asleep. Why had they stopped crying?

"Cover them back up. Hurry," Haus ordered. "No need to let the little things get rained on." The rest of the men rowed laboriously away from the storm, toward the glow of sunlight on the horizon.

Eventually the rain stopped and the waves calmed. Haus ignored his own hunger and longing for dry land in favor of his interest in the babies they had so curiously found way out here—on the ocean of all places. For the moment, he forgot they were lost. "Open it again," he said. "Show me."

Jiminick opened the lid wider this time. Four babies, indeed. Haus's bushy eyebrows rose in bewilderment.

"My lord, they look all similar, like twins…but four of'em," Jiminick said.

"*Four* twins?" Gilqured said, holding the helm and leaning far over to peer into the crate. Even injured Warren stretched his neck to see the oddity.

"They're called quadruplets when four of'em look alike," Haus told them.

Jiminick shook his head. "These babies are strange, my lord. Let's throw them into the water."

Haus leaned over the crate in study of them. They were all alive and quiet now, but they had sounded so odd before. If they were still alive, they couldn't have been floating out there long. Any normal baby wouldn't last.

"Don't throw 'em overboard; we may need to eat 'em if we stay lost," Gilqured said. "Those blasted brutes from House Perkins may have run us clean off the land for now, but the Great Sea made sure we'd have something to eat."

"Shouldn't do that," Haus said. "These aren't human babies…" A murmur swept through their company at his words. "They are *devils*." Grinning fiercely with all the anger and frustration of the skirmish he'd survived today, Haus raised an infant up and removed its stained swaddling. It was a boy with his umbilical cord fragment nearly ready to fall off. "See here. Long, pointed ears. They are devils, and they are *my* devils. My sons."

"Sir?" Jiminick said, staring at the naked creature small enough to fit into Haus's two cradled hands.

"You heard me! They're my sons… I can't make children otherwise."

"But what about Tobas?" Gilqured asked.

Haus snorted. "That little snot? The only child to come out of one of my hundred concubines? His whore mother deceived me. You know Tobas isn't mine, but these devils are." His eyes burned into the tiny creature sleeping in his grasp with its little round head resting atop his knuckles. He snapped out a joyful shout. "Row harder, boys!" He gingerly returned the first devil to the basket and proceeded to check on the other three. All boys, perfectly alike and the same number of days old by the look of all their umbilical cords.

Jiminick sat on the deck, eyeing the baby Haus cuddled to his whiskery face. "I guess we'll need to set up a nursery in the manor and find a wet nurse fast, my lord."

Haus popped his head up. "We're doin' more than that, boy." He turned to survey the long stretch of land growing larger on the horizon. "We're gonna remodel the whole place." That earned him a few extra eyes. Haus put his other hand in the basket to share love with the three babies who weren't on his lap. "I want a new system of underground apartments. Complete with a kitchen and a breakfast room—and a veranda overlooking the sea! And I want a special training room."

Jiminick mouthed the words *special training room* as he kept up with what Haus said.

"That's right. An underground one. And a new trainer."

"What kind of trainer?"

Haus smirked. "The best fighter in the Darklands. I want him found. He'll train my sons to be killers."

Haus's men went silent, including the rowers' grunting.

"Assassins!" The word emerged from Haus's mouth as a passionate hiss. "You think House Perkins's dogs were frightening today? Wait till I unleash my *devils*. My devil sons will protect me and destroy my enemies. They'll cut them down so far I'll be the most feared man in Kell's Key—maybe the whole of the Darklands!" Haus cooed at the babies again and put down the one he was holding in exchange for another. The little thing mewled as if in annoyance. Haus barked out a laugh after glimpsing its unusually bright green eyes before they closed sleepily again.

"Look at 'im," Haus said. "I'll bet this one came out of his mother first. He's a hellion, this one! He probably knocked his brothers on the head to be the first to see the world. The deadliest devil. Quick and cunning. This one's name is Poison."

Haus's men all shared looks with each other, staying silent.

He put Poison down and picked up the next baby, the one he had held prior to Poison. "Bleed."

"He's bleeding?" Gilqured asked, pausing with his oar.

"Keep rowing, you idiot! No, he's not bleeding. His name is Bleed."

The men murmured the name around to each other.

"I know it's an odd name, but he'll live up to it. I'll make sure." He exchanged Bleed for the next baby. "Bludgeon!" he declared. "I can't wait to see this one's skill. He'd be fun to watch, yes indeed. Maybe he'll carry out private executions of my worst enemies for my entertainment." Haus chuckled and picked up the last baby. "Hmm…"

"What's this one's name, my lord?" Jiminick asked.

"Hold on, hold on. I'm thinking. This one's lighter than the others. I'll bet he's the runt. But it won't matter because he's as coldhearted and bloodthirsty as the rest of them. This one I'll name Arson."

"Arson?"

"The fire starter. That's my Arson."

One of the younger oarsmen piped up. "My lord, my aunt would make an excellent nanny! And her daughter is currently nursing a new babe. I can fetch them both as soon as we hit dirt."

"No!"

The oarsman snapped his lips shut.

"Well, you can bring the wet nurse but no other women!"

"But don't you think the…devils will need a motherly figure around?"

"They need a full tit until they're old enough to chew meat and nothing else. No women. They'll have a trainer, and that'll be enough." He followed up under his breath, "Can't trust a damned woman anyway."

"No women," Gilqured murmured behind the helm in echo.

"None. I can't have my expertly trained assassins getting all soft over pretty faces and shapely bodies. No mothers. No women. No coddling." Haus spoke with a firm lip. "They'll be taught discipline from the moment they can walk and then on to weapons and agility and empty-handed fighting. They won't be seen by anyone but me after the nursing years. They'll keep to their special apartment complex under the manor. They'll get all their praise and warm love from me but not enough to overshadow their creed of respect, obedience, and loyalty. Other than me, they'll have the influence of their trainer."

"Land, sir!" one of the men shouted and pointed.

A dark line stretched across the horizon. Haus smiled. "Indeed. It was the luck of the devils that brought the land to us."

"So." Jiminick swallowed. "You really intend to…raise them as…"

"Devils," Haus finished for him. "I'll say that word once and I'll say it again. My sons will know who they are. No one will ever cross me again."

Chapter 1

Arson

Twenty-three years later...

Arson tiptoed through the corridor of Elkleon Manor, which belonged to one of the wealthier lords in Kell's Key. Too wealthy, his father had said. Getting too big for his pants and earning too many friends. Not to mention he was late in paying his loan and he'd been talking foul things of House LinGor at the governor's ball last night. Though Father sometimes dispensed these kinds of details, Arson and his brothers never questioned a mission. Father's word was law, and it was the devils' sole purpose to carry out the mission.

Arson's soft leather shoes were perfectly silent. He kept his face covered and his hair bound tightly in a plait. His fitted clothing, reinforced with leather plates, had also been worked into an efficient, silent form. All four brothers looked perfectly alike in these black uniforms. They could sneak past anyone still awake at this hour and subdue those who got in the way by sticking them in their necks with sleeping serum. Those who got the serum would awaken in the morning, totally oblivious to what had happened and who had done it.

Haus had ordered a special death for Lord Elkleon, hours of pain, so Poison carried a deadlier serum. Bleed currently searched for the vault, and Bludgeon kept watch at the other side of the manor.

Arson continued along, often having to duck his head under

the shorter doorframes of the servants' wing, and jumped when an unaccounted-for girl stepped around the corner.

Her eyes bulged brightly in the moonlight from the window. So did his. How had he not heard her footsteps? Before she could scream, he lunged forward, snapping his arm. At the end of his gloved finger, a thin, protruding needle coated with the sleeping potion pricked the artery in her neck.

She had seen him. That was a problem. It should look like their master had died accidentally, in his bed, and though all the residents were supposed to chalk it up to either a terrible misfortune or the curse that tended to fall upon those who crossed Haus LinGor. This girl could tell the tale tomorrow about a shadow man in the corridor, and it would be too much insight as to what might be causing the mysterious "curse."

He had to kill her and make it look like some form of accident or suicide, perhaps by throwing her body down the well in the rear courtyard. He reached for her neck to suppress the blood flow to the brain and paused at the look on her face. Though he had scared her, a peaceful expression graced her sleeping face. She was full grown, possibly fourteen or so, but still so small in stature. The pose she had fallen into interested him too, twisted like an S shape with knees crooked and one hand up by her face. Arson removed a glove and flipped his soft leather mask up to catch his breath. He knelt beside her and looked some more. They were on a tight schedule and were supposed to leave this house as quickly as possible but...

Her dark brown hair, spread across the floor, curled about in interesting, flowing shapes. He took a deep breath, extending his study. He'd seen and killed plenty of women before but had never taken such a good long look at them. At home, the devils weren't allowed to talk to Haus's servant girls. He'd spy them through the eyeholes of his mask but couldn't make eye contact or any other fleeting type of communication.

"Arson!" hissed the frantic voice of Bludgeon. He approached while rewinding his tiny hand crossbow. "What are you doing? Put your mask back on!"

In one quick motion, Arson did so and sprang back to a ready standing position. "What is it?"

"The Elkleon knights are coming home from the look of the line of torches marching through the city. Time to go." Arson glanced down at the girl and then back to Bludgeon. As skilled as they were, the Elkleon knights were too much to handle right now. They had to finish off the lord and flee before the knights arrived, but this girl would remember what she had seen...

Arson left her and hurried down the corridor behind Bludgeon. A garderobe door slammed open, startling both of them. He caught Bludgeon's quick glare beside him. He'd get all sorts of chastisement from his brothers tonight, and they'd get most of his dinner to keep them from telling Father about his sloppiness. He pressed against the wall, Bludgeon aligned beside him. Lord Elkleon himself stepped out of the garderobe—their target. Where was Poison?

No need to worry whether the lord of the manor would see them in his sleepy daze. They stalked him on his bumbling way back to his chamber, keeping coordinated steps with each other.

Poison came around the adjacent corner just as the lord approached his chamber door. One long-legged step placed Poison in the spot where he extended his hand, to which was strapped a severed snake head. Its fangs, dipped in the killing serum, extended as his hand did. He slapped the snakehead across the back of the man's neck. His expert precision buried the fangs right where they needed to go. The mixture immediately put Lord Elkleon out of his wits and would kill him eventually. Poison caught him as he fell and dragged him into the chamber to place him in his bed. For the sake of evidence, Bludgeon opened a drawstring bag he carried on his belt and dumped a live snake onto the bed with the dying man. The death adder was common to the area, but Poison's serum had less remorse for its victims than the cold-blooded creature. The three nodded to each other and then darted for the prearranged escape route.

Bleed met them in the corridor, toting what had to be a hundred pounds of baggage draped over his shoulders and to his belt—gold from the vault. Father had told them to take exactly what Lord Elkleon owed him, no more, no less. This cloud of confusion they'd created for the household, with the lord's death and exactly the right amount of money gone, would make it seem like some supernatural force had come to put them all in line. The devils of House LinGor were more than assassins; they were a godlike wind of punishment.

They hurried along, and once back in the dark corridor, Arson spotted the sleeping girl again. His throat tightened up.

A slap on his shoulder jerked him alert. "Hurry, fool," Poison said.

The sound of voices echoed closely outside. The knights would soon enter through the kitchen. The four brothers would have to exit through a second-story window and traverse the rooftops to make their way to the ground.

Arson left the girl lying there again as Poison pulled him toward the chamber with the window of choice. An old woman sat snoozing in the chair by her bed, a sewing project lay across her lap, and her lamp's flame flickered on. The brothers had deemed she didn't need the sleeping serum when they first climbed in there.

Arson lurched for the lamp, sprinted back to the corridor, and slammed it against the floor next to the girl who had seen him. The flames instantly caught her dress.

The eyes of his brothers were all staring at him coldly when he turned back around.

"I'll explain later; let's hurry," Arson said, and they piled out the window to the cool night air.

"A fire?" Haus said and followed up with a roaring laugh. "A fire, my sons, you know my heart, bless every ugly one of you, you bastards, a fire!" They stood in a line stiffly, as they had been trained to do since they could stand, and he wrapped his meaty arms around each of them in turn. His head could only reach the height of their sternums. His affection brought Arson a world of relief after he had sweat the whole way home, hoping his father wouldn't see the stunt as sloppy.

"Let's hope a lot of the Elkleon knights died putting it out, eh?" Haus couldn't wipe the grin off his pocked old face; he put his hands behind him and paced back and forth. "A manor in chaos, a dead Lord Elkleon—bit by a snake—a careless girl with an oil lamp. It's as big a confused mess as I would hope for the Elkleons." He sighed in delight. "This is what I've meant for you devils. The way you can get in, stir the place up and then get out—with my money—without being seen and leaving dread and fear behind you. The LinGor Hex. That's what I'd like to call it. We'll spread those words as whispered rumors throughout the Banishtere Marketplace."

Haus spread his proud eyes across all four of them. "And to think, you were only sixteen when you completed your first big mission of eradicating the Perkins. I must say, I believed in you, but when it finally happened…what a magical night—and the beginning of my power and fortune! And we're not done yet, boys. We've only just begun."

His eyes sparkled over his smile as he gave them a nod. "As usual after a mission: the pleasure box—you can all use it tonight; you've earned it."

That made Arson and his brothers smile and make eye contact with each other.

"And tomorrow—boy, I won't be able to sleep—by tomorrow I'll have all the money counted up and hear the sweet news of the devastating accident of House Elkleon." He roared another laugh.

Arson, Bludgeon, and Bleed lounged on the big, fluffy cushions in the secret lounge of the manor's basement, eating cakes and fruit and conversing softly. In the open nook to the side, Poison stood before the pleasure box, chin lifted high, eyes closed as he enjoyed his fellatio, performed by an unknown servant within the box. He tended to make a lot of humming or groaning noises that were hard to tune out, but Arson and the others were used to it.

"Better than last time," he said loud and shamelessly, brushing a hand along the box's green silken covering after he finished. "Who's in there?" He stepped away and fastened his codpiece closed but kept his attention on the box, which delivered no answer to his question. Arson bit three grapes off the stem and watched his antics. The little sliding window snapped shut when he withdrew from it, as always.

Typical Poison behavior to cause such tension in this place. Bludgeon and Bleed carried on, both reaching for a date from the pile on the table of delicacies. They were never allowed alcohol, not even in this special room, because they were expected to remain ever alert. This particular apartment was their reward for every job well done though. In here, they could relax and drop their stern, disciplined demeanors for a few hours. At the end of the night, they would return to sleep within the foyer leading into their father's bedchamber, to protect him as he slept.

Poison banged a fist on top of the pleasure box. "Who is it? Answer me!"

"You know they're not supposed to talk to you, Poison," Bludgeon said over his shoulder, having already enjoyed his turn.

Poison ignored him and persisted. "Are you young or old? Is it Gert the maid? Or Ingel the washing girl?" His eyes brightened as the idea sparked, and he pressed his ear to the box to wait for an answer. The household staff weren't allowed to see the devils, but it didn't stop them from spying on the women in their chores now and again. He forced the window open, but it didn't matter: after the last time he became curious about who hid inside, they started covering themselves with a blanket to avoid his prying eyes. "Answer me now!" he shouted straight into the slot.

"Poison!"

"If you're a man, I'll kill you!" He began to rattle the box, and its wooden frame swayed and creaked.

"I'm a woman, sir!" a frantic, muffled voice replied from within, and he calmed himself with a deep breath.

"Then which one are you?" He forced the lid open, dragged the swaddled figure out, and tore the linen shroud off her head. He paused and gawked. "Nanelle, the servant who puts extra blackberries in our muffins every Sunday morning." A cautious smile lifted Poison's expression. She trembled in terror at his feet.

Arson sucked in a breath. Poison had done it now! No one in the manor was allowed to see the devils' faces unmasked. Arson and the other two all stood up at once. What did this mean? The devils also weren't allowed to see who performed fellatio on them either. Their father would say, "The pleasure box is just a tool. Who cares what mouth is waiting on the inside?"

Poison obviously cared. He closed his own gaping mouth, eyes unblinking. "What else can you do?" He grabbed her arm and she squirmed and resisted, which seemed to make him more excited. Before he became too violent, Arson signaled the others not to bother moving and stepped forward. Father didn't need to find out about this incident. They'd simply send her on her way.

Arson whipped out his dagger and put it across Poison's throat.

"Your foolishness is going to get us in trouble," he growled.

Frozen in his manhandling of the girl, Poison shot him a hot glare; his face red in his excitement.

"Besides, it's my turn," Arson added. She could go on her way but not before finishing her duty here. Smirking at Arson, Poison opened his hand to release Nanelle's wrist, and she dropped back down to her knees. Arson snatched it back up and pulled her to stand. She yelped, and he ignored her discomfort as he led her toward an adjoining room rather than back into the box. Poison didn't stop him, which relieved Arson of having to engage in yet another argument about whose turn it was or if Poison could get away with using the box twice. By their father's rule, they only got one use each.

"He always hated being watched," Bludgeon murmured behind him before he closed the door.

In the new dark space, Nanelle laid her hands on Arson's waist. "My lord."

A fiery sensation shot through him. He snatched her hands. "What are you doing?"

"Thank you," she said. "Um—"

"So," he said simultaneously. He would've followed up with the order to do what she always did, but he paused at her sound. "What?"

"Do you like the extra berries? I make sure to…anytime I'm the one preparing your breakfast."

Arson scrunched his nose. "Are you going to do it?"

"My lord?"

"What?"

"Um…" He couldn't see much in the dark, but he imagined she twiddled her fingers. By the angle of her vocal vibrations, she pointed her face downward. "I know how you like my mouth, my lord, but would you…?"

Arson's heart pounded for some reason. He genuinely couldn't guess what she was trying to say. He waited, wholly interested in this situation.

"I can always tell it's you, particularly when I'm in the pleasure box."

"What's that supposed to mean?"

"Well, I…"

He had no idea what this was about, but the longer the conversation continued, the harder his cock grew. Something deliciously wicked presented itself, something he knew he wasn't allowed to feel. Father would be furious if he found out Nanelle had come out of the pleasure box, so he certainly couldn't find out that Arson had been speaking to the woman like this. They weren't allowed to speak to anyone in the manor beyond Father and their trainer. He had never wondered why.

She fought through her stuttering to say, "I don't know any of your names, and I'm not allowed to know. From being in the pleasure box though, I can tell you all apart, and I know *you*, my lord, in some bizarre way."

He jumped at the light touch of her hand to his. A warm contact. It soothed—not a sensation he was used to. They were raised on hardness and discipline. Haus had forbidden this kind of friendly contact. The devils of House LinGor were supposed to be mysterious and terrifying. No one could touch them or even talk to them. Their father or trainer talked for them. Yet out of total fascination and overwhelming lust, he allowed her to take his hand and graze it down her body from her lips to her skirt. His fingertips strummed the strings crisscrossing down her bodice.

"You're my favorite, you see. While we're in here, why not…" He could hardly hear her voice over his pounding heart. "Since we're in private…" She placed his hand on her skirt, about where her crotch should be. "You might like to try my pussy instead."

He shook so violently and so notably that he had to take his hand away. He couldn't let her know of his weakness. He didn't exactly know what a "pussy" was if not a cat, but whatever she meant, it was probably forbidden. He and his brothers had earned the pleasure box ever since they were sixteen, well old enough to enjoy fellatio and also skilled enough to accomplish missions. Fellatio through the pleasure box was all he knew when it came to the matter of his lower body. Father had explained to them how the cock needed to be upkept, and fellatio could only be enjoyed after a mission. He had no idea what kind of trouble he'd face if he let this servant have her way with him.

Father had some pretty harsh punishments for the devils when they were naughty. When they were ten, Bludgeon had to stand in the training hall with his outstretched arms holding up weights all day after sneaking into the kitchen to get cookies off the counter for all of them. Poison, always looking to skirt the rules or snatch some kind of luxury they weren't allowed to have, had talked him into it, but Bludgeon got caught. Throughout that day, anytime his arms drooped or he dropped a weight, he took a beating. The devils had grown up with this sort of disciplinary treatment. They were used to it, and it had shaped them into the fierce and strong men they were today.

Through the door behind him, his brothers argued. They were trying to repair the damage Poison had done to the pleasure box so Father would never know.

Terrified of Father's wrath and also of this shaken new feeling, Arson reached out and took Nanelle by her hair. "Do your job," he growled and then pushed on her head to make her kneel. He couldn't disobey Father any more than what had already been done.

Chapter 2

house LinGor

Bludgeon nudged Arson awake, sitting straight up at the end of their four-man formation, the way they guarded their father's apartments. Poison, at the opposite end of the line, usually woke up first, elbowed Bleed, Bleed elbowed Bludgeon, and then Arson woke up. All looked well. The servants stood before them, waiting to bring in Haus's lavish breakfast spread but not until the four masked devils rose and moved on with their routine.

The devils enjoyed their own meal in a spotless nook with gilded frames around paintings of animals being slaughtered by proud hunters and big windows with heavy drapes pulled back to allow in the soft glow of the morning sun. Outside the windows, the blue ocean spread wide across the scene and into eternity. Every day they were reminded of their origin: four infants from another world, bestowed as a blessing upon Haus by the Great Sea.

Haus, their beloved father, had started out with a mere glassblowing shop, but through seedy dealings and sneaky wiles, he'd grown a fortune and wormed his way into the lofty network of powerful houses that controlled Kell's Key. He upheld a certain honorable appearance on the outside of his dealings. On the inside, he got his real work done, lending money and destroying enemies as favors to his friends. Haus himself was the devil of their society, feared by all and protected with love and devotion by his otherworldly quadruplets.

Arson could hardly note the beautiful blue scene outside, though, or the tasty meal on the table. His three brothers sat silently, hidden under their deep hoods, which they all wore to breakfast. They couldn't let the staff see their faces. The wide hoods allowed them to eat unburdened. Rather than keep his eyes low, however, Arson couldn't resist peeking up anytime a pair of footsteps entered the room—someone to add a last-minute pitcher or bowl of jam to their table. Nanelle hadn't shown up today. No telling if anyone found out what happened in the rewards room last night.

With the table complete, the last servant scurried out and Arson's three brothers commenced murmuring to each other, snickering and recollecting.

"Arson." The deep voice of Poison hit, and Arson popped his head up from his fish pastry and his orange juice. Poison had pushed his hood back so his entire face and front of his loose hair could be seen inside his hood. "What did you do with her last night?" His green eyes flashed inside the shadow of his hood. His teeth seemed to glow with them in his wide smile.

Arson pushed his own hood back a bit and shrugged. "Same as you'd expect. Did you fix the box?"

"Poison had only loosened some nails," Bleed said with a mouth full of bread and jam. "We hammered them back in with a boot."

Arson sighed. Hopefully Nanelle hadn't gotten in trouble. He had awakened thinking of her and wondering why he had refused her offer of some other, different kind of intercourse. Father's punishment was frightening, and Arson couldn't stand the idea of disappointing him, but was he missing out on something worthwhile by obeying him?

Poison laughed in that low hiss of his. "If only it had been my turn, I can't even tell you… Did she say anything to you in there?"

All the confusion of last night's feelings flared up with the introduction of sweat at both of Arson's sides. "No," he lied. "I just told her to do her job." He had to wonder what Poison would've done if in Arson's place. Obviously he would've been up to the adventurous temptation the woman had offered. Had Arson made a mistake by denying himself such an adventure?

Poison shook his head, beaming his mischievous mirth. He acted as if he'd say something, but the look on his face dropped to blank and he pulled his hood forward in a snap. The rest of them followed his action, and the door swung open.

Arson's heart pounded. His brothers continued to take small bites under the cover of their hoods, but Arson could only make dry swallows of nothing. He didn't dare peek at who had entered.

A platter landed on the table with a light tap of porcelain against wood. Muffins were stacked as a pyramid on it—muffins with many dark purple clusters.

"I…" A female voice.

You're my favorite, you see, he remembered that exact voice saying to him.

"I made sure to wake up in time to make these. I know you like them." Hurried footsteps tapped away, and the door closed again.

Poison threw his hood off and reached to grab the blackberry-riddled muffin at the top of the pile. "I think we all like her muffins," he said with a grin.

When outside their apartments, the brothers wore special clothes, richly decorated with gold and silver threads, and birdlike demon masks encrusted with colored jewels so no one could mistake Haus LinGor's devil sons—not that they would have. The masks' different colors helped Haus tell the brothers apart: Poison wore red, Bludgeon wore dark green, Bleed was orange, and Arson blue. Their masks were sculpted expertly in wood and clay with cloisonné finishing; and the jewels embedded corresponded to the painted base colors with the addition of black onyx. Ivory made up the lighter parts of the individual characters' features.

In this garb, the quadruplets stood beside their father on his self-appointed throne while he listened to requests from certain privileged individuals bearing invitations. Though today Poison had dressed in another type of assassin's uniform; it was red with a mask made of iron-enforced wood; not so many jewels decorated this one. The demonic character's mouth gaped open with the tongue rolling out as if dying of strangulation, but the piece was beautifully crafted. His red pants were more casually fitted than the tight black uniform they wore last night; they hung off the hips and thighs loosely but were bound tightly around his calves and topped with boots and armored knee guards. Poison stood proud and tall as they were trained to do, but Arson could feel his aura of beaming pride more than usual. He'd always envied Poison's unwavering confidence.

Arson harbored whirling thoughts today, which he couldn't seem to suppress. Nanelle mostly, but there were also flashes of that girl he'd set on fire last night. Her big-eyed stare laced into and confused his memories of Nanelle attempting to make some kind of intimate advance he didn't understand. Despite his burden, he dared not tell anyone those things in an attempt to unload the turbulent thoughts.

Arson put his worries aside when Haus's other son strode up the red carpet toward the throne. Tobas. This man, Haus considered to be his fake son. Though Tobas stood a bit taller, he did possess a similar wide nose and broad brow, quite like Haus's features. He was a young boy when Haus tossed his favor for Tobas aside and replaced it with the four devils. Now Tobas must be about thirty-four years old, but he looked more like forty-four with his tired dark eyes and stringy, oily hair. His clothes were dingy too, as Arson knew Haus made him run petty errands around the city, breaking people's fingers when they didn't pay Haus the money they owed or at best dropping off the weekly supply of banalweed to be sold illegally through Haus's glassblowing shop. Apparently banalweed, banal as in ordinary and boring, was just a nickname for the narcotic, as if it could fool the city guard.

"Father," Tobas said. "My mother sends you a letter from the dungeon. She's sick; please have mercy." He knelt and held forth an envelope in both hands.

Twenty-three years ago, Haus had decided Tobas's mother had betrayed him but held no evidence for the case. Today he didn't even keep concubines around. Only the occasional prostitute was invited into Haus's chambers every few nights. Arson and his brothers had often wondered what went on behind that door they guarded and why he didn't have a wife like other men about the city they had seen. When they'd ask him, he'd bark an expletive and say, "Can't trust a woman, boys! The pleasure box gets it all done for ya!"

Haus remained unimpressed at Tobas's display today. He waved his hand, and his secretary stepped forward to take the letter and pocket it. When Tobas raised his head, there were tears running down his cheeks. Didn't he know tears were a sign of weakness? Haus had told the devils such things from birth. No wonder Tobas couldn't seem to keep up with their excellence.

"Father," Tobas began again, "I still love you and would do anything to remain with you, but since you took in those…those *monsters* of yours, it seems I can do nothing right. I've carried out every job you've ordered me and will do so again. Please, Father, send some medicine to my mother. I don't ask for inheritance, only that you allow my mother to live." He lowered his head again and struggled through some more pathetic weeping.

Arson and the other devil sons didn't flinch or make a sound, regardless of what Tobas said about them. They knew words were useless as weapons anyway. Tobas obviously didn't know how to impress Haus LinGor.

Haus cleared his throat and sat forward on his gaudy throne. "Tobas, you're a good tenant, and you were just eleven when I found my real sons, a babe, and nothing here is your fault, but your mother betrayed me by sleeping with another man to conceive you. And though she's in prison, I'm doing her quite a kindness by keeping you here and letting you be my subject."

"But you're my f-father."

"I *was* your father, boy, before I woke up. Now get back to your work."

Tobas didn't argue.

A messenger wearing the badge of Lady Lexion stood next in line, a closer ally to the LinGors than many. "Come to hire one of my boys then? I'm lending you Poison this time." Haus waved, and Poison went down the steps to join the messenger, who lurched a little under Poison's impressive height and glare of his menacing mask but tried to hide it with a cough and a bow to Haus. "Bring him back in one piece, and then we'll discuss the lady's debt. Got it?"

"Yes, m'lord." The messenger bowed again and walked away with Poison striding proudly behind him. His platinum braid shone down the middle of his red-clad back.

The long line of people stepped aside, creating a wave effect as the red devil passed. Arson hadn't been out of Kell's Key yet, and Poison was second, after Bludgeon, to be hired out to another manor lord.

For that first outing, Bludgeon had shown the skirmishing Darklandic houses out east how fearsome the LinGor devils were. It was their debut, besides a prime victory for Lady Lexion against her biggest rival, and had already started a region-wide interest in the secret house of LinGor. Only those with a special invitation could contact the devils' proud house. A more exclusive privilege permitted renting the devils. Their great campaign of underground power had only just begun.

No telling when it could ever be Arson's turn to shine. Though he'd love to experience such a thrilling adventure and glory for himself, he wished so with hesitance. He'd never worked without the support of his three brothers before. He envied Poison and Bludgeon, sure, but even more so, Arson revered their bravery.

The double doors to the practice room slammed open two nights later, startling Arson out of his exercise routine. Poison stood in the frame, his head bandaged and his platinum hair hanging out in strings. He held a tight frown below fierce eyes. He walked stiffly into the middle of the room to join his dumbfounded brothers. A frantic servant scurried in soon after with a roaring Haus LinGor leading the way.

"She'll pay, I swear it!" Haus yelled. After the servant left, they sat in a circle on the training room floor. "I know she hired your protection service, but for all her riches, doesn't the woman have her own guard as well?" Poison kept calm despite Haus's anger, carefully unwinding the bandage from his head. The dried blood on it gleamed with a coppery sheen when the light hit it. He had already been stitched up by Lady Lexion's surgeon.

Poison explained, "She wanted me to escort her to Wormsbury. I rode right in her carriage with her, and as you would expect, we were attacked by bandits. I think this group had caught wind of her trip. They knew exactly where to hide for the ambush, and they had everything from crossbows to magical explosives. She may have a mole among her servants." He exhaled, able to keep calmer than Haus even though he wore the injury. "This group turned out larger than I expected. She lost a few men, and I was struck so hard that my mask broke off, though it did save my life." He still had the mask fragments with him, which he passed to their father from hand to hand through his brothers. Arson observed the clean slice of a sharp blade, which took a swipe off the mask demon's cheekbone when the fragment passed into his hands, not the damaging blow though. Poison's face remained pristine and handsome. His stitched gash went along his hairline.

"Thank the Great Sea for that, my boy!" Haus took the fragments and nodded sternly. "I'll get my smiths to improve these masks."

"She apologized and promised a great compensation, so don't worry, Father," Poison said, and Haus nodded. "But there's something much more interesting…"They all leaned in. "When my mask broke off, she saw my face, of course, and when we had a quiet moment to dress my wound, she told me…" He took a deep breath. "We aren't devils, we are something called *elves*."

"Elves?" Haus said. "What in blazes is that, and how is it not a devil?"

"Elves are a race, like human, but not human. They have a kingdom beyond the rock forest."

"But you came over the sea."

Poison shook his head. "Perhaps so, but she was quite sure about my being an elf."

Haus leaned back with a pleased smirk on his face. "Elf, devil, I don't care what you are; just knowing there are more of you is the real news!"

The four brothers' eyebrows all rose at once, and they shared looks with each other.

"We'll go there, to the elves," Haus declared. "And I'll barter with them to get wives for ya."

"Wives?" Bleed blurted. Arson knew they all probably wanted to repeat it. "But I thought you didn't want us to associate with women."

Haus sat cross-legged, a short little man, with his arms crossed and a tight smirk on his face. "I know. I've told you time and again how you can't trust women. But listen, you don't have to. A wife is an asset, and though I don't need such an asset anymore, it's different for you boys."

"How?" Bleed asked.

Arson looked to Poison for his impression. He held a certain kind of smile. He knew something, but Arson chose not to ask him quite yet.

"You four boys are my heirs. Wives might be a good idea for you after all. The elf women can bear children for you. That's why they're assets."

Arson's heart sped up. "Children?" *Wives?* he followed up in his head. He'd never considered such a thing. The idea sounded as queer as opening up a flower shop or writing poetry for fun. He couldn't imagine life taking such a sharp turn. *Children?*

Haus's face was brightening up red with the tightness of a huge smile. "Why didn't I think of it before? I was wrong to deny you boys wives! With some wives of pure elven blood, you can breed me an army of devils, and then we'll be the true power in the region! I'll conquer all the other houses and forge a real throne!"

"Father!" Arson snapped before the man could get too excited to hear him. "I've no experience with women. How are we supposed to breed an army?" Of course, he didn't count a few moments of interaction with Nanelle as experience with women. They had all agreed that Haus didn't need to know they all had seen the woman in the pleasure box and she them.

Haus waved a hand at him. "Don't you worry a second about that. You'll find it to be the easiest thing in the world. You'll love it even! You just swagger right into the bedroom, do your business, and then get back to the practice hall to sharpen up your skills for the next mission. Your wives will do the rest of the work." Haus stood up, and the brothers remained seated, sharing all manner of expressions of shock and awe at Haus's sudden change of plan for them. He leaned down to kiss the tops of their heads in turn, being extra ginger with Poison's slashed scalp. "I'll tell you all about it soon. Ah, the Great Sea did bless me that day." He rushed out of the room, his positive attitude restored and complemented with a new youthful energy, to plan their trip to the elves' kingdom.

The door boomed behind him, and with him gone, Poison's eyes brightened to a level of mischief he only let his brothers see.

"You've been uncharacteristically quiet, Poison," Bludgeon said to him. "What are you holding inside that grinning mouth of yours?"

"Excited about getting a wife to get you off instead of a stranger in a box?" Bleed asked.

"I think we all are," Bludgeon told him.

Poison sat in his place, smiling bigger, waiting patiently for everyone to shut up. His smile infectiously spread across the rest of them in the anticipation.

"Are you idiots done yet?" he asked.

Bludgeon leaned over and punched his shoulder. "Hurry and tell us! You're terrible at keeping secrets."

Arson asked him, "Are you happy about Father's new plan?"

"Of course I am, little brother."

Arson hated it when he treated him as if he were younger, but that was Poison. He assumed leadership over them, and none had bothered to challenge him on it.

"Getting back to my story about my assignment with Lady Lexion…" Everyone leaned forward a little. Arson thought they'd heard it all, but apparently he had more to share. "When we arrived at her manor in Wormsbury, she told me more about the elves and took me up to her chamber. And we had sex."

"She gave you fellatio?" Bleed said.

"No, the actual kind—*body* sex."

Arson's mouth dropped open. "You're already well ahead of us all on the wives front!"

"Oh, she could never be my wife. We merely did the thing Father didn't want us four to do. It was marvelous!"

"Do you think Father would get mad if he found out what you did?" Arson asked.

"Maybe not as of today," he said and followed up with a bark of laughter pointed toward the door.

"O Great Sea, say more," Bludgeon said, rubbing his face with a groan of frustration. "You have no idea how deeply I've dreamed of sex with a woman. My imagination runs wild almost nightly, trying to piece together how it works, wondering what in the world it's about, and why we can only do it through a damned box! Tell us, Poison. Don't be a prick! What was it like?"

Still smiling like a bobcat, Poison told them and spared no detail.

Chapter 3
hanhelin

"Ameiha? have you finished packing yet?"

"Just about!" Hanhelin shouted back but needlessly.

Yhulin strode through the door and paused to click her tongue at the scene.

Hanhelin blew out the flame under the flask holding the boiling leaves of various types she'd picked yesterday. She paused in her work to observe Yhulin's unpleased expression. She looked around herself, at all the books she'd left lying about. The trunk stood open, half-full of her clothes, more books, and her boxes of paints and powders she'd been using to practice her Desteer makeup. She hadn't donned the face paint today. Instead, she'd chosen to twist her black hair up into a messy bun, tie back her long sleeves, and get to the bottom of her *most* important invention—the one which would save Norr and all of elvenkind for good!

Pulling down her magnifier over her eye, she leaned over the table to cut more herbs into the smallest slivers she could manage.

"Ameiha?"

"What, Yhulin?" Hanhelin snapped her face up again. She sucked in a deep breath. No need to bark at the young *faerhain*. Yhulin was a good handmaiden of only seventeen but mature beyond her years. Hanhelin wouldn't have her forever. It wouldn't be long before Yhulin would go on to choose a husband and build another proud Norrian household.

Yhulin knew her well too. "Would you like me to pack the rest of it while you finish your invention?"

She hadn't yet told Yhulin what she was on the cusp of creating, so the lass couldn't know the importance of delaying her departure for a paltry few hours.

"Princess!" boomed a male voice, which startled both her and Yhulin together.

Hanhelin shot Yhulin a frantic stare. "Has it been so long already?"

Smiling in a nervous light, Yhulin nodded.

The door flew open, and Cavlihen marched in, spurred boots hitting the slate floor with a sharp *kap, kap, kap*! And Hanhelin winced at every one. Cavlihen's face tweaked harder at any disarrayed thing he saw on his way to Hanhelin's side, especially the alchemy lab she'd failed to clean up on this day in which they were supposed to leave for home.

"I can explain…," Hanhelin said. "It's *very* important—"

He kept walking, acting as if he hadn't listened.

"Cav—"

Yhulin jumped far across the room from the angry captain, and Hanhelin had nowhere to flee to keep him from sweeping her up and hanging her over his shoulder.

"Oh, that's mature, Cav! What's wrong with you? I'll tell my father! When I'm finally Grand Desteer, I'll order your head on my desk! Cavlihen! Stop it!"

"Yhulin!" he barked at the younger lass and pointed across the room. "Get the household *saeghar* to help you clean this mess up. The elder is waiting to see us off."

Yhulin leaped to go and find the nearest young lad Cavlihen spoke of. The youngest son of the homeowner had demonstrated a fervid interest in all of Hanhelin's strange gadgets, and he shouldn't be far off.

"Well, you have to put me down, Cavlihen!" Hanhelin warned from over his wide shoulder. "You can't treat me like this anymore. I'm thirty-two, fool! I'm almost Grand Desteer."

"Well, act like it then," he grunted. He carried her as far as the corridor outside her room and put her down, taking a moment to survey her messy appearance.

"I didn't have the time to don all my fineries, okay?"

Scowling, he reached out and pulled the cord holding her hair up, and it all tumbled down in a silken ebony waterfall. She pouted, looking up at him before taking it upon herself to untie her own sleeves to let them fall properly over her wrists.

He let his face relax and nodded.

"I hate you," she said.

He tightened his lips. "Are you done?"

"Yes, I am."

"Then let's go say goodbye to the elder. As soon as you get home, you can play potions all day long." He pulled her by her arm and they started moving along the corridor which wound around the curved side of the house. The steepled windows on the outer wall were all framed in leafy ivy growing all over the outside.

"No, I can't," she argued, still pouting. "I've gotten more work done on my research during this tour than I had ever gotten at home. I'm about to make a breakthrough, and you'll be so sorry that you ever interrupted it!"

"I thought you said you were done." Nonetheless, he kept walking.

The long stone hallway gave her enough time to compose her face. This house, the elder of Lockheirhen's house, had been chiseled out of a solid stone hill. Maybe a lot of the rooms were actually natural, open formations in the rock. Normally, she would stay in the Desteer Halls at every clan village, but for this one she stayed with the elder because his house was safer by all calculations—even though it technically lay inside the earth and the ground was where the trolls were coming from.

"You're just anxious to get back to the palace," she said.

"I keep to a schedule, *Ameiha*, and so will you when you are Grand Desteer."

He opened the front door to a scene of well-formed groups of royal Tinharri *saehgahn* and her own expertly honed sect of White Owl guardsmen—of which Cavlihen was captain.

The elder also boasted a fine collection of strong *saehgahn*, male children to guard his household—no *faerhain* or *farhah* daughters though, so the elder's wife must feel pretty outnumbered.

Now in the public eye, both their demeanors shifted to graceful and gracious. She slipped her hand around his arm so he could escort her.

"Thank you, Honorable Elder Lockheirhen, for your hospitality, your music, and your stories."

Lehomis, the elder and his little wife who complemented his own small stature, both bent a knee together, hand in hand. "Yer welcome la—I mean *Ameiha*. You'll visit again soon, I hope."

"Possibly sooner than you'd think, if the truth were to be told." For that line, she couldn't shake the images of the troll raid aftermath she'd seen along her tour. A great number of elves had died in the past year and a half because of them. Those creatures were notorious for bursting out of the ground and wrecking the forest. One large chasm they created swallowed up half an elven village! As Grand Desteer, she'd make it her first priority to fix the horrible injustice.

Hanhelin held her hand out to make contact with Kristhanhea, Lehomis's wife. This *faerhain* had endured quite a rough life in the Darklands before Lehomis found her on his travels. They'd kept Hanhelin up for hours most nights during her stay, recounting all the wild adventures that had led to their union. "I hope you enjoy a long life with many sons to protect you and daughters for your company."

"*Harrenhenni, Ameiha*," the shy Kristhanhea said, doing her best with the Norrian language as it wasn't her original tongue. She'd been an elf raised among humans in the Darklands. She and Lehomis made the perfect couple with their nearly matching hair colors and similar heights. He stood rather short for a full-grown *saehgahn*, even among his own sons.

One of Hanhelin's attendants approached with the tea of goodbye from inside the house. Before Hanhelin could leave, she had to sip one more taste of tea with her hosts. She took the first sip and handed it to Kristhanhea.

While he waited for the cup, Lehomis drew Hanhelin's attention to the tall, black-haired *saehgahn* standing beside him. "By the way, this is one of my older sons. His name's Horse."

Hanhelin hid her smile behind her long sleeve. "Horse? Like the common tongue word for what you breed in this clan?"

"*Ah,*" Horse confirmed with a formal bow to her. "My father named me, *Ameiha.*"

"I could've guessed easily enough," she said, shooting a sly smile at Lehomis, who beamed. This must be his favorite son.

"He's the pride of Lockheirhen," Lehomis put in, confirming her estimation.

Hanhelin did one more visual sweep of Horse in a manner she wasn't supposed to as future Grand Desteer. She took in his colors and angles. He was excellent. She almost asked Lehomis why his son appeared to be yet unmarried. He resembled Lehomis in most ways except for height; he towered over him, and his black hair shimmered like the coats of the clan's best horse stock. It's as if Lehomis knew how this lad would grow up.

"Well…Horse. I am pleased your father introduced us. If you are available, maybe my handmaiden can ride you home."

At her joke, Lehomis choked on his sip of the goodbye tea and followed through with laughing coughs he tried and failed to hide in a handkerchief. Kristhanhea slapped him on the back. Horse, himself, smiled brightly and bowed again.

She couldn't stay much longer than that, as much as she hated leaving this particular clan, and Cavlihen's nudge on her shoulder confirmed the parting words were over.

She'd spent the whole year in preparation of becoming Grand Desteer of Norr, to tour the country and visit every clan, to get to know her people on a personal level, hear their concerns, and guide them in prayer. Today it ended, and it was time to go home to Ko Hanilkha, home of the Tinharri clan.

Chapter 4
Elves

Arson followed the voices to find his father and brothers bent over a large map on the table in the breakfast nook.

"Down here on this side. All this is Norr, the scholars tell me."

Poison stood with crossed arms, staring down at the blotched old parchment map. "No wonder we've never heard of this place," he said. "It's all the way south of us, across not only a sea but the whole damned rock forest."

Bleed shuddered. "Remember when we approached the rock forest on the Shirigen mission?" He shook his head and observed the rocky drawing.

"Well, if we can brave through the whole thing, there will be a great reward on the other side, lemme tell you boys," Haus said. "G'morning, Arson."

"Good morning, Father." Arson stayed back away from the table. From this distance, he could see the big blotch of drawn Norrian forest well enough, plus the bay gaping between the Lightlands coast and the rock forest, which isolated Kell's Key from that region. Kell's Key folk didn't have much reason to venture south, Arson understood. They enjoyed a lush and sunny climate with plenty of natural resources and more than enough trade with the Darklandic folk east of there. Kell's Key was one of the richest cities in the Darklands, second only to Ilbith on the far side of the continent.

"So are you boys ready for the adventure of your lives?"

"Yeah!" the three shouted at once.

"Yeah," Arson echoed afterward.

"That's my devils!" Haus barked but paused. "I mean *elves*." Stifling a giddy outburst with his lips pressed together, Haus rolled the map back up and headed to the door. "Get yerselves ready. We leave tomorrow."

Bleed and Bludgeon burst into excited chatter in Haus's wake. Poison stood by, listening with a mood as light and pleased as the others. Arson, for some reason, couldn't manage to match their enthusiasm. He tugged Poison's sleeve.

"Poison."

"What?"

Arson led him a few paces away as the other two carried on, talking about "beautiful elf girls." Apparently they expected to find their future wives running merrily on the beach half-naked when they would hit the shore. The Norrian forest looked vast. Surely they'd be trekking through dangerous tree and plant growth for days before they found any elves—and who knew if they'd be greeted with kindness?

He leaned in to ask Poison, "Aren't you a little worried about this trip?"

Poison shrugged. "It'll take more than deadly rock cliffs to scare me away from this venture."

Arson swallowed, a difficult effort. "But don't you… Do you ever see people you've killed in your dreams?" Even as he asked it, that girl from the Elkleon manor, her big eyes stared back at him, a vision renewed this morning shortly before he woke up.

Poison frowned and cocked his head, considering Arson's question while staring toward the window. "No. It's interesting though…"

Arson leaned forward again close enough to whisper. "What is?"

Poison turned his gaze on him and smiled. "Ever since my night I spent with the Lady Lexion…"

"Yeah?"

"Ever since, I've dreamed of nothing but her shapely, naked body quivering beneath me and screaming 'Devil! Devil!' in her passion for what I did to her." At Arson's silence, he laughed and put a playful slap on his cheek. "Lighten up. You'll be glad we did this. Trust me." Poison smiled, turned his back, and started toward the training hall, swiftly plaiting his pale hair as he went.

Maybe Poison was right. They were all strong enough to brave the terrain ahead of them. And why wouldn't four women from the elf kingdom want Arson and his brothers? Yet regardless of how hard he tried, Arson couldn't shake his dreary mood.

Even though they had surveyed the rock forest from the horizon in the past, it couldn't have prepared them for how treacherous hiking through it could be. The rocks jutted up from the ground like giant knives and towered overhead, casting all manner of jagged shadow this way and that. They really were sharp—and brittle! A surprisingly moderate level of noise had already caused three or more pointy rock peaks to topple down toward their heads. They'd already lost one soldier to a falling rock. Plummeting themselves was the other hazard, as the trail wound up and down through the spires, often turning unpredictably into cliffs that were also slightly too brittle to tread over.

Haus had packed up a large caravan of fifty men, horses for the quadruplets, and two carts of supplies for the long journey to the elves, all many things to have to look after. Keeping all cartwheels on flat ground became the challenge the farther up the winding cliff faces they trekked. If anyone were to fall off such a cliff, they'd get impaled on the sharp rock spires below.

"I do apologize," Poison said to his father and brothers from atop his horse, "for my cockiness in the face of this landscape."

Haus shuddered. "I know I ordered you boys not to wear any masks on this venture, but now I wish I'd had you geared up in *something* more protective than a hood.

"Why didn't you have us cover our faces, Father?" Arson asked. He tried not to look down from his seat on the saddle at the cliff drop mere inches from where his horse's hooves touched down. In a situation like this, he preferred to trust the horse to use its instincts and find good footing.

"Better you not hide your proud elven heritage," Haus explained. "We wouldn't want to scare your new wives with your devil masks.

They'll want to see your handsome faces instead. By the way, Poison, how's your head?"

Poison reached up and grazed the length of his stitches with his fingertips. "Well, Father. I'm not expecting much of a scar. If there is one, my hair will hide it."

"Good," Haus yipped. "Can't believe that...*witch*, Lexion, let you get such an injury!"

Poison sighed with a smile. "She hired me to protect her, remember, Father? Not the other way around."

"Yeah, but still..." Haus continued his grumbling for some minutes before a new sharp shriek broke through the wind and caused another distant break in the rocks.

Arson squinted. All the white rocks reflected the bright sunlight and made it hard to look in any direction. However, the shady sides of the rocks cast gorgeous purple shadows, adding beauty and mystery to this treacherous region. He caught the faraway rock fall from the tip of one spire, but it wasn't caused by their chatting.

At the back of their caravan, Haus's hired scholar—who knew more about the elves and the map's landmarks than anyone else—stuttered and pointed. Arson squinted in that direction again in time for another piercing cry to cause more cracking and snapping of the chalky rocks. "S-s-scouel!" he managed.

Everyone stood and gawked.

Haus began, "What's a sc—"

His question was answered by the outstretching of huge white wings and the sudden swoop of a sleek body cutting the air above them.

"A dragon?" Arson blurted.

"No, it's a scouel, my lord!" the scholar shot back. "A white one! I wasn't expecting to see one at this side of the rock forest—thought they'd keep to the deeper corners!"

"I'll bet it's hungry!" Haus warned. His men were winding up their crossbows, and Arson's brothers unsheathed their swords. Arson did the same, feeling an intense surge of adrenaline typical to the high point of any mission he'd been on, except this creature's cries made his hair stand on end.

The scouel circled around and flew over them again like a hungry vulture, except five times bigger. On its next round, it opened its jaws and flashed long canine teeth despite the more hawklike sounds it made.

"Manfred!" Haus shouted at his scholar. "What do we do about it?"

Manfred could only work his jaw uselessly for the moment.

The scouel, with a wicked snarl, did another pass, this round dipping low at the party and then weaving expertly between the rock pillars. It spooked a few horses so badly one of them danced off the path's edge and the broken ground caused another horse and rider to follow. Thankfully none of them were any of Arson's brothers.

"Move now, beast!" Poison roared at his horse, urging it to sidestep away from the edge and get closer to a soldier with a crossbow poised. He sheathed his own sword and wrenched the crossbow out of the man's hands, pointed it, and fired the bolt at the scouel.

The flying creature flinched at the hit but continued, letting out a louder shriek that panicked all the horses. The bolt appeared to bounce off its large, scaly hide.

"Probably best to continue our way, my lord, under the cover of the rock wall ahead," Manfred suggested. Down a dip in the path, the rocks were more fused together like a canyon.

"You heard 'im, men!" Haus waved his arm ahead, and the caravan moved on. The new break in the path proved a problem for the second wagon, behind which Arson found himself waiting. Ahead of it, Bludgeon dismounted his horse and took the wagon horse's bridle, hopefully to help it pull the wagon's right wheels over the triangular-shaped break in the path. As expected, the first wheel fell into the divot and stayed nestled. Those riding in the wagon jumped out.

"Better leave it here!" Bludgeon suggested.

"No!" Haus argued. "We need our supplies and wealth to barter for your wives!"

Getting more anxious by the instant, Arson dismounted too and approached the back of the wagon as if he could help somehow. Farther up in the caravan, Poison and Bleed shot more crossbow bolts at the creature. No matter how many hits it took, it neither slowed nor lost interest in the caravan. One shot finally lodged into it, releasing a ribbon of blood flow to stream down its pearlescent scales and white fur. Still the creature shrieked and flapped and flashed its teeth at the terrified men.

Arson shook his head at the back of the wagon.

"Driver! Whip the horse!" Bludgeon ordered the last person on the wagon. "The rest of you push!"

The surrounding soldiers made their way around to Arson's end, and the whole handful of them pushed the back of the wagon. With enough grunting and abandonment of all self-awareness, the right-front wheel rolled out of the divot with a great feat of everyone's combined strength, but the right-back wheel would be next.

"We'll have to push this one over it too," Arson told them. "Keep the horse going!"

The driver whipped and shouted urgently at the poor animal, but everyone's lives depended on it.

Krrrraah! The scouel called, dangerously close. The monster, wearing another bolt like an irritating toothpick in its skin, swooped over the stuck cart. Arson and all the men ducked down beside the cart for cover. When he rose again, the driver was gone.

In initial confusion, Arson squinted and looked around. It finally occurred to him that the scouel had snatched him. There! With the man's lifeless body in its talons, it landed and gripped the side of the rock with its other foot. The back talons appeared like a massive bird's and the front feet were more like paws with sharp claws.

Another monstrous call announced a second scouel, eager to share the fresh meat the first had claimed. It landed precariously on the narrow formation and snapped its doglike jaws at the poor dead driver's body. It picked his clothes off with a few careless rips and then fought the original scouel for the meat, tearing an arm off.

Arson's stomach churned to watch until Bludgeon leaped on top of the wagon.

"Bludgeon!" Arson protested.

"Shut up and focus!" he reminded Arson.

"No, boy!" Haus yelled to Bludgeon. "It'll get you too!"

Bludgeon ignored him and signaled to Arson and all the men behind the wagon to push again while he whipped the horse.

"Hold on!" Arson said to them. He put his hands underneath the structure instead, between the large wheels. "Lift it, all of us together!

Ready?"

With one great heave, they gave it a try. Ten or so men plus one devil lifted and pushed, and the heavy cart ever so slightly obliged enough to get it out of the hole in the path. Over that hole, Arson could see straight down with a dizzying clarity. Dust billowed up from where the fallen rocks had hit the bottom. He persisted, regardless of his fear, and held up the wooden planks until he and the others had stepped well over the gap. He had never thought to guess how unstable the rock forest would've been. At least the road ahead appeared solid enough.

Leaving the two scouels to feast on their man, Haus's caravan hurried forward, horses and all, down into the crevice for safe hiding from any more flying killers.

Chapter 5
Norr

Twenty-three years ago. Tobas: eleven years old...

The door to their private family wing flew open. "Make way!" Gilqured shouted as soon as he stormed through the doors.

The maid who scurried along the hall had to leap and flatten herself against the wall. Tobas, sitting on the floor with his collection of wooden horses and the little wagon with lifelike moving wheels also shuffled aside. Gilqured kicked his bunch of toys, and they clattered in all directions.

"Hey!" Tobas fussed and stood up.

Gilqured ignored him, grabbed the next nearby maid, and demanded fresh milk in four suckling skins. Tobas reared his head back to hear that. His father, Haus, came through the hall next, toting a bundle of rags close under his chin. A baby? The three men who came in behind him also had what looked like sleeping babies.

"What happened, Father? What do you have there?"

Rather than answer his innocent question, Haus shoved Tobas away with a rough palm to his forehead. "Keep out of the way, boy," he ordered and paused. "See me later." He left Tobas blinking.

The next man with a bundle passed him, and Tobas caught a mewling sound. It was indeed a baby! His father marched on into his inner chamber, and the men with the three babies followed. The door slammed behind them.

That wasn't the end of the alarming new hurly-burly in House LinGor though. Maids were running everywhere. A younger man burst in with a young woman toting yet another baby. "I got her! The new wet nurse, sir!" He hauled the confused woman all the way into Haus's apartment without any hesitation, and the door slammed yet again.

"I don't care!" Haus came out yelling another minute later. "Get everything needed. Take it out of people's houses for all I care. I need cradles! Four of them! In fact, get absolutely anything pertaining to babies you can think of!" At that, he shoved out the men who'd gone in with him, allowing some of the maids to stay in. The men stormed past Tobas, paying no attention to him.

Tobas gawked at all the activities. What in the world was happening today? He'd ask his mother if she weren't currently out at the market shopping. Tobas moved forward, deciding to go in and see for himself.

The scene on the inside was a little calmer. One maid was putting clean swaddling on one of the babies. The wet nurse untied the front of her dress to offer a breast to another. Haus was cuddling the third one, and the last one lay on the bed over a fresh blanket spread out beneath it, awake, as the second maid stroked its light-colored hair and let it grasp her other finger. Tobas approached that one slowly.

"Come to see yer new little brother, Tobas?" the maid asked. When Tobas got a close look, he grimaced. It was cute…if not for its bright green eyes and oddly shaped ears.

"It's a monster," Tobas uttered. The thing's ears possessed a very defined shape with a long, pointed tip.

"Yer father says it's a devil. The Great Sea gave them to him."

"*That's* my brother?"

She nodded. "He says this one's name is Arson."

What a strange name! Tobas could only frown down at it. He'd played with a baby or two before, but this was just too ominous for him to get into that playful mood today.

A large hand suddenly landed on his shoulder, and Tobas whirled around. "Father?"

Haus stood over him, frowning, and still holding a bundled creature. Tobas didn't like that frown. "We need to talk, boy."

"About what, Father?"

"Yer going to have to stop calling me that."

"Why?"

"Because I'm not yer father anymore."

Today...

Tobas sobbed over his mother's fresh corpse, lying limp on her straw bed in her dungeon cell.

"I'm so sorry, Mother! I tried! I really tried!" He didn't care how weak he appeared before the dungeon guards. His poor mother had never done anything to anyone, only serve Haus during her best years as his concubine. For most of Tobas's childhood, she'd enjoyed Haus's favor, being the only one to ever give him a child, but Haus was a madman.

After Haus came home, toting those four strange-looking babies, he had just as quickly thrown Tobas's mother into the cell, and Tobas found himself sleeping in the smelly stable.

Ever since that fateful day, Haus had doted on his fake sons, four creepy, pointy-eared "devils" instead of his real son. It took all of Tobas's best efforts to be good and do his work and reclimb the ladder of Haus's secret kingdom to gain a better status and get a real room outside the kitchen. His days of boasting the status of Haus's son had long ended.

But at least the others weren't as mad as their master. Tobas had friends throughout House LinGor, men and women working for Haus who knew the truth and sympathized with Tobas. Tobas was obviously Haus's son, and everyone could see it in his features: the reddish hair, the wide nose, and the stalky stature. Everyone but Haus.

Tobas put his mother's head back down to the straw and wiped his nose on his filthy sleeve. He observed his dingy clothing, how horribly Haus had treated him and this poor, dead woman.

He nodded to her as if she could hear his thoughts. Maybe she could, considering her ghost could be standing right next to him.

Haus was a madman, and Tobas knew what to do with dangerous madmen. From here, he'd go and talk to Jiminick, one of Haus's leading men who held great authority over the rest. Haus had left Jiminick home in charge of them. Since the madman had departed with only a modest entourage, Tobas had found his hour to act.

"So Norr is on the other side of that water, huh?" Poison said next to Arson as they all stood together on the last stretch of cliff, at the other side of the rock forest, overlooking a huge body of water inside a bay.

"No sense in standing around this forsaken pile of rocks any longer," Haus replied and started down the slope to solid ground. "C'mon, my boys!"

Arson followed behind him, but Poison sprinted past to be at the head of the adventure party.

"I'm not looking forward to traversing back this way," Bludgeon said behind them. "How many people have we lost?"

"Six," Bleed answered. They had replaced the wagon driver with a new soul brave enough to sit up high, as Haus wouldn't allow any of his devils to do the job.

"Maybe we don't need so many men after all," Haus said to them. "I just need my devils, Manfred, and a few to drive my wagons full of goods."

Arson trudged along, feeling a lifetime wearier than when he'd set out. It didn't matter how much sleep he'd managed to catch last night. He didn't like not knowing how things would go with the Norrians, a race of people they'd never met.

"What does *Norr* mean anyway?" Haus asked Manfred, his scholar.

"It means 'north' basically," he answered, "by orientation to the kingdom south of it: Sharr."

"Now Sharr, I've heard of," Haus replied. "Norr must be on Sharr's side against the kingdom of Neitherban and Ilbith."

"A wise guess, my lord. You're right," Manfred confirmed. "Norr acts to divide Neitherban from Sharr, being such a wide mass of trees with hidden elves within. Norr stretches mostly across the whole continent. It has upheld the alienation of the north and south for millennia, I'd think."

At the foot of the sloping terrain, they quickly found a small settlement with a dock and a big boat. "A bay ferry," Haus called it and eagerly strode forward to find its keeper.

The first sign of life they found was chopping firewood beside one of the little earthen houses, a man in ratty clothes. Up closer, all hushed themselves to see that it must be one of *them*, an elf, for his pointed ears and slanted eyes above high cheekbones mirrored the devils' easily.

The elf noticed them and started aback, squeezing his axe in his hand, held down by his side for now.

"Greetings," Haus said with a smile. "Are you the ferry's owner?"

The elf sized them up, his eyes lingering on Haus's sons from behind his long, stringy hair. "My grandfather owns it. Are you…traders?"

Haus nodded deeply with a slight laugh. "Yeah, indeed we are. We need to hire your ferry to get us across the bay into Norr."

As pale as the young elf man looked, his face drained a bit more.

"Why're you blinking so much?" Haus asked. Behind him, Arson exchanged looks with all of his brothers. "Isn't it normal for traders to come through your country?"

The elf dipped his chin. "Yes."

"Then may I have a word with your grandpa?"

As if in surrender, the elf slogged off toward the bigger house at the center of the small complex, and Haus's party followed. A few more male elves working the homestead gawked at them along the way, but so far, no women could be seen.

"Wait here," the elf told Haus and went into the front door, giving it a generous bang against its frame. It didn't take very many minutes before the door opened again and a more mature-looking, though no less youthful, elf appeared in the doorframe. This one's sharp eyes scraped across Haus and his sons—especially his sons. Arson did the best he could to keep from shrinking under that scrutiny.

The mature elf's stare settled on Haus. "You're the leader of this party?"

"I am," Haus said.

"Please enter for a word. Just you alone."

Poison bristled beside Haus, not because they had any reason to be jealous but because of their lifelong dedication to protect their father.

Haus patted Poison's arm. "It's all right, my sons. I'll be back. Wait for me here."

Before they went through the dark doorframe, the elder elf whistled a few specific beats, calling several other capable elven specimens to stand around the devils and their men and wagons. Still bristled, Poison whipped his head around rapidly, and Arson tried to give him a silent message to be calm by widening his eyes and pulling in his lips. The elves were merely worried for their own safety in the face of this load of strangers—that's how Arson chose to believe it. Without any weapons or obvious hostile signals, they gave Haus's party no need to panic yet.

The tension made the time feel triple long, however, and at the end of that eternity, the door swung open again and Haus exited first, smiling.

"We're in," he said. "They're going to ferry us to Norr, and they're even sending a guide who can translate for us."

The original young elf and his grandfather stepped out behind Haus.

"Prepare to launch," the elder ordered the other elves, and the tension dropped. The elder carried on with Haus, doing the usual business: inspecting the size of the wagons to see if they'd both fit on deck and counting heads and whatnot.

"What did you talk about, Father?" Arson asked Haus, and the three other devils gathered around to hear his answer.

"Usual business of payment and all, but he had some awfully strange concerns."

"Like what?" Poison pressed.

Haus hissed and rubbed his balding pate. "Don't take this poorly. We've got a mission here, but"—Haus shrugged—"he didn't like your hair color."

The devils all regarded each other, at the platinum locks they all boasted. Haus had always told them they were gorgeous men, when not playfully calling them ugly. Every local elf in sight had dark hair. Why would a ferryman be concerned about their hair color?

Bleed asked the very question in Arson's head, and Haus answered, "He didn't say why. I reassured him we had a wealth of trade in our wagons and we wouldn't be long in his country. In the end, he gave up, saying something along the lines of he had no say in it anyway.

Basically, we may have to meet with Norr's official councilors or whatever, but otherwise we're fine. We're in, as I told you."

Being aboard a ship made Haus extra giddy, aside from the attitude of success, finally on a clear path to Norr after three days of struggling through the rock forest. He used to sail around a lot in the past, which led to finding his quadruplet sons by sheer luck. The elves had a ferry large enough to hold both wagons at once—so everything unfolded smoothly.

"We all need to lighten up," Haus said to his men as well as the boat's elven crew, who rowed and worked the small boat's sail. "Let's sing a shanty! Elves, repeat these lines. You too, boys. I never taught you these songs before." And so he began a song, fast-paced but light and bouncy. It lifted the soul.

"Oh, the Great Sea roars with a voice so bold, and the sailors they tremble as the winds take hold— C'mon, Arson!"

Arson had never sung before, but he liked the faint music either coming from his father's inner chambers or the one adjoined to the devils' reward room, which had no singing, only string and wind instruments. Joining in with one's voice was a curious thing to experience. Arson concluded that this could be a prime means for people to entertain themselves when far out on the ocean. Being stuck on a vessel like this in the middle of the ocean should get mind-numbingly boring.

At his father's nudge, he opened his mouth and tried to mimic the tone they used. "Winds! Take… Hoooold."

Haus roared with laughter and elbowed him again. "You'll get it! Here's the next part: For he rules the ocean with a power untold, this fearsome sea god with a heart so cold."

Arson kept up with the words as best as he could, juggling them with the rhythm needed. At first the elven ferry crew refused to participate, but after a while, when Haus's men were laughing out loud, they gave it a try. These Norrian elves obviously knew music better than the devils.

Despite his difficulty, Arson was laughing by the end of the song. "We'll brave the storms and the wild, wild tide!" he sang loud and proud. This made for the first day the devils had ever been allowed to relax in the company of others. Being among a load of happy men was so different from having to keep his back stiff and look imposing to anyone else in the space. When he checked his brothers, Poison was looking toward the land ahead, elbows braced on the boat's taffrail, and Bludgeon and Bleed were speaking softly to each other near the stern. Out of the devils, only Arson cared to try singing.

Haus announced the next song and belted out a line but paused when Poison shouted, "Look!"

The whole ship went silent at the huge cloud spilling through the trees off the land.

"Not good," the ferry captain grunted.

"What's not good?" Haus asked him. "Mist?"

The captain said, "It's a cloud from the Darklands."

Poison twisted around. "A walking cloud? I've seen those at least twice."

"We don't get 'em in Kell's Key," Haus told the captain. "It's really sunny where we're from. Beautiful beaches and palm trees, we got."

The captain dismissed Haus's rambling. "We've only been seeing this cloud in the past few years. It means bad things."

"What does it mean?"

"Trolls."

Haus's lips rounded as he mimed the word.

"The mist can hide much," the captain told him. "Trolls can roam in it, hiding from the sun. It shields them. Sometimes we see them. Sometimes not. Be wary on your way."

Haus followed him to the helm where another elf steered. "Well, hold on now, you can't just leave us with 'beware.' What do we do if we see a troll?"

"Run."

"That's it?"

"Run toward light."

"*Ameiha*! Did you hear?" Yhulin swept into Hanhelin's tent. "They've spotted another one."

Hanhelin didn't bother to look up from her limited alchemy set she'd erected in her tent. "Spotted what?"

"A walking cloud."

Hanhelin's heart dropped. "Another one?"

"It's drifting between Clans Nerry and Omihen."

"Any trolls?"

"Not yet."

Hanhelin looked back down to her cutting board with fresh herbs and bowls of different salts around it. "They're getting closer together."

Yhulin nodded gravely.

Hanhelin wound her arm in beckon. "Come, Yhulin, and help me. Cut the rest of these *sigmarhen* stems."

"What are you making, *Ameiha*?"

"Something that will change Norr forever."

"Oooh." Yhulin took special care to cut the herb exactly as Hanhelin had. "You know though…"

"Cavlihen will be in soon to whisk me away to safety, I know."

Yhulin nodded, confirming her guess. They worked in silence for a minute, as if to savor the peace. Yhulin's knife made a soft tapping rhythm against the wood.

"Yhulin," Hanhelin said as she ground the *skrin* salt in the mortar. She'd made good use of her campaign, gathering up all of these ingredients from every corner of Norr.

"Yes?"

"Have you decided yet?"

"Decided on what?"

"You know. The *big* decision."

Yhulin giggled, still such a young *faerhain*. She'd actually made the leap into adulthood earlier than most. Seventeen was quite a young age to decide on a husband but not too young by what Yhulin proved. "No. I'm not in a rush."

"You probably should be. I did some mathematics last night, and it looks like it should take a mere three generations or less for Clan Tinharri to hit a wall."

"How so?"

"My great-aunt had mentioned it briefly before I departed. This happened at least once before. Caused a civil war too."

"Because of a shortage of females? And it will happen again?"

"As Grand Desteer, I'm going to do as much good for the elves as I can. I'll try to solve the imbalance problem *and* eliminate the troll threat. In the meantime, let's plead to the Bright One to give us more *farhah* births. We need to marry off as many *faerhain* as possible, or our race will be in danger. Again. In times like this, we need fewer Desteer maidens and more mothers."

"Well, you can count on me, *Ameiha*. I've already chosen the home. I'll be sad to leave your service though."

Hanhelin gave her a smile. "I envy you."

"Really?"

Hanhelin nodded. "I used to dream and wish for it at age six or seven. I used to think I'd choose Cavlihen as my husband because he was always there outside my chamber, protecting me. That's what husbands do, right?"

Yhulin put the knife down. "You're going to make me cry if you keep talking like that."

She motioned the lass to keep working. "It's all right. I took the news hard when I learned I was born to be Grand Desteer, but it's for the best. It suits my personality and interests. If I were running a household, I'd be too busy for my studies."

"True," Yhulin said. "And let's not forget this most important invention you're making here—the one which will 'change Norr forever.'"

"Indeed." Hanhelin pointed to the largest beaker. "Put the herb in there."

When Yhulin did, the hot liquid already bubbling in it flared green. "Ooh." Yhulin ogled the color, set aglow by the candle beneath the faceted bottle. "It's like an emerald."

"And now this." Hanhelin added all the different salts she'd been grinding into fine powders all morning, and the color turned to something like gold. She blew out the candle flame, and though the tent went dark, the liquid in the beaker still put off thin glints of light from its glass corners, shining on the tent walls.

"Why's it glowing?" Yhulin whispered.

"Because it's working," Hanhelin answered in her own whisper.

She gave it several minutes to cool and had Yhulin light a few new candles so they could see to pour the beaker's contents into a smaller, more manageable vial. It wasn't as much content as the thick glass made it appear, but she did manage to fill two small vials, one of which she took outside.

Cavlihen caught her outside, and she put up a hand. "Yhulin told me," she said.

"We may have to seek shelter in a clan nearby," Cavlihen said.

She gave him her warmest smile. "Give me five minutes and I'll go wherever you bid, my dear *saehgahn*, but for now, watch this." She took one of the vials out of her pocket, stoppered with a cork. The concoction didn't look as luminous as it did while hot. It had more of a dull-brass look now. She searched around her, seeing a lot of trees and dead leaves. She considered objects she had on her but no need to ruin a good slipper or purse. She couldn't use something made of stone or metal already. A dead log lay on the ground, the best test subject she'd find for now.

Hanhelin approached the log's end, uncorked her vial, and tipped it over the barky surface.

"Are you sure you should waste it, *Ameiha*?" Yhulin asked. "It looked so precious in your tent."

"It *is* precious," Hanhelin said as she finished pouring out everything in the container. The potion, thick and shiny like liquid metal, seeped into the soft decaying tree like water. For a brief few seconds, she swallowed a knot of doubt stuck in her throat, but then the glow began.

Cavlihen lunged forward and yanked her back away. She only fought him partially, needing to see her work—if she'd succeeded. The log's surface turned a dark color right before taking on a smooth, matte appearance, like polished iron. Hanhelin exhaled the breath she held throughout the transformation and stepped forward, jerking out of Cavlihen's hold.

"*Ameiha!*" he roared when she reached to touch it.

Too late. She put her hands on it, confident it had worked. She twisted around and smiled at them both. "It's okay, you can touch it."

They both did. Cavlihen moved first as if the concoction could yet be dangerous.

"It feels like stone," Yhulin said.

"It's petrified," Hanhelin explained. "Something that happens to trees buried in the ground over a very long time and with the right conditions in place. Here, I've made it happen instantly."

"Why did you do this to the tree?" Cavlihen asked.

"I'm hoping it will work on more than trees. I created this to better fight the trolls."

Cavlihen's eyes sprang wide. "Like what sunlight does to them."

Hanhelin nodded to him. "It won't matter anymore when they claw up through the ground at night or stay inside walking clouds. I call this 'liquid sunlight.'"

Chapter 6

Maidens

The trees were different in Norr, enormous, white-trunked, and with big white springtime blossoms. Once Haus's company reached a certain depth of the forest, much of the landscape started to look artfully sculpted. Enormous woven walls made from a skinnier type of tree appeared. The newer the wall, the easier they could see through the holes in the weaving. Older "living walls" had thick trees fused solid. It appeared as if the elves wanted to guide them through some areas and confuse them in others. How the elves made all the trees bend in unison to form shapes and paths went beyond anyone in Haus's convoy. Giant roots also sprang methodically out of the ground to arch over the path, and some avenues passed between perfect rows of trees, planted purposely.

"Is the whole forest like this? A garden?" Haus asked the grandson of the bay ferry's owner.

His name was Deveghen, and the "ferry clan" sent him in good faith to escort Haus's party to the first available clan and help translate what they meant to achieve in Norr. "No," he answered simply. "Some parts fashioned. Some parts wild."

So far they hadn't had to cross the densely lush forest underbrush with its thorns and berries they'd seen so much of here. The path they tread seemed well upkept. Deveghen had already explained to them about the common road on which they traveled; traders and other visitors to Norr mostly used it, and the elven citizens had more secretive roads.

"How do they make the trees do this?" he asked, and his attempt at conversation gave Arson a bit of comfort. It had been a pretty awkward journey for the past two or three hours.

Their guide posed his hands in his difficult effort to try to explain in the common tongue how such feats of topiary were achieved. Many of his words were lost in translation, and he eventually gave up, admitting that he didn't know enough to fully explain. He had grown up sailing the ferry.

Deveghen's inept attempt to explain Norr's amazing forest shapes was the high point of their conversations. Otherwise, he often looked over his shoulder to spy the quadruplets again and again.

"What do you think his problem is?" Poison murmured to Arson.

Of course, he didn't know, but Arson didn't like it. The devils hadn't bothered to speak to their guide. Haus always spoke for them as a basic rule, and the devils listened and obeyed. So Arson, and his brothers too, kept quiet and let their father handle things. The elf's body language showed clear enough that Haus should also be aware of it.

Not far past the forest's border, they were met by a stern set of soldiers with pointed ears and tall, thin bodies, like Deveghen but much better specimens of male elves. They were quite unlike Haus's devils too, with their darker hair, larger eyes, and longer noses.

They received the quadruplets with less enthusiasm than the ferry people. Much less. Their average, unthreatening linens and uncovered faces helped nothing.

Arson blinked, watching these stern guardsmen scoff and keep their distances. Their white-knuckled grips around their spears and bows only made his hand itch to reach for his own sword, and he knew his brothers felt the exact same phenomenon. These elves didn't like them. If they couldn't gain their trust, a deadly skirmish could easily erupt and it would carry through to the end as easily as breathing for the devils.

Finally Deveghen stepped into the elves' foreign-spoken conversation with a gesture toward Haus's party and soothing-sounding words. Half the guards sneered and spat at Deveghen's statement.

"Are they...?" Haus murmured. "Are they putting our guide down for being a sailor and not a warrior?"

"How would you know that, Father?"

Haus blinked. "I don't. It's a feeling and not hard to conclude they would do that. Doesn't matter where you go, there's always class snubbing going on."

Deveghen put his hand to his chest and spouted one more strong sentence with conviction behind it. The leader of the guards nodded at last.

"Deveghen will take," the guard leader said, pointing to Haus in the most broken common tongue they'd heard yet.

Haus mimicked Deveghen's gesture. "He'll take us to a village?"

Deveghen took over the explanation. "I'll take you, yes. Before you can trade with us, you have to visit the Desteer."

"Who's he? Your king?"

Deveghen shook his head. "The Desteer talk to the Bright One. They will evaluate you and decide if you should trade here or not."

"Sounds fair to me." He observed Poison's look of impatience. "It's all right, boys. This is somewhat common. When we get new traders to Kell's Key, they first must join the league and be accountable. It keeps everything legal in our bustling city." He pointed to Deveghen. "Get on with it then. Take us to the best and closest village."

Half a day later, they arrived at a village jumping with life, especially around the hub. No market stalls stood, which was the first odd thing. Trading goods was only their front, but after setting out, Haus had explained to the boys about commerce anyway and markets and bride prices. Instead of market stalls in the town square, this village had a huge dirt clearing with more warriors like those rangers they'd encountered earlier today. This must be where they practiced their martial arts and weaponry.

"Must not be a market day," Haus said to his sons as they traversed around the wide area of grunting male elves doing their exercises under the noon sun.

Many eyes shifted warily to the devil brothers since their entrance here. Arson eagerly scanned to see a female among the busy crowds but couldn't pinpoint one quite yet—just loads of frowning long-haired males armed down to their skintight leggings.

Deveghen pointed to the biggest building in sight and most likely the center of the whole village. "You'll begin your journey here in this clan," he said. "Every village is also a clan. You must pass the judgment of the Desteer before advancing to the next clan to be judged by that Desteer and so on. The clans that approve you will trade with you."

Haus smirked and nodded his head. "It won't matter," he said under his breath. "If this clan approves our stay here, we'll get your brides and hurry on our way."

Inside the big, round house, the newcomers were given cushions to kneel on and were instructed on how to sit: on their knees with their hands lying politely on their laps. Opposite them waited a set of other cushions under the tall domed ceiling. The spacious room didn't offer much for distraction. A warm fireplace flickered behind the hosts' cushions with a kettle hanging over it. Otherwise, tall windows loomed on the curved outer wall behind the guests.

Poison and Bludgeon started bickering about who would get to choose their bride first when Haus snapped at them. "Let's see how this will play out, all right? Don't be stu—"

His words slacked off, and his stare drew Arson's to the group of *stunning* female elves coming around the corner from a side corridor. They made swift work of the journey yet somehow managed to look like they were floating instead of walking. Hard to tell because their feet couldn't be seen under their long silk dresses.

Haus's eyes were grazing across them, most likely picking out wives for his sons already.

The women knelt and settled upon the other cushions, sitting straight and tall, displaying a sort of discipline not unlike the kind the devils had grown up with. They kept their faces, painted white with a purple stripe across their eyes, solemn under veils of dark hair in different shades of brown and black. Arson could never put a label such as "old" on any of them, especially with the face paint, but some put off auras of wisdom others couldn't seem to master yet.

The one at the center of their wedge-shaped formation rose, stepped forward a few paces, and then knelt again in the center of the room where her cushion was positioned closer to the visitors. Her dress, identical to the others', flowed long and loose and had a little jacket covering her arms and a wide sash around her waist. All their hair hung loose, pooling around them.

"I'm the head of the Desteer maidens for this clan," she said, finally breaking the silence. "I can tell you are new to this place and will inform you first that visitors are mostly welcome but heavily watched, so do not be offended by our customs."

"This doesn't feel very welcome to me," Haus said. "I mean no offense either; I only want to talk to your lord, if not your king."

The Desteer maiden nodded. "I can fill this position for you. Each clan has a counsel of Desteer who handles important judgments. What have you come to talk about?"

"We'd like to trade goods with your people. And there is one important matter we need to discuss: my sons." He motioned to them, who sat straight-backed and solemn-faced—their best show of discipline, two on each side of him. They'd left the rest of their men waiting outside, most likely under a heavily bladed guard or at least stares sharp enough to kill.

The head Desteer maiden lowered her chin to shoot a pointed look to each of them, her eyes glowing creepily from the dark painted stripe. Once again, not a favored body language they'd received ever since they started meeting elves in this land. Arson shrank when her stare passed over him.

Dismissing the sullen faces the women made, Haus continued, "I found them when they were infants. I knew they weren't human, and recently we learned they're elves—like you people."

"Indeed they are," the head Desteer maiden said.

"Because of that, we came on a friendly venture to get them some wives. I need to barter four females from you."

All the maidens' faces soured instantly. "We can't do that," the head maiden replied quickly.

"I have gold," Haus said. "I brought a good quantity with me, but there's more back home."

"We don't need gold, sir. We can't let any females go with your sons."

"Why not?"

She explained patiently, keeping the sour look off her expression unlike the others. "It's against our custom to marry females to outsiders."

Haus stammered for a bit, working his jaw up and down before getting out, "That doesn't sound right; these boys are elves."

The head Desteer maiden shook her head. "Our situation is complex. To our race, there are more males born than females, so we can't afford to marry outward. There are too many males dying in loneliness as well as *of* loneliness here. Besides, your sons are…" She bit her lip.

Arson's heart increased in speed to hear this, and Haus's explosive reaction conveyed his alarm at this turn of events. "They're the finest specimens of manhood I've ever seen, madam!"

"Don't raise your voice please."

The devils had trouble keeping still at that point, but they tried. Bludgeon and Bleed fidgeted at Haus's opposite side from Arson, and Poison was balling his fists over his lap.

"Poison," Arson whispered softly to try to calm him.

"Tell me what problem you have with my sons!" Haus demanded, always prepared to speak on the quadruplets' behalf.

The Desteer maiden lowered her chin again. "They are not kin to us Norrians; they are from over the sea."

Arson sucked in a breath. How did she know that?

The woman continued, "And they have in their blood a corruption which we in Norr take great pains to avoid mixing our blood with. To mix their blood into ours would mean disaster."

Haus looked to his left and right at his sons. Arson and the others had all lost their stone faces, though they were not about to act out of line—not until Haus would give them the signal to move.

The Desteer maiden continued, "I will give you one chance to turn back and take your…sons out of Norr. Otherwise, we will kill them."

Chapter 7
Tensions

"My invention, liquid sunlight," hanhelin told Cavlihen and Yhulin as the three of them rode side by side on their horses, "we'll use it to destroy the trolls." The grinding and rattling sounds of the caravan moving ahead and behind them filled her ears, a constant sound she'd gotten used to. "When we arrive home, I'm going to set up a permanent alchemy lab and we'll create a great store of it."

"You said you hardly get time to work on your alchemy at home," Cavlihen said.

"In the past, yes. You saw what I've created," she replied. "My father won't have any choice but to allow me the time and space to nurture this invention—to perfect it."

"There'll be troll statues all over the place," he said.

"Better than having live trolls roaming around, hurting our people."

Yhulin, riding beside her, shuddered. "I wish we wouldn't talk so much about it, *Ameiha*. Why do they come to our country anyway? Isn't the Darklands a better place for their comfort?"

"They're coming because they like the taste of elven flesh."

Yhulin gagged slightly and covered her mouth. "It's so awful to think about."

"You asked, *guenhihah*," Hanhelin told her with a frown. "Nonetheless, I expect this is an age for their awakening. When they wake up from their long, hundred-year slumber, they feed, recede into their caves again, and do whatever foul things they do. They worship Wikshen. They craft spells and count the enchanted items they collected along their raids, then they seem to go back to sleep."

"Is there not enough people to eat up north in the Neitherban kingdom?" Cavlihen asked her.

"Elven flesh is sweeter," Hanhelin said. "Not to mention Wikshen. With the mists floating around down here, it seems like he's driving the trolls south. He probably thinks he can conquer Norr—and perhaps Sharr."

Yhulin shivered again and rubbed her arms. "Now we're talking about Wikshen."

Hanhelin gave her a soft smile of reassurance. "Trolls are for me and the *saehgahn* of Norr to deal with, young one. Not you. You have a more important task."

Yhulin nodded. "I'm looking for a husband as we speak, but with no luck yet, *Ameiha*."

"Don't rush it," she said in turn. "You have the power to change a *saehgahn*'s life forever and to carry on the future of us. Don't take your task lightly."

Yhulin didn't speak but put her hand to her heart. At least she rode more sturdily at the change of subject.

A rumbling in the earth threw off her renewed posture, however.

Hanhelin hunched over, holding her reins warily below her chin. Cavlihen's eyes were popping. He didn't speak, but she knew they shared the same word in both their heads: trolls.

He kicked his steed and shot forward to bark orders at the other *saehgahn*.

Hanhelin regarded Yhulin. "Don't fear, but it appears we're about to increase our speed."

At the sound of horns, they did indeed accelerate to a gallop after the several minutes it took for the heavy caravan with its many riders, runners, and wagons to pick up its pace. Hanhelin didn't worry for Yhulin in this task; the young *faerhain* could handle a horse, for it was one of the requirements for working as a handmaiden to the princess.

What is going on? Hanhelin thought. *That tremor didn't seem too far off, and there's no mist around here.* But the sun was setting fast. As long as the moon dominated the sky, the trolls had free range of the land, and Wikshen would surely be there to protect them come morning.

"There was something wrong with that meeting," Haus grumbled as they rode back up the trail. "I demand another meeting with another leader!"

The devils rode deflated in their saddles; the four of them had not said a word since the meeting with the Desteer.

"I was afraid of something like this," Arson finally expressed. He hadn't felt nearly as much grief about the thought as he did now—now that the rejection was real. A bizarre loneliness nagged him. Being raised so closely to his brothers, this pain was new.

Deveghen nodded along with Arson's words. "This is what I expected too. You four are strange elves. Human traders are one thing in our lands, but strange elves are something my people don't like. Not at all."

"It doesn't make any blasted sense!" Haus argued. "My boys are good! They're strong and sensible and trustworthy."

Deveghen sighed. "Maybe foreign elves don't know the threat they pose."

"What threat?"

"No one in my country wants your sons or anyone like them to breed with our females."

"The Desteer lady said something of the sort. Why?"

Deveghen shrugged. "I don't even have to go into that part of the argument. A better reason we don't want strange males here is because there aren't enough females for us as it is."

Haus's brow furrowed, and he regarded each of the devils. Come to think of it, Arson had already seen the density of males walking around in town earlier. No females at all, except the ones in the Desteer Hall.

"What's that supposed to mean?" Haus asked.

"In an average elven family, if they have three children, one is a girl and two are boys. Never any more females than that."

"And it's true, you know it?"

"It's proven every time a baby is born." Now Deveghen stared off into the forest. "Most Norrian males die lonely."

Arson's stomach dropped. His brothers showed similar distraught on their faces. They all knew what a wife was: a companion to a man and the one who bore the children. At least once in their assassination career, the devils had crept up on a target as he slept in bed with a woman beside him. Arson used to be at peace using the pleasure box and knowing the devils of House LinGor wouldn't live the married life. However, all of a sudden, his world was crashing down to find he couldn't have what he'd been promised only since last week! They had all enjoyed the pleasure box up until now, but Poison's story about Lady Lexion was too enticing.

"Father!" Poison barked. His stone face now pinched in hurt. His eyes looked reddened from Arson's vantage. He, least of all, would not go back to that tired old pleasure box.

Haus raised his hand to calm Poison. "Stop the wagon!"

The driver pulled on the reins, bringing the whole caravan to a rough stop. "My lord?" the driver asked as Haus climbed to the back and opened a chest among many others.

Haus took out a smaller box with iron feet and a little latch. He stepped off the wagon and opened it before Deveghen, revealing a wealth of gold coins.

"What is this?"

"What do ya mean, what's this? Don't you know gold when you see it, boy?"

"I know what gold is."

Haus shoved it closer to him. "What I'd like is for you to show us to another village—one with lots of beautiful females. This box o' gold is enough to buy your grandfather a new ferry—a bigger one!"

Deveghen stared at the gold. "We do have use for gold, my clan on the bay."

"Good!"

The young elf accepted Haus's gift upon two open palms. "Tell the next clan it was not me who brought you to them, or they'll shave my head."

Haus smiled. "I'll take full blame."

Sitting before another set of Desteer maidens, much like the first group, Haus trilled his lips. "Isn't there a man around here I can talk to?"

"There are no men living in Norr, sir," the head Desteer maiden of this clan said. They were in another big round house, though there weren't as many elf women sitting in this one as there were at the other village.

"You know what I mean."

"We have an elder presiding over our village, but he will be less compliant than I am to let your sons take wives from our village."

"What?" Haus gasped. "Madam, I haven't told you why we're here."

"No need. I sensed your intent when you arrived."

Haus stuttered. "I see a few beauties behind you; won't four of you come with us and mate with my sons?" A round of frowns and pouts appeared on their gorgeous, painted faces.

"We can't do that, sir. Several of us in this generation born with Desteer talents have chosen to ignore the Bright One's calling and settled down with husbands instead; only us few chose the Desteer Hall. This means we are married to the Bright One, and it's our civic duty to serve our clan. Sir LinGor, please leave and don't visit any more villages on your way out, or the order of the *saehgahn* will kill your sons, who are lucky to be alive as it is."

Haus's face boiled red, but he rose and jerked his arm to signal his devils.

He ranted and raved all the way down the path and into the fields beyond Norr. "Don't despair, boys, we'll work something out," he said after Deveghen parted from them. "Maybe they'll wake up in the morning to find four girls missing; that'll show 'em." Haus's face took on a hateful smirk. "They think we won't reenter their forest."

They did that very thing when a new path appeared along the road. Arson's heart pounded. This was the mission of a lifetime, sneaking into a huge forest kingdom to steal women. To steal someone he'd cherish for the rest of his life. For once in the devils' career, they were on a mission that benefited themselves rather than Haus's coffers.

A meadow soon opened up along their way where they spied exactly what they'd hoped to find: an elf woman—alone—with a basket, picking berries. The devils charged their horses at her, as if they'd all been thinking the same thing, leaving Haus stuttering behind them.

"Why aren't you running?" Poison yelled, full of spirit and virility as he reached her first.

She didn't bother, only stood and watched as he slid off his horse and dashed to snag her wrists. He threw her across the saddle like a load of skins, and they all rode away with haste.

Arson panted, full of adrenaline, when they slowed down a ways away from the meadow and hopefully anyone who could've heard the commotion.

"One down, three to go, my boys," Haus declared.

Poison whirled off the horse and pulled the woman down with him. She still didn't offer to struggle and didn't even show a frightened expression to boot.

Poison grasped her jacket-like bodice and jerked her closer to him. "Are you not scared?" He smelled her hair.

"Poison, be gentle!" Haus said and rubbed his sweaty, bald head. "I'm gonna have to teach you four about courting and sex soon. It's all sinking in now."

"I can't mate with you," the elf woman said to Poison, looking calmly into his eyes as if to let him down easy. "I'm already married to the Bright One."

"Another Desteer maiden?" Haus asked with a sneer. "No wonder there aren't enough females for marriage; you're all marrying your god instead! Listen, madam, you're going to have to marry a real person for once and tell us where we can find three more eligible girls like yourself."

"We can't be called girls; we are *faerhain*. Please respect our custom. And when you blaspheme, I will no longer talk to you. Now please take me back, or I'll alert my sisters telepathically. They'll send out the *saehgahn* to retrieve me."

"What is the say-gawn?" Haus asked.

"The male elves. They will be far less gracious than the females of authority have been to you."

"You must be witches," Bleed said. "Father, what shall we do?"

"I don't care. I'm keeping her," Poison said, holding her tightly against him.

Haus nodded to Poison. "Tie her hands and put her into the wagon with the most room."

Haus resumed his seat next to the driver and twisted around to speak to her after the wagon took off. "Now tell us where to find a village with other women like you."

The creature remained as radiant and graceful as ever, even tied against her will. The golden grass straws in her honey-brown hair seemed more decoration than mess.

"My name is Linhala," she said. "Please listen to my counsel because you are on a destructive path. I can surrender to spare my fellow *faerhain*"—she paused to suck in a breath—"but, sir, your other son is coming your way." She clenched her eyes closed and shook her head as if struggling internally. "You should meet him kindly and spare Norr of violence it does not need."

Haus gaped at her. "So you'll come willingly now?"

She took the next few seconds in silence before nodding. "If it will serve my people, we can discuss it, but the *saehgahn* will search for me when they notice me gone—it won't be an easy transaction at all."

Arson rode next to the wagon, listening to the conversation and staring at the female. He didn't like seeing her tied up like that, but her words kept his feeling in waiting. "Father," he said. "She said your other son—"

"Alert!" Bludgeon, who rode at the head of the procession, called. A horn sounded in the forest behind them.

"Too late, someone must've heard your shouting," Linhala said and then leaned over to hide her head low in the wagon.

Arrows flew from the trees. *Knock, knock, thunk-thunk!* Two of Haus's men went down.

Poison stood up on his horse's saddle and leaped into the wagon with Linhala, ready to destroy anyone who attempted to take his bride. Arson dropped from his own horse to avoid getting shot and stood ready to defend his father when the elven warriors charged from the forest.

He engaged the first one to dare an approach. Their blades clashed. The elf looked positively savage with his hair swept up on one side with spiky feathers of it sticking out and his enraged expression. He wielded two short blades similar to how Bleed fought—nothing Arson couldn't handle after all his years sparring with his brothers. He slid his blade against the elf's throat and focused on the next to approach before the first could fall. Two more came at him! Arson parried and danced side to side, repelling their swords while keeping his father safe behind him.

"Get under the wagon, Father!" he ordered.

Clash-clash-clash! Arson had to work his arm fast against the two warrior elves.

Poison's voice rang out to compete with the ferocity of the Norrians, and somewhere unseen Bludgeon called out for assistance.

Arson's hands were too full, and he worried about his father first and foremost. The two elves keeping him busy were advancing on him, backing him up against the wagon! He lost sight of his father. When his back met the scratchy wooden slats, he dropped and rolled. His father wasn't under the wagon like he'd told him to do. He rolled all the way to the other side to emerge behind it and possibly gain some space, but things were getting more and more heated around him. He did find that space he'd hoped for, and his two opponents each ran around the wagon in opposite directions to try to close him in again. Arson backstepped, keeping them both in sight.

During his distractions—and the confusion of more incoming enemies with the worry about his father's safety—a great blow hit the back of Arson's head from an enemy he failed to detect. With the explosion of pain across his skull, his vision winked out.

Chapter 8
A Strange Elf

hanhelin"s caravan galloped for a long time, exhausting their horses, until Cavlihen deemed they could slow up. Hanhelin drooped and ached in her saddle; she'd missed a night of sleep to gain distance from the tremor they'd heard. The light of dawn finally winked through the tree leaves. They hadn't seen or heard of any trolls since, and she opened her mouth to call for some rest, when a faint shout through the trees made her pause.

Ever on alert this night, Cavlihen whipped his reins once again and galloped up the length of the caravan, leaving Hanhelin to gawk in her mix of surprise and exhaustion.

After the caravan's long, slow stop, she listened hard for whatever might be spoken or shouted in the distance. She leaned over to Ari, her accompanying *saeghar* page. "Go and listen for me."

"Yes, *Ameiha*." The lad followed Cavlihen's path up the long procession of guardsmen, horses, and covered wagons.

She squinted for a glimpse of where Cavlihen might've paused, but the trees were too dense.

After about a minute, Ari came sprinting back, his shoulder-length hair flying horizontally in his speed. His rounded eyes glowed in the morning twilight. "*Ameiha*! The scouts are back!"

"What is it?" Now she stretched her neck as far as she could to see, fruitlessly.

Her page stuttered. Yhulin, on her own weary horse, kept silent behind her.

Mouth hanging open, Ari pointed backward. "*Ameiha*, they've found…"

"What? What did they find? Trolls?"

He shook his head and blinked. "No, but they've found someone. A strange elf."

Hanhelin frowned. "A strange elf? What does that mean?"

"They pushed me back and told me not to let you— *Ameiha*!"

She was already sliding down the curve of her horse's midsection. "Yhulin, stay on your horse. Ari, show me."

"I can't—!"

It didn't matter because Hanhelin marched forward. The lad could only follow, half-heartedly gripping one of her long sleeves. He wasn't *saehgahn* yet, but his eagerness to take his vows showed clearly. He followed her closely, maintaining that connection. She allowed it so long as she could get away with making her way up to see what kind of "strange elf" her *saehgahn* had found.

At the front of the procession, Cavlihen and a handful of the other White Owls argued over a large sack with a humanoid shape within. They'd caught him like a criminal, whoever this strange elf was.

"What's going on?" Hanhelin demanded, and at the sight of her, Cavlihen swiped a hand at young Ari. Hanhelin blocked the strike with her own wrist. "I asked you a question!" The *saeghar* retained his grasp on her sleeve so she hooked her arm into his to let him be her living shield if he saw necessary. The lad would eagerly die for her. Every male here was expected to.

Over the sacked person stood a guardsman with a club, as if he'd beat the captive to death if he moved. In addition to that, five *saehgahn* stood formally in a row with spears poised.

Hanhelin made her way closer to the spectacle, and Ari added resistance to her movement. "Tell me who you've captured," she ordered again.

Cavlihen moved over to guard her other side, wedging her in between two sweaty bodies. He flipped her veil over her face. "Don't let him see you if he wakes up."

"It doesn't matter if he wakes up!" the *saehgahn* with the club spat.

Hanhelin opened her mouth to ask yet again, but Cavlihen beat her to it. "Our scouts got into a skirmish at the border. There's a strange entourage of traders, and a few of them are elves. They appeared to have a *faerhain* among them."

"Why are you bothering elven traders?"

"They weren't all elves; most were human. There's no reason they should have one of our females with them, but there's one particularly ominous detail..." He presented the sacked person.

"Who is it? Show me. This is one of those elves?"

"Yes."

"So show him to me! I'll use *milhanrajea* to look inside his mind and see what he's about."

"You've told me you haven't mastered *milhanrajea* yet."

"I'm close, but— It doesn't matter. As Tinharri princess of Norr, I order you to show me your captive."

Cavlihen huffed, took a second, and then led her closer to the sack. Her page maintained his protective hold on her arm.

The *saehgahn* with the club tightened his grip and held the weapon ready to bash the captive's head should he awaken too soon. Another stood by to open the sack. Hanhelin nodded to that one. Cavlihen nodded at the same time, and none could tell which one's order he obeyed, but he finally untied the top of the bag and pulled it down over a blood-matted head...with shining platinum hair. This elf's hair was paler than his skin!

Hanhelin flipped her veil back to see better. At first she couldn't form any opinion, too confused at such different coloring. Norrians had black hair, or at least brown. Hanhelin searched this person for as long as they would keep the sack open. The profile. The closed eyes. The ears' slightly different shape.

"We find this elf to be very foreign, *Ameiha*," Cavlihen said before her thoughts could finish developing.

She whispered to herself, "A foreign elf with pale hair." She checked her guardsmen, who stood as if awaiting her order to kill the captive. "Is he alive?"

"He's breathing," the one who held open the sack answered.

"We're going to kill him though, *Ameiha*," Cavlihen replied.

"No!" She shot out the word.

The bystanders all gawked, including Ari.

"Why?"

She grabbed Cavlihen by his leather pauldron. "Listen to me! Don't do *anything* yet! Hold on!"

"Ameiha?"

Ignoring any further word, Hanhelin flew back to the cluster of wagons, which had stopped a fair distance away from the potential threat, yanking the page along with her. "Help me," she ordered him. "Get the trunks open."

"What are we looking for?" Ari asked.

"A book! Find the trunk with my books."

The lad leaped up on one of the denser-packed wagons and handed down heavy boxes and sacks to the other *saehgahn*. Yhulin appeared at Hanhelin's side.

"I thought I told you to wait on your horse."

"Which book do you need, *Ameiha*?" Yhulin pressed.

"The one with the gilded cover. The myths of Norr."

"The myths book?"

"Didn't you hear me?"

"Here, *Ameiha*." Ari placed a heavy chest before her with the help of an older *saehgahn*. "This one has books."

Hanhelin and Yhulin both plunged their hands in and sifted through, stacking tall towers of books on the ground around them.

"This is what we collect on every tour of Norr, more books from the Lightlandic traders," Yhulin mused.

"And what a good habit it is, I've developed, because right now the book I need is the most important thing…" She let her thought trail off in her concentration.

A distant, growling male voice shouted behind her. "He groaned. The beast is waking up!"

"Don't kill him!" she shouted over her shoulder. "If I could just get my bearings…" She dropped the two books she'd lifted and stood up, looking off to the farther side of the caravan. She took off running.

"Where are you going now?" Yhulin called after her.

"Keep looking!" She might've stowed a book or two in her box of more personal belongings.

Ari was panting at this point as he followed faithfully behind her. Yhulin had spoken correctly about her shopping habit. Norr's grand library had filled a whole new shelf since she'd been born into the family.

Behind her and Yhulin's vacant horses waited another, smaller wagon loaded with her clothing and alchemy set. With Ari's help, she stepped up onto it and threw open the wooden chest with blue painted orchids all over. Within it she pushed aside her box of Desteer face paint and powders, her silk fan gifted to her by Clan Kanarihen, her comb... There! Some books sat at the bottom of this chest. *The Questionable Tales of Lehomis Lockheirhen.* Lehomis himself had given this to her one night when she told him about how she loved to buy books when on the road, but that wasn't the book she needed. Lifting it up, another book with flashy gilding winked at her in the morning sunlight. "*Norr na Lornigah,*" she recited the title. Unlike Lehomis's book, this one was written in her native tongue.

Flipping through it, her stomach sank at the density of the text. She sent Ari running back to the front of the caravan to make sure they hadn't and wouldn't kill the captive elf yet. She turned page after page, sighing, feeling like a critical piece of her kingdom's great puzzle was falling through her fingers.

She paused at the next chapter, gawked at it actually. She whispered the words of the chapter's title, "The Foul Overseas Taint." Dizzily her eyes took in the text below those words. Her lips numbly sounded out some of them, but she didn't have to actually read them. She'd read them before. This couldn't be happening. What were the chances? Foreign elves with a negative quality in their bloodline, which caused them to act out differently than an average Norrian, and who possessed negative magical abilities, would be a great danger to her kind. These foreign elves with blond hair brought disaster and bred it right into Norrian bloodlines. Today she'd found the real thing. This legend was one of the major reasons her society could be so strict. Norrians practically lived by the fear of foreign elves—and with few texts to guide them around it. She scanned the book's pages as she started walking back up the caravan, needing to refresh on this information as much as she could before engaging in a critical argument with her protective *saehgahn* entourage.

"Blond hair," she breathed the words from the book. "Green eyes. Cocky attitude. Beware these features as they could mean ruin for our descendants, turning future Norrians away from the Bright One and embracing the sin of the Swine." That quickened her pace. Apparently a historical wonder had fallen right into her lap. A horrible thing her people had feared for a thousand years or more. A foreign elf. An elf bearing the Overseas Taint.

Book in hand with her finger holding the chapter, she trotted to rejoin the confusion at the head of the caravan. The captive groaned loud enough for her to hear, and they all came into view right as Cavlihen threw a heavy punch down on the side of the foreigner's head, knocking him out cold again.

"Stop!" Hanhelin barked, dropped her book, and sprang to stand over the captive, now only half-covered by the sack. From what she could see of his upper body, he wore human-style clothing, so he definitely hadn't been living in Norr recently.

"Get away from him!" Cavlihen roared and lunged to grab her.

She dodged and nearly tripped over the sleeping person. "I command you all to freeze!" She put her entire soul into the yelled order. Everyone did. Cavlihen, among the rest, stood staring.

"We will not senselessly kill this newcomer."

"*Ameiha.*" The word steamed hotly up Cavlihen's throat.

She dropped her arms and stood as a pillar over the unconscious elf. Checking herself, she found she actually straddled him. She took a deep breath to try to control her blush and squared her stare on Cavlihen.

"I am the third Tinharri princess of Norr," she reminded them, "which means I am destined to take up the mantle as Grand Desteer. Do you all know what that further means?"

Most of the males with their hostile stances around her nodded, but they wouldn't be able to guess what she would propose next.

"I can't marry, so instead I will dedicate my life to knowledge—for the good of my people." She motioned downward. "We will restrain this elf. We will not kill him senselessly. Understand?"

"Why, *Ameiha*?" Cavlihen asked, calmer but no less ready to strike the captive if needed.

"I will evaluate him. When he wakes up, I'll question him. I will find out if he means us harm. We must keep him in custody for as long as we need."

She spotted Ari standing in the tight cluster of *saehgahn*. They had all packed in tightly, all of them poised to defend her. Keeping his eye contact, she pointed to her book on the ground, and he lunged to pick it up for her. "I will study the Overseas Taint and use this person as my subject. I'll find out just how terrible it is. *If* it's terrible. Maybe I can eradicate it even. From him. From our population... We won't know unless I'm given the space to try."

By the end of her speech, her guardsmen were blinking. She jumped at the sudden feeling of Cavlihen's arms coming around her. "Well and good, *Ameiha*," he said softly in her ear. He lifted her up and removed her from the captive's body, putting her down at a safer distance. "But how will you hash this out with your father? And the current Grand Desteer?"

"My father, I don't know," she answered honestly. "But I'm hoping my aunt will agree or at least form a sensible understanding about the proposition."

Cavlihen's quirked mouth indicated doubt.

"While we're out here, I'm in charge and I'll study him as long as I can. Disarm him and lock him up," she said.

"Oh, we've already disarmed him," Cavlihen said.

She stood with her clenched fists hidden under her long sleeves, awaiting Cavlihen's support for her plan. Though she was technically in charge of this venture party, in dire situations his word could still trump hers—and the matter of a male with the Overseas Taint was a dire one indeed.

His shoulders ever so slightly deflated in his next exhale, a movement only she would catch. "Clear out the smaller wagon. Tie his hands and lock the cage with two extra padlocks. The princess has spoken."

Chapter 9
Shackles

haus rose from huddling behind a tree and strained his good eye to survey the tail end of the violent scene. Three platinum heads he counted. The last elven soldier died, gurgling blood in his throat with Poison's foot planted across it, twisting and grinding his sword deeper into his lung. "Who do you think you are, trying to take my bride away?" he growled, gnashing his teeth and grinning. They definitely won the fight and with men to spare. Bludgeon stepped back from his recent kill, and Bleed emerged from the forest, soaked down with blood and sweat.

"Arson!" Haus shouted. "Where are ya? C'mon, boy, how many did ya get?" Arson's three brothers looked around where they stood. "Arson!" Haus yelled again. "Dear Great Sea, he better not be dead." He followed up under his breath, "Thought I was doing him a favor by hiding… Find your brother, ya bunch of louts!"

Everyone searched the area thoroughly, calling and checking all the dead bodies. No sign of Arson.

"Arson!" Haus yelled. "My son, where did he go?"

"Be calm," Linhala said, still in her bonds as her people had failed to rescue her. She sat calmly in the wagon, completely forgotten until now.

"Arson is alive. And you have a greater problem coming toward you."

Haus turned to her. "He's alive? How do you know? Did you see him? Is he captured?"

"Yes." She showed an odd void of emotion considering what they'd been through. Maybe elven women were more unlike human women than they thought.

"Ya hear that?" he roared to his party. "We'll arrange search missions to sneak around and see where they took him."

"That won't be so easy, my lord," Manfred said. He'd been hiding under one of the wagons to keep from getting hit by flying arrows.

"Ah, Manfred," Haus said. "Glad yer still with us. Pull out your map."

"My lord?"

"Hurry and find it! And this girl!" He reached over to jostle Linhala by her shoulder. "You and her are gonna work together to help me figure out where the clans are and which one has my Arson. We're gonna find him, or this whole damned forest is going up in flames."

Arson woke up in a swaying, bumping wagon, definitely not his father's wagon. Wooden poles bent all around him and were covered over by a linen tarp, lightly glowing with sunlight on the other side of it. He quickly found his hands and feet tied. The world spun around his throbbing head. He tried with all of his will to focus his crossing eyes on a bright sliver between the fabrics at the back of the wagon through which angry eyes glared right at him: an elf riding on a horse behind the wagon. They had captured him, but there wasn't anything he could do now in his daze. He dropped his head back down to the rough, bare boards and let his eyes fall closed.

He came alive again to leather slapping on his shoulder and piercing shouts in another language that stirred his headache. What could he tell them when he couldn't even understand them? The elf lowered his horse crop and cleared his throat.

"Why are you in our land?"

"I don't know," Arson responded, too drowsy to think properly.

"Where did you come from?"

"Over the sea…" was all Arson could tell him as he drifted away again.

"Let me see the foreigner now," a female voice commanded sometime later, during the nighttime. Arson opened his eyes and groaned. He managed to sit up and rubbed at his face. He ventured to touch the back of his head and found it tender underneath hair matted together with either mud or dried blood. He couldn't tell yet. Two of every person and object distorted his perception and kept him swaying dizzily.

"Please go back, *Ameiha*, or I will have to call on Saehgahn Law and force you to turn away from this creature. He is dangerous." Arson tried to crawl to the back of the wagon but found it hard. He collapsed in his effort.

"It is my final order as third Tinharri princess, future Grand Desteer of Norr, to let me look into this elf's eyes, or I'll remember you after my ceremony."

"Uh…" The male voice stuttered a bit. "Do be careful, *Ameiha*— *Ameiha!*" The tarp flap whooshed open, and there stood a heavily decorated feminine figure, her face covered by a thin black veil attached to golden pins sticking out from her thick black hair. Her white gown and scarves glowed in the torchlight of night. Behind her stood one horrified male, seemingly frozen in place, and several other males with stiff expressions and weapons poised.

The woman kept silent for long moments, and Arson knew she was studying his every feature.

"Colorless eyes, save for a hint of green, like a new sprout," she finally said and then held up her hand. "You are indeed a carrier. Touch my hand so I can know a bit more of you."

Arson reached despite his throbbing head and dizziness.

"*Ameiha!*" the guard cried but was obviously too afraid to grab her person.

She stuck her delicate hand through the bars, and Arson feebly reached his bound ones toward it. When she took his hand, his head flooded with a sense of calm, illogically overriding the urgent notion that he'd been taken by a hostile enemy party. He gasped and stared at her, eyes wide, trying to penetrate her veil as best he could. His effort helped to realign his vision.

She let out an uncomfortable sort of hiss. "You…," she murmured. "You're a devoted warrior."

"We knew that already, *Ameiha*."

She spat a few hard words in their foreign language at the elf beside her and turned back to Arson. "I won't let them kill you," she said in the common tongue. "I've performed on you only a slight graze of *milhanrajea*. You must go to meet my father and be evaluated deeper by the Grand Desteer. The taint is mysterious, and I wish to lay bare its facts. It's something we've worked hard to guard against for centuries. If you are as obedient as the hint I've gotten from my evaluation, and will comply, maybe we can learn what it really is. You'll be treated well, so please be calm and cooperative."

As she turned her back, veils and gown swishing and golden hair decorations glimmering in the moonlight, Arson began to breathe, finally realizing he'd been holding his breath.

Arson didn't see the mystery woman again the next day after the wagon started rolling. He endured another day of riding and stopping, and they fed him a crude diet of nuts and roots. He missed the food his father provided almost as much as the camaraderie of his family. Besides whatever time he'd spent unconscious, this would be his first full day apart from them all. It racked his nerves, but he had to keep himself calm. Patience and logic were crucial in these uncertain hours.

Another day passed. He spent it nursing his sore head and getting his strength and equilibrium back while waiting for his brothers to rescue him. They didn't show. He didn't want to think about the possibility of them getting killed in that skirmish and he being the only prisoner of war taken. He refused to consider his brothers were dead.

On the third day, the elves flung open the tarp and hauled him out and down a steep bank to a creek where half the male company, a great number, were bathing. His guards ordered Arson to bathe too, though after his clothes were off, they retied his wrists to keep him from getting far if he tried to run. It made it impossible to bathe properly. The rest of the bathing company glared at him throughout, and a handful of fully clothed elves stood guard with their weapons trained on him.

Blood matted large locks of hair at the back of his head, a nick to his scalp really, but the bump's tenderness lingered, and untangling all the matting made it so much worse. He managed despite his tied hands.

He considered the nearest guard to him. How easily could he take him down and seize his weapon in his state? His calculations pointed to his success, but even if he did get the elf's spear, fighting through this large number of others and then running off into the woods naked with tied hands and a long spear probably wouldn't work very long.

Instead, he asked that elf, "Where is the woman?"

His questions earned him a good thump on the head from the bow of another elf standing behind him. The sting overlapped with his bruise, and he winced but otherwise managed to hide his pain.

When they deemed he was finished with his bath, they dragged him out of the water and up the bank without a stitch on his body. They took him through the camp, earning many stares, especially to his light-colored hair, until they wound up in a heavily guarded clearing. A little fire flickered beside a canopy draped across the limbs of two trees. Under the canopy sat that grand female elf who had so intrigued his base instincts despite his head trauma. She still had her sheer veil obscuring her face and wore a dark blue dress with gold trim that blazed in the daylight.

Beside her sat an unveiled female, poised at a little table with paper and ink at the ready. A gorgeous creature with soft brown hair. Her bosom was smashed down under a tight bodice, but the garment helped to accentuate her narrow figure, like an hourglass in her kneel. Arson would steal her as his bride easily. And gladly. But the one under the veil…

The guards marched him right up to the females' canopy, seemingly without a concern for his absence of clothing. He wasn't sure if he should feel ashamed or not, but his rising cock at all his thoughts about these beautiful creatures made him wonder in the moment.

The younger scribe girl's eyes were all over his body, lingering on his naughty appendage, and her mouth dropped open.

"Yhulin, stop that. This one is off-limits. Consider him *sarakren*—

unmarriageable—until further notice," the prominent female said, and the younger one dropped her eyes to the papers before her.

Now Arson slowly moved his bound hands to cover his genitals, embarrassment remedying his excitement, and the prominent female spoke again. "No need, Arson, you are not out of line. It's common for young *faerhain* to see *saehgahn* as you are in our society." The veiled figure stood up and walked toward him. At a certain point she veered around him to study him from all angles.

"You are similar enough to our kind aside from your great height. I see the main differences in your coloring."

"Are you going to kill me?" he asked, and she stopped walking.

She studied his face through the filter of her fabric. "So long as my authority can keep you alive, you'll live as long as that."

He stared at her face, trying to see it through the veil but could only make out soft shapes. A male elf approached and handed her his clothing, folded neatly.

"Your clothing is strange," she noted.

His clothing was strange? All of her male associates walked around in detached leggings with only a little loincloth to cover their pelvises. Their ass cheeks showed on either side of the narrow strips of cloth.

Hanhelin followed up. "You are from the human lands?"

Keeping his thoughts to himself, Arson nodded his head once.

"Where did you come from? Who are your parents?"

"My father is Haus LinGor of Kell's Key."

"Is he an elf?"

"No."

"You don't know your elven parents?"

Arson shrugged.

"But you know that you came from over the sea? My guard said you murmured it." He nodded again, and she did the same, thoughtfully. "Arson."

"How do you know my name?"

"Because I'll become a Desteer maiden soon, which means I have special abilities the position calls for. Listen now. My company stares at you because you are strange. We have warnings in our texts about the Overseas Taint coming here. These records have helped to shape the way we live today. It's our solemn onus to guard against and eradicate it from our populace lest it taint our bloodlines and cause disorder to take root within our very selves and threaten the strong foundation of our societal discipline. However, the fact is we know little about it; what it really is, if it can be cured. So I'm going to make sure you are allowed to live. I want to take off your bonds, but I can't yet. You must answer a few questions."

"How do you know I even have it?"

"Your pale hair color and glowing green eyes are the first clue. Your affirmation of traveling from over the sea worsens such suspicions. Now please answer my questions. My vision of you revealed that you are a warrior of some sort. You've killed before."

He nodded his head firmly.

"Why?"

"I do as my father asks."

"Your father asks you to kill?"

He nodded again.

"It's not unheard of here to extinguish life if it means protection of the females. *Saehgahn* are all warriors too. Born into their station. I must ask you now though: Do you enjoy it?"

He hesitated a long minute before finally offering, "I… I don't know. I do as I'm told."

"Has anger ever made you kill?"

"No."

"Do you consider yourself important?"

He quirked his mouth at these strange questions. "No. My father is important, and I'll defend and obey him until I die."

The veiled figure dropped her chin and put her hands together. "Do you often become angry?"

"No."

"No?"

He shrugged, so confused he was forgetting about his nudity. "I have three brothers and a father. I love them, and my life is complete so long as they live well." He thought his life was complete, but he never actually knew what it meant or if it were true.

"I like hearing that, Arson. It sounds similar to a *saehgahn*'s peace, but…your three brothers? Are they elves too?"

"Yes. We're identical." The female gasped, as did all the males around her, and her female companion covered her mouth. They murmured among each other and tightened their bowstrings around him. The veiled female kept her composure, but her deep breath pulling in sounded clearly. Something about that made him feel excited, like the pleasure box did, but Arson tried to subdue the feeling. Regardless, his cock offered to rise halfway. The veiled female raised her arms to calm everyone.

"Are you saying… Did you and your brothers share your mother's womb?"

"Yes." Arson couldn't figure out why this was so strange to them.

"But you…*you*, Arson, are not generally angry or think yourself important. Are you?"

Keeping his eyes high to try to dissuade attention from his renewed erection, Arson clicked his tongue. "You're trying to assess my general temperament?" he said. "The angry one, I'd say, is my brother Poison. He can be easily excited or quick to get mad. I'm the one who is often forgotten. The quiet one, I suppose. I was born last. You want angry? Go find my brother Poison and leave me be!" Ironically, her persistent questioning nudged at his anger. Poison would probably be lashing out already if they had captured him instead. Once again, Arson envied Poison for his incredible nerve. He'd have not only the balls to take these men on right now, he would probably also succeed and escape with a female draped over his shoulder—all done while in the nude!

The veiled female let out a deep breath. She raised her veil, and Arson froze, his annoyance and readiness to try walking off the scene with whatever dignity he had left went forgotten. Instead, her large eyes, wreathed in long dark lashes, made his heart sink. Her black and shiny hair, like a horse's coat, threw off hot red flashes in the light's angles.

"That's good to hear," she said. "I think you will be all right here for a time. It's another hint of the taint to be born in multiples. The way you describe your temperament next to your brother's suggests that you may not have as much of it as he does." He didn't miss her eyes' quick tour around his body before rising back up to meet his.

They had a long way to go as he exceeded her height by a good foot and a half. "My name is Hanhelin. I'm the third daughter of the king of Norr. Customarily, the third princess is destined to be the Grand Desteer, and I'm no different. I'd like to talk with you more, but my *saehgahn* don't trust you. It would make things much easier if you can swear allegiance to me. I can induct you into the order of the *saehgahn*, and hence you can walk free and serve me. Would you agree to this?"

He could walk free? That would greatly increase his chance of escape. He'd be stupid not to agree. "Yes," he said.

Chapter 10
The Study

"Induct him into the White Owls are you insane, Your Majesty?" Cavlihen barked in Hanhelin's tent later that night. She helped Yhulin to arrange her bedding as he yelled, something she normally didn't do, but in this case, she needed a chore to help her feign nonchalance.

"We won't consider him quite a *full* member yet," she said. "He'll need training anyway so he knows how to be a White Owl. He'll be closely watched, of course."

Cavlihen pinched his nose bridge. "Induction or no induction, the minute you take those shackles off him, he'll run away…if not kill us all while we sleep."

Hanhelin sucked in a breath, standing up straight from her stooped position after smoothing out her side of the top blanket. "I just…" She huffed. "I used the lesser version of *milhanrajea* on him, and I don't think he'll do that—escape *or* kill us."

"Then what will he do?"

Hanhelin's cheeks warmed. She didn't have an answer for Cavlihen, but she knew she could definitely form a plan for what to do with Arson to keep him alive and conduct a long study of him. She might have to make him *sarakren* properly and later graduate him to being a White Moth—the personal guard of the Grand Desteer. But before she could proceed in any way, she had to make him a *saehgahn*, an idea

Cavlihen and the rest of them hated.

"I'll see about him," she told Cavlihen.

"What does that mean?" His face had gone red, and she knew he had every reason in the world to be in a raving panic right now. The Overseas Taint was not an issue to trifle with.

"I'll need to do another physical examination, followed by several mental examinations."

Cavlihen roared instead of grunting his displeasure. "We have no luxury to pause; there're walking clouds spilling down from the north. We have to get you home!"

She knew as much, and she couldn't let it happen. Delaying their trip out there in the forest would provide the best opportunity to perform this most important examination.

Yhulin's sweet voice piped up. "What about your alchemy study, *Ameiha?*"

Hanhelin closed her eyes. "That's important, but this might be more important." How could one weigh the two: troll attacks or the Overseas Taint?

She dished out the easier answer first. "I've made great strides to fighting the trolls." The harder answer to formulate was how she'd use her authority to delay their trip so she could do her most important study of all. Back at the palace she was princess number three. Out here she was Hanhelin, third princess of Norr, the highest-ranking person in the caravan. She had more authority out here than at home. She couldn't begin to wonder how Arson would be received in her home clan with her father staring down his nose at the foreigner. They'd easily kill him on the spot and not give a sniff at what Hanhelin thought of it, but their situation in this moment was different.

She nodded firmly to Cavlihen. "I know what to do."

"What the hell are you doing now?" Arson demanded as they stripped his clothes off yet again but this time with no body of water in sight but a small, sunny meadow, exposing him to all eyes of the camp. They put heavy shackles on his wrists with chains extended to the sides, fed over tree branches, and two strong elves pulled them taut.

Strung up like a clothesline, he longed for the stretch of trees in the background. *Where are you, my brothers?* If they could only find him, the four of them would tear right through this caravan.

Hanhelin approached him calmly, hidden under all those veils, and her maidservant got straight to setting up a writing table with a stack of loose-leaf parchment and a quill, often sending intrigued glances right at his vulnerable body. A young male elf working with the girl opened a small, dusty box with lumps of charcoal and graphite within.

"Be calm, Arson," Hanhelin said as she waited for everyone to get situated. "I told you I'd like to know more about you."

"Well, I talk better with clothes on," he shot back.

A smirk might have quirked her delicate lips, but he couldn't be sure from this side of her dark veil. "Today we're doing a physical exam. Mental exams will take place in my tent, away from so many ears."

"A physical exam?" In utter confusion he regarded his exposed flesh. "Didn't you see enough of my cock yesterday?"

Hanhelin sighed. "Your 'cock' looks about average to me, but you'll need to understand that you are different from us in a much deeper way."

Arson scrunched his face and observed the other males around him. Besides his pale colored hair, he couldn't fathom how much difference she saw in him. He was an elf just like everyone else here. Actually, at this point, he grew weary of being an elf. If he could go back in time to being a "devil," he'd do it in a heartbeat.

"Are we ready?" Hanhelin asked her attendants.

"Nearly," the young boy answered. He appeared to be sketching something with the graphite. A human figure?

"All right, we'll start simple. Arms."

At her order the two chain holders tugged his wrist restraints out tightly, forcing Arson to reach out to the sides.

"Kneel, you fool!" A guard at his back kicked the crook of Arson's knee and he dropped. Arson growled out his anger aside from the pain at the rude attack. An elf with a thin length of leather, like a belt with painted stripes, approached and extended one end at his shoulder and ending at his wrist. He counted the painted stripes on the rope.

"Four *krons!*" the elf declared, and the maidservant dipped her quill into the inkpot and labeled Ari's drawing accordingly.

"Legs," Hanhelin ordered, and they made Arson stand up so his leg measurement could be recorded in the same way. It took an awful lot of willpower to keep from kicking the idiot in the head while he was in range.

"What's the point of all this?" Arson asked the princess.

"It's science," Hanhelin told him. "We have to tell the books of history exactly what we've found here. You see, most of what we have written about the Overseas Taint are stories and vague accounts of meeting elves of your like. You are a rare find, so I will write all I learn about you for future generations to benefit from my findings…if I don't manage to solve the taint's mystery entirely."

Arson scoffed. "This is stupid."

"No, it's not."

"I'm not tainted! I'm just a person. I must get back to my fa—" The guard behind him ended his complaints with a knock to his head with a wooden spear shaft.

"Please comply, Arson," Hanhelin said softly in an attempt to soothe him. "You don't know anything about the taint, which I understand, but it's a deathly serious matter. Perhaps it's thanks to the Bright One I've found you. It's probably thanks that *I* found you before anyone else in my country—for your benefit as well as Norr's!"

Arson hissed now. His irritation at all this harassment was mounting too high.

"What next, *Ameiha*?" the measuring elf asked.

Hanhelin dropped her chin and gave a stern nod, obviously frowning despite the obscurity of her black veil held down by a gold circlet.

The elf nodded back and then held the leather end up to Arson's flaccid penis.

"Oh my god, Great Sea, really?" He spat at the princess.

"I'm sorry if this makes you uncomfortable. In Norr, it's our custom for males to be brought up without shame. I know you were raised elsewhere."

"It's okay," Arson barked in all-out embarrassment. "Let's see if it's a good fit for your mouth, hah!" His incredulous, scoffing laughter turned into a growl when the guard behind him let loose, banging his head with his spear shaft until Arson fell to the ground to fend off the blows with his forearms. The chain holders pulled his arms out again.

"That's enough," Hanhelin ordered. She stepped closer to him when all had calmed down. Arson kept his chin tucked in a measly effort to protect himself with his arms pulled out. "Since he's down here, let's go ahead and count his teeth." She said to Arson, "Open your mouth and behave yourself. Ari, sketch!"

Mercilessly, the elves followed every whim the princess's sick mind conjured up. After counting every tooth in his mouth, they measured the length of every finger and toe, the palm of his hand and width of his heel. Any detail they could think to record on paper about Arson, they did.

When they finally let him close it, Arson clamped his mouth shut. It was probably better to get it all over with, or they'd knock him out again if he put up any more resistance. But the minutes turned into two hours or more! The princess's little page boy sketched all of Arson's features down fast, and her handmaiden labeled it in ink, all for the good of the "future of Norr." Arson couldn't wait to get back into that musty covered wagon and be shackled down to its frame.

He couldn't even get all the way through processing his feelings of violation once left alone, because after only another hour or so, they hauled him right back outside as soon as the sun offered to dip and chained him up tighter than ever to enter the biggest tent in the camp. At least they let him wear his clothes this time.

Hanhelin paced around, shaking her hands feverously inside, less calm than when she put such humiliating torture on him throughout the daylight hours.

"I think I'm ready to try it," she said to Cavlihen, her guard captain, the one who sneered hardest at Arson anytime the two were in the same space.

"Are you sure?"

Hanhelin pointed to the two big trunks at the center of the space. They locked Arson's chains to the trunks' handles to help prevent him from running away.

"Sorry my hands are tied," Arson said. "I won't be able to whip *it* out for you right now."

Cavlihen grunted and lunged forward to put another blow on Arson's head, but Hanhelin leaped between them and pushed him back with two firm palms to his chest.

"No! Cavlihen. Calm down. He needs to be calm for this, and I need concentration. It's a dangerous experiment since I'm a little green yet."

Arson lowered his eyebrows. "What is?"

Hanhelin turned around and flipped her veil up to give him a rare view of her face. Arson swallowed at the sight of her soft edges and radiant eyes. In this dimly lit tent, her hair looked blacker than ever, like a void he could fall into. She smiled at him! Suddenly his throat dried. Arson could no longer speak. *These* were female elves—marvelous and unearthly! His own species. He'd seen a good many women out on his missions. He'd seen Nanelle briefly, someone who often manned the pleasure box, but this…these females he was compatible with were something else!

"That's right," she said. "Let's all be calm." She turned her smile to Cavlihen. "All of us. Now please, Cav, go and sit over there."

He did so, kneeling in a position which made it easy to spring up again in case Arson tried something. Hanhelin's handmaiden, Yhulin, also a fine thing to behold, fidgeted in place nervously. She'd make a good wife for him if he could figure out a way to get free and whisk her out of there.

"Arson." That deep, sensuous voice of the princess snatched his attention back. She took a prim-looking position on a cushion opposite him. "I'm going to perform *milhanrajea* on you."

"I don't understand."

"It's a mind-viewing technique. It will help me get to know you and to make sure you mean us no harm."

"Does it matter? You've harmed me already."

She sighed. "All for necessity. You are a strange—"

"A stranger, I know, and in this land, you beat up on strangers. I get it."

Hanhelin fell silent but did have to raise her hand ever so slightly to signal Cavlihen not to punish him. Arson didn't bother to turn around to view that bastard again.

"I mean you well, I really do," Hanhelin said in her soft feminine voice. Bizarrely, it put him off guard again. She had such a soothing quality he'd never picked up in another person before. "I want to help you."

"There's nothing wrong with me."

Silence.

"This feat I'm about to attempt. It's dangerous."

"How?"

"Mind viewing is better accomplished by experienced Desteer maidens. I'm yet in training."

"How's it dangerous?" Arson demanded.

Hanhelin raised her hands and formed them like crescents, as if to cup someone's face on both sides. "It involves an electric shock shared between us. It won't hurt, but it will be a startling, cold jolt. If I do it wrong in any way, it may kill you."

Arson stiffened up.

"I want you to know that I've no ill will toward you. You being born with the Overseas Taint was never your fault. I meant the best for you. To help you—if you don't mind my repeating myself."

"You're talking as if I'm already dead!" Arson rose up on his knees as high as he could against his short chains.

"Please calm down. You're not dead…yet."

"What will you do if I die?"

"Give you a proper burial at Laugaulentrei as an honorable *saehgahn* deserves. And then…"

"And then?"

Hanhelin tightened her lips. "You said you had three brothers. We will go and catch them, and I'll continue my study with them."

Arson jerked against his bonds, his stomach boiling at the thought of harm coming to his loved ones. "No! Leave them alone!"

Hanhelin bowed her head at his emotion. "Forgive me, but we're searching for them anyway. We've alerted the nearest clan of their impending danger. They are a grave danger to our people indeed."

"Just let us go! We'll leave, I promise!"

"I admire your honor for your family, Arson."

He swallowed the lump in his throat, panic still on the rise.

"I shouldn't have told you this yet. I do need you to be calm."

"You can keep me if you let them leave in peace."

Hanhelin began folding up her long sleeves, revealing thin wrists and forearms wrapped in skintight inner sleeves. Her nails were manicured with jewels and enamels. "I intend to keep you alive and healthy, Arson. I would honor your request to let them leave the country with a promise to never return, but that decision will probably belong to the Sa-Destrai and my aunt, the Grand Desteer."

"The Sa-Destrai?"

Hanhelin hummed. "Let's see, you wouldn't know these words. The Sa-Destrai is like what in the Lightlands they consider a king."

"King, yes," Arson said.

"And for your information, his consort is considered Fa-Destrah."

"You mean the queen. And now what the hell is a Grand Desteer?" he asked, hoping to prolong his impending death.

"She advises the Sa-Destrai sometimes as well as lead the country in spirituality," Hanhelin answered. Flexing her fingers, she moved closer to him. Arson leaned back. "The Grand Desteer is also the head of the Desteer cult," she continued, a bit vacantly as she prepared to perform her dangerous magical feat.

Arson tightened his lips. He might've asked more questions, but if this was inevitable, it might be best to let her concentrate.

"I've never successfully performed this rite," she murmured.

"Why'd you have to say that?" he responded, staring past her graceful hands to her stunning indigo eyes. They caught Arson's like a magnet. He held his breath. She slid her hands into his hair, and putting aside the terror of what he knew it meant, it exhilarated him. Aroused him! This woman! He didn't blink—he couldn't!

Those indigo eyes closed…

Arson's closed but not to follow hers. A bright flash of light filled his head. A splash of cold water hit, but not a physical one. He flinched and shuddered and fell slack. His shackles kept him from crumpling entirely to the ground. A groan creeped up his throat involuntarily in the residual chills, like icy razors, rushing across all his limbs.

"I saw it!" Hanhelin shrieked. "I saw…"

"Is he alive?" some male elf asked.

A harsher male voice barked, "Yhulin, don't touch him!"

"Arson?" Hanhelin said frantically. Hands patted his face, maybe hers, but maybe not. "He *is* alive. Give him space."

The icy razors persisted. Arson didn't want to move.

"See? He's breathing." Regardless of her order to give him space, the heat and breaths of many bodies hovered over him.

He flinched. Drool had streamed down his cheek. He offered to move, and everyone sprang backward.

The princess was staring at him when he focused his eyes. She whispered his name, "Arson," as if in amazement rather than inquiry.

"Whah'd you do ta meh?" he asked, slurring the question up with a numb tongue. He righted himself and wiped his drool along his sleeve, needing to lean his head over to do it. Hanhelin held her hands over her mouth. Tears had wet her own cheeks.

"*Ameiha*," Cavlihen said. "Are you all right?"

"Is *she* all right?" Arson mocked. "Hah!"

Yhulin answered his comment, "Well, at least Arson bounced back quickly enough."

"He survived because of his evil power—"

Hanhelin snipped off Cavlihen's comment. "No! He survived because of my successful effort."

"What did you see, *Ameiha*?" Yhulin asked.

As if reminded, Hanhelin took a deep breath and beheld Arson once again. "He's…" She nodded her head. "He's honorable."

"What?"

"He's loyal and strong and hardened—as can be expected of a *saehgahn*." She spoke her words with conviction but bit her lip and returned to staring at Arson right after.

Cavlihen, Yhulin, and the page boy all gawked for a moment.

"So… What does that mean?" Cavlihen asked.

Her answer didn't wait to pop out of her mouth. "It means it would be shameful of us to senselessly kill him."

Another long silence. Why should they think Arson was evil anyway? He'd only done right by his family all his life. He loved his father and brothers!

"He wasn't raised as an elf," Hanhelin explained. "His so-called father is a man who adopted him and raised him as a warrior— No! An assassin."

Everyone blinked at him, and Arson blinked back. How could she know?

Hanhelin looked down at her hands. "He lives a life of discipline, just like a *saehgahn*." She trailed her gaze to Yhulin. "Prepare my vestments."

"For what, *Ameiha*?"

"For a *saehgahn* naming ceremony."

Cavlihen worked his jaw before stammering, "N-no!"

Arson could only watch their exchanges helplessly in his chained-up state. Her mind-viewing spell left him feeling shaky and exposed. Those things she said about him. It was as if she'd seen everything in his head. Didn't she say she'd do that very thing?

Ignoring Cavlihen's protest, Hanhelin stood up and faced him. She snatched the small ring of keys off his belt and he let her, having suddenly lost his strong reserve to argue against her. She used one of the keys to personally unlock Arson's wrist shackles.

Quickly he glanced around the tent, gauging the amount of armed people, the unarmed, and whether Arson stood a chance against them all. It would be a long shot unless he could get one of their weapons. His heart sped up, preparing the attempt. He had to get back to his family!

Hanhelin's eyes met his, and his heart skipped and slowed. She held his stare for the time it took to unlock his second shackle. He swallowed, forgetting about the hasty decision to fight his way out. His heart continued its decline, and he couldn't understand why. Trying to fight right now would've ended in his death anyway, by all likelihood. A gentle smile graced her soft, pink lips. Did she know that she was affecting his heartbeat and emotions?

"You'll be all right among us now, Arson."

He might've shot back something cocky, but his throat dried. He nodded. She stood back to observe him and he sat there, free, but he didn't make any move. Not to attack, not to snatch her or her handmaiden, or even to speak.

"You'll go back to the wagon you've been riding in and prepare yourself mentally while I get ready for the ceremony." She nodded again, as if for herself, smiling with a confident warmth—a favor graciously extended to him. "Tonight I'm going to make you *saehgahn*."

Chapter 11
Initiation

haus paced by the campfire, wringing his hands. he waited for Bludgeon or Bleed to return from their scouting missions, refusing even to eat until at least the two returned. They were covering two different directions today to try to catch a hint of Arson's trail. They had been so fazed since the elves' ambush they had missed which direction Arson's kidnappers had taken off in. Right now Poison was trying to charm Linhala, but the woman was cold as ice. Not that Poison had any experience to help his task—the kid made Haus cringe. Of course, it was his own fault for refusing to teach his boys about how to handle women all those years.

Haus bypassed his group of men by the secondary fire who'd already dug into their big slabs of venison they'd hunted out of the forest. The aroma of cooked meat teased his nose, but he refused to partake yet. He decided instead to march over to Poison by a tree where Linhala huddled with her hands held up by her face as if to shield herself from his purred speeches as he tugged at her wrist. Haus yanked Poison's wrist.

"What's the matter, Father?" he asked in an annoyed whine. He couldn't blame Poison's frustration. Haus had been a horny virgin once upon a time too.

"Aren't you worried about your brother?"

Poison took a step back and acted offended. "Of course! But it's not my turn to search."

"Well, maybe you should be out there anyway. If I don't have all four of my boys back safe…" He shook his head with his mouth hanging open. "I just don't think I'll be all right."

Poison gave him a smile with a hand on his shoulder. "Found or not found, I know Arson's fine. He's as strong as any of us."

"Sure, but he's also more on the sensitive side."

Poison laughed out loud. "Since when do you worry about our feelings?"

Haus felt himself blush. "Shut up! By the way, what the hell's going on with your wife?"

Poison snatched a glance at her behind him. The woman was glaring at them both. "I'm working on it."

Haus threw his arm around the tall kid and guided him back toward the fire. "Women are a funny breed," he told him. "You can't trust 'em."

"Yes, you've told us. How do you get them to the point of marriage if they're acting like her?"

"You gotta bargain with 'em, you get me? Find out what she wants, and then get her to give you what you want in return for it."

In Poison's silence, Haus could almost see the puzzle pieces moving around in his pretty head. "But when I was with—I mean it seems like…"

"What are ya trying to say, boy? Out with it."

"Um… She won't talk to me. How am I supposed to find out what she wants if she won't tell me?"

"What has she said so far?"

"'I want to go home. You'll be destroyed by the *saehgahn*. You tread a dangerous path and there's a forceful wind creeping behind you.'" Poison finished with a shrug.

"Okay, well. Here," Haus began. "She said she *wants* to go home." Poison waited.

"So tell her you'll take her home in exchange that she lie down and let you do your deed."

Poison scrunched his nose. "But I don't want to take her home."

"She doesn't have to know that, which is the beauty of it!" Haus elbowed him in the hip, the highest point at which he could reach.

"Trust me when I say, she'll do the same thing to you."

"She'll what?"

"She'll bargain with you for sex just to get what *she* wants out of *you*. Women do it all the time. They know that we want something far simpler, and they'll use their bodies to rob us blind."

Poison grimaced and glanced back at his wife again. "That's horrible."

Haus nodded with his eyes closed. "I know, I know. They're a sneaky kind, but you can be sneaky too."

When Poison turned as if to get back to it, Haus pulled his wrist again. "Nah! Give it a rest for tonight. Come sit by the fire with me. You should have something to eat, though I'll wait for your brothers."

"I'm back," Bludgeon said in a low voice as he tromped through the tall grass from the forest.

Haus leaped forward on his short legs. "Where's Arson?"

Bludgeon shrugged. "Haven't seen any life out there."

"Damn!"

He went straight to the fire to kick off his boots and rub his own feet. "But I found the trail where a caravan went through. It's taking a faint road through the woods. A less used one than the common road."

Haus and Poison joined him. "It must be them. Which way is the caravan going?"

"South and west."

"Then that's the way we'll go," Haus declared. "We'll wait to see if Bleed found anything and then form a strong plan."

"It was a big caravan, Father," Bludgeon warned. "I'd hate to think about attacking them for revenge."

"I don't need revenge. I need my Arson back," Haus said. "It'll be a stealth mission."

Poison grinned from his seat across the fire from Haus. "Stealth is what we're all about."

Arson sat in his muddle, unchained, in the covered wagon for another hour before they called him out yet again, not so forcefully but with the same stern expectation. Spying them through the flaps, he found the elves kept their close watch on him. Without any bound limbs though, his chance of escape was already greatly improved.

Forced to walk across camp, his moment of chance had yet to reveal itself. The guards, with the princess's head man at the lead, escorted him—probably to her. Arson checked to his left and right at the darkening forest for any clue or path to get the hell out of there. If and when he made the attempt, he figured he could easily follow the caravan's trail backward to reunite with his family. But soon a big familiar tent came around the bend. Indeed, he'd see her again.

They didn't take him to the tent though. Its cold, dark appearance announced the princess wasn't in. Instead, they took him wordlessly past it into a little clearing in the brush where a beautiful voice hummed long notes.

"Arson." The voice snapped his attention to the pale figure standing between two trees.

Three male voices hissed before a sharp exhale preceding the startling ignition of colored light, orbs of it, floating over three stones. One of the elves proceeded to light a fourth, and in this light, Hanhelin's white robes blossomed in three shades: red, yellow, and lavender.

She wore no veil tonight. Instead, her long black hair draped heavily over her head like a hood of hot tar. Her beauty seemed to have been overtaken tonight, however, by a stern mien under a thick layer of white paint covering her face. A purple stripe had been drawn across her eyes, obscuring their otherwise beautiful shapes and thick lashes. Suddenly Arson remembered the "Desteer maidens" he and his family had spoken to when they first arrived in Norr. Hanhelin was yet another one of those women. She frowned as if Arson deserved a severe beating, and after she'd removed his shackles and showed him some sense of favor earlier when he'd survived her mind-viewing trick.

The male elves took him to the center of the clearing, and Hanhelin approached, gliding gracefully over the mossy ground.

"It's easy to assume you've never had a *saehgahn* naming ceremony," she said. "Have you?"

Arson didn't know what that was, so he shook his head.

"Kneel down. Your becoming a *saehgahn* is crucial to your survival in Norr. Becoming a White Owl will be the next important step."

Arson swept his stare around the present company. "A White Owl?" he murmured. He had noticed a good number of male elves wore special white uniforms and cloaks. Cavlihen, for one, wore a mantle of white feathers over his armor.

Hanhelin continued, "The *saehgahn* are not merely the opposite sex to females in our culture. They are an order all their own, a sacred order to which all male elves are inducted." Over his lowered stance, she raised her hands high. A set of extra-long sleeves hung from them, waving gently in the breeze like colorful flames themselves in this magical lighting. "Bright One, our Forest Architect, this is Arson, and he is stricken with a foul disease."

Arson furrowed his eyebrows. "Disease?" he whispered.

"And though I intend to learn about his disease, I beg You to cure him of it. You sent him to us, and I thank You! He will now be a *saehgahn*. Never let his hair be cut, and never let him stray off the path of honor. Because on his journey he will be met with many temptations. Give him the strength to resist!" She looked down to him. "Arson, the world is harsh, but serve me and the Bright One well even if you are stricken with pain and suffering."

Yhulin approached with a bucket and dumped its freezing contents over his bowed head, and then without warning, Hanhelin slapped his face with her hand. It stung—a lot! More than he'd guess. The rings on her fingers didn't help.

Stunned and gasping, Arson might've roared and maybe struck back, but he couldn't. He fell backward, frozen in some unexplainable paralysis. This was like the experience in her tent earlier but so much worse.

The minute he hit the earth, his ability to move returned and he collected himself, though a persistent cottony blankness stuffed his mind, smothering his previous anger and offense and leaving him at a loss for opinion at the moment. He lost all composure of his expression. After all those years of practice in appearing stoic before other people, these elves were seeing how dumbfounded he could be.

Hanhelin reached down to his face, and he recoiled. He tried to scoot backward, to avoid her touch, but found himself a little too weak and disoriented. Her fingers grazed his face, and he paused at the feeling.

"Don't disappoint me," she said.

Stupidly he nodded, staring up at her, but only seeing a dark stripe across her oval-shaped face, between two thick curtains of hair.

"And also, be wary around the other *saehgahn*. They still don't like you. They don't trust outsiders who weren't brought up among them. They will be harsh with you, but that's how they are. They're harsh with each other too."

One of the *saehgahn* approached bearing a folded set of white clothes.

"Stand up and receive your new station, Arson," Hanhelin ordered, and he scrambled to his feet to obey. "You are one of mine now."

The sound of his wagon doors slamming open startled Arson awake. "Get out," a harsh male voice barked. "Today you must train."

"Train?" he mimicked groggily. Finally something familiar. He moved eagerly now, dressing in the Norrian White Owl uniform, getting frazzled at how the leggings worked. The elves called it *sagarhik*, and it covered less around the hips than the clothing of Kell's Key: just a pair of braies to cover what mattered, paired with a separate tube for each leg to be tied to his belt. This breezy garment left a bit of his behind cheeks visible. He overcame the initial embarrassment and ventured outside with this on. Everyone else wore the same thing anyway.

The Norrians' training regimen turned out much different than expected. The elves prepared no decadent breakfast to lovingly greet him to the new day. None of his brothers were present to chuckle and reminisce with him—the missions they'd accomplished and the women they'd seen. No beautiful training hall with gilded doorframes and murals of victorious warriors wearing devil masks on any plastered walls. There was mud, there were trees, and lots of growling male elves who hated him. Nearly every one of them took some sneaky chance to shove or trip or knock him in the back of the head when they caught him not paying enough attention. After the first of one such attempt, he blew off and attacked the elf, only to be piled upon by the rest of them, all of them so angry and fierce they would not have cared if he suffocated.

Cavlihen leaned over to view him at the bottom of the pile. "Behave," he growled in broken common tongue.

The rest of the morning offered a grueling regimen of drills consisting of running, jumping over obstacles, and tediously working with a partner, punching at his open palms and then reversing the roles. It took a lot of Arson's willpower not to punch the scowling idiot in the face. Several times he looked around him, at the forest, and longed for freedom, but these elves were constantly staring at him, openly distrustful.

"The princess orders our departure," Cavlihen announced. *"Enherahp!"* At his formal word, all the elves paused, performed some fast handwork, which ended in a bow, and then all moved on to other chores. Arson blinked at them before copying their bow. Cavlihen approached him, shaking his head. "No, like this." He raised one hand and held it. Arson did the same. Cavlihen laid it across his chest, clicked his heels together, and folded his other hand behind him. Arson definitely struggled with getting it right. "No, reverse your hands, idiot."

Flustered, Arson did so, and Cavlihen went through the rest of the motion slowly.

"What am I doing?"

"Honoring the princess."

"But she's not here."

Cavlihen reached out and slapped a flat hand across Arson's forehead. He endured the blow with tight lips, watery eyes, and more pent-up anger than he'd ever had to bear.

Cavlihen left a stiff finger in his face rather than take his hand down. "The princess is *always* with you!" he lectured. "She's the reason you are alive—literally—and the reason you will go on living. That goes for all of us. We will all die for her someday and better sooner while we're at our strongest."

Arson blinked at him, his anger dispelling at the realization. He really was a *saehgahn* now. She owned him. He'd even agreed to serve her last night when she had him all dazed and intimidated in her little ceremony. Though he'd prefer to keep to the belief that he served his father, he couldn't deny this new feeling that had befallen him. A feeling he couldn't quite place, but when he tried, it felt like he...

needed Hanhelin. Knowing he couldn't have her made him sad. How bizarre. His urge to escape faded under this new need to be near the princess, but he could put it back if he tried hard enough using his logic. His libido was certainly still in place—complemented by his yearning to obtain a wife. Too bad it couldn't be Hanhelin.

He no longer had to ride in the musty covered wagon. For a day, they walked, and though Arson walked on his own, the eyes of his fellow Owls followed him wherever he went, eliminating any possibility of escape while on the move. The daylight wouldn't be a good time anyway. He would need the cover of night if he were to make any move at all.

During a brief pause, it occurred to him to sketch out the familiar outlines of his devil mask in the dirt among some clustered bushes in case his brothers were tracking him.

Back on the move, he twisted around to view the princess's entourage behind him. Her handmaiden rode before her, dressed bright and beautiful, but not nearly as richly as Hanhelin dressed. That handmaiden…

"Face forward, fool!" the elf behind him snapped and clipped a fist across his chin to set him straight.

Arson ground his teeth, holding in more of his anger and frustration at having to take hits without hitting back in order to keep out of trouble. His patience wouldn't last much longer.

Nonetheless, he didn't have to stare at her to know what he needed to do next. His father had brought him and his brothers here to retrieve elven wives so they could breed more devils to strengthen House LinGor for all ages. Elven females had proven to be a rare sight here, but he'd get one. He made a silent vow to leave here with that handmaiden—tied up if need be—and go back to join his family triumphantly.

For the next whole day, Arson helped pitch their campsite, and then he trudged about it, enduring lectures he barely understood and carrying out menial tasks not worth his time, like gathering firewood and fetching buckets of water for the cook.

Though Arson was free to walk around now, no one had handed

him a weapon yet. They drilled him with a wooden sword, not an uncommon practice, but when traveling, a steel sword would work much better for defense—even to defend the princess's caravan. He quickly got the feeling they weren't going to give him a real weapon at all. Perhaps Hanhelin herself would have to give them the word first.

Anything given to him was thrown at his head instead of handed, like his bedroll and kit of grooming tools, consisting of a comb and soaps for keeping fresh and clean. The only thing they didn't chuck at him was all the proper pieces of his White Owl uniform. The white cloak had a mantle attached to it with embroidery on the back of each shoulder: a royal seal and a stylized owl emblem. This marked the royal family's elite guard, a duty bestowed on a concentrated number of elves. Looking around him, most of the elves wore green or blue. He knew Hanhelin had given him the honor to help keep him from the chopping block, but he knew he deserved the station anyway and had proven himself in the drills and practices both days so far.

During such practices, he often twisted around to check for Hanhelin's impression at his ability, but she wore her veils during such occasions and appeared blank under its obscurity. She was studying him hard, he knew it. Anytime he gazed at her added a new starch to his back and shoulders, and he worked harder.

As the sun waned, Arson moved about the outskirts of camp, picking up twigs for the fires, and the darkening forest suddenly occurred to him. He could make a dash, right now, as fast as possible.

Just drop the sticks and go! You're better than all this menial work and abuse, he told himself. Arson bit his lip, staring into the deepening shadow. He still needed to claim his wife, but these stupid elves were taking him farther and farther away from his family's location every day.

"Arson!" Cavlihen barked.

What now? Instead of barking back the answer, he merely twisted to view him, holding an armful of smelly old branches.

"The princess is summoning you to her tent."

Arson lost his blank mien. He couldn't think of anything to say back, so he followed the captain and dropped his load on the pile along the way.

In her tent, Hanhelin sat formally, as always, with her handmaiden poised at a short writing desk and her page boy arranging charcoal sticks and cloths for drawing.

"Welcome, Arson." She extended her hand in a gentle and practiced way to the cushion across from her. "Sit."

Arson did, ogling all that went on in here. Both candles and magical light orbs provided light to last them however long they'd be.

"Don't worry," Hanhelin said as he continued to eyeball the people and things, checking to see if there were any chains or barrels they might decide to chain him up to. "I'm not going to touch you tonight, body or mind. Instead, I want to hear you speak."

"You forgot what my voice sounds like?" He snorted.

She cleared her throat. "Forgive my common tongue. I'm trying to master it as a Grand Desteer should. We shall have a talk, and I will know more about you on a personal level."

He spread his hands. "Nothing to talk about."

"On the contrary, there are lots of things to talk about." She grazed her fingers along a decorative book beside her. "You have the Overseas Taint, and though I saw into your mind, there's so much I still need to know about you." Arson waited until she cleared her throat again. "Also, during our conversation, I must ask you to hold perfectly motionless. Ari will be sketching your portrait—for our history records."

Arson scoffed, put up his knee, and rested his arm across it. "That kid has already sketched every inch of me."

"Not necessarily," she countered. "He hasn't done a detailed observation of your face. Future generations will want to know exactly what your face looked like."

"Once again, you're talking as if I'm already dead. I'm *alive* and glad for it. I don't want to think about death yet. I don't like the way you've been treating me. Okay?"

An uncomfortable silence. Hanhelin's veils were beginning to seem like a security barrier for her. She pulled her lips in and blinked her dark eyelashes. "I apologize."

"I just want to go home," he added.

"Why did you come here, Arson?"

Yhulin tucked down tightly to jot his answer.

"You saw inside my mind. Doesn't that make this meeting pointless?"

She shook her head, veils swishing slightly. "No. I glimpsed images but not reasons. I did hear voices, from which I might glean reason, but I'll still need to hear your answers to my questions."

"My father and me and my brothers came here to trade goods with your people," Arson said.

Hanhelin stuttered and blinked again. She shook her head a bit firmer. "Cavlihen."

"*Ameiha?*"

"Step out."

"I can't... *Ameiha*? Are you sure?"

"Yes. Step out. I'll call you if I need you. Yhulin and Ari, you may also go."

Cavlihen clicked his tongue. "The princess has spoken." He shot her an intense stare. "I'll be standing *right* outside the flap."

"I know," she said in a breath. "You always have been."

Yhulin didn't look so certain either as she crossed the space, walking gingerly over the rug, passing Arson as he stared at her. Her eyes flicked to him briefly, and he gave her a flirtatious smirk. He observed all her comely angles and movements. Her long, dark hair was half swept up in a fancy arrangement along her head, the other side hung down mysteriously. Arson sniffed her air in her passing, flowery and fresh, and it turned him hard with a sense of needful delight. It had been a pretty long time since he'd used the pleasure box. He shamelessly watched the shape of her backside as she exited.

"Arson," Hanhelin whispered with a rough edge.

He snapped back to attention.

"You don't realize how deeply you endanger your own life."

He reared his head back, frowning. These elves were so confusing and filled with mysterious rules. All of this exhausted him.

She leaned forward, baring intense seriousness. "As you've said, I *have* seen inside your mind, and it's not good. Just now, you have lied. Tell me the real reason your family is in Norr."

He sighed. "We need wives," he said. "When we get one for each of us, we'll leave your country forever, and I mean that. I will never return."

"Wives." Her voice grew harder each time she spoke.

He nodded, spreading his hands, oblivious as to why this was such a problem. "We thought we were devils, but we're elves. The Lady Lexion told my brother so when he slept with her. When my father heard this, he decided we should have wives of our own species. What's the problem?"

The princess huffed. "I'm trying to understand," she said. "Maybe your culture being so different from mine is making it hard."

"I could've told you that up front," he said. He waved a hand along his own face. "You've studied my appearance extensively. Am I not a good specimen to woo a wife here?"

Hanhelin's shoulders slacked. If she could finally give up her stiff social proprieties, maybe they could have a fruitful conversation.

"Am I wrong for wanting a wife?" he pressed.

"By all natural inclinations, no," she finally said. "But in Norr, it's a sin to 'want a wife.'"

Arson wrinkled his nose.

She leaned back as if in an effort to relax. "I'll try to stay calm, Arson. I'll explain things to you and try not to take offense or disgust at what you tell me about yourself. Your culture is vastly different from ours, and I must receive your information scientifically, but Arson…"

She threw her veil back and sat forward again. She tapped the back of one hand into the palm of the other. "You must keep your voice low and stop acting so arrogant. The things you say offend your fellow *saehgahn*."

Arson lowered his brow. "But I haven't—"

"They will *kill* you, Arson, the moment they think you mean to do me harm, and they *do* think that. Your attitude and your lying and your comments edge them closer to striking." She sucked in a long pull of air through her nose. "I have a lot of authority as Tinharri princess, but my authority only goes so far against that of Saehgahn Law." He opened his mouth to ask after the definition, but Hanhelin kept talking. "Saehgahn Law is the loophole the males have to take all authority over the females. It's enacted in the presence of danger. It means Cavlihen will override my orders to spare you if he deems you a threat to me or Yhulin."

Arson blinked. "The handmaiden?"

"Yes."

His face remained contorted in his everlasting confusion. The muscles began to hurt in some places. "The handmaiden," he murmured. A handmaiden was merely a servant. Why would this princess, such a high office, be so worried for a simple handmaiden? He couldn't make any guesses about these crazy people. Arson shrugged. "Princess," he said formally. "My family and I mean you no harm. We're actually quite anxious to leave. My father is very rich and we need some wives, so…"

"So?"

He continued, "So how much gold would you like for Yhulin? I need to take her with me so we can leave as soon as possible."

In the candle light, he could see well enough how red Hanhelin's face grew. She dropped it into her hand, and her silky black hair spilled down around it, enshrouding her emotion. She sucked in air through her mouth—loudly. Was she crying?

"You can go."

"What did I say?"

"Go!" At her raised voice, the tent flap flew open and Cavlihen stormed in, reminding Arson what the princess had said about him, that he wanted to kill him at the first sign of danger. He threw his hard, hooked hands along Arson's arm and jerked him toward the exit. Arson still couldn't guess what he'd said wrong and how he'd made her so upset. He'd thought making marriage deals was a perfectly normal thing to do with people of high rank. Haus had told him and his brothers about bride prices on their way down here.

Sheer confusion and disorientation kept his limbs limp enough for Cavlihen to steer him straight out of the tent.

Chapter 12

Culture Shock

"Did you hear me, Ameiha?"

She didn't. Last night's conversation with Arson proved too distracting to entertain Cavlihen's breakfast-hour concerns. He spoke of Arson, of course, but Hanhelin and Cavlihen's thoughts about him were vastly different.

"Hmm?" she hummed back.

"I was saying, he's so strange. He sleeps sitting up—all night long. Each morning, he awakes at our nudge. We use a stick, of course."

She gawked at him. "A stick? Are you afraid to catch his Overseas Taint at the slightest touch of his sleeve?"

Cavlihen pulled his lips in. His tobacco pipe smoldered, forgotten on the stump beside him. "Yes, to be exact. We are worried to have him among us."

Hanhelin half stood up and pointed at him. "Well, stop it! He's an elf like us, and it won't make anything better to treat him as anything less. It can and will and is making matters worse." She shuddered upon sitting down. The way Arson spoke last night: wanting to *buy* Yhulin from her. As if Yhulin were a goat or a sack of grain! This foreigner put Hanhelin on edge same as he did to her *saehgahn*.

"We must all understand," she said for herself as much as for Cavlihen, "Arson was raised in the human lands. He knows nothing of elven ways. He knows human ways. His father is a man. Not a *saehgahn.* That's why he talks like a man and expects…"

"Expects what?" Cavlihen leaned forward, biting down on his pipestem.

"He expects us to deal in trade the way men do, but it's not quite the same here as where he grew up. That's why I need you to be patient. I'll tell him about our ways. This is a learning experience for him and all of us."

Cavlihen sniffed and sat back again. "I've seen him staring at Yhulin."

Hanhelin shuddered again. "I know. I'll talk to him." As soon as she gets over her ghastly dismay at his attitude toward females. "He simply doesn't understand Norrian conduct. It looks vile to us, but to him it's normal."

She caught how Cavlihen fingered the sheath of his dagger hanging on his belt. "I doubt you can fix him. Nonetheless, I'll be watching him."

"I know."

He stood up and stretched, dumped his pipe's bowl, and smashed his boot into the embers. "We must move again today."

"No!" She stood up too.

"Why? We're still not safe. Our scouts have estimated we're a day or two ahead of the fog."

He made a good point, but Hanhelin couldn't let them leave yet. If they could only camp here one more day and maybe spend an extra night at all future campsites, she might scrape together enough time to study Arson. She also needed to school him on the proper behavior of *saehgahn* before they reached the palace. The more he knew about the way to act, the longer he might survive in the palace. Otherwise, even as an inducted *saehgahn* and White Owl guard, Arson's life hung in the balance.

"I have much to study today, especially since it's such a clear day."

He huffed and peered around them. "They told me the winds might be pushing the fog back northward. Also, they've yet to see any trolls."

"One more day here?"

"If you insist, *Ameiha.*"

Right on schedule, night fell and Cavlihen directed Arson to Hanhelin's tent. His heart pace sped a bit, unsure how pleasant or unpleasant this meeting would be. He entered her tent to find her sitting where he last saw her, veiled once again. She sat behind the short-legged writing desk Yhulin usually manned. No handmaiden in sight to Arson's dismay.

"Where's Yhulin?"

"She won't be attending me tonight. In her stead, I'll be recording important notes for this meeting." When he continued looking around, she added, "Ari won't be here either. It will be better for him to sketch your likeness in the daylight."

"Fine by me," Arson said and plopped down on the cushion across from Hanhelin.

Cavlihen roared behind him, "Did the princess give you permission to sit yet, you worm?"

Arson winced and rolled, ready to fight off his attack, but Hanhelin shot up to stand behind him. All three of them froze.

"This is why I requested more time tonight, Cavlihen. Arson needs to be educated on conduct."

Cavlihen pointed a stiff finger at him. "Lesson one: Princess Hanhelin tells you when and where you can sit."

Hanhelin twisted around. "Arson, say these words to Cavlihen: *Awl don eh tarhonon*. 'I made a mistake.'"

Arson parroted the words, and Cavlihen relaxed but didn't wipe the scowl from his face.

"I'll be right outside as before."

Hanhelin sighed heavily at his parting. She motioned to the cushion. "Take your seat."

"Did I upset you last night?" Arson asked as she claimed hers.

"Yes," she said. The elves were a very honest sort of people, Arson was coming to know. "But I will try to ignore my discomforts. Your culture is vastly different from mine."

"Why is it bad to ask for Yhulin to be my wife?"

She raised her veil again, to his surprise, and he got the delight of gazing at her stunning face. A face more radiant than Yhulin's could ever be—considering the handmaiden herself was a world more gorgeous than the women back at home. Arson struggled to control his erections these days, especially considering how long it had been since his last release. Haus had explained to the boys long ago how important it was for a man to be "satisfied" and so had arranged a decent schedule for the pleasure box's use, not too many and not too few. Even during longer periods between missions, when affairs between houses were quite peaceful in Kell's Key, Haus arranged challenging games from which the quadruplets could earn the pleasure box and keep themselves "satisfied."

"I forgive you for asking such a foul question—to try to buy a female from me." She swallowed. "In Norr, males are not allowed to ask females for marriage or to bargain for them."

"Why?" Instead of waiting for her answer, he followed up. "In my culture, we have something called a *bride price*. It's good for matchmaking when a man wants a certain woman as his wife. Sometimes her family really needs the money. I only offered you gold as a courtesy."

She countered. "But in Norr, we have an imbalance under which my people suffer. To every three males only one female is born. If males were given the freedom to choose females, then they would wind up fighting over them. The scarcity would cause violence among us, and it already has in the past. We've remedied the violence by leaving the decision wholly up to the females. They are the ones who ask the males for marriage. Your 'bride price' is no good here."

Arson shook his head. "I don't get it. So how do I woo Yhulin?"

"You don't."

He shook his head in confusion.

"In a normal situation, Yhulin would watch all the *saehgahn* around her, either here on the road or at home in our clan. She would see their physique." This made Arson remember that initial meeting when Yhulin stared so shamelessly at his exposed body. Hanhelin continued, "She would listen to them talk. She would decide which one is her favorite and then send a token inviting him to the Desteer Hall. That's where he would formally be given a choice, to accept her proposal or not."

"So…," Arson began. "What if the *saehgahn* she chooses doesn't like her?"

"He's free to reject her proposal. However, as it goes in my country, by all likelihood, he would accept her invitation anyway."

"That doesn't sound good."

Hanhelin spread her hands. "*Saehgahn* live long, lonely lives, most of them. To avoid such brutal loneliness and also driven by his desire to"—she hummed—"breed, he is most likely to accept the proposal."

"Breed? You're talking about his sex drive actually."

"I don't understand some of your common tongue language."

"He wants to have *sex*," he reiterated. "We all do! That's what you're talking about. It's satisfaction."

"Satisfaction?" she mimicked. "Is this what you think of married couples' relations?"

"No. It's what I think of being male. It doesn't need to do with being married. It's the reason my brothers and I love accomplishing missions."

Hanhelin's face lit up red, and she quickly flipped her veil back over to hide it. "You speak of a concept that is foreign to my culture and by all fact and opinion *disgusting* to fathom."

Despite her opinion, Arson smiled in amusement. "That's why I want Yhulin. You see? I need satisfaction. My father says all men deserve it. With Yhulin as my wife, my father will get the grandchildren he wants. He wants lots of 'devils' in his household to protect him."

"Stop it!" she snapped.

At her sharp voice, the tent flap swung open.

"No, Cavlihen," Hanhelin called. "Everything's fine. Go stand outside."

His smile dropping, Arson licked his lips and leaned forward with a dip of his head. "What's the matter?"

She shook her head under her swishing veils. "You can't have Yhulin…or anyone."

He leaned to the side to try to see her face better under its obscurities. "Why?" he asked. "Can't I persuade her to choose me?"

"No."

He blinked at her, more confused than ever. "Then can I leave and go home with my family to Kell's Key?"

"No, Arson."

Miles away from the amusement he felt a minute ago, his heart sped again but not for the same reason. They weren't going to let him leave, and they weren't going to bargain with him for a wife. He was a prisoner. Trapped. His hands twitched, and a strange new hot feeling radiated within them. He needed to get out. A weapon. He could fight his way out. He might die trying but better that than being forced into the life of a celibate prisoner!

"Arson? No! Sit down!" Hanhelin rose and threw out her hands to stop him before he even realized he jumped up in panic. "Arson!"

He grunted and pulled away from her reach. Cavlihen met him halfway to the tent's opening, and they locked hands. His panicked state flying into wild abandon, he fought the elf, dropping and pulling his opponent with him where he rolled on top of him and pinned him down by his throat.

"No!" the princess yelled. At all the loud sounds, more hostile elves entered the tent. One threw himself in front of the princess, and the others worked together to lift Arson off Cavlihen.

"I told you he was dangerous!"

"Be calm!" the woman ordered.

Three against one proved too much for Arson to fend off. The elves overpowered him until he found himself pinned down similar to what he dealt the other elf.

Hanhelin stepped in close and prevented one elf from punching him in the face and two others from drawing their daggers.

"It's all right! He's not dangerous; he only tried to walk out. Something I told him upset him. He didn't attack me."

"Are you sure, *Ameiha*?"

She nodded. Her veil had fallen completely off her head and now lay forgotten on the ground somewhere. "I promise you, he wasn't being harmful. I overreacted."

After a good bit of argument between his captors, and those heavy trunks being dragged back into the tent, Arson found himself chained up as before. Hanhelin insisted again and again that she needed this night to study Arson. Cavlihen finally agreed but under the term that Arson be restrained.

Arson, himself, no longer had anything to say. His face burned, but he hadn't been hit in it. His eyes threatened to cry tears, something he wasn't allowed to do as one of the devils of House LinGor. Hanhelin sat across from him, frowning, as he stared back at her—actually he glared. She'd cleared out everyone in the tent to leave them alone again.

"Tell me about your father," Hanhelin said in a weak voice after a long and awkward silence since the last person walked out, begrudgingly, and clinging tightly to an unsheathed sword.

Arson didn't answer, too pissed to care about answering her pointless questions.

She waited. And waited.

"How about your brothers?"

He held his vow of silence.

"You said your brothers are identical to you?"

As silent as he kept, he openly glared at her, right at her eyes. He knew she feared him. She turned her head in search of her veil but didn't bother to retrieve it. Instead, she fidgeted her hands on her lap and cleared her throat with her eyes cast down at them. She observed the little writing table in front of her, quill and paper ready to go but yet unmarked. She reached out and took the table at its sides, lifted it, and set it aside. In all these actions, and without the veil, she finally looked like a normal person to him, not an otherworldly priestess like she had meant to resemble.

With the table out of the way, she moved her seat cushion closer to him and knelt down on it properly, knee to knee with Arson. He might've lost his angry edge at this turn of events but wasn't willing to change his attitude yet.

She whispered his name, "Arson," and the sound of it made the rest of the muscles in his face go slack. "Listen to me." She reached a hand toward his face, and he tensed up, terrified she'd send another magic shock through his skull like before to steal all the thoughts and memories out of his head.

Her skin connected with his along his cheek. She spoke again, just as soft, as if she meant to soothe him. It did. It did more than soothe though. His tears broke free and rolled shamefully down his cheeks.

"I don't like this either," she whispered. "When I found you, you were lying on the ground unconscious. They were going to kill you. I did all I could to save you. That's why you're here now, being treated in this way. The other way was death. Please understand."

"I want to go home."

"I know. I know…" She huffed. "It's very important to me and my people that I study you. I intend to find a way to know all about your tainted blood. I want to know if it can be neutralized. If we can do that, we might be able to go back to a happier state than we've lived. We won't have to have such strong feelings against elves like you."

She lingered her hand on his face and trailed it up to his hair. A warmth followed it, sending pleasurable trails of tingles behind all five fingertips. This touch was somehow more special than Nanelle's lips on his member, but he couldn't fathom why. It was less erotic, for sure. Could she be using a different magic now?

"Don't tell them I've touched you like this."

He opened his eyes from having them closed, so confused by all the feelings she caused him, from anger to sadness to pleasantness. This woman, who had seized him into her custody and subjected him to such embarrassments and torments, now captivated his mind and body all at once, and she wasn't even inside a pleasure box.

"I've never been touched like this," he caught himself saying.

Her hand paused its movement through his hair. "Really? What about your mother?"

He shook his head. "Didn't have one."

She removed her hand, and he watched it return to her lap.

Will you do it again? He couldn't manage to make himself ask for more due to the thickness in his throat. He'd told her the truth. He'd never known such a simple yet oh-so-pleasurable contact before. Haus used to tousle his and his brothers' hair when they were young, and that was about it.

"What happened to your mother?" Hanhelin's eyes bored into his.

He shrugged. "My brothers and I were found at sea. In a basket within a crate, strapped down to a raft."

Her eyes rounded and watered. This attention… What was going on?

"What's the matter?" he asked her. The attention kept him nice and hard down below, yet it also flattered his ego and made him want to share her emotion, but he shouldn't let himself cry again.

She shook her head, hiding her mouth behind her long sleeve. "Go on. Tell me more."

"Our father loves us. He's the only person we can trust."

"Did you not have a nanny or grandmother?"

"I don't really know what those things are."

"I see." Hanhelin sniffled and dabbed her eyes on a handkerchief. "I've seen many things in your memories," she said. "They are a bit confusing to me, but that may be because I'm unfamiliar with customs outside of Norr. Yet there are things I know about you that match our customs. Like your honed discipline and physical fitness. The *saehgahn* train and practice hard all their lives as you do, but they have mothers, you see, not just fathers. Their mothers cuddle them at young ages and comb their hair and touch them as I've touched you. They are not starved of affection as you are."

Starved of affection? Arson had never known of such a concept. All his life he'd been kept busy with training and discipline. He had run around and played games with his brothers from the time they could walk, but there was no female person around to touch his hair like Hanhelin had done. He still wished to ask her to do it again but didn't need another fight with her captain. How sad though, that he should've been getting this type of "affection" throughout his life! Why? Why did Haus not let him have a mother or a grandmother— or a nanny?

"And what about your father?" Hanhelin asked again in the same instant he thought of Haus.

Caught off guard, Arson blinked and recited the basic knowledge he knew of the man. "He's a powerful man, and a lot of people fear him." Arson suddenly found it easy to answer her questions. He wanted to answer them for some reason. "He raised us to protect him and to punish his enemies, so we do."

"I saw in your mind that you've killed people."

Arson nodded. "We do it for our father. When we please him, he lets us use the pleasure box."

She wrinkled her nose. She'd shown more facial expressions tonight than any other time he'd seen her. "The pleasure box?"

"That's where we get our satisfaction. It's the best," he said honestly. Her face twisted at what he said, so he said more to try to fill in whatever gaps dotted her understanding. "The missions are tough. Only my brothers and I can accomplish them. When we do, it makes our father so happy he hands us the key to a special room, actually a set of rooms only we can go into after a mission. There's food, and music comes through a grate in the wall where people play instruments in another room, and there's a pleasure box. Sometimes we fight over who gets to use it first—which is usually my brother, Poison. Last time Bludgeon beat him down to the carpet good enough to earn the first use."

"Beat him down?"

"Well, not badly. We like to tussle together. It's fun even though Poison usually comes out on top. One night I got to use the pleasure box first though." He smiled brightly at the end of that comment.

When he opened his mouth to say more, she stopped him. "Hold on. You didn't tell me what the pleasure box was yet. How do you use it?"

"Oh right." He described the shape of it and its beautiful brocade fabric covering to make it look pretty in the room and then its usage. The little slot where the devils undid their pants and put their eager cocks into the dark space to be serviced by a faceless person, usually with full lips and a skilled tongue. He went on to recount their last use of it, with Nanelle, and how Poison almost broke the box. Though that was a little bit of a stressful night, Arson laughed through the end of the story. It made a better story than a present happening.

Hanhelin didn't laugh though. Her face had gone pale.

Arson simmered down and asked, "What?"

Her hands trembled as she brought her handkerchief up to cover her mouth. He could only blink, chained to the two trunks as she rose and paced around, making *ick* sounds aside from soft sobbing she obviously didn't want her men outside to hear. She gasped and collapsed to her knees at the corner of the tent, facing away from him, her shiny black hair spilling down her back.

Arson fell silent, watching her, oblivious to her problem now, but it hurt his heart all the same. She didn't seem to like anything he told her, including his best stories, and her disproportion of positive to negative reactions was starting to get to him. His stomach dropped in grief. What could he tell her next to make her feel better? Which story might earn the return of her fingers to his hair?

Arson waited awkwardly for her fit to blow over. "Are you all right?" he said.

She let out one more drawn-out moan, having given herself over to a deep cry, but trying to stifle the sounds. From his vantage, he could see her shoulders shrugging and elbows working as she wiped her face, trying to bring back her composure, and then she rose and calmly glided back over to reclaim her cushion before him.

"What did I say wrong this time?" he asked honestly. He really wanted to know. This odd air between them wouldn't get her fingers very close to his hair.

"You didn't say anything wrong exactly..." She shook her head. Her eyes were red. She dabbed them again with her handkerchief. "Arson, that's not how males and females are supposed to interact," she said. "When I peered into your mind..." She shook her head, looking up toward the tent's ceiling. "I noticed a decorative box but no clue what it meant. What you've told me is awful." She buried her face again but held in any further outbursts of tears. "Arson, a *saehgahn* must work hard—*very* hard to earn marriage."

"Well, I *do* work hard," he said. "And I earn the pleasure box."

She shook her head again. "No. It's not the same. It's not right."

"But I do want marriage—which is why I asked about Yhulin. I want more than the pleasure box."

"No," she countered. "It's so much... It's so much more than what you call *satisfaction*."

He frowned. "You confuse me." He was honest about his hard work. Those missions were all death-defying accomplishments, and they made him worthy of his reward. He didn't know how to frame his explanation to her though.

"Have you ever thought about the girl in the box? Her feelings?"

"I..." He hadn't thought about her until he saw her face. Aside from the strange fact that she liked to spoil them with extra sweet muffins she made, Nanelle had said some strange things to him: *You're my favorite. You might like to try my pussy.* This woman he didn't even know… She liked him. She wanted to communicate with him. She wanted to establish some kind of relationship, but he didn't understand how and why. Haus had always taught the quadruplets that women couldn't be trusted and they were subordinate to men. Before she emerged from the pleasure box, revealing her pretty face and her voice, she was somehow not human—by Haus's design.

His father's rules kept him afraid to think about too much. Until they discovered their true race, marriage was off the table for the brothers. If they hadn't learned about elves, they'd still be devils and they'd live out their entire lives earning the pleasure box. Knowing what he knew now, he could probably never be comfortable using that thing ever again.

"I don't know," he whispered.

She nodded and met his gaze at last. Her lip quivered as she reached out to him with one hand. She grazed his hairline and his breath caught. He closed his eyes.

"You're just a child, really," she whispered back to him. "I can't blame you for any of this. Like any *saehgahn*, you've held your discipline and carried out your duties, and that's why I think you are good. I think you can learn how to live better. Anything about you we may find horrid is only due to your upbringing and your position."

She pulled her hand back and he whispered, "Don't stop." He opened his eyes to lock them on her.

"I have to." She dipped her chin, breaking away from the message he tried to silently send her. "They don't want me touching you."

His tears threatened to come out again and he held them in. Right when she had him at his most vulnerable, most open to communicate, and wanting, she opened the tent flap and told Cavlihen she had finished with tonight's inquiry. She told them Arson had behaved himself and not to harm him.

For that night, they made him sleep locked up in the wagon, alone with his thoughts. The thoughts proved too powerful for sleep to conquer. There was Haus, ever standing in his consciousness, reminding him to *shape up, boy! Stand tall! Close your mouth! You don't ask questions, you only obey! The man in that other manor must die! Make your father proud! Don't you want to earn the pleasure box?*

Yes, he did! He wanted it so bad! He wanted that touch. He wanted to be touched. He wanted…

Hanhelin's fingers grazed his scalp. He wanted more. Please! Why? Why couldn't he just ask and receive? There was so much he needed and no one to hear him! No one cared what a devil wanted. He had to carry out the mission, and then maybe, if Father felt generous, the slot would open and he may find someone's gentle touch within the box—and that was the only way he'd ever know the feeling of tenderness.

Father, why?

Chapter 13
Message

Arson awoke to the sound of groaning metal. They were opening his cage on wheels. "Time to move," Cavlihen, standing on the other side, said. "The princess says you are forgiven for acting out last night and you're to return to our ranks today. We're headed out again. Know what that means?"

"Um," Arson said with a groan. He might've toppled over anytime he managed to fall asleep last night, in his sheer exhaustion.

"It means you are to march and keep your eyes and ears open. You will die for the princess if needed today. Understand?"

Butterflies flared up in his stomach at the word "princess." Their conversation last night was a little…strange.

After announcing that she'd ride in a wagon today rather than on her horse, Hanhelin sought out Yhulin at the creek where the young *faerhain* bathed inside an enclosure of hanging linens. Four *saehgahn* stood guard around it, looking outward from a respectable distance. She moved one sheet aside to spy her in the act of tying her linen undergarments in place, standing on the bank with the water lapping at the other side of the makeshift bathing tent.

"Yhulin," she whispered.

Yhulin twisted around. Her hair sat tied messily atop her head, and at the moment she only had on the thin chemise with its drawstring fastened over her breasts, the first layer of her proper *hanbohik*. Her skin glowed radiantly in the morning sun, a stark contrast to her dark brown hair. In her twisted pose, her elbows winged out like a dancing swan, her bosom thrust forward.

Hanhelin paused in thought of Arson, whom she knew had been looking at Yhulin so inappropriately. She had to wonder why. What was there to look at? A queerer thought shot briefly across her mind: the wonder if Hanhelin had shapes he would like also. In their own culture, *faerhain* could ogle *saehgahn* all day, making note of their trim waists and long legs and all the shapes and lines detailing a male's naked body. She'd never thought to wonder if a *saehgahn* would also find interest in looking at a female. Arson had taught her that they would indeed—if allowed to do so.

"*Ameiha?*" Yhulin asked, and Hanhelin finally noticed how hard she was staring.

She swallowed in embarrassment. "I want you to ride in the wagon with me today. I need someone to talk to."

"About what?" Yhulin clamped her mouth shut as soon as she'd spoken that second word. They both knew "what."

Though she'd been blushing, she suddenly went dizzy. "About *him*. I really don't…" A knot pulled tight in her throat.

"Oh dear." Yhulin dropped her faintly interested expression and extended her arms for a comforting embrace. At the sight of her handmaiden's body under that gown, Hanhelin couldn't shake Arson's echoing voice saying, *That's where we get our satisfaction.*

She feared vomiting her breakfast at the rushing ill feeling. She threw her hand over her mouth and pushed Yhulin away, leaving her to her privacy and probably confusion.

The rolling wagon was a better place to have a conversation on the road. All of its noises helped to cover their voices. Hanhelin and Yhulin lounged in its bed, on cushions and blankets between cargo trunks. Sometimes the two of them rode like this when Hanhelin wanted a break from riding horseback all day, although the wagon couldn't offer much more comfort considering its bouncing, clattering movement over the uneven ground.

Arson walked near the front of the caravan for a few reasons. From there, the majority of the *saehgahn* company could watch him, it left a good distance between him and Hanhelin—whom the *saehgahn* still didn't trust him around—and if they were attacked, he might be one of the first to die.

"I had a strange conversation with him last night," Hanhelin whispered to her handmaiden, hoping her voice would be lost to the wagon's driver.

Yhulin piped up quickly. "I wondered how it would go since you barred me from attending. You've yet to tell me why."

"He doesn't understand our customs. It's jarring and, honestly, distracting."

"What does he say?"

"The absolute truth of what's on his mind. Things which would get him punished if anyone else heard it. Things which would get him branded *sarakren*."

Yhulin reared back. "Really? Can you tell me what?"

"Well, he's…a little more experienced than an average unmarried *saehgahn*."

Yhulin covered her mouth and slid her eyes toward the front of the caravan.

"The whole thing makes me ill. He's so preoccupied with the business of married couples."

"Is he?" Yhulin said. "That's such a folly for *saehgahn*. Yet you don't think he should get *sarakren* status yet?"

"Not if I'm to study him," Hanhelin said. "Besides… He's only being honest, which is what a *saehgahn* is supposed to do. This all leaves me in a difficult position."

"So you *would* brand him *sarakren*, or perhaps shave his head or put him to death, but you'd rather study him?"

"It's more complicated." Hanhelin huffed. "Last night, he told me dreadfully sad things. He never had a mother or a grandmother. I don't think he's ever associated with a female person in a healthy way." His story of the woman named Nanelle was far too ill to share with Yhulin.

"It does seem odd. Sad too."

Hanhelin continued. "I touched his hair."

Yhulin dipped her head low, holding her stare on Hanhelin. "Why? You still don't know how dangerous his taint is."

"He was chained up." She shook her head and shrugged. "He needed to calm down, or I would've never acquired an answer from him. He…" She swallowed, and Yhulin appeared to hold her breath. "He took to my touch a bit desperately. And the way he stared into my eyes. I don't know. I've never shared such a deep connection to a *saehgahn* before, who wasn't a close family member."

"But it's not proper for a *saehgahn* to stare at us or at our eyes," Yhulin pointed out.

"I know. It's like I said, he doesn't know our customs. The way his eyes made me feel though…"

"How?" the handmaiden pressed.

"Nervous—I think. And a little sad." Hanhelin blew a breath out, relieved to finally be able to get these things off her chest, but it also added another layer of frustration at how she didn't understand much about Arson and what exactly to do with him. The closer they drew to the palace, the worse she felt. She couldn't guess what would happen once they arrived. She'd already done her best effort in making him a *saehgahn* and also a White Owl, not quite an impenetrable plan. She'd have to learn as much about him as she could out here. If her father put him to death, she would have done all she could to help her people.

Then it hit her. "Stop!" she ordered, and their driver pulled hard on the reins. He called her order forward, and the word was passed all the way to the front.

"What's the matter, *Ameiha*?" Yhulin asked, clinging to the nearest trunk until their wagon had stopped completely.

"Get out the writing implements," she ordered.

"Oh dear," Yhulin said. "I'm not sure which trunk they're in at the moment."

The driver stepped into the wagon bed to help them search. They just so happened to ride in the same wagon that carried Hanhelin's personal items. While they rummaged, she looked ahead, shielding the sun off her eyes with a hand and noted a bright speck waiting far in the distance. Arson's platinum hair waved in the wind among all the black-headed Norrians in the caravan, his stance relaxed and cocky. Hanhelin's stomach fluttered.

The princess had decided to bring the whole company to a halt at her royal whim. Nonetheless, Arson took the moment to comb his fingers through his hair. Three bright strands fell out and waved on the wind from his fingers. He lowered his hand and released them, hoping they'd snag on a bush by the trail. He didn't have much to drop as clues to his brothers for where he'd been, especially since the elves had confiscated everything he'd had on him when he was captured, but if they were keen enough in their search, and if they scoured this road, they might notice the unlikely blond strands. Otherwise, he'd ingeniously thought to draw a picture of his devil mask in the dirt before they left their campsite. He knew his brothers were smart enough to check those stirred areas of wilderness.

But what about her? The thought struck him, and he wasn't sure where it had come from. Who? Hanhelin? The one who held him captive and had subjected him to all that humiliation? He blinked as he looked back toward her end of the caravan again. Leaving her felt strange. He belonged with his family and would be glad to finally bed Yhulin as his wife, but…why was he wondering how his leaving would make Hanhelin feel? It didn't even bother him how she'd argued against his taking Yhulin as a wife, but leaving the princess's service gave him quite a nag right now.

He shook off his odd feeling and tightened his lips. He was so out of place in her service; he really should go back home.

"Here they are," Yhulin announced.

"Good," Hanhelin replied. "Set me up a desk."

Her great-aunt, the Grand Desteer, might be her best hope. Though Hanhelin had always considered herself more intellectual than she—spirituality was the standard required trait for that office—surely the Grand Desteer cared enough about the future of Norr to take Hanhelin's side on the matter of studying Arson. So Hanhelin made them all wait for her to compose her letter detailing everything from Arson's capture to how he proved no immediate harm and why they should keep him alive for study of the Overseas Taint.

While her ink dried, she ordered her own horse to be readied for a rider to take her letter ahead of them. Better to have one such as the Grand Desteer to know what would approach the palace's doorstep than it be a surprise.

She took a deep breath to watch the rider gallop away on her horse. The fate of Norr lay in her aunt's hands now.

At the next campsite, the *saehgahn* busied themselves, unpacking, pitching tents, grooming horses, sharpening tools, and oiling weapons. When someone noticed Arson standing idly, they threw a rake at his head and ordered he clear the leaves for tonight's fire.

Arson, one of Haus's four beloved devil sons, had grown so weary of this menial work. His body had been sculpted for optimum fighting ability, not work like this. Enough was enough. He threw down the rake.

"Are you deaf, tainted one?" The upper-level *saehgahn* barked.

"I'm not your lackey!" Arson barked back. His hands were heating up again; his rage seemed to trigger the sensation.

The elf's lips stiffened into a fine line.

Knowing this body language well, Arson opened up his senses. He could map out the vibrations of all bodies around him, which was helpful in sneaking around dark manors. Rather than commit to engage the *saehgahn* in front of him, he ducked under the spear shaft swipe of the one behind him. Arson rolled to the side, reclaimed the rake on the ground, and sprang up. From there he swung it around and knocked the spear out of the elf's hands with the rough-hewn handle. He hit him on the head and twirled it boastfully. He and his brothers were skilled at every basic weapon. Bludgeon wasn't the only one who could raise a large hammer, and Poison didn't stand alone in his ability to strike like a snake. Arson was right there with them for all those twenty-three years of deep physical training.

"Ah!" one elf yelped and went down.

Arson carried on with the rake, lunging to gut jab another elf and whack the opposite one along his head. Moving around like this energized him. Escaping didn't feel so impossible anymore. Maybe he could snuff them all out and walk away with his prize bride if he could capture one of their spears. Maybe he'd take the exquisite Hanhelin with him!

Just then he spotted Yhulin, who had fallen against a barrel with her mouth rounded and her hands to her bosom in surprise at his sudden violent outburst. He shot her a grin and pointed right at her.

But now the elves were growing angry and many more of them charged at him from various angles.

They flooded around him and took control of his rake. Arson snatched one elf's mantle and wrapped it around his neck for an efficient strangulation death, and probably ten hands reached in to pry him away, leaving his victim to gasp for breath.

When they finally had him pinned to the ground, Hanhelin approached. Her cool and smooth air had restored since their last late-night meeting.

"Arson," she said without quirking a single muscle on her face. "Why are you disrupting camp?"

"I told them. I don't rake leaves!" he spat back.

"Listen," she said calmly. "When you rake leaves, you do it for me. Not because you were told to. When you gather water, you do it for me. When you collect firewood, you do it for me. And when you lash out in violence, you do it to protect me—not to turn on your brother *saehgahn*. Do you understand?"

Caught on her voice, Arson blinked. His anger suddenly lifted from him. Maybe because of her words but most likely because of her bewitching voice. Once again off his guard and dominated by a handful of other people, he relaxed. He had known better than to attract all this attention to himself if he ever hoped to escape this group. One by one, the hands released him. He stood up with a cautious slowness, located the rake, and began clearing the leaves. Hanhelin smiled and walked away with her handmaiden in tow.

"Explain to me why you were fighting this afternoon," Hanhelin ordered him that night when he sat down before her. They let him sit unchained, despite how he'd acted earlier.

First he answered, "I don't know" but thought better of it and described his thoughts in that moment about being Haus's cherished son and whatnot.

"Yes, I remember you describing your father as rich. Noble, I suppose is the word for it where you come from."

"Not really," Arson said.

"Explain then." Though she didn't bother with a veil tonight, she kept her face cool and aloof.

"A noble is someone born into a high class, I understand. Someone with political power," Arson said. "My father is a self-made rich man with lots of power, but he operates more on the underground. His mystery apparently is what helps to strike fear in his peers. We, the four devils of House LinGor, are what help keep that mystery terrifying." He smiled, despite Hanhelin's clear displeasure.

"Your father has no power, but he has fear?"

"On the surface, he runs a glassblowing shop. On a lower level, he lends money. Underground, he has people killed, and that's where me and my brothers prove useful."

"Is it not enough to trade his glass?" Hanhelin asked.

"Not if you want total fear and limitless gold. We're very carefully building a reputation. I don't know how much Lady Lexion paid for my brother's service as a bodyguard, but we know it was an enormous amount. She needed top-notch protection, so she came to our father."

Hanhelin hummed. "The world outside of Norr is wicked and greedy, I hear."

Arson crossed his arms and leaned back casually. "Well, aren't you people the same? You dress pretty well yourselves. Quite unlike the ferrymen we met at the border."

"The ferrymen are of their own clan. Tinharri is the ruling clan."

"The ruling clan," he parroted. "So did you hoard gold and unleash your own devils to get your high status?"

Hanhelin flinched but otherwise kept her composure. "No. We, Tinharri, lead the other clans because…"

He waited, smiling.

"I don't know why—but we are good. The clans of Norr are united and charitable to each other."

Arson barked a laugh. "So are all the noble houses of Kell's Key."

Hanhelin watched him as he laughed a few more beats. She leaned over and rapidly shuffled papers to jot something down. "Ouch!" she cried.

Arson flinched, feeling a sting on his finger, and jerked his hand up to place it in his mouth. He looked around him for whatever insect might've bitten him. "Damn," he mumbled, finding nothing.

Hanhelin hissed, having also stuck her finger in her mouth. "I cut myself on the crisp page," she said. "What's wrong with you?"

Arson checked his finger, and nothing marred it. No sting spot or hint of redness. "I don't know. First you cut your finger, and at the same instant I thought something bit mine."

Hanhelin's mouth corners turned downward. She placed her bleeding fingertip back into her mouth and got back to her scribbling with the quill.

"What are you writing?"

She hesitated to speak for a brief minute. "This and that. Mostly my observations about your behavior."

"And what have you observed?"

"I'm gauging your boastfulness."

"My *boastfulness*?"

"Yes."

"Why?"

"I'm finding you very boastful."

Arson waited.

"I'm also comparing it to your other traits to see the balances on plain paper."

"I don't understand."

"It's about your taint," Hanhelin explained.

"That thing you think I got across the sea?"

"The fact that you were born across the sea. This is what I'm studying. Appearance-wise, you hit all the trademarks of having the Overseas Taint. I'm calculating your personality traits."

"And how many of my traits align with the taint?"

"So far, not many," she said. "Your pride is also a trait of the *saehgahn*, and I'm sure you get a great amount of boastfulness from the society you grew up in: your 'rich and powerful' father particularly."

"What are the recorded traits of the Overseas Taint?"

Hanhelin opened up her little gilded book and pulled out a leaf of paper she'd jotted things down on. "A keen love of self, so keen that it creates a barrier of hate to those around him," she read. "Highly aggressive, a loner, a pronounced ambition—usually a desire for material things, power, and overall things normal elves know that don't bring happiness." Hanhelin took a breath. "Delusion, anxiety, paranoia. Also a vast magical ability, stronger than elves should normally be born with."

"So which one of those do I have?" Arson asked. "I hardly know what most of them mean."

Hanhelin shook her head. "You've rashly attacked the other *saehgahn*, and you're a little boastful, that's all. As I said, so far these faults might not be at the taint's level."

"And you still think I have this thing?"

She spread her hands. "Well, I can't ignore the other signs, particularly the factor of where you came from. But…" She lowered her eyes in thought. "I'm inclined to believe you are a carrier but not one affected by the symptoms." She batted her eyelids, and it lit Arson's stomach on fire and trailed straight to his loins. His mouth dropped open. "Aside from your vulgar way of speaking, I find you far from odious. Your air is actually a little…pleasant." She gazed up at him through her eyelashes. "Arson."

He smiled at her. "I like it when you say my name. You do it a lot."

"We tend to be straightforward in my culture."

"At home," he said, "I'm the last born. I don't know how my father would know that since he found us in a basket, but I tend to feel forgotten. Especially with Poison in the lead. With you, you speak my name a lot. It makes me feel front and center."

She gave a light laugh. "You are front and center to my attention these days. I found someone with the Overseas Taint."

He shook his head.

"Why do you disagree?"

"The taint is a fairy tale. I even see you reading it out of a book of whimsy."

"We'll have to be in disagreement then. Even if the taint doesn't exist and is only a tale…" She extended her arms as if to bring in the camp or the whole of Norr. "My people believe in it, and that puts your life in danger."

He lowered his chin now. "So why don't you let me go?"

"Because you'd still be dangerous."

"Because *you* believe in the taint."

"Yes." After a short silence, she asked, "Arson, how do you feel about me?"

"Annoyed because you won't let me go."

"That much is obvious."

"Well, actually…" He shook his head. "I don't know. I've felt odd ever since you slapped me and dumped water on my head."

"Your *saehgahn* naming ceremony." She nodded. "How do you feel now?"

"Sad, I think. Or…"

She wrote something else down.

"Now what are you writing?"

"I'm comparing you to the average *saehgahn* too."

"And how similar am I?"

"Tell me more about how you feel—about me."

He smirked and studied her up and down. "I think you're beautiful. I like beautiful girls. My brothers and I have been talking about beautiful girls ever since we set out to find our wives."

She batted her eyelashes again in her blush, and it illustrated his point.

"But you're the princess of this country, so I haven't entertained any thoughts about taking you home with me. I'll settle for Yhulin if you could ever decide to work with me on this issue—"

"You're back on that again?" she shrieked.

He blinked at her raised voice. "Yeah. I want her. From what I've gauged through those clumpy dresses you two wear, she may have a nice, shapely body under there."

The slap she delivered to Arson at the tail end of his sentence shouldn't have been too much of a surprise considering how he noted Hanhelin's shoulders rose and fell with her heavy breathing building up to that outburst of emotion, but it did startle him backward. The ensuing pain elicited his own anger, and he considered grabbing the bitch's hair and maybe twisting it while telling her not to do that again, but the strange new side of him said no, that he didn't want to cause her pain and it would somehow reflect back on him and make him feel worse. His logic dictated he'd get in serious trouble if he struck back at the princess too. He'd rather she caressed his hair tenderly like before.

He simply cupped his face and growled, "Don't do that."

Hanhelin stared back at him, her flat hand still poised, her posture starched with anger. "I told you, you can't have her! You can't have anyone. Ever. Even if you join our society, you may never have a wife."

"Why?"

"Because your Overseas Taint will poison our bloodlines. You will breed evil into us. The elves will wither into vile, hateful creatures who would destroy each other, maybe the world too."

He swallowed, rubbing his stinging face but watching her with his untouched eye.

"You *might* be able to live with us, but you will never marry. The best you can hope for is the *sarakren* brand or castration."

"What does *sarakren* mean?"

"He who is forbidden. It's a warning to all eligible *faerhain*, not to choose this elf."

Arson sniffed and stood, leaving her gawking on the ground. "Shut up," he said. "It's a fairy tale. The reason you're so mad right now is because you're jealous of your handmaiden."

He walked out of her tent, deciding for himself that the meeting was over.

Chapter 14
The Taint

That familiar annoying poking at his shoulder woke Arson in the morning, sleeping straight up on the ground as always. "What are you up to, fiend?"

"What do you mean?" Arson countered with a groan. After rubbing his eyes, he found he wasn't where he had fallen asleep, which would've been the designated area among the rows of *saehgahn* in their bedrolls. He sat instead at a different end of the camp, right outside Hanhelin's tent.

Arson surveyed the area, squinting. "How'd I get here?"

"Exactly what we were hoping you'd tell us," the *saehgahn* said.

The princess's handmaiden was looking through the front of the tent, keeping meekly behind the flap in this early hour, most likely to report what she saw to the princess who waited inside.

"I watched the whole thing," Cavlihen piped up, returned from the woods. "My guard mate and I." He motioned to the spot he usually sat to guard Hanhelin's tent throughout the night. "If he hadn't been wearing his White Owl uniform, I might never have detected him."

"What did he do?"

Cavlihen pointed at the path along the outer bounds of the camp. "Arson moseyed up along there. I called to him softly, and he didn't respond. He just walked over and replanted himself right here where he slept sitting up for the rest of the night. I decided to leave him there to see if he tried anything, but he only kept sleeping."

"I don't remember a thing," Arson said. "And I've never sleepwalked before in my life." After he finished the statement, he went over the scenario again and again. "I've always slept outside my father's chambers with my brothers." He observed the girl eyeballing him from the big tent, and her head popped back inside. "But my father's not here." He couldn't imagine why he'd want to sleepwalk back over here though. He knew he didn't want to see the princess again for as long as possible after those awful things she'd said to him.

He stretched and worked his way dizzily to his feet. "I don't care," he told the elves. "Aren't we leaving again today?"

"We are," Cavlihen answered, piercing him with squinted eyes.

"Good," he said, feigning comfort in this group of people he'd suddenly found himself a member of. "I don't like this wing of the forest. It stinks." He didn't lie. Something odd hung in the air with the morning mist. He got to fiddling with his elven pants on his way off the path to take his constitutional piss before he was even out of Yhulin's line of view. He knew she watched him, and he pretended not to notice.

On his way to a private area in the woods, he bent branches and tore fresh leaves down all the way, anything to help his brothers discover his trail. After doing his business, he swiped a small patch of earth clean and drew another devil mask symbol in the dirt.

Another long day of walking in Princess Hanhelin's caravan brought Arson to another exhausting evening of running this way and that to get her camp set up. He raked the leaves like before, hearing her voice in his head reminding him, *You do it for me.*

He did it for her. For the woman who said she'd cut his testicles off. He'd hoped to achieve the opposite outcome on this trip to Norr. Arson took it all in stride. He had drawn a devil mask at the base of every tree he pissed on all the way over here. He had also made note of everyone else's daily patterns. Where they all walked or stood. Tonight he'd observe where they slept. The plan for escape was already formulating in his mind. He'd next have to start watching Yhulin's patterns. So far, he knew she slept in Hanhelin's tent—the most guarded thing in the camp, naturally. After his sleepwalking incident and Cavlihen's seeing his white uniform, Arson now knew to smuggle away some forest-colored clothing for his big escape and kidnapping. Rope! He'd need rope and a gag to restrain the girl if necessary. It was all coming together.

Hanhelin had yet to call him into her tent for the nightly discussion, and the sun had already retired. Maybe he'd get a break this time. The forest darkened down to a black curtain after sunset, showing only the first layer of brush at the outskirts of the campfire glow. The darkness looked inviting. How easily could he get away if he dashed right now? Arson shook his head and picked up another stick to supplement their supply for the fire. He shouldn't make a run without darker clothes.

"Psst! Arson," hissed a voice from the shadow, one that made his heart leap.

Arson dropped his bundle of twigs. "Bleed?"

"Yes," his brother said. He wore a proper hood and cloak to keep him invisible to most eyes. The firelight flashed on the strands of blond hair wisping out of the hood's shaded space. "I've finally found you. What's going on?"

"It's a long story," Arson said. "How did you find me all this way?"

"You drew your mask in the dirt, ya kunk." He made a slight laugh, and it eased quite a bit of the tension Arson carried.

"Yeah, I did." He chuckled back.

"So come on," Bleed urged. "It's clear. Let's go."

Arson's body jerked to do so, to spring into that inviting shadow with his brother—a sight for sore eyes, but something held him back with a tug at his heart. The camp, more like one certain tent, made him feel as if he stood on the edge of a cliff. He could jump into the water or stay on solid ground. If he ran, the elves would hunt him down and also his family. He wasn't sure how hard Hanhelin's men hunted his father and brothers as of now. They were quite concerned, not only with keeping him in their sight but about the thin mist that had been seeping over the land for the past few days. The stink he'd complained about yesterday smelled worse in this area.

He told his brother, "You know where I am now."

Bleed cocked his head, most of his features hidden in the shadow of his hood.

Arson continued. "I'm a prisoner here, but strangely I've also been made a member of the royal guard."

Bleed's facial expression twisted by the way his shadows shifted. They couldn't stall to discuss the peculiarities though.

"There's a young woman here who's deliciously eligible, so I'm going to steal her before rejoining you."

Bleed's eyes brightened. "A woman? How many of 'em?"

"Two, but one is the princess of this country. I figured I might get her servant to be my wife. The princess won't bargain for her though."

"As expected," his brother replied, rolling his eyes. "Women have turned out to be so rare here we haven't seen one since Linhala." Bleed gave him a bow of camaraderie. "I shouldn't linger then. You can find us on the northern border."

Arson nodded. "We're headed toward the palace, in case I can't get away soon enough. It's on the west side. They call it Ko Hanilkha."

Bleed reached out and slapped his arm firmly. "Godspeed. Get your wife." He darted back into the brush, leaving Arson now with a mission and a renewed sense of strength. He suddenly didn't feel like a prisoner anymore.

"Kinda late, don't you think?" Arson asked when he was finally let in to speak to the princess.

She moved about the small space, putting away large glass vials and little oil lamps for heating them. One of the smallest vials she appeared to have finished corking and wrapping a cord around it.

Cavlihen growled behind him in response, and Hanhelin raised her hand. "Arson, I'm the princess. You can't speak to me as such. It's improper, and it angers your fellow guardsmen."

Arson shot Cavlihen a bland stare before moving forward and plopping down on his designated cushion. He turned his stare toward her and detected the flare of a blush in her cheeks. "Let's get this over with," he said.

Hanhelin waved to Cavlihen again, and he swept out of the tent with an obvious air of reluctance. She closed the trunk where she'd loaded up the potion bottles, hung the corded bottle around her neck, and tucked it into her bodice. "So...," Hanhelin began to Arson. "I hear you've been sleepwalking."

He shook his head and shrugged. "It's never happened before."

"Do you know why you did it now? And to my tent of all places?"

"No."

Hanhelin hummed after his short answer. "They said you mentioned how you used to sleep like that outside your father's room?"

He nodded once slowly. "Yes. We're bound to protect him."

Hanhelin hummed. "How interesting."

"What is?"

Her long eyelashes batted, pointed down to her papers on her writing desk. "I can't help but notice you are now sleeping outside my tent."

"It only happened once," he said, defensive.

"Please let me finish." She cleared her throat. "It's as if you have replaced your father with me."

He leaned forward, sneering. "You think *you* can replace my father?"

"Not exactly, but you're my *saehgahn* now."

An icy chill shot down Arson's back. He used to protect his father, and now he was protecting Hanhelin—without realizing it.

"I'm pleased to have found you, Arson."

He huffed, so tired of all of this "study" she put him through. She thought of him as nothing but a project.

"Do these discussions bore you?"

He threw his hands out. "They're starting to. If you don't mind, I'd like to go get some sleep. It was restless enough last night, and to be perfectly honest, you make me uncomfortable."

"How?"

Avoiding her gaze, he sniffed. "I haven't forgotten what you said to me last time."

"That you couldn't get married and you could get castrated."

He slicked his tongue across his teeth, holding his stare on the tent's center pole behind her.

"You have the Overseas Taint, Arson."

He barked out a laugh of anger and pinched his nose bridge, bracing his elbow on his knee. "There's that word again. I wish you'd leave me alone. I don't have this taint you're so afraid of."

She breathed the words, "You have all the signs."

Once again, Hanhelin didn't bother wearing her veil. Her eyes were large and glossy in this lighting. She wore a slight frown, but he couldn't tell if she actually was sad or if she acted. He lost his confidence after a whole afternoon of planning his escape and reconnecting with Bleed and daydreaming about his first intimate experience with Yhulin. Seeing Hanhelin now though, without her veil, his thoughts of Yhulin evaporated.

"When you were brought to me, you had taken on a head injury."

Hanhelin moved toward him on her knees and put her hand on his head.

"Bow," she ordered, and he did, desperately hoping she'd stroke his hair. Close enough—she parted his locks to look closely at his scalp. "It has healed well," she reported. Her fingers continued to move, and they did take on a soothing motion.

Tingles filled his scalp. Relaxation and utter relief. He closed his eyes and enjoyed.

He tilted his head and chanced a peek up at her. Warm serenity doused her expression. A slight smile curled her soft lips, but when their eyes met, she stopped and scrambled back to her cushion.

She cleared her throat and then said loud enough for anyone outside the tent to hear, "There, I've written so much already. Now we must talk fruitfully, Arson. My study goes well."

Arson checked the tent's entrance again. No one had come in, and Hanhelin now stared hard at her lap with a bright blush. Arson blinked in confusion.

"What do you want to know next?" Arson asked. Her caress of his hair did so much to improve his mood, and obviously Hanhelin knew it. She blushed so brightly though. Did she also enjoy doing that to him?

She raised her finger and leaned over to actually write something down. "Your hair has an interesting texture," she murmured. "Thin though. Fine strands." After describing his hair on paper, she returned her hands to their folded position on her lap. "Arson. Tonight I'll tell you all about the Overseas Taint so you'll at least know what it is and why we fear it."

"You could've done that sooner," he said with a grunt.

Her shiny storybook sat beside her as always, and she opened it up. She closed it again with a sigh and rested it atop her thighs. "It's a tale," she explained. "But we Norrians take it as fact, and your taint—people like you… You are a punishment on my people."

He scrunched his nose. "A punishment."

She nodded deeply. "I'll recite the tale to you as I understand it. This book is written in Norrian, but I'll recount it better in your language if I do a recital instead of a reading." She took a deep breath, and Arson waited.

"Long ago, when Norr was a new kingdom, it boasted many beautiful *faerhain*, proud *saehgahn*, and a grand palace in the lush green forest. In those days, everyone lived a blissful life of happiness and fulfillment. We had plenty of *faerhain* to go around, couples would run and play in the forest. They married and threw lavish parties for their friends and families. It was an opposite to our outlook on life today, and I can't imagine what it could've been like to live back then. Anyway…

"Our king of that time beamed with pride at the number of daughters he'd been blessed with, balanced by an even number of eligible sons he knew would protect the kingdom long after he died. He picked his youngest and prettiest daughter and decided she should be gifted to the Bright One as His bride and as thanks for such a glorious and bountiful life all the elves enjoyed.

"The Bright One, though He never took in brides, decided to accept the king's gift and at least take the girl to His kingdom to live, but the girl didn't know His plan and feared marrying our deity.

"On the day of the Bright One's arrival, the girl sat in silence inside a gilded box for a grand reveal. She wept and worried over what would become of her. That's when a court *saehgahn* walked by her box and heard her weeping. This *saehgahn*, though good in his heart, was a known flirt about the palace grounds and had been with many *faerhain* by that point. 'Why are you crying, Princess?' he asked and tapped on the box. She opened the door and invited him in. In the dark, tight space of her enclosure, he sat on the bench beside her and she spilled all her worries and was weeping on his shoulder by the end of it. 'I'm afraid. I don't know what will become of me in the Bright One's palace,' she said. The *saehgahn* smiled and petted her hair. 'You've no need to fear,' he said. 'I can show you what to expect of physical love and maybe you'll feel better about it.' This made her rise back up and look him in the eyes. 'Really?' she asked, and he said, 'Of course. Shall I show you?' She nodded her head. 'Yes please!'"

Hanhelin sighed and frowned at her lap. "That's when he took her chin between his fingers and said, 'It begins with a painless kiss.' And he seduced her." Hanhelin spread her hands.

Arson shook his head, shrugging. "So? Did she feel better about her marriage afterward?"

"Of course she did. In fact, she loved the *saehgahn* after that. But her dire mistake doomed my people's existence forever."

Arson lowered his brow as he waited for the coming explanation.

"The princess was no longer a virgin, and even worse was that she *loved* the *saehgahn*—in her heart. When the Bright One appeared and strode down the long throne room toward the king and his waiting gift, he opened the door of the gilded box to see the princess sitting there, smiling. She'd gained her confidence, but the Bright One knew everything she'd done and everything she felt in that moment. 'Why did you ruin my gift?' the Bright One asked the king, who stammered nervously for a response. The king didn't know what the princess had done with the *saehgahn*. 'I thought this princess had been named for Me,' the Bright One reiterated. The king looked to the princess for an answer. He looked to his advisors for advice, but the mistake had already been made. The Bright One left the princess where she sat and transformed into a whirlwind of light in search of the naughty *saehgahn* who'd spoiled his gift. The whole palace wailed and ducked for cover in the chaos. The Bright One snatched the *saehgahn* up and held him like a chalice in a massive glowing hand atop the vortex.

"'If My bride was taken away, so shall the brides of two-thirds of *saehgahn*. From this day forward, if My children can't figure out how to communicate and allocate their pairings, they'll instead destroy themselves to the very end of them.' And with that, he took the mischievous *saehgahn* away, disappeared, and two-thirds of all the *faerhain* in Norr dropped dead."

Arson reared his head back and sneered. "What did He do to the bad *saehgahn* after?"

"That's where the Overseas Taint comes in." Hanhelin nodded her head with her eyes closed as she said it. "The Bright One dropped the *saehgahn* on an island somewhere. Somewhere *over the sea*, you see?"

Arson shook his head.

"On the island, one of the Swine's daughters lived."

"The Swine?"

"The Swine is an evil being," Hanhelin explained. "A demon and the king of Kullixaxuss—or *hell* as you might call it. He delights in trickery and tormenting the innocent. He sets his fiendish minions on the land of the living to see what mischief they can find, all for the delight of his own malicious sense of humor. He works opposite to the Bright One, who has made it his goal to help and guide us, regardless of our inclination to falter.

"Anyway, the *saehgahn* had to survive in the wilderness now. A terrible place. The sky was always grey and his feet sank into the boggy terrain. He tread through thornbushes and across sharp rocks under his bare feet. Did I mention the Bright One took his clothes away?"

"So what about the Overseas Taint though?"

"Patience, Arson, I'll tell you. Luckily, the *saehgahn* found fruit trees growing here and there across the land, and one day, when he was harvesting a few pieces for his dinner, a woman stepped out from behind the tree."

"The Swine's daughter?"

"Yes. She was pale and shapely with platinum-colored hair. She easily seduced him. For a little while after that, the *saehgahn* figured life wasn't so bad on the island. He had trees which bore fruit year-round and a beautiful companion who would visit him every once in a while… And then, one day…" Hanhelin sighed again. How seriously did she take this story? "He found a basket with a note."

"What was in the basket?"

"Babies, Arson."

A chill ran up Arson's spine. *Babies in a basket.*

"The note read that the Swine's daughter had lovingly given birth to the *saehgahn*'s offspring—a litter of them, like, like *animals*!" Hanhelin shivered despite what she knew about Arson's birth. "The *saehgahn* picked one up and hugged it to his chest. What father wouldn't? But as he did, a wise old man appeared—the Bright One in disguise. He told the *saehgahn* to kill all the babies. If he killed them, it would prevent a horrible calamity on his people. He also warned the *saehgahn* never to make love to his friend again."

"So did he kill them?"

"He didn't have the heart! They were just babies. What harm could they do? He loved them because they were his sons. He dearly wanted to keep them, but…" Intensely into the story, Hanhelin wrung a lock of her black hair in her hands. "He wanted to take the wise old man's words to heart. So instead of killing them, he built a raft. He put all the babies in their basket on the raft and set it afloat on the ocean. He assumed they'd go to some other land to live better lives or maybe die at sea, but they, indeed, floated straight to Norr where some kind and lonely elf most likely raised the boys. Obviously, the boys would go on to grow up here among my people and eventually breed their bloodline—the Swine's blood—into the Norrian bloodline. Thus we have the Overseas Taint."

Arson blinked. "It's an outlandish story."

"Prove it wrong." In waiting for his reply, Hanhelin crossed her arms, hidden under her long sleeves.

He shivered at this tale as she did, and the ill feeling replaced the comfort she'd given him earlier. "So did the *saehgahn* resist the Swine's daughter's next allure?"

"Of course not. He's weak. And when he meant to resist her allure, she'd go and turn herself into a tree or some such."

"How did that seduce him?"

"If you were walking around, naked in the wilderness, and came across a tree with a moist vagina, would you resist trying things on it?"

Arson just stared at her with his mouth open.

"The Swine's daughter has all kinds of tricks up her sleeves, Arson. That *saehgahn* is hopeless, and because of him, we have to stay on our guard!" She pointed to his head. "Pale hair!" She moved her point down a bit. "Green eyes! You have so many clues about you. You obviously don't look like us, and you even came with the tale of how *you* were found at sea!"

Arson shook his head. "I mean you no harm though. My brothers and I just want wives. If we can get them, we'll go back home to Kell's Key and never return."

Hanhelin shook her head, returning her arms to their crossed position. "That's exactly the problem. Breeding your bloodline. You mustn't do it." She huffed. "I'm afraid of this taint." He avoided her gaze now, regardless of what she said. "But I feel for you and have long decided to protect your life. I'll get to the bottom of this mysterious taint. Maybe there's something to be done about it." She shook her head. "Neutralize it or perhaps at least manage it. That's why I need you to let me study you."

He pulled his lips in. What kind of shit had he fallen into these days? Because of this fairy tale about a bright person, he had lost his freedom in the blink of an eye. How long and how far would the Norr elves hunt him and his family if he ran away?

"I don't know what to tell you," he said. "I don't want to be a prisoner."

When he met her eyes again, she was crying silently. She really *did* feel for him. "Listen," she said. "I will soon be promoted to Grand Desteer. I intend to keep you with me as my guard, always. You'll be transferred to the order of the White Moth."

"What does that mean?"

"The White Owls protect the royal family and the White Moths serve the Grand Desteer. You'll be untouchable as a White Moth; it's an extremely elite sect. You can live out your life serving me. I'll protect you in turn and study you. But you can't get married and you certainly can't…" She grazed her eyes down his form. "You can't *use your body*."

Arson huffed. Maybe he'd rather die than go the rest of his life without *that* type of pleasure, the type he worked to achieve. The pleasure box was fine, but he'd been so excited to *use his body* ever since Poison told them about what he did with Lady Lexion. He couldn't go back to the days before his adolescence now! Even in this moment, all this talk of seduction and body use perked his cock to readiness. How could he ignore such a strong urge for the rest of his life?

"I can see you are suffering." Hanhelin spoke after a long moment of silence. The tears continued to stream down her cheeks, and she let them. "As a prime Desteer candidate, I can sense your feelings, and it burns me so deeply." She made a fist at her stomach. "It hurts."

She wasn't kidding. Arson had nothing to say back to her though.

His crossroads right now showed him death or celibacy. If not run for a slim chance of escape, it might be better if they went ahead and executed him instead of this madness she wanted to put him through. He didn't want to die though. He wanted to live, and he wanted to live fully.

When the tears began down his face, he swiped them away. "What do you want next?"

"Nothing," she breathed. "You can go and rest now."

Arson walked numbly toward the area where the *saehgahn* slept. He couldn't figure out if he was batshit pissed or depressed. He was both. Maybe tomorrow would be a better day. He'd get back to his plans and forget about that stupid story Hanhelin told him. First he headed to the woods for one last pee before bed, and that's when he saw her. Yhulin. She traversed the narrow trail toward the stream, uncharacteristically alone.

She moved slow and casual. Arson kept low to stay out of her sight. Confirming her solitude, she made a little smile, apparent in the moonlight, and stepped onto the muddy bank of the stream. Arson finally noticed how lightly she dressed tonight, only wearing a blue robe-like thing with a snug sash around her waist, showing how narrow it was. She untied the sash, and Arson's heart sped to an unfathomable speed.

The rest of it unfolded beyond his ability to keep up. In all his years of sneaking into manors, he'd yet to see a naked woman, and now it was finally happening. His penis thickened up, and she'd only let her robe drop to her elbows. It went farther than that.

Her pale back glowed almost as brightly as the moon, and she even went so far as to remove the thin bindings around her chest. On her lower body, she wore a little white undergarment similar to what Arson and the *saehgahn* wore as standard uniform, except hers covered less—at the back, a thin little strip went between her buttocks.

Arson caught himself rubbing at his own crotch and halted it. He could easily jerk off right now and get a little taste of relief from his ever-growing sexual tension, or he could award himself better.

Long forgotten went Hanhelin's dark tale about a lusty elf as Arson stood and stepped over the bush to join the sweet little handmaiden, peeling off layers of his own clothes. When he reached her, he'd undressed down to his white elven leggings, boots, and his sleeveless white undershirt. His tunic and cloak lay forgotten on the ground.

He put his hand on her naked shoulder and squeezed.

She gasped and whirled around. "Arson?" Somehow her eyes didn't match her reaction of surprise. "What do you want?"

"Your body." He pushed her down to the ground and mounted her—awkwardly. He'd never done this before. Poison had described to him and their brothers how Lady Lexion invited him to get between her legs and that's how they were able to "have sex." Hearing someone's account of it and actually trying to do it were two different things. He clamped his hand over her mouth, expecting her to scream, but she didn't try.

She didn't struggle either but lay on the ground, watching him with those same bland eyes. He lifted his hand off and she said, "You frog! I'm not allowed to consider you for a husband, and even if I was, you're doing it wrong."

Arson paused, heart hammering, but confusion quirked his mouth. "Then how should I do it?"

"You shouldn't do it!" she hissed. "You'll get in so much trouble. I haven't chosen you."

"Shut up," he said and smooshed his lips against hers. Poison had described this. He'd said that he kissed Lady Lexion's mouth, and afterward he kissed her between the legs, at her direction, and then she let him put his cock inside. That's how it worked, and that's how Arson wanted this to go with Yhulin. Despite her disagreement, she let him brush his mouth against hers, maybe as curious as he. He tasted her lips, lightly brushing his tongue against and nibbling them. They were amazingly soft and a little salty in this humid night. She opened her lips, and the kiss deepened. She groaned against his mouth.

She likes it! That thought stiffened him up perfectly.

"I have to tell you though, I've been watching you bathe. You're so... tall"—she did her best to explain all this throughout their kiss—"and you have defined muscles on your stomach and..." She was panting by the time she decided to grind her crotch against his.

"Will you choose me for marriage? You're the reason I'm here," he grunted against her mouth.

"I can't." Nonetheless, she put her hands to his hair and it felt so good! "I'm doing something very wrong right now," she said, all the while pushing his head downward until he had a mouthful of her small breast.

He moaned around it with a spread of fire over his body.

"Why are you doing this?" He had to pause to ask, though he knew he was positively stupid for bothering to question a good thing. Who cares, as long as it happens?

"Because you're so— Ohhh." Her answer melted into a sigh. "Just don't tell the princess." When he didn't respond, she grabbed the hair on both sides of his head and jerked him to meet her now intense glare. "*Don't* tell the princess."

Her order caused him to pause. That princess. He wanted her too. If only. "I won't," he agreed.

"Good. Now hurry. Bring it out."

He paused and then suddenly realized what came next. She reached for his braies and yanked it sideways until his huge erection popped out. His heart sped ever more. This really was happening.

He leaned back.

"What are you doing?"

He shrugged. "Don't you need your lower kiss?"

Leaning up on her elbows, she twisted her intense glare, the tension from her warning lingering. Perhaps it had shifted into the intensity of her carnal urge. "I don't know what you're talking about. Nonetheless, you'll surely die if anyone in the world happens to wander over here or if Hanhelin suddenly wonders where I've gone, so hurry!"

Nodding rapidly, Arson bowed over her again, and she loosened her own underwear for him. "Do your *er* and hurry and leave me." She stopped him again and put a finger in his face. "This does *not* mean we are married."

He only got hung up on the foreign word she used. "Er?" he asked.

She lay back down and raised her knees around him. "It's the Norrian word for what we're doing. Actually it has many meanings, but it's forbidden. Don't ever say it around the others."

"Right."

"What are you waiting for? I said hurry."

She'd gotten awfully bossy since deciding she wanted to do this. Arson had no idea what exactly to aim for and couldn't see enough under the moonlight. Poison had said that he pushed and his cock went right into Lady Lexion.

Yhulin's lower body radiated heat against his member and greeted it with a thick moisture. Using his best intuition, he shoved forward and it slid inside. In the next instant, he hung in disbelief.

"Hurry," she whispered, a little breathier than one second prior.

"Have you ever done this?" Arson whispered.

At first she kept silent and then said, "Once. It was unofficial like we're doing now. He died a few days after in an accident. Regardless, I've been taught how this works. All the *faerhain* learn it, but the *saehgahn* are taught nothing about it. Move it in and out."

Arson tried that, and it was the greatest sensation in his life. He sighed initially, but his breath picked up heavily and so did his speed. Yhulin clung to him and he loved it! It made him feel so strong.

Sex. This was it. Yes!

When he began to grunt in delight with his thrusts, she shushed him. "Make no sounds," she whispered, struggling to speak properly as she received this treatment, which mounted more raucously the more excited Arson became. He pushed her along the dirt, vigorously increasing his speed and force. Any glance he got of her face, she was clenching her eyes shut but did open them often to look at his face.

"Beautiful *saehgahn*," she cooed, and he loved that!

"You're a wicked little handmaiden, aren't you?" he said back, and she put her hand over his mouth.

"Don't speak," she warned despite what she'd proclaimed about him. She gasped again and again at his forceful thrusts. Feeling so virile and alive, he tried it harder and then more so, hitting against her, and she took each blow with a sigh or hiss. He leaned up on his knees and got a moonlight view of her naked body bouncing horizontally, breasts going up and down. Without having him to hold on to, she grasped the dirt with her clawing hands, digging her nails in and groping up clumps.

Suddenly the wet sheath around his cock squeezed, and it sent a new tingly thrill throughout him. She let the earth go and clamped her own mouth. A few pulses followed and Arson didn't know what it meant, but it must feel good to her.

He focused his thrusts a little firmer, hitting where it felt best to him. Time for his satisfaction. His breathing rhythm flew out of control and pumped out ragged. His orgasm ensued.

Yhulin pushed away from him. "Don't!" she warned.

No? She didn't want him to finish? Did she want to send him back to camp aching? No way in hell he'd deny himself this part. He pushed her down and she fought. She did all she could to wiggle off his cock but to no avail. He pinned her shoulder down with one hand and pulled up her leg with the other, holding her tiny willowy body down under his rock-hard force and let the cum flow. He savored every second.

He took a moment to pant in exhilaration before pulling his spent and very happy appendage out of this beautiful morsel of femininity. He'd keep the picture of her splayed on the ground in his head forever, even long after he took her to Kell's Key to be his wife.

"You fool!" she hissed. "You weren't supposed to do that."

"Do what?" he said as he worked his genitals back into his loin cloth. "That thing you practically asked me to do?"

"I mean spend yourself inside me. You know how dangerous that is?"

Arson frowned. She just didn't want him to come inside her? Was that even possible? "Oh," he said, blinking. Finally Hanhelin's story about the Overseas Taint returned to his mind's forefront and he dismissed it, but then their conversation about the pleasure box churned his stomach. He had blatantly set aside Yhulin's feelings in that moment in favor of his own needs. "Might've been nice if you had explained it to me beforehand," he grumbled.

In reply, she huffed and hugged herself with a shiver.

He didn't appreciate the attitude. "Look, you asked and I delivered. You're welcome—" He paused, realizing how rough he was being right now. "Yhulin…"

She glared up at him.

"Thank you." He had no idea what he could say to smooth this over. They'd done it and there was no going back. Nonetheless, he meant it. He really was grateful for what she gave him. It was something he could've only wished for once upon a time in Haus LinGor's world of isolation.

Still, she didn't answer beyond an exhale through her nose.

"My brother Poison said he and Lady Lexion were appreciative of each other after they did it." Arson opened his arms to hug her, and she shoved him away with both hands.

"We've done a forbidden deed," she snapped. "Keep it in your heart as you live your vow of celibacy but never speak of it and *never* touch me again."

Chapter 15
Fog

hanhelin opened her eyes a bit early. A soft blue glow against the tent announced the young sun. Her sleep had been restless and full of dreams. Dreams about Arson but also about her great-aunt and her father and a huge wall of smoke keeping her from getting home. As troubling as that image was, she couldn't deny how silly it also was since seeing her father and aunt in the dream did signify she'd gotten there. Difficult challenges faced her these days. She didn't need a dream to warn her of the drama of Arson's arrival at the palace.

Deciding not to catch a few more minutes of sleep for fear of another odd dream would hound her, she sat up and found Yhulin staring at the tent's wall.

"Yhulin?"

Usually the handmaiden rose earlier than she to fetch her some breakfast and lay out her *hanbohik*, but right now the lass just sat there quietly.

"Yhulin," Hanhelin said again, and she finally snapped to. "Are you well this morning?"

"*Ameiha*," Yhulin peeped. "I think I'm… I'll need some string and a small piece of wood. Or leather would do."

"Why?"

"I need to craft a token for my future husband. I'm ready to choose him today."

Hanhelin reared her head back. "So soon? How long have you known?"

"Since last night."

Something didn't feel right about this conversation; it churned Hanhelin's stomach. "Who have you chosen?"

Yhulin tucked her chin. "I'm afraid I can't say yet."

"Nonsense," Hanhelin countered. "Say who he is and we'll bring him into the tent right now. I'll evaluate him, bless your marriage, and let the two of you use this space to enact the marriage rites. What a happy day it will be." Regardless of what she said, Hanhelin couldn't manage a smile, and disturbingly, Yhulin had none to show either.

"Kamneigh."

Hanhelin squinted and tightened her lips, focusing hard on the young *faerhain*. "Kamneigh," she mimicked. "The one who cooks for us? He's a little on the young side. He has skinny legs too—and I don't recall hearing or seeing you speak anything of or to him. Why haven't you at least asked me about him?"

"I was a little embarrassed, but I've been watching him lately. He's tall."

"He *is* tall. Almost as tall as…" Hanhelin closed her eyes, and the bright image of Arson with his light hair flashed in her eyes like a burned impression of sunlight. "You're not being truthful."

At that, Yhulin's demeanor shifted from cautious to teary and afraid, like a child.

"Why would you hurt a good *saehgahn* by lying to him about marriage?"

Yhulin cupped her face and erupted in tears. *"Ameiha!"*

Though she usually might've embraced Yhulin at that point, the lass's actions were making Hanhelin's hair stand on end. "What've you done?" she demanded with the authority of a princess and not the kindness of a friend.

"Ameiha." Yhulin sobbed again. "I did a foul thing."

"What did you do?"

"I seduced Arson."

Arson woke up once again to a different setting than he went to bed. "What the hell?" He breathed the words sleepily. Cavlihen stood off to the side watching him.

"Good morning," the elf said. "You did it again. Have you any enlightenment as to why?"

"No," Arson said. Behind him, of course, stood Hanhelin's tent. He found himself closer to it than before.

Cavlihen marched over to him and stood like a pillar with crossed arms. "I'm watching you. Every day and every night." He left Arson on the ground, blinking. He obviously didn't know what Arson had done last night besides sleepwalking, and remembering it now tugged at Arson's mouth corners. He barked a private laugh and got up to start his day.

Arson beamed all the way to the part of the river where the *saehgahn* took their baths. Just upstream, his life had changed. He couldn't suppress his smile and often flashed it proudly at the scowling Norr-men who moved around him in their daily chores. From what he'd learned of their culture, he'd done something many of them would never be lucky enough to do. He couldn't decide which reason made him more giddy, the personal threshold he'd crossed or their obliviousness to the gift he held over them. Yhulin had strictly told him to never tell, however, and he'd honor her command.

When he came back around to Hanhelin's tent, strained voices and whipping sounds abounded inside. They made Arson's stomach drop. A guard stood outside, cringing but otherwise ignoring the sounds, and when Arson drew near, he shot him the usual glare.

Whack! "Ah!" a feminine voice hissed, and Arson hated the sound. He swept past the guard and lurched inside the tent.

"Hey! You're not supposed to—"

Ignoring him or whatever consequence he'd get for barging into the princess's space, Arson lunged across the rug and pried the switch out of Hanhelin's hand before she could land another lash on poor Yhulin's backside. The girl only wore a simple robe to shield the strikes.

The guard entered behind Arson, and after the initial beautiful and deadly glare the princess gave him, she turned it to the guard and said, "Leave us. Step far away from the tent. I need to talk to my handmaiden." Regarding Arson she ordered, "You stay."

Gawking, the guard took a moment and finally bowed, reversed his direction, and went back outside.

"What's going on?" Arson asked, still holding the weapon away from Hanhelin while also fighting back the horror boiling up in his stomach that she probably knew what he did to her handmaiden.

Yhulin shrank into a ball, clenching her averted eyes shut, especially when Arson tried to look at her.

Hanhelin gave up on the switch in Arson's grasp and wiped her forehead with her sleeve, but her anger was building and somehow Arson could feel it radiating. "Yhulin has been making bad choices," she said awkwardly. "I awoke to find her acting strangely and talking about choosing a husband on this day."

Arson's eyebrows rose. *Does she mean me? Has she changed her mind? Why wouldn't she after getting a taste of what I have?* He wanted to smile in hope, but Hanhelin's burning anger kept him sober. It scorched his flesh metaphysically, a sensation he'd never felt before. He decided to wait before blurting out anything foolish.

Hanhelin's gorgeous face scowled harder. "She named off some random *saehgahn* outside—probably the first name to pop into her head!"

Arson's hope deflated. Yhulin didn't name him? After their intensely intimate episode? He scoffed. "Too good to be true, I suppose," he murmured.

Hanhelin continued in her hard voice. "So rather than alert the poor lad to this sham she wanted to drag him into, I pressed her for answers. It's a heavy decision to choose a husband in our culture, and it didn't take a seasoned Desteer to pinpoint the oddness in her sudden confirmation." Hanhelin huffed and closed her eyes. She swayed as if dizzy. Arson put his arms out to catch her if she passed out. Hanhelin widened her stance, opened her eyes, and stabbed Arson with them. "She told me you had come upon her like a husband would last night."

Arson froze like a statue. His mouth dropped open. He blinked, turned, and said to Yhulin, "You told me not to tell, and now you've told already? And the morning isn't even over yet!"

Yhulin didn't bother to respond, only curled tighter as if her pain persisted. Yet somehow Hanhelin's hurt expression made him sad, far sadder than Yhulin's pain.

"She told me because I asked and Norrians don't lie, Arson. When asked, they answer."

"Well, look what good it did you, Yhulin. I was perfectly willing to keep our secret."

"Silence!" Hanhelin commanded after a shudder. She squared Arson in her icy glare. "Listen to me, you fool."

He clamped his mouth shut and watched her eyes like a young calf at the slaughterhouse.

"I will not judge you as harshly as I would have because Yhulin tells me that she invited you. She explained how she'd been secretly looking at you and feigning disinterest, as I had told her you were off-limits, but apparently…" Hanhelin sucked a breath through her nose. "Apparently you looked so 'beautiful' and 'glorious' to her she wanted to have you for that moment. And she has experienced such weakness in the past too. She is mostly to blame in this case. I know that any and all *saehgahn* would oblige such a request."

Arson let out the breath he'd been holding.

"But we have a complicated situation today." Hanhelin shifted her eyes from Yhulin to Arson a few rounds. "She tells me you spent yourself inside her, quite spiritedly and against her advice. Do you know what this means?"

Arson shook his head.

"It means you've done *exactly* what I told you not to do—breed your Overseas Taint into our population!"

Arson put up his hands and shook his head. "She… she… I mean… I didn't…"

"She may or may not be pregnant after that. We'll have to see. It's the reason she wanted to choose a husband right away and marry him on the road. She would've carried out the rite and perhaps your child would be born later. We'd all assume it belonged to her new husband. Her idea was foolish though, because I'd expect the child to be blond if it were yours."

"I think you're really jumping ahead here, Your Majesty." Arson immediately regretted saying that.

"Am I?" Hanhelin's eyes flashed at him, her pupils shrinking to dots. "You're still in trouble, Arson. You disobeyed me after I told you the story of the Overseas Taint! You marched right outside and put yourself on Yhulin without a thought. I'll bet you spent no time either."

She guessed right. Though it should've been an easy assumption, her rightness chilled Arson's bones nonetheless. He really hadn't been thinking. Neither had Yhulin.

"*Ah-Ameiha…*," Yhulin whined, now in a weeping fit. Her hands were shaking violently, and she had been staring at the thick dirt lodged under her nails. She tucked her hands under her arms and asked, "What will happen to me now?"

Hanhelin did another sweep from one person to the other. "This wouldn't be such a bad situation on a normal day with two perfectly normal elves." She gestured to Yhulin's pathetic pose. "Since she lured you into this sinful situation, she could get a beating, as I have already delivered."

Arson realized he still had the switch and dropped it. *Lured?* he thought. Had she really lured him? He thought he'd followed her against her wishes and then attempted to force her into the situation. Had Yhulin told Hanhelin that she *lured* him—under their austere Norrian vow of honesty? That must make it true.

Hanhelin went on, "And after the so-called unofficial marriage rite, an evaluation would be done of the *saehgahn* involved to make sure he is of sound mind. If he is, the Desteer would declare the two married whether they meant that or not. But *you*"—Hanhelin turned on Arson again—"you are no normal elf."

She paused to take in a deep breath. "I just can't believe it. I can possibly believe it of Arson, but not of you, Yhulin. I…" Yhulin didn't see it from her crouch, but a tear rolled down Hanhelin's face. These two were pretty close friends from what Arson had observed. And Hanhelin did appear obviously jealous at Arson's open ogling of the younger girl.

Arson's heart pounded. He had no idea what had become of this travel party. Would they not be friends anymore? It didn't matter of course, especially since he still needed to kidnap Yhulin for his wife, but Hanhelin's sadness put a burning in his gut. There was no reason for all this emotion!

"Hanhelin," he said.

She bared her teeth similar to what the *saehgahn* did at him. "You spoke my name?"

He ignored her selective offense. "Why don't you let me take Yhulin to Kell's Key?"

The two women gasped. Finally the red-faced Yhulin twisted around to stare at Hanhelin in horror.

"I'll take care of her," he said. "All we want are wives, my three brothers and I. My father wants elven grandchildren. We came to your country peacefully, but you have only shown us rejection and violence. It can all be over if you cooperate."

"No."

He was watching Hanhelin, but her lips didn't move. He whirled around to view Yhulin.

"No," Yhulin said again. "I will not be the wife of a tainted elf. I will not bring shame upon my people by denying a good *saehgahn* a rare opportunity to enjoy a wife."

Arson stuttered. "Then why did you do that with me?"

Hanhelin's bland voice cut off whatever bickering they'd raise. "You've already brought shame on your people, Yhulin." She huffed. "Arson. You will remain in my custody, and I'll continue my study of your taint, but when we reach the palace, you'll live locked behind bars. I obviously can't trust your self-control. I can't trust the palace *faerhain* not to be enchanted by your exotic features either. I happen to know most *faerhain* are looking for variations in the available *saehgahn*. It's amazing how easily differently colored hair can trump a loveable personality or strong body."

Arson's face twisted. Things really were worse from this day on. He'd better get his escape in motion before she decided to chain him up for the rest of the trip.

"And Yhulin."

Yhulin shivered, teary and pale on the tent's floor. Arson had done this to her because of his ignorance to some technique of not ejaculating inside of his sex partner. If only she could've explained it to him beforehand, they might not be in this predicament today. She had her past experience and told him that she'd learned of sex in her schooling—something he'd never had. How could he have known that he was supposed to pull it out a second earlier than he did? Also, having to adopt the technique right as he was in the act was the worst of times! No. He couldn't blame himself for this too harshly. Both of them played a part in this spiral of confusion.

"I'm going to keep you close to me too," Hanhelin told Yhulin. "We'll see if you're pregnant. If not, I will banish you from the Tinharri clan. If you are pregnant with a tainted blond child, we'll marry you off quickly—to a light-haired *saehgahn*—and I'll keep you close for a secret study. I'll deliver the child and then study him throughout his life to see how the taint behaves in a second generation. Understand?"

"Yes, *Ameiha*." Yhulin bowed over, forehead to the floor. How graciously she took that harsh sentence. It certainly sounded more complex than Arson "living behind bars."

Though Hanhelin's grief weighed on his mood like never before, Arson couldn't deny his sympathy for the first woman he'd ever made love to. And his guilt for her current pitiful state.

"Hanhelin," he murmured, unsure what he'd plead for exactly.

"Silence," the princess ordered. "Yhulin, leave us now."

Wincing in pain, Yhulin finally straightened her spine, rose, and scurried past Arson, avoiding all eye contact with him and the princess.

"Yhulin," he whispered, and she ignored him. He might've followed her outside, but Hanhelin meant for him to remain in here.

Now alone together after last night's incident, with emotions running raw, Arson stood and waited for whatever Hanhelin intended to say. For a long few minutes she said nothing and paced around, often looking down at her writing desk. Would she record for the history books what the elf with the Overseas Taint did so sneakily?

"Why are you so sad, Hanhelin?" he asked.

She sniffed in an attempt to appear haughty instead of miserable, as he knew she was. "I'm angry."

He shook his head. "I've been feeling these..." He frowned in frustration at his confusion. "Vibrations off you. You're sad and I know it. It goes deeper than seeing your tears and body language."

She turned halfway to eye him. "You feel that?"

"I do."

She regarded the writing desk again. She needed to write it down?

"Is that something odd?"

"Do you..." She swallowed to fix her croaky voice. "Do you not feel these vibrations around your brothers?"

He shook his head.

"Do you feel it around Yhulin?"

"No. Only you, Hanhelin. Ever since you mind-viewed me. Or maybe after you started touching my hair. I'm not sure."

Finally she dropped down before the desk and dipped her quill. The scratching sound indicated her writing.

An idea entered his mind, and he used his silent stepping skill to traverse the space and kneel behind her. He put his hand on her head and cascaded it down her soft, flowing hair. The strands streamed through his fingers with a magnificent silkiness. It truly surprised him.

At his touch, her quill stopped moving and she tensed up. "What are you doing?"

He pet her again, repeatedly, as if she were a cat. "It does something special when you caress my hair. I'm returning the favor."

"Arson."

"Hmm?"

She didn't follow up. He shouldn't interact with the princess like this. Maybe last night's boffing had bestowed on him a greater sense of pluckiness than he knew.

"I can feel your suffering," he explained, "and I don't like it."

When she offered to duck away from his hand, he caught her between his arms and slid them around her. Bafflingly, she didn't get angry and call her guard. How far could he take this before she did?

"I think I know what your problem is," he whispered into her ear from behind. Only the pointed tip of it poked out from her hair, which he breathed against to spread heat along her ear and face.

"What do you think is my 'problem'?" She mumbled the words, but her tone implied he hadn't relaxed her well enough.

He kept his whisper going, liking this tender conversation a little too much. "Like I said before, you're jealous of her. Not because of me but because she's free and able to choose whom she wants. You were born to be Grand Desteer, someone who can't marry."

Hanhelin swallowed so hard he heard it plainly. She budged to move away from him, and he tightened his arms. She gave up and let him hold her longer.

"There's more," he whispered softer than before, and he knew she listened carefully. "I actually like you better. You're more beautiful, and it's obvious Yhulin doesn't like me. She liked my body and hair, but you've shown in subtle ways that you like me. Truly, I'd like to have you and can treat you to the same I gave to her—better actually—if you'll let me."

Did he really just say that? It was the truth. He did like her. Though his captivity was in her hands, she obviously felt for him. She'd been the one who saved his life and continued to keep him alive. She actually cared about him, and he appreciated that. The other day, she'd only said she'd castrate him out of anger. He hoped she didn't actually mean it. In a perfect world, *she'd* be the handmaiden and he'd kidnap her instead of Yhulin.

She elbowed him in the ribs, and he loosened his arms. She twisted around to stare at him. He couldn't guess what she thought, but her raw emotion had lifted. Her eyes roved over his face. Arson thought fast. What to do next? He put his hands up and carefully seized her face. Time to act, as she hadn't yet rejected his offer. This tactic had worked on Yhulin last night after all.

Leaning forward, he pressed his lips to hers. She tensed up like a tree, lips stiff under his. The breath from her nose stopped. Arson put a knee forward to get his body closer to hers, pressing her against the table until she leaned backward, bracing her elbows on it.

Clink! Glunk-glunk-glunk.

Hanhelin gasped and shoved him away. "Now look what you've done!" The inkwell got knocked over and spread its black stain across the page she'd been writing on.

Before bothering to clean it up, she shoved him again. "Get out!"

Arson didn't push his luck. On the outside of her tent, he stood disoriented and raw in all his raging feelings. Had he gone crazy? If he weren't careful, his lust would get him killed. He'd have to save it until he got back home to the land of the sane.

Hanhelin stood alone in her tent, lost and mind spinning. Earlier, when she had performed *milhanrajea* on Yhulin, she captured visions of what the young *faerhain* had done with him last night. His face hovering over her, his loose hair dangling. His sculpted, smirking face with its high cheekbones, eyes spaced in delirium. His arm muscles had bunched, braced on either side of the lass like two hard pillars locking her in. Hanhelin saw it as if she were Yhulin.

She swayed and let herself drop to her knees. Arson had just now used that same pushiness on her—Hanhelin!—as he'd used for Yhulin. The third Tinharri princess! He had filled her with a new sense of... No. She had to be strong. She could *not* entertain such a dangerous notion. This must be what Yhulin felt when it happened to her.

The ink from the little pot spread far over the table in her negligence. From her spot she could tell it had already spilled over the area of the page where she had arranged his imprisonment and possible castration once they arrived home. She took a long deep breath. She wouldn't rewrite it.

His odd statement: that he sensed her sadness. It meant something extraordinary, something the Desteer had taught her about. Even though he'd done *er* to Yhulin, he strangely received that sensation from Hanhelin. It didn't make much sense. Not at all. But it did mean that Arson really was kin to the elves of Norr. And though he talked and acted otherwise, it meant that he had "chosen" her. He'd made his decision unconsciously but deep in his heart. The one Arson really wanted to be married to was Hanhelin.

Hanhelin cleaned up the spilled ink and donned half her royal garments right before Cavlihen stuck his head into the tent. He was the only male person who could enter while she changed. "Princess, please hurry."

"What's the matter?" she asked as she started tying off her belt.

"It's time to leave."

"So soon?"

Cavlihen frowned deeper than he had been. "The fog is here. You know what it means."

"Trolls," she said in a breath. Why now—the worst day to deal with such a calamity? Once again, she stood torn between the trolls' impending destruction of her country and the need to keep Arson closely under her watch. The Overseas Taint could be a worse danger than the trolls. The trolls could snuff out a number of elven lives with their violence, but the taint could overtake her people generation by generation, starting with Yhulin's offspring.

She rushed through the last loop in her intricate belt knot and left it looking however it looked. Shuddering with thoughts of the trolls, she hastily located her vial of "liquid sunlight" and hung it around her neck from its cord. Outside, her *saehgahn* had already broken down most of the camp, her tent being the only one left standing, and as soon as she stepped out, four *saehgahn* stepped in past her to commence its disassembly.

Hanhelin surveyed the scene of elves working briskly, keeping their emotions under control but putting off anxious auras. Arson moved among them, full of more pep than he'd ever shown among his new company. Once he noticed Hanhelin had emerged, his head spun back to view her again more than once. So far, no sign of Yhulin.

Hanhelin caught Cavlihen's sleeve as he swept by her, holding a heavy crate. "What can I do to help?"

"Just take your place in the wagon and keep your head low, *Ameiha*," he said.

Before he zipped away, she caught him again. "Make sure Yhulin rides with me."

"We were going to require her to, *Ameiha*." He left her at that.

As much as Hanhelin hated the idea of riding with the lass who had done the forbidden deed with Arson, and after this morning's confrontation, it was imperative to keep her safe. All *faerhain* needed to be kept under the utmost protection, as they carried the future of Norr. Yhulin particularly could be more than one person this day. As a future mother of Norr, whether already in that role or not, Yhulin was actually more valuable than Hanhelin.

Hanhelin made her way up the steps to board the wagon with her skirts hiked, and her page stood by to catch her if she fell. Arson had made his way over to her wagon, still watching her. He absently carried around a small frying pan after breaking down one of the campfire setups as he made sure to kick the rocks and branches out of the way of Hanhelin's vehicle's wheels. There was so much she wanted to talk to him about, but they'd hit the end of their easy time frame for an interview. He couldn't answer her intimate questions in front of the other males for fear of their offense. Arson's brute way of talking could easily get him killed.

"Look what I've found," a young *saehgahn* said, who stood amid a stack of boxes waiting to be loaded onto another wagon.

Arson snapped at him, "Hey, that's mine!" The things they'd taken off his person when he was unconscious had resurfaced. Currently the young *saehgahn* fiddled with what looked like a tiny bow in his hand, with a small arrow loaded into a groove in the wooden handle. "Be care—!"

Too late, the lad accidentally triggered the mechanism, which released the string's tension. The arrow flew—toward Hanhelin!

Clank!

Hanhelin stood dumbfounded. Arson's masculine scent wafted up her nose, and his hand rested along her breast, his frying pan laid across the other. Hanhelin blinked. Everyone around stared. The urgency to leave the area for the thickening fog forgotten for an instant.

Arson had managed to spring up the side of the wagon, using his long legs to do it easily, and extended the frying pan to shield her heart from the deadly, sharp projectile.

Sneering, Cavlihen struck the *saehgahn* on the head and dragged him away. The lad dropped the small weapon, and Arson leaped off the side of the structure to sprint over to the box that held his things.

In that initial stun, one elf offered to stop him and Arson pushed him away. "Fuck all your distrust!" Arson scolded. "I'm taking my things back if there's going to be monsters rampaging through this forest. Do you want your princess to survive or not?"

No one tried to fight him.

"Arson…," Hanhelin began, heart pounding hard. He was so quick! Expertly. He had told her of his upbringing, an assassin who'd helped to make his father the most feared man in Kell's Key. As of today, he made an excellent White Owl. "Arson," she said again.

Scowling about his fellow males, Arson fastened the tiny bow in a holster at his belt. He glared up at her, and it made a spark shoot through her.

"You'll travel as my bodyguard." That simple command was all she needed. After his lightning-quick reflexes literally saving her life today, no one would dispute it. Cavlihen pouted in his full-body tension at the situation but didn't offer a word.

Neither did Arson, who proceeded to fasten his own sword to his belt.

As if the company wasn't tense enough, a new, thicker wave of fog rolled in through the trees. Snapping out of his pout, Cavlihen yelled, "We're out of time!"

Arson looked around him and then to Hanhelin. He leaped up the side of the wagon again, and the two shared eyes for one intense second before Hanhelin said, "Wait. Where's Yhulin? Find her!"

"Shit!" Arson hissed and dropped back to the ground.

A rumbling began under everyone's feet, of a boom that escalated louder and deeper until they could stand it no more. It morphed into a high piercing shriek that shook the trees so intensely their fresh green leaves and white blossoms rained down. Some of the younger, thinner trees snapped and toppled.

The incredible vibrating sound roved over them like an ocean wave. Elves fell, clutching their ears, including Cavlihen. Arson dropped to one knee but otherwise stayed erect. Hanhelin fell flat to the wagon bed and didn't even remember doing so.

When she rose again, grasping the rail to pull herself up, three ominous giant shapes had appeared. The mist kept them cloaked, but she knew who approached. Trolls. A stranger figure stood with them, a smaller one. A person. A woman. An evil one.

Hanhelin gaped until Arson grabbed her wrist. She didn't notice when he had climbed up her wagon again. "Find Yhulin!" she reminded him.

He pulled her off the rail. "I will, but you're coming with me."

Chapter 16

Yhulin

The wagon began to dip under Arson and hanhelin"s feet, and the motion blended oddly with the sound of an elven distress horn in the distance. The ground was churning up beneath them! Forgetting about any proprieties or whether the other males could get angry, Arson wrapped an arm around Hanhelin's waist and lifted her high to balance her on his shoulder. She squeaked in his ear at the sudden motion.

The wagon sank lower by the second. With the princess in his care, he leaped off the side, away from the trolls and other elves. They didn't fall far with the movement of the structure. In fact, the wagon and ground it stood on reversed direction and pitched like an ocean wave instead. On either side of it, two giant curved, branch-like things emerged, like goat horns or something, lifting the wagon high. Under those arose a head spanning wider than the wagon. Long tendrils of hair like thick roots hung down it.

A troll had burrowed up right under Hanhelin's wagon. Arson only took a second to observe the enormous, steaming, hooked nose with mossy rock-like skin and deep-set shadowy eyes rising out of the earth before deciding the show wasn't worth it. He put Hanhelin down, took her wrist, and dragged her off into the forest.

"Yhulin!" Hanhelin shouted with a frantic squeal on the end as they went.

Though Arson preferred she keep quiet, he knew they needed to find the girl. She'd make a good wife for one of his brothers, and Arson now decided to claim Hanhelin for himself.

The mist thickened around them, swallowing the trees. Sounds alluded to the elves fighting frantically and suffering behind them, making Hanhelin weep and shiver.

Arson suddenly decided to turn toward the creek if he could get his bearings on it. His guess proved right when a slender shape broke the swirling mist and ran toward them.

"Yhulin, where've you been?" Hanhelin demanded.

"Bathing off my shame." Her dripping hair could've told them that. Her comment stung him a bit. He was so confused about what had happened and their awkward new triangle but no longer had time for all that nonsense.

Hanhelin took her by the shoulders. "Trolls are here, and Arson's taking us to safety."

Yhulin regarded Arson with a displeased frown. Last night's big event was a little soon for him too, but remembering it and seeing her all fresh and groomed this morning added a virile, new alertness and exhilarating new emotion like he'd never known before.

He tightened his grip on Hanhelin's wrist though. "Time to go."

"Wait!" Hanhelin protested. "We can't leave my *saehgahn* behind. Cavlihen—and Ari! We must find Ari; he's only *saeghar*!"

Yhulin put her hand on the princess's shoulder. "No, *Ameiha*, Cavlihen won't want you to be anywhere near the danger, even concerning Ari."

Hanhelin huffed. "You're right. We'll let Arson take us to safety, and then we'll double back around to rejoin them after everything has calmed down."

At Hanhelin's utterance of Arson's name again, Yhulin shot him a hard stare. She really was mad at him for doing to her what she had clearly agreed to do last night. And today her haughtiness didn't help his lust very much.

At Hanhelin's nod, Arson pointed the way they'd go, but he didn't tell them *where* he would eventually take them.

Hanhelin grabbed the girl's wrist. Another horn sounded in the distance, and both their eyes bulged. Arson took off, and they all ran as a chain. Hanhelin's silken robes proved horribly troublesome. Yhulin's were less grand but as inconvenient. The underground thundering shook the earth again, nearly to the point that even Arson couldn't keep his footing.

"Oh please, Bright One, no," Hanhelin said breathily as they gathered themselves up after the tremor. The mist condensed so thickly they could barely see each other. The earth shifted again and knocked them off-balance.

A great cracking sound hit Arson's and the girls' ears—it rattled his teeth!—and something emerged from one of the ridges on the turf. Another set of giant horns, followed by a huge hand with thick, chipped fingernails as long as a human leg.

Hanhelin and Yhulin clung together, and Arson shook them loose so they could all run properly. He pulled her along, and she hung onto her handmaiden just as tightly.

"Let her go so we can run freely!" Arson barked.

Hanhelin didn't listen, more concerned with Yhulin than herself.

"He's right, *Ameiha*, don't worry about me!"

"You're more important than someone like me!" Hanhelin argued.

Yhulin insisted on gathering Hanhelin's robes and running behind her, but Arson disagreed with this clunky procedure. While the troll worked itself out of the ground, he drew his sword, snatched the robe end from Yhulin's hands, and sliced off the hem.

"How dare you—"

Arson cut Yhulin off. "Shut up!" He checked the troll's status as it churned up dirt into huge mounds to squirm free. It resembled a man with bluish skin, a huge nose like the others', yellow eyes, and a long grey beard.

Arson yanked Hanhelin to run again. Now with her skirt shorter, perhaps Yhulin would worry about herself. She persisted in doting on the princess too much, and annoyingly, Hanhelin continued to return the sentiment.

Up the slope ahead, the shouting voices of the *saehgahn* stirred the peace; some were calling for Hanhelin and some wailed as if dying. When Arson put a foot to the ground's upslope, a new rumble began with a set of horns bursting through, right between his legs. The trolls were sprouting up everywhere!

The three of them were thrown backward. Arson and Hanhelin rolled into a tangle of limbs. He couldn't tell the status of Yhulin until he removed one of Hanhelin's silken cloths from his face and witnessed the newly arrived troll reaching its great arm out of the ground and sweeping her into its massive hand.

Time slowed.

Arson froze.

He and Hanhelin had to watch the beast bite over her upper body. Its mouth engulfed the whole section, clothing and all, and closed its flattened front teeth over until blood seeped up and soaked her fabrics, dying it all red in its torrent. Her muffled scream inside the troll's mouth ended there. It snapped her in two like a carrot, chewing her upper body and holding her legs in its bumpy hand. Her blood ran down its lower lip and into its wiry beard in rivulets as it chewed.

Now content with finishing off her legs, it remained half-buried in the ground. The sound of her bones crunching between its teeth chilled Arson's skin. He knew he'd puke sooner or later, and Hanhelin had already started heaving. She shook against him, and he finally noticed she clung to him.

The previous troll who had dug onto their path now barreled toward them with its short, tree-stump-like legs. Arson didn't give Hanhelin the chance to vomit or cry or however she'd deal with what they had witnessed. He pulled her onward, checking to make sure his sword remained in its sheath after all his running and stumbling. They sprinted, hand in hand, leaving the two trolls and struggling elves behind.

By the sound of it, more trolls were emerging in their wake. It was difficult to predict what would become of the rest of Hanhelin's people, as the fog prevented seeing the battlefield and the trolls just kept coming, but it didn't look good. Arson had Hanhelin all alone now and wouldn't concern himself with those complexities anymore. This was the time for the devils to get out of Norr with their lives and each with a wife too.

The guttural laughing and stomping of troll feet raged in the distance. Hanhelin's jerky body movements showed clear her worry for her *saehgahn*. She wanted to let them know her status, but she was also sharp enough to know they shouldn't dare go back. At least they could run faster than the hulking trolls. He allowed her a moment to catch her breath and listen to the faint violence. A short moment.

Even before he decided it had been long enough, another tremor started near them and the earth began to churn; another troll would emerge. Arson pulled her on before it could pop its head out and see them. His foot slid on the dead leaves and dampening soil, and he fell down an unexpected, massive land shift caused by the trolls' tunneling. Hanhelin tumbled after him.

They rolled uncontrollably down the new bank, through fresh earth and upturned roots, until one of the fallen trees stopped them, and there they lay for the moment. Arson groaned, feeling stretched and worn and jabbed by the terrain. Hanhelin had landed on top of him, not in a hurry to move either, but the trolls could emerge from anywhere.

He made an effort to rise, nudging her off, wincing from the new bruises on his back. Once on their feet, he guided her down the rest of the newly formed bank to a calmer section of the forest. They had left the chaos far behind, and could barely hear the violence any longer. Maybe it was over.

"Yhulin!" Hanhelin paused to lament. "Poor Yhulin!" She knelt down as if to pray, but Arson grabbed her arm and pulled her up again.

"Not yet," he said. "We have to walk. The farther we get from there, the better." Nonetheless, he harbored his own nausea at seeing the young girl die in such a hideous way. The same girl he'd lost his virginity to not twelve hours prior. He ground his teeth against the persistent emotion. It was all over though. He had Hanhelin now.

"You're right," she said with a sniffle. Her tears were running freely, leaving trails on her dirty face. "We shouldn't be too far from the palace at this point—all we have to do is walk west. We'll surely find a *saehgahn* ranger or two if not better. Arson." She stopped walking, causing his arm to stretch until he stopped.

A roar of pain shot up his arm; damage to the tendons must've occurred during their fall. He twisted around and raised his eyebrows in annoyance. She stepped closer to him. "Though we lost a female today, you've managed to protect me. Thank you. You've done well." She patted his chest with both hands. "You are a good *saehgahn*."

He nodded and continued walking, taking her by the hand.

She spoke again, somberly. "Though I wish Yhulin had lived instead of me."

Yhulin was a bit of a complicated subject for him right now. His first real sexual partner, who treated him so rudely afterward. Now she was dead, so he saw no reason to think about her anymore. Instead of voicing that opinion, he asked, "Why?"

"Because she wasn't a Desteer maiden like me. She was a future mother."

"I told you, she probably wasn't pregnant."

"That's not what I meant," Hanhelin said. "She was the kind of *faerhain* who get married and make children. Those are the most valuable."

"But you're the princess."

"And a Desteer maiden," she countered. "I'm in this world to serve my people. Yhulin was the one worth saving." Hanhelin whimpered again by the end of her statement.

Arson firmed his jaw at that nonsense. "Don't cry. Crying would be stupid right now."

"I'm sorry. It's just so sad."

"Stop thinking about it!"

He didn't look back, but Hanhelin seemed to clamp her mouth shut, leaving only the sound of her sniffling.

Arson observed the position of the sun through the trees. They had left the battle behind now, and he preferred to go north, toward the border, not west. He shifted their path.

"Where are you going? The palace is that way." Hanhelin pointed, but Arson didn't bother to look.

"We're not going to the palace."

"Where then?"

"Back to my father. We're going home to Kell's Key."

"What?"

"We came here to find elven wives, and now I have mine."

She began with a stutter. "M-m-me? I can't marry you. As future Grand Desteer, I'm married to—"

"Who?" Arson snapped, suddenly finished with all her cultural restrictions and difficulties. "The Bright One? Time to grow up. I have better plans."

Hanhelin jerked her hand away, and he turned around, ready to tackle her, but she wasn't running. She hit him with one of the hardest glares yet. He mirrored it in challenge.

"You stupid fool!" she hissed hotly.

His white cloak waving in his peripheral vision reminded him of how she expected him to act as her people. He wasn't one of her people. It took a lot of willpower, for all the intense emotional vibrations he caught from her, but he untied the cloak, which bore the royal seal and white owl symbol, and threw it on the ground.

Her face turned red, and her knuckles whitened by her sides. "You took the *saehgahn* ceremony. Do you know what happens to males who deceive?"

"I said I would protect you, and I did. And I'm not being deceitful. I'm truthful when I say that I'm taking you to my home."

"But I won't—I won't marry you!"

"Is it considered deceit for me to disagree?"

"No, that begins a series of new crimes!"

"Don't yell," he reminded her. "One of those creatures might hear and burst through the ground and gobble you up just like Yhulin." He crossed his arms. "They could be all over this forest. They could be tearing up your castle right now. You can run if you want. I'm tired and honestly don't want to chase you. I may find another female along my way back. A motherly type perhaps. I'll take her whether she wants to come or not. I don't care if she screams or cries. I wasn't brought up to care for such things. So go ahead. In the best of cases, maybe you'll find some *saehgahn* to protect you." Arson turned and started walking.

For the next moment, his feet tread loudly through the leaves. He didn't look back to check Hanhelin's expression, and he didn't hear a sound from her until another tremor occurred, this one in the distance. The sound of feet kicking up leaves came up behind him. She took his arm and huddled close, walking with him, though she scowled up at him with her face dirty and streaked with tears, her hair a mess. Some princess now.

"I'm doing this to save an innocent *faerhain* from your slimy paws," she said. "But now I'm holding out hope for a *real saehgahn* to save me from *you*."

Arson didn't respond but started walking. He fought the welling guilt inside him for the way he had made her feel, but this was necessary. He was rescuing her from the trolls. Besides, he longed for his family.

"So those were trolls back there?" Arson asked a long way down the path. They walked north at Arson's insistence. Hanhelin allowed him to have it his way, but he didn't trust her not to call on her men if she got the chance.

"Yes," she said. "You're from north of here; haven't you ever seen one?"

He shook his head.

"Well, I suppose Kell's Key is quite isolated from the dark region," she reasoned. "Trolls avoid the sun if they can help it. They are the bastard children of the Swine. The trolls are a bane upon our kind; they like to feast on us. And that mist… It meant Wikshen mustn't be far off."

"Who's Wikshen?" Arson asked.

Hanhelin nodded sharply. "Another abomination. Wikshen is their god, a man possessed by one of the worst evil spirits to touch the earth. He's chaos on two feet, and he has befriended the trolls. He seems to share in the trolls' appetite for elves. In an ancient age, he brought rats. Huge flesh-eating rats."

"You often have to fight off Wikshen and trolls?" Arson said.

"Wikshen, trolls, humans, and other threats. We need all the *saehgahn* we can find. It hurt me to my core when you tore your cloak off."

"Not much I can do about that," he said. "Besides, your people treated me badly. You told me yourself they wouldn't accept me. You told me I couldn't get married and that you might cut off my testicles. What motivation do you think I have to stay in your kingdom?"

"Honor," she said. "You might have had it rough, but you don't know what could have been. Maybe you have the Overseas Taint, but if you had displayed yourself admirably for long enough, maybe you could have broken a barrier or two. Maybe my father—or I, as Grand

Desteer—would have granted you a pass for marriage, but I couldn't have gotten your hopes up yet. *Saehgahn* have to perform with all their might without the promise of reward. I wanted to see you shine. I wanted to prove that the taint isn't what we think it is."

"It's nothing, that's what it is!" he said. "I feel nothing. There was nothing wrong with me until I met you, and now you want to learn about it by locking me up. When you come home with me, you can ask all your odd questions to my brothers and learn four times better." He waited for a response, but she had none.

She frowned, angry about his plan. He knew none of these elven girls would be happy about being kidnapped, but what was he to do when obtaining a wife the nice way was barred to the quadruplets?

When night fell, Arson located a place for them to rest. He no longer wanted to trust hills, mountains, or the earth in general but decided to settle in a shallow cave, more like a nook, on the side of a hill anyway. He didn't want any elves to find them either. The air cooled down dramatically, and Arson went against his better judgment and decided to build a fire. Collecting the wood put a terrible ache in his bruises. He set it all up and then found two twigs to rub together.

"Look now, you stupid elf," Hanhelin said, coming to his side. She rummaged through his belt pouch. "Those *saehgahn* you hate so much supplied you with a survival kit." She brought out flint and kindling from one of the pouches hanging off his Norrian belt. Arson took the flint and struck it over the kindling but growled in pain and hugged his side. Leaning over, he dropped the two stones.

"What've you done to yourself now?" She finished taking off her slippers and placed her hands on her hips. Hanhelin took over the fire, and once she got it going, she knelt beside him and pulled at his shirt until he relented to help her. "You scraped yourself up. Lucky for you, the survival kit includes a salve." She popped open a bottle, and a leafy smell wafted out. She dipped her fingers and then rubbed the concoction into the scrapes on his side. It was cold first, and a hot stinging came after. "It's important to keep it clean," she said.

Arson blocked the new pain from his mind and suddenly noticed her hands caressing his body. Yet another new confusion. His father's surgeon had always tended his wounds, and right now this work being done by a woman registered quite differently.

Arson took great pains not to look at Hanhelin while she worked. After the stress he'd caused her today, he couldn't figure out what would make it more awkward, looking or not looking. Talking or not talking. So he kept his seat, stiffly, not looking at her, but savoring the moment while it lasted. How might he get her to touch his hair next?

Her hands slowed down after a while, and by then his cock throbbed with need. Merely last night he'd done his pleasurable deed with Yhulin, but already he burned for more. Hanhelin just so happened to be the available candidate this time. Would she let him though? She had said that line, which sounded like capitulation: *I'm doing this to save an innocent* faerhain *from your slimy paws*. He'd take it, of course, but he did lament their strain.

Hanhelin, I'm sorry, he practiced in his head. Could simple words patch up such a deep gash he'd created in their relationship? He wasn't sure how else to start. Heart pounding, he turned his head to view her from the corner of his eye. "Hanhelin…"

She suddenly paused in her work. Her hands stopped moving. Her eyes widened and her pupils shrank. "Arson."

"What?"

When he turned forward again, he finally noticed the two trolls—trolls? No. Women. Smiling women were standing there. No! Not even women! He couldn't tell what had found them. Feminine creatures with rough scales that flared up at their shoulders and other corners. They were scantily clad, one wearing only a bunch of feathery necklaces over her chest, with a stringy, feathery skirt to match. The other's neck seemed broken, constantly held to the side, yet she smiled like the other. They were both holding…vines? More like metal wires, which glistened in the firelight. Thorny wires.

Frozen in his seat, pain forgotten, Arson cued his mind to react in a series of ways. He would lurch for his sword and swing forward to kill these creatures…

But he wasn't fast enough. At his mere flinch, the scary women flew at them with the spiky wires poised. They had Arson's arms pinned down under the painful lasso faster than he could calculate. The devil from House LinGor had met his match. Somehow they doused the fire in that same instant, leaving him blind and disoriented. Hanhelin screamed in the darkness, but he couldn't help her.

Chapter 17
Darkness

So shocked and pained, hanhelin couldn"t think. One moment,
she's rubbing salve across Arson's hot skin, and in the next she's snagged
up by cold, looping wires and yanked across the earth, leaving Arson
behind to roar in his own surprise and appall.

The thorny lengths of metal tightened as if they'd squeeze her limbs
right off! They kept her perfectly helpless, bound up inside her own
dress. Pointy barbs, like thorns on a rose branch, stabbed through her
fabrics and into her skin in hundreds of places, stinging so badly, but
she couldn't dwell on the pain. Her long hair wasn't her ally tonight
either. It wrapped around her along the journey of being dragged over
the ground, also catching and ripping against any root or twig she
passed over.

Female laughter taunted above, and Arson's growling sounds of
distress faded behind her. "Arson!" she called. She'd give him a pass
for the way he had treated her today if he could manage to get her out
of this. The attack had happened so fast though, and she knew they'd
caught him in the wires too. Whatever these female creatures were,
merely one of them flaunted enough strength to overtake a *saehgahn*
like Arson, and Hanhelin had seen how strikingly acute was Arson's
performance at morning practice.

"Stop this now!" Hanhelin warned in the common tongue, but it
made the woman laugh louder. Hanhelin was too wrapped up in her

own fabrics and hair to see much, but it appeared the creature wearing feathery decorations had taken her. The one with the crooked neck must've stayed behind with Arson. She had no way to tell if there were others unseen in the shadows.

The "Feather Witch," as Hanhelin chose to call her, kept walking pointedly for a long distance, ignoring all protests and warnings about the wrath of the king of Norr Hanhelin spat at them. Feather Witch would laugh back often but never spoke.

When Hanhelin's arms turned numb, something finally dissuaded Feather Witch's progression: the rumbling approach of a troll stomping through the trees. One of the thinner trees fell over at his nudge, cracking and tumbling loudly. If Arson survived Crooked Neck's attack, at least there'd be a well-defined trail for him to follow to find her.

Through her own hair and from her compromised angle, Hanhelin couldn't see much of the troll or Feather Witch, but the booming masculine rumble of intelligent speech ensued, to which Feather Witch didn't seem to answer. In this darkness, Hanhelin remained oblivious to any body language the creature might be using to communicate with the troll.

The troll's voice rose and turned frustrated. When Feather Witch started to walk, the troll lunged with a roar.

Hrrreee! Feather Witch shrieked, the first sound she'd made since her petty laughter.

In the confusion, Hanhelin's spiky wire bonds went slack and the sharp points pulled away except for the ones she lay on. The sound of large wings flapped, and Feather Witch's shrieking altered with the jerky movements. Hanhelin frantically worked to free herself from the wires and then from her own clothing and hair. The wires were a brutal thing to fight out of, scraping up every edge of her and pricking her hands, but she fought them as hard as she could.

A smidgen of hope sparked within her when she realized what her pains and distress would do for her: alert Arson to her plight. Hopefully they were still within range of each other, and she didn't exactly know the rules, but Arson had told her of his sensitivity to her emotion. Arson really was her *saehgahn*, and if he could sense her pain at this distance, he'd fight for her—considering he got out of his own capture. She believed in his skill to do so.

With her long black locks finally out of her face, Hanhelin saw the struggle. Feather Witch had sprouted wings Hanhelin otherwise didn't see, and the troll tried to bat her out of the air as she zipped this way and that, trying to get back to Hanhelin.

Hanhelin had already seen what a troll could do to a *faerhain*, and so she oddly rooted for Feather Witch, but she'd use the distraction to sneak away.

She dropped her outer robe to lose a huge drape of fabric as well as about a pound of weight and took off, hiking her remaining skirts to her knees.

Not enough luck was on her side this rotten night. A huge hand enclosed around her as she ran blindly over the noisy terrain. Feather Witch's screaming receded into the distance, whether she was flying away or running in defeat, and absolute terror replaced Hanhelin's frantic planning. She couldn't move—the fingers were enormous and hard as stone!

The image of Yhulin being crushed between the troll's teeth flashed. It would soon be Hanhelin! It took the next second to wonder if this was the same troll, willing to fight the birdlike woman for another taste of elven flesh. Hanhelin wiggled and screamed and called on the Bright One.

At the thought of her god, she went quiet. In her bodice…

She worked her arm to try to wiggle it out of the troll's grasp. Indeed the creature meant to eat her like her poor handmaiden. It opened its enormous mouth. This troll had tusks like a boar sprouting out from its bottom jaw, unlike the one who had eaten Yhulin. Its breath reminded her of stale moss and rotten meat. It might've eaten *someone* earlier today.

Its fingers were looser around her right arm, thankfully. Hanhelin grunted and struggled and worked until she had it free. She had one chance, and it was slipping through her fingers.

Her head went into its foul mouth, hot, moist, and dark. Against her ability to control it, screams erupted from her own mouth, deafening only herself in the small enclosure. Her hand quickly grew slippery in the troll's steamy breath, but it worked its way down her bodice— she wasn't even sure if she controlled it anymore! She pulled out her "liquid sunlight" potion on its cord and yanked it loose. She'd been carrying it on her person because of how precious it was, the prototype which would save Norr. The troll's tongue slicked across her, tasting her sweaty skin and dragging her hair painfully with it.

The troll rumbled in delight, and it brought a rancid new breath from deep in its lungs. In the total darkness of the beast's mouth, Hanhelin threw the bottle forward without taking the time to remove the cork. Hopefully something would happen if he swallowed it.

Crack! Something better happened. At the explosion of light that burst in the small space, Hanhelin saw she'd thrown it between the troll's back teeth and he crunched down. He froze in all his motions as the potion immediately took effect, spreading its golden light along the surface of the inside of the mouth and leaving solid stone behind.

The troll gave a helpless wail but could no longer move to take Hanhelin out of his mouth; his hand solidified around her, locking her in!

Through one agonizing minute, the troll turned half to stone, the important half considering its brain turning to stone meant death for it, but Hanhelin was now forever trapped in the mouth of a stone statue.

The whole creature fell over backward, its knees collapsed beneath it, and Hanhelin found herself suddenly in silence.

"Hello?" No one was out there, not even Feather Witch. Hanhelin's legs were dangling, bent forward, and her head and torso were upside down in the troll's stone hand. Blood rushed to her head. Panicking would be a bad idea, but what could she do?

"Arson!" Her voice echoed around her ears. It wouldn't vibrate far inside this enclosure. The longer she waited, the more uncomfortable the position grew.

"Cavlihen!" she tried, although she hadn't seen him since this morning. No voices answered. "Ari!" She'd even take her faithful page—anyone would do! Her voice feathered out into a breathless sob. "Yhulin!" She cried. She hadn't luxury enough to cry for her friend so far.

"A-A-Arson!" she tried again through her weeping. It did her no good, of course. The blood pooling in her face plus the stress of weeping caused a headache. She stopped herself and took a deep breath with barely enough space in the stone grasp to do so.

Fingers on her toes tickled. She froze, curling them in.

"Arson?"

A deep laughter reverberated in the stone around her. Not Arson's laughter. The hand snatched her foot, and then the feather of a breath touched her sole.

"Hhhurh," the breath sighed. The hand slid up her calf from her foot, grazing the fingers delicately along her skin. "No hair on this one. What nice thing have I found now?" She'd never heard a voice so deep.

A shrill feminine laughter replied to the rumbling voice. Feather Witch was back? Somehow Hanhelin knew Feather Witch hadn't been the one handling her foot.

"I don't know how this troll petrified in the dead of night, but I'm glad he did." The hand left Hanhelin's leg alone. "Let's see…"

Too terrified to try speaking to this new person, Hanhelin waited, mostly holding her breath. An odd silence followed but not for long. Grinding sounds around her accompanied the vibrations in the rocks. The troll's stony fingers around her cracked. One finger broke off. Another.

The grinding and cracking continued until the last finger fell apart, more like it disintegrated into sand and rained down against the rest of the troll, and Hanhelin also fell a short distance, now lying draped over the troll's bottom jaw instead. She had hung upside down too long and couldn't bring herself to move very fast in her dizziness.

Did that person just…break the stone troll's hand? She shivered, ready to squirm her way free and make a mad dash for safety once on the ground, but Feather Witch pulled her down roughly and planted her oddly shaped foot onto Hanhelin's chest.

Another taller, darker figure moved in to hover over her, his features obscured in front of the fog-filtered moonlight. Already Hanhelin knew that Feather Witch answered to this much larger person, who had broken the troll.

"Look at this," the deep rumbly voice said with naked amusement, probably through a smile. "Exactly what I'd hoped to find in the troll's mouth." He took a moment to look over her. Hanhelin could *feel* his grin even though she couldn't see it. "How'd you like to be in *my* mouth?"

Arson couldn't see a thing, and he couldn't move. The barbed wires dug deep into his flesh. When the initial shock wore off and Hanhelin's sounds of distress faded into the distance, he decided to wait and listen.

A strained breath filled the silence over the breezy forest sounds. He concentrated on it, easily able to use his well-honed skill as a stealth assassin to place it, its distance from him, which way the person moved, and when "she'd" make any other move. He considered his creepy new companion a "she" because he had seen only two disturbing women before they put his fire out, and the pitch of the breathing. Those lungs really struggled. Or maybe her throat pipes. He must have the broken-neck woman.

"What do you want?" he asked the creature, taking the chance to let his mind race over his options.

"Elven flesh," the woman whispered. Her voice, probably as damaged as her neck, could only make this type of whisper when speaking.

He jumped and shivered when she put her hands on him, on his collar, to pull it wide open where the thorny wire wrapped along his throat. He endured the next beat when she moved her head in, breathing loudly in her strained way, and her foul sound filled his ears.

The smell of her breath was noxious enough, but it intensified when she spread her saliva over his skin. He heaved but fought it. Offending this witchy thing could be dangerous.

Nonetheless, she laughed at his reaction.

She tore his sleeve at its shoulder seam and licked another place where a barb pierced his skin. She was tasting his blood in these small places. Her gentle hissing laughter and deep, ragged breaths gave away her delight at this game. Soon her hands were in his hair and he fell over at her push. She straddled him without any apparent worry for whether she sat on his barbed wire bindings.

Arson struggled now, beginning to feel too overpowered, but when he offered to wiggle, she lurched with one arm and his wires tightened. So strong, she kept control over them and could tighten or loosen them with ease.

This'll be tricky, he told himself. Keeping calm trumped all in importance. He let her continue to explore his body, ripping open more places on his shirt and licking little bleeding spots at her whim. Where had he left his sword? Also, where had he fallen in orientation to it?

At this point, Crooked Neck circled her tongue around his nipple. She went beyond her interest in his blood and sucked it.

His mind scrambled and he sighed. "What the shit is happening?" he asked, and she giggled. His blood flowed south. This might not have happened quite the same way if he had light to see her by.

Her tongue felt normal enough. She tickled him with it here and there, all down his arm, up to his shoulder, back to his neck, and his cock stood indiscriminately. It had become quite bothersome lately.

The raw stench of the spit trails she left on him easily kept him from considering ludicrous ideas though. If she wanted to lick his blood now, chances were good she'd want to do worse if he continued to let her.

Then it occurred to him: a horrible idea, but any idea would do. She ripped his shirt open wider and searched his chest for more blood spots. When she found none there, for the way his shoulders were folded in, she settled for tasting his sweat instead.

"You whore," Arson said with a sensual purr.

At his bold statement, she reared back, braced on her hands on either side of his face and spat dead between his eyes. At her work, she hissed a laugh, which sounded like it spilled through a smile. He didn't miss how she dragged her crotch along his leg.

He recoiled against the putrid attack and recovered as fast as he could. "You want blood?" he continued. "I can tell you where to find a lot of it."

She hummed, and it sounded like leather rubbing against steel. "Where?" she whispered.

"My dick, stupid. It's all in there. You can suck it if you like."

She sighed and rubbed her crotch against him harder. Her sensual treatment proved quite a distraction from how ugly he knew she was. "Deceiver," she answered.

"How?"

"I only worship Wikshen."

Wikshen? Hadn't Hanhelin used that word? "Didn't ask you to worship me, I said you can suck me off."

She hummed a grating laugh. "That's how we worship Wikshen."

A shiver ran through Arson. "Is… Is Wikshen here? Tonight?"

"He's come."

Blinking his eyes, Arson had to focus. "Where did you take the other elf?"

"Wikshen," she said as a soft hiss and bowed down to lick his nipple area again, which had spouted a new stream of blood under the barb's pressure.

Arson lay back in a torrent of emotions and feelings. His cock stood persistently at her continued teasing, but he really had to get up fast and go after Hanhelin. She had told him in the past that Wikshen partook of elven flesh or blood, as the trolls did.

Hanhelin…

"Take your clothes off," he whispered as she continued her play.

She hummed another laugh and made her way to his face where he had a few stinging scratches on his cheek. She licked them.

"Take your clothes off," he whispered again, half acting and half-genuine about the state of mind he displayed. "I wanna fuck you."

"I told you," she whispered back.

"What? About Wikshen? Will he really care when you're already grinding against me?"

"Wikshen is my living deity. I would never defy him."

"So what do you want with me?"

"Elven flesh."

Through a new horrible anxiety at his failing plan and growing concern for Hanhelin, Arson made a nervous laugh, trying to let it sound cocky.

She paused in her licking. "Although… You told me there was blood in your cock. I wonder… How much would I get if I bit off the tip and then sucked…it…dry?" She dragged her words out long, grating her voice right by his ear.

Arson immediately went cold and dizzy at her words. They were enough to shrink his cock back down to normal size and beyond. Crooked Neck considered the idea for the next few seconds.

She dismounted him and leaned toward his lower half, holding his wires painfully tight. Arson reared his leg up and bashed his heel into her face. She flopped backward and might've screamed but had little voice to do so.

Arson did a roll and shrugged out of the coiled wire. He had one good chance to guess where he'd left his sword because he could already hear Crooked Neck lunging at him from where she'd landed. Her broken neck made no difference to her agility.

He was close, he knew, when he stepped right into the cooling ashes of the small campfire Hanhelin had helped him start. A quick wind whipped at his back—she narrowly missed a lunge at him. Her fingers caught his hair and pulled a few strands out. No time to consider any pain or whether she'd snagged him. He reached…

Clank! His sword fell over onto the ground at his touch. At least he'd guessed right. Keeping its position in mind as part of a mental map he was drawing, Arson whirled around to fend off the witch, who approached with her next attack. He heard it but couldn't see how!

He chose to drop and roll.

She fell against the ground with a *thump!* and hissed in pain or dismay, he couldn't tell. Arson took his chance to reach for the sword, and she snagged his ankle. He went down and hit his chin hard on the dry dirt. Too seasoned a fighter, he didn't concern himself with the pain. He flung his long legs in two complementary arcs, kicking her in the face at the same instant as he hauled the greater weight of his body up to a standing position. He put his hands up and caught her next attack rather than resume his search for the sword.

She now breathed heavily, and her voice took on the characteristic of a disturbing cat's growl. He had her head in his hands, and it gave him an idea. Before she could bring her own hands into play, he dropped to the ground again and twisted her head along the way.

Crack! Her neck broke—again. She didn't bother to scream, but it put her on the ground, breathing heavily, leaving Arson to spring up and leap back toward the faint campfire embers. He roved the ground with his searching hands and finally found his sword again. He unsheathed it, *ssshring!*

He opened his senses as far as he'd ever practiced. He'd never been in a fight so frantic before, or with such a strange person—or even with a woman! Her breathing sounded from her place on the ground and alerted that she was quickly rising. Tracking the level of her head by her throaty sounds, he tried a swing. *Hhwoop!*

The heavy weight of his blade found resistance in its target. He'd won and didn't even need to wait for the feedback sound of her head hitting the ground followed by her body. Such a fine blade. The expertly forged House LinGor blade had made its journey easily through her neck.

Thump—thump…

Arson stood panting, almost as if he waited for her to get up again. His adrenaline surged. He almost wished she could continue the fight but quickly snapped out of his trance and remembered Hanhelin.

The moon finally made an appearance through a break in the clouds, revealing the dark shape of Crooked Neck's fallen head and body. Scattered around the area were his and Hanhelin's things. He picked up his belt and its pouches, fastened his sword and dagger back to the belt, spotted his hand crossbow, and threw it in his bag.

Whatever Wikshen planned to do with Hanhelin, Arson wouldn't let it happen. He flew off into the night to recapture his future wife.

Chapter 18

Wikshen

Wikshen and Feather Witch had brought hanhelin to a strange area of the forest where tall black obelisks, a natural-looking formation, jutted up from the earth in a circular group. Wikshen had quickly receded into the shadow as Feather Witch got to tying Hanhelin to one of the thinner obelisks with the same piercing barbed wire she had been wearing for the past hour.

The strange-looking human squatted before her and began straightening Hanhelin's hair and clothing. Actually, she removed some articles which came off easiest, particularly her sleeves by pulling the knots which held them to her bodice, leaving Hanhelin almost down to her undergown. Hanhelin had never gone around in the open forest in such minimal clothing before.

Now she sat there, bound like a bundle of twigs, and watched Wikshen eat from baskets of fruit and freshly cooked animals, particularly the leg of a Norrian deer and carcass after carcass of pheasants. She winced at his every bite, for her people didn't eat these animals when they had such a plentiful bounty of herbs and fruits growing here, mushrooms too. During the winter, they caught fish from the frozen rivers and settled with those. In truth, they couldn't eat a deer or pheasant if they wanted to, as the elven digestive system struggled with it. Only a desperately hungry *saehgahn* caught out in the wilds for too long might consider eating an animal—at the expense of stomach trauma, of course.

When not sympathizing with the dead animal, she couldn't not look at him: a huge man, settled down between the two tallest obelisks. He had lit up ethereal blue flames to hover in the air by which Hanhelin could study him. His stringy hair hung long and oily down his face and spilling over his shoulders. All his features were dark, particularly the long length of fabric wrapped around his hips. And his arms, both working to hold up the meat he consumed, were huge. He was bigger than Arson and any male elf Hanhelin had ever seen. She had to wonder if all male humans were this size or was this one odd?

The distant tremoring announced the approach of more trolls. Hanhelin recoiled against the stone pillar as far as she could, which wasn't much. Feather Witch moved to take a sack full of more food the trolls must've foraged from high in the trees. They also brought steaming platters of more deer carcasses and some pieces that looked to be parts of some poor beautiful Norrian ox. The trolls had cooked them and now laid them before Wikshen gingerly with an air of respectful fear.

Raising his head from his current piece of food, Wikshen gave the troll a grunt, and the much larger beast backed away into the shadow.

Feather Witch sat on her hands and knees a fair distance from Wikshen, pointed toward him. Murmuring. She was…worshipping him.

Hanhelin had heard enough stories about past Wikshens to know that he was an everlasting spirit acting as "king of the Darklands" who frequently possessed new host bodies for each generation. Apparently some people regarded this possessed person as a deity.

It suddenly hit her. This erection of black stones was a shrine. He sat at the center, the figurehead, and ate bountifully of the offerings the trolls brought. Hanhelin, tied to a pillar, was an offering too!

Wikshen gazed at her from across the way, as if aware of her heart speeding up. Impossible though. His big mouth spread into a smile, and his black eyes narrowed, but he didn't stop devouring leg after leg, pear after pear, and on to the huge ox ribs.

Feather Witch finished her prayer and got up to arrange the things the trolls brought into tidier piles. Wikshen caught her arm as she passed him, and she started with a gasp.

He jerked her violently, and Feather Witch fell like a pile of sticks to the ground. Wikshen reached out and slapped her exposed thigh. She shrieked in pain, and Hanhelin winced, now sympathetic to the creature who had captured her.

Suddenly disinterested in food, he stood up and towered over her. Feather Witch twisted on the ground and shot him a feminine eye, the back of her hand covering her mouth coyly. She made a soft groan.

Wikshen lurched as if he'd attack her again, and instead of cower and cry like Hanhelin would expect, she caught the woman smiling in the instant she launched off the ground and sprinted away.

Wikshen laughed primally and chased her. She didn't get too far into the shadow beyond the blue lighting for Hanhelin to hear clearly what went on next. Sounds of distress rang out, sometimes pain, and then an odd, rhythmic moan carried on until the woman let out another frantic scream.

Hanhelin's face drained of its blood to have to listen to the creature's grisly progression. Wikshen's black hair shimmered blueish in the light when he rose from the ground and backstepped into the altar's lit circumference. The movement on the ground he left behind confirmed that Feather Witch still lived. She made a satisfied sigh behind him when he turned and strode toward Hanhelin.

Already queasy from those sounds, Hanhelin found no comfort in knowing that he hadn't killed the witch as he approached. It was awkward enough how he hadn't bothered to speak to her since bringing her back here, and the ominous way he stared at her now, with his all-black eyes, brought her near to fainting. Vomiting could be the alternative outcome.

He worked his hand under his long kilt-like thing. "There's more left," he finally said, staring straight down at her. With his free hand, he grabbed the barbed wire at Hanhelin's bosom. It made a shrill scraping sound when he dragged it up, with her in it, along the shaft of stone it was wrapped around. Hanhelin could imagine sparks flying at the back of the obelisk. Wikshen pulled slowly, causing the horrible noise, which he didn't seem to mind, all the way up to make Hanhelin stand. He raised her higher than that. Her toes left the earth, and he didn't stop until he had her at his face level. His true height grazed her awareness; he must be seven feet or more!

Now she could see his face up close and quickly wished to forget it. A thick, black ooze dribbled from both corners of his grinning mouth, and the same substance trickled from his eyes beyond his control to stopper it. When he smiled deeper, his teeth were huge and some of them pointed like an animal. This human—or this creature—was not natural.

"Look at this," he said softly as he observed her features. "No fine women like this in Alkeer. Or even Wormsbury." He used the exact opposite tone with Hanhelin to the one he used with Feather Witch, despite its natural gruffness. "Not that it matters. You're a valuable commodity to me."

He touched her face, smoothing his rough, dirty fingertips along her cheek's curve. His hand down below kept moving, massaging, touching himself for pleasure—which was a forbidden deed to *saehgahn*. He did it so blatantly in front of her!

"Where can I find a few more elves like you?" he asked. "Hmm?"

Hanhelin clamped her mouth shut. She'd die before handing over any member of her country to the likes of him!

"You won't answer? That's okay," he said. "I can sniff 'em out easily." He put his cheek alongside hers as if to feel its softness. His was so oily and rough to the touch, and the black ooze rubbed off on her. "You'll be my first treat, but I'll need much more elven blood than what you have to achieve my goal, ya see?"

Hanhelin didn't "see." She knew a Wikshen or two in recorded history had come to Norr, looking to slay some elves, but the details in common Norrian storytelling were vague. He seemed to either want to kill elves for fun, or he wanted to feast on them with his troll friends.

"How'd you like to do it, my dear?" Wikshen asked her.

"Do what?"

"You're going to do me the honor of spilling your guts." A smirk quirked his grimy face. "But first I'm thinking a little fun might be in order."

"Fun?"

He flourished his hand toward the dark area where he left Feather Witch. "Before you become my honorable sacrifice, it's always practical to get in a good, hard worship session."

Hanhelin sealed her mouth and blinked, unsure what to say back to these odd things he suggested.

"Of course, elves are different from human women," he said. "They can't become dreadwitches, so there's really no point, but still…"

Maybe that explained why Feather Witch looked so strange; she must be a "dreadwitch." Wikshen must've made her one through some sort of magical practice, giving her the strength she had used to kidnap Hanhelin. Her shrill voice too, but perhaps it also stole her ability to speak. Wikshen had turned some regular woman into a foul creature and stationed her as his minion. It didn't help to find any hints as to what he wanted with Hanhelin though.

"A chase is always fun," Wikshen went on. "Or we can get straight to the bloodletting."

Feather Witch had finally collected herself and come back around to this side of the obelisks, limping and favoring her left arm. Wikshen had injured her, whatever had gone on back there.

Hanhelin swallowed in the next moment. He'd asked her if she'd like to run away and have him chase her or just die right then and there. Neither. At a loss, she pouted and put out a whimper.

Wikshen's smile brightened. He turned to say to Feather Witch, "Oh, look now, she's singing my song! She must want me so bad!"

Feather Witch cackled in delight at his jest, and he barked his own laugh.

Pumping his legs as fast as he could and hurdling over logs and brush, Arson focused all his senses.

Hanhelin. If anything happened to her… If she couldn't be his… He didn't know. The thought of her being stolen by such ghastly unknown creatures put a new rage inside him like he'd never experienced. He couldn't very well be madder right now than if one of his brothers were murdered.

His hands burned. He'd been feeling many new phenomena since he left Kell's Key. He wasn't the same person anymore, especially after Hanhelin entered his life, and he'd never be again. He couldn't stop and ponder what he'd done to his hands. Behind the sounds of wind rushing by his ears and his feet stomping down on leaves and branches, his ears tuned out far, farther than he knew how to control.

It would serve his purpose. Every night bird, every sneaking raccoon to take a nearby step, and even the fluttering wings of a moth past his ear, Arson heard them all but wanted to detect Hanhelin, her voice, or her breath. He ran on, ready to pinpoint any possible hint. He would.

Wikshen waited, showing a gentle smile on his otherwise hard and rugged face. Hanhelin held her breath in a desperate attempt not to cry.

"Here's the difference," Wikshen told her when she never got around to answering his question. "A chase would be the most fun for me. I'll catch you in the woods and have myself a good time, but it'll hurt for you. I'll be as rough as I please, because that's how I get my entertainment." He turned again to show her Feather Witch, who carefully continued her tidying tasks one-handed since Wikshen injured her arm. It could be broken for all Hanhelin knew.

"It'll be as bad as that. Maybe worse, I don't know. I get a little too excited sometimes. And then afterward, I must collect your valuable elven blood."

Now Hanhelin trembled visibly, and Wikshen watched her.

He hummed a laugh and grazed his large hand over her quivering shoulder. "A formal sacrifice will be quicker. Calmer." He reached up and caressed her hair. "You're so pretty, unlike these sluts I brought with me. I'd spare your nice face any abuse and just get straight to the cut. You won't feel a thing. I promise."

He lowered his brow and scanned the forest behind Hanhelin. "Taking that other strumpet quite a while to get back, isn't it? My poor dear broken tart. I had a little accident the other day with her neck." He smiled largely and shivered in delight. "Snapped her neck right at the moment of climax." He held up his hand to show Hanhelin his palm. "I used her hair for leverage. This is what I'm trying to tell you. You could take some horrible injuries in the chase. My girl didn't die because she was already a dreadwitch at that point. Her neck fused back together the way it broke, but yours won't. It could be a long, slow death for you. Sometimes people don't die instantly when their necks break. I've seen some gruesome stuff along my campaign. So you might want to choose wisely. The chase could mean hours upon hours of torment before the kill." He stepped back and flourished both hands, one pointed toward the forest and the other to the altar place where he'd been sitting like a deity. "Hurry and pick."

Hanhelin's heart raced. She had to say something! He was exceptionally bigger and stronger than her, so he'd get his way, and her choice was whether she wanted to be raped with lots of pain and terror or a quick death. Hanhelin pouted again. Tears would come so much easier than an answer.

Wikshen put his hands together and rubbed them. A renewed flow of black sludge trailed off his chin as if he were salivating like a hungry dog. "Hurry or I'll choose for you."

"I'll run." Hanhelin's eyes sprang wide. What had she just said? The words had popped out on their own!

Wikshen's wide smile returned. "Really? Are you stupid?"

Hanhelin nodded rapidly. At least she'd have a chance at escape. A slim chance at freedom was better than giving up willingly.

"I want the chase," Hanhelin said with a better sense of conviction.

Wikshen slapped his hands together. "Good choice!" He took a few graceful steps toward her, his naked thigh emerging through the slit in his kilt with each step. Strangely he walked around without shoes, instead wearing a pair of toeless socks and a black band around his exposed thigh. He wore no shirt and acted as if the night chill didn't faze him. If it didn't, Hanhelin wouldn't be surprised. So far, everything about this legendary enigma was all oddities and strangeness.

"You won't regret it—" He stopped himself. "Well, actually, I mean me, *I* won't regret this." Laughing at himself, he touched a finger to the wires around Hanhelin's torso, and the whole thing suddenly disintegrated. Hanhelin dropped and collapsed on impact, forgetting how far up she was hanging.

Her nerves danced high. "Wh-what are you doing here in my country?" she dared to ask up at Wikshen's grimy, smirking face.

"Besides having fun? I came for elven blood, as I've said."

Hanhelin blinked. "Why do you want our blood?"

"I'm counting, you know."

"Counting?"

He nodded over his confidently crossed arms. "I'm giving you a head start to make the chase more challenging."

Although she would've liked to gather his reasons, she instead turned and ran, her body making the wiser choice for her.

It didn't take long for her to become winded; she'd been in such distress for all of the day but was at least glad her clothing was now lighter.

She no longer noticed the air freezing her arms and legs as she worked her way across the land, dodging trees and branches. "Help!" she cried. If some *saehgahn* could be near the area, whether a ranger or someone who'd straggled away from her caravan's disaster, she stood a better chance at standing up against Wikshen. "Arson!" she tried, knowing they'd parted somewhere close. Hopefully he'd survived whatever the witches had planned for him.

Hanhelin hit a hot, slimy surface and fell backward in disorientation. How odd, the path had been clear, and then suddenly it wasn't. Deep masculine laughter hit her ears.

She blinked and stared up at the impossible looming shape. "Wikshen?" Where did he come from?

"Maybe this game is too easy for me at night," he mused and leaned down to grab her.

Hanhelin rolled away frantically and dashed to the side. An unseen fallen branch tripped her, and Wikshen laughed again. She collected herself and relaunched. She limped from there. To her this was survival, but a petty game to him. When she'd gone all but ten feet farther, he appeared again before her—out of nowhere!

"Let me help you over the obstacles," he said with an outstretched hand. She slapped it away and continued.

She chose a route through densely growing trees, knowing it should be hard for him to squeeze his massive shoulders through tight spaces. She could get through easily though—she was an elf after all— and just because she'd been a heavily educated princess didn't mean she didn't get her daily forest recesses growing up. She'd spent many hours a week, running along trails and through meadows with her *saeghar* brothers and cousins. Fun time like that balanced well with her learning. The only thing she'd ever lamented was how those days made her so fond of male company. They were caring and protective of her. They showed her snakes and insects and pointed out birds flying overhead or perched in the trees, making her outings as educational as any. How nice it was going to be when she'd be able to marry. How privileged was a *faerhain*, to be able to pick out any *saehgahn* she wanted and have him all to herself. That's what she thought in the years before her parents told her what her destiny would be. Long before birth, she was destined to become the next Grand Desteer just because that seat was given to any third born princess available.

Making her way through the many thick tree trunks, Hanhelin snapped out of her memories. She must be about to die for the way her life flashed before her eyes.

An arm snaked between two trees and grabbed the back of her gown, her hair too. "Ah!" she cried with a jolt.

"Maybe you should give up," Wikshen taunted.

"No!" She fought forward, against the pain, trying to pull or rip her way out of his hold. She squeezed through another pair of trees, and he let go.

"You think you've got a good strategy here?"

She didn't listen, only moved forward, taking the narrower openings over the easier ones.

A sudden sharp sound with the cracking of wood broke the otherwise quiet air of the forest. The long creaking of a slow-falling tree followed, and Hanhelin twisted around in disbelief to watch it struggle its way through the other trees into its new horizontal position. Had Wikshen broken the tree?

He stood behind her, next to the splintered stump, ever grinning in the moonlight. He raised his hand and swiped it. In a flash a reflective surface winked and cut through another tree.

The second tree fell alongside the first. Wikshen raised his hand. "I'll cut them all down if I have to."

Hanhelin caught herself gaping. Where had that blade come from? How could it be sharp enough to hack through a healthy and mature tree? She shook out of her bewilderment and continued, now looking for a wider path as the narrow squeezing had only slowed her down. She broke into a dead run as soon as her feet found clear earth. She sprinted, ignoring her discomforts—her sore ankle and her windedness. Whimpers escaped her throat, but she ran as hard as she had ever run.

She slammed into him again. Wikshen had some magical way of appearing in front of her. This chase wasn't really a chase. After she bounced off of him yet again, he lunged forward and grabbed her before she could recover.

"This isn't actually as thrilling as I thought it would be. Let's go back to the shrine." He lifted her high and draped her over his shoulder like a sack and caressed her hind quarters all the way. The ground moved far below her face. She grabbed a fistful of his long black hair and considered ripping it out of his scalp, but paused. A white speck reflected moonlight between two of the trees near the fallen ones. A person. Arson!

He's here! He found me! She opened her mouth to call out to him, but he put his finger up to his lips. She'd been right to make him a *saehgahn*. Her effort had gained her a certain level of his allegiance. She knew he meant to kidnap her for his wife too, which would at least work out to her favor in getting away from Wikshen. At his order, she kept her mouth closed and rode on Wikshen's shoulder, anticipating Arson's move.

"I guess this'll be the end then," Wikshen said with a sigh. "I'm disappointed at how much the chase bored me. You'll die a good death though."

Once again, Hanhelin shivered. Maybe Arson had a plan. For now, she'd lost sight of his white clothing. Hopefully he could follow Wikshen, even though he wore darker clothing, through this night atmosphere. She knew enough about Arson's life that he had honed his sneaking skill. She trusted him, yes, but he was a mere elf, and Wikshen was something far more abominable.

If only Arson's brothers could be with him right now. The four of them could surround Wikshen and take him by surprise. But they weren't. All alone, he kept as far behind as he could without losing contact. Wikshen's feet tread heavily across the terrain. Arson held his hand on his sheathed sword. He might have one shot to make his strike.

He tailed Wikshen for a good distance, sometimes having to watch Hanhelin dangle miserably over the brute's shoulder, her hair hanging long down the back of his legs. The sight stirred Arson's heart with a peculiar pain. Why he suffered such discomfort about this went beyond his knowledge. All he knew was that he must have her. Knowing someone else carried her around so carelessly right now fed his heart's pain into a burning rage, like oil in a lamp. He couldn't bother to care right now about Wikshen's height and girth, how easily Arson could leave and meet up with his family and get the hell out of this forest, or how he could die on this dangerous undertaking. He *needed* to get Hanhelin away from that beast.

A light glowed up ahead, faintly behind so many rows of trees. Arson quickened his pace and veered off to move in a wide radius, to bypass Wikshen and Hanhelin. He might find a way to hide and wait for his chance.

He slowed his pace again when the source of the light drew nearer. Better to see what manner of henchmen Wikshen kept before taking his place. A strange collection of tall black stones with floating blue orbs drifting smoothly around them materialized from the mist as he approached. No trolls in sight yet, but a woman moved about. It must be the witchy woman who took Hanhelin away from him, making the mistake of leaving Crooked Neck with Arson.

He moved swiftly toward her while she hobbled around the place. He got back into the state of mind of the legendary killer—one of Haus LinGor's devil sons. The pitiful but repulsive creature never stood a chance. Arson moved from tree to tree until he had a clear shot of her. He sprang up behind her and sliced her throat open across his sword's long blade. She could only let out a gurgle, choking on her own blood before going permanently silent.

Like in normal assassination protocol, Arson dragged her away to a hiding place. He couldn't take her far before Wikshen arrived and put Hanhelin on the ground. Arson ducked and made sure to position himself behind one of the tall stones.

"I suppose if you can tell me where to find the next village, I'll give you the quickest death I know how," Wikshen said as Hanhelin stood on her shaky legs. She eyeballed the forest path from which they came, hoping Arson had kept up. "I can feel vibrations," he explained. "So I'll find them nonetheless, but I'd like my visit to go quicker than that."

Hanhelin asked in order to stall him, "Before I tell you and also before I die…" She spoke slowly to buy the most time possible. "I must know, why do you need elven blood?"

He crossed his meaty arms and laughed through his nose. "For more power," he said. "If I absorb the rare mineral found in elven blood, I can erect a special tower through a practice called *geomelding*."

She mimicked with enough interest to almost distract her from her fear. "Geomelding." It was a very rare magical practice, and it made sense that Wikshen could use it, considering that it was known how Wik was a "spirit of the earth."

He pointed to the ground before him. "I go barefoot to get minerals out of the ground. And the element in your blood…" He grinned.

Hanhelin knew what he referred to there as well. Elves had a glittery substance seen plainly in their blood, which wasn't apparent in any animal or humans. Elves had something different about their blood, and it had much to do with their natural magical abilities.

Wikshen paused and yelled, "Tart?" He was calling for Feather Witch? The woman didn't come at his call. "Tart! Where are ya?" He shrugged. "Maybe she went to take a piss, eh?" He lowered his brow at Hanhelin. "I suggest you kneel."

Hanhelin dropped before him so as not to anger him but continued the conversation. "What is the tower you plan to build?"

"You still haven't told me where to find a big lot of other elves."

"I hesitate to do so."

He snorted another laugh. "How honest. Regardless, I can see that and it's getting annoying."

"How much elven blood do you need?" She'd ask as many questions as she could to give Arson the time he needed to catch up.

"I'll settle with one hundred dead bodies to fill my store. Should give me enough juice to erect the tower and grow the reach of Wikshonism across Kaihals. But each new question you ask will add ten more lives to my body count. How do you like that?"

Hanhelin cringed.

"I'll give you this one," he said. "The tower's power will spread a magical outbreak of fear across the land, potent enough to get me more…" His voice trailed off curiously. He sniffed the air. "Iron," he said.

"You need iron?" she asked.

"No, stupid! I can smell it. If I didn't know any better, I'd say someone got gutted to hell." He chuckled, but his mirth quickly faded.

Hanhelin brazenly reached out and put her hands on his leg. Whatever Arson had done out there, she couldn't let Wikshen catch on to him. "My lord, I feel I am growing intrigued by this prospect of Wikshonism. How could it help the peoples of the continent? Please explain so it's easy for me to understand."

He shook her hand off his kilt and moved around to stand behind her. Now sweating in terror, Hanhelin stared into the forest, hoping Arson was close.

"Ech. What do you care when you're about to be dead? Hurry and tell me which direction to go for more elven blood. Now."

He leaned over behind her, looming his dark shadow and making her feel small and insignificant. She wasn't sure when or how he'd kill her, but she knew one thing: she would die with the stench of his noxious body odor in her nose.

With Wikshen's attention concentrated on Hanhelin, Arson made his way closer. He needed to make one killing blow, much like he'd done to Crooked Neck.

Wikshen raised one hand, and in it materialized a long, thin blade, as if he'd stab it into the side of Hanhelin's head. Hanhelin didn't see it from her vantage. She stuttered out a bunch of nonsense after Wikshen demanded information. Arson's time to act was now.

A few long-legged lunges carried him clear across the space to the center of the altar area, his poised sword still dripping with the witch's blood. He put his foot down beside Wikshen, cocked back, and swung with expert precision—execution-style. *Hhwoop!*

Clank! His sword ricocheted off Wikshen's neck so hard that he too bounced backward. Wikshen recoiled, releasing the blade, and grabbed his neck. He twisted around and eyed Arson, who scrambled back to his feet, shocked.

"I thought I smelled putrid man sweat." His words grazed so cold and calm that it dropped Arson's stomach.

He looked down at his sword, still intact and sharp, but it had failed to cut Wikshen's skin. A chunk of oily black hair did fall to the ground, but Wikshen put his palm up to show that he hadn't even drawn blood.

Nonetheless, Arson resumed his swordsman's stance.

Showing absolutely no intimidation for Arson's threat, Wikshen switched his glare between Hanhelin and Arson. "Well, here we have another elf to donate his blood. Now just ninety-eight to go."

"Did he hurt you, Hanhelin?" Arson asked in a bark, shoving aside his fear.

"No." She had sprung away from Wikshen in the confusion and now stood off to the side, wringing her hands and dancing in place. She worked her jaw as if she'd say more but didn't.

"So," Wikshen said amid the tension of the moment. "Is she your wife?"

Arson didn't hesitate to answer. "Yes, she is!"

"Well, how nice." Wikshen grinned. "Your blood can be spilled together. It can mingle on the ground before I take it into myself. How romantic would that be?"

Arson ground his teeth but stood firm. Wikshen wanted him to attempt another strike; he could tell by the way the beast eyed him throughout his laughter. The mirth didn't touch his eyes, which was why Arson didn't bother; if he charged into his trap, he'd be dead. Instead of charging forward, Arson, holding his sword poised, inched to the side. A little farther. Farther again. He made his way slowly toward Hanhelin.

Wikshen noticed this as he knew he would, and he wound up making the first strike, throwing himself forward and stopping short.

Hwoop-hwoop-hwoop! Some blade flew out of nowhere and spun end over end toward Arson, who leaped and rolled to the side.

Wikshen laughed again. "You've done this before," he said.

Arson rearranged his stance and made himself ready again.

"How long have you been practicing the sword, elf?"

"I was raised by it!" Arson yelled, at the edge of his wits. He'd already learned that his sword wouldn't cut Wikshen's skin, and this monster had some way of throwing blades—from where, Arson couldn't tell!

"Hanhelin. Run. Get out of here," he ordered.

She took a few steps back but stayed.

His hands burned again, and Arson took a short instant to shake each one and return it to his sword's handle.

"Raised by it," Wikshen parroted. "Interesting." He put his hand out with the palm up and flat. "Would you say that it's a part of you?" As he spoke, a large, curved, barbed, black blade emerged from his hand, straight up toward the sky. As the end came out, Wikshen snatched it from the air and gripped the blade so tight that thick, black blood ran down his wrist. Apparently *that* blade could cut his skin.

"What are you?" Arson asked in bewilderment.

Wikshen smiled and jerked his head in Hanhelin's direction. "Tell him, my love. What am I?"

Hanhelin's shaky breath sounded first. Arson couldn't spare a look away from his opponent, or they'd both be in trouble. "He's possessed by a dark entity, a pixie named Wik," she said. "He is considered a deity to some people in the Darklands. He came to Norr to wreak havoc at his own sick entertainment. And to drink elven blood."

"Ha-ha-ha-ha," Wikshen began. "Not a bad definition, but something about it is a bit off. I am a deity but to more than some and will soon be to all of Kaihals—"

Arson watched every movement of Wikshen's face. For one second, his eyes turned in Hanhelin's direction, and that's when Arson decided to throw his sword, as one would throw an axe, and it landed in Wikshen's face, cleaved into the softer tissue of his upper lip and through the thin bones along his nose. The blade had also destroyed his eyeball to go so deep.

Wikshen stood, still alive, with his face almost chopped in two.

Arson ran for Hanhelin, ready to grab her hand and run, but she threw both hands up and said, "Give me your belt pouch! Do you have the fire kit with you?"

Arson had two belt pouches, which he patted to remember which was which. "The fire kit?"

"We need to make fire! A torch!" she urged.

He ripped the belt pouch off its strings and tossed it to her. She shot for the pile of fragrant herbs lying in a neat pile by the other offerings the trolls had left for Wikshen. Arson made his way around behind Wikshen while he worked the sword out of his own face and kicked the back of his knee. Wikshen went down heavily. Arson grabbed the back of Wikshen's long, black skirt, pulled it over his head, and attempted to tie him up with it.

But the fabric moved as if *alive*! It slid right out of his hands like a slimy, live octopus and dodged all of his further attempts to snag it.

"There!" Hanhelin had doused the herb pile with some oil from the altar and clicked the flint over it, creating a small, quick-burning bonfire.

Wikshen threw Arson's own sword at him, flying end over end, and Arson dropped flat to avoid taking the same damage he had dealt Wikshen. Rather than go in for the next attack, Wikshen perked up at the sight of the flames with the first look of alarm Arson had seen. Even the huge bloody gash running across his face didn't appear to bother him, but the fire obviously struck some kind of nerve. Arson left him there and dismissed his sword, which had flown into the dark forest brush.

"Use fire!" Hanhelin told him, but Arson was catching on already. If a blade couldn't faze him, could a flame? He grabbed up the first bundle of whatever looked flammable, grass or some other kind of dried herb. Hanhelin's use of the oils gave him an idea. He dipped the end of the bundle in the fire to create a torch and then snatched a bottle of rum from the collection Feather Witch had neatly arranged. One night on their way back from a mission, Arson and his brothers had stalled to perch atop a roof to watch a performance of jestmages. They were putting alcohol in their mouths and spitting fire to the awe of the audience. After yanking the cork out of the bottle with his teeth, he poured a large amount of the burning liquid into his mouth.

Wikshen made a dash for Hanhelin, knowing she was Arson's weakness, but Arson leaped into his path and blew a big spray of rum over the torch. A cone of fire erupted in Wikshen's face, and the man staggered backward with a gasp.

"Just as I thought—fire!" Hanhelin shouted. Finally Hanhelin's exasperating book smarts proved useful.

In a panic, Wikshen changed direction and dashed for the dark forest. The small fire Hanhelin had created spread and grew. The flames jumped across the oily foods and other bottles of alcohol, which exploded one by one. The grass also began to catch. Arson grabbed his sword in one hand and Hanhelin's arm in the other to lead her in the opposite way Wikshen had run.

They dashed off, practically clinging together. The bitter residue of the rum had doused Arson's teeth.

"You didn't swallow any of that, did you?" Hanhelin asked him.

"No. My father doesn't want us to drink it. He wants us to keep our senses sharp."

"Good," she replied. "It kills elves."

He gawked at her and skipped a step. "What?"

"You didn't know?"

"No!" He spat off to the side and then tried to suck more of the residue off his teeth and eject it.

"How lucky that your father gave you that rule. Did he not know?"

"He didn't even know about elves until three weeks ago!"

"Anyway." She panted between words. "We can't relax."

"What the hell is going on around here?"

"I don't know." She slowed down a bit, breathing hard. He would've pulled her on, but she obviously didn't have as much stamina as he. "But if he happens to—" Her warning ended in the shrill squeal of a huge bird diving through the air over their heads.

"Get down!" Arson pulled Hanhelin's gown, and she fell with him.

It wasn't a bird flying overhead, it was Feather Witch!

"Why's she still alive?" Arson asked, rising and drawing his sword.

"Dreadwitches don't die so easily," Hanhelin said. "Wikshen told me he had broken the other one's neck and it didn't kill her."

Arson spat a swear and held the sword ready for if she intended to dive at them again. For now, the woman squatted on a tree limb, as if trying to mimic a bird. Her arms had morphed into big black feathery wings. Maybe that feathery costume she wore wasn't actually clothing. She glared at them from under black painted eye sockets, sneering at Arson. She wore a large dark stain of blood down her mostly naked front from where he had slit her throat.

Arson grabbed Hanhelin's hand. "Let's run," he suggested softly, pretty certain his hand crossbow couldn't kill this creature if his sword through her throat hadn't.

But at his first step, Wikshen appeared right before them, face already mended back to perfection save for a dousing of drying blood. Feather Witch erupted in laughter to cheer her deity on.

So surprised at this sudden happening, Arson dropped his sword and he couldn't form a thought before Wikshen mauled him. His force knocked Hanhelin out of the way. Arson put his hands up in defense. This was it. He was dead. Wikshen got him.

Feather Witch made a dive for Hanhelin, who screamed off to the side at both shocking threats. She managed to drop and avoid Feather Witch's talons—apparently her feet had morphed as her arms had. In fact, her face was slowly morphing too, into something birdlike. Hanhelin managed to get ahold of Arson's sword before rising again and swiped it at Feather Witch. She tried to mimic the stance of a swordsman, but she had no experience with a blade.

Wikshen squeezed his hands around Arson's throat, tighter every second. Arson's hands heated again like they had been doing off and on for the past hour. He exhaled, pushing out a primal roar through the constraint, wanting Wikshen dead, *willing* him to die.

Feather Witch made another dive and screamed when Hanhelin nicked her wing with the sword.

Wikshen increased his pressure even more, releasing barbed wire from his hands to snake around Arson's throat.

Arson's hands burst into flames.

Wikshen's loosened. The barbed wires vanished in his onset of confusion.

Flames. Arson let them flow. He made them. They turned hotter and hotter. They singed Wikshen's face; his eyebrows burned off. The flames crept into his hair and ignited it. The burn spread down Wikshen's body. The temperature kept increasing. So desperate to destroy this monster, Arson never stopped to think how or why, or would he die this way too? The temperature grew to an unfathomable height.

"Arson!" Hanhelin yelled. "Stop! Get out of the fire!"

He was in the fire? Was he *on* fire? He couldn't feel it, nor could he stop his hands from burning. He still didn't trust Wikshen not to come back, especially after seeing how well his face healed such excruciating damage in that short amount of time.

"Arson!"

Finally he let go of his thought and then his anger. He released the tension in his hands and pried them away. Wikshen's skull disintegrated into ash when his hands disconnected, leaving behind naught but a body. The burn crept down the neck. Arson crawled backward, out from under the smoldering carcass. Char marks spread over the outside of it. The black cloth Wikshen wore around his hips gradually evaporated into the air like smoke. The rising sun showed a bit of what was going on in this early hour. The rest of Wikshen vanished in a moment. His body's ash joined the breeze with the oily black smoke of the battleshift, which danced away into nothingness. A big, dark burn mark marred the ground where he'd been.

Feather Witch, now alone, watched her master go up in smoky flying ashes. She gave a mournful call and took flight, high into the sky, finally leaving Arson and Hanhelin in peace.

Arson's hands had blistered up intensely but would otherwise be fine.

"Are you all right?" he asked Hanhelin when he noticed her staring at him in shock.

Her eyes shifted to his hands and back to his face.

"What are you looking at?"

"You *do* have the Overseas Taint."

Chapter 19
Allegiance

Arson shrugged off hanhelin"s statement and grabbed her wrist but winced and gave up. His hands were horribly burned.

"I'll wrap them up for you," she said.

He started walking, hands held carefully open. "I want to move away from that black smear first." He shuddered at the long, human-sized scorch on the ground. Arson's fire had even singed the leaves and branches bowing over the spot. "Do you think he's really gone?"

Hanhelin kept up behind him. "Yes. I mean. I've never seen a Wikshen, but I recall his being weak against fire from the legends. I'll be sure to write about him when I get back, to warn future generations of his want for elven blood. Right now I'm more worried about you."

"I'm fine." Although he knew it would be too painful to wield his sword for a while.

"We have to talk about what you did," she said, panting behind him. "Please stop. We haven't slept at all. Both of us need to stop and breathe."

They hadn't gotten very far from the spot Wikshen burned away, but he did so. He put his back against a young tree and slid down into a seat. Hanhelin nestled down beside him.

"So I have the Overseas Taint, huh?"

"Do you believe me now?" she countered.

He studied one of his damaged hands. The outer layer of skin had already started peeling back to show the underlayer, bright red and as tender in appearance as it felt. It wasn't as bad as Wikshen had taken. He huffed and threw his head back to rest against the tree.

"I'm dedicated to knowledge," she told him. "I'd like to try to help you."

"How can you help me?"

"I don't know yet."

He watched her face as she took one of his hands and inspected it. He stared at her openly, noting the thickness of her eyelashes and the poutiness of her lips. They were shapely and plump and a deep rosy color in this dawn lighting.

She opened up his remaining belt pouch for that salve again and a roll of linen bandage. "What are you looking at?" she asked.

"My wife," he answered, dead serious.

She paused and met his eyes. Searching them. They held the stare for a long moment until she broke away and started working on his hand. "Tell me about this magic you just used," she said.

He'd expected her to deny his claim or argue. He was proud to proclaim her as his wife. It might not be custom—they hadn't gone through any sort of marriage ceremony—but he believed his own words for some reason.

"What do you want to know? I'm also curious about it."

"How long have you been able to channel fire through your hands? How old were you?"

"About twenty-three." When she looked up again with a raised eyebrow, he said. "I'm twenty-three now. That was the first time it had ever happened."

"I see."

"I don't know how I did it, but I'm glad. He was choking me with those wires coming out of his hands. If I hadn't burned him, I'd be dead and you'd be..." He grazed his eyes up and down her beautiful image. She mirrored the discomforts his thoughts gave him.

"I know," she said. "I'm grateful that you saved me. But you used a sort of negative energy magic. Another hallmark of the Overseas Taint."

"Are you looking a gift horse in the mouth?" He smiled despite his annoyance. It was bizarre and alarming what he'd done, and his blistered hands were standing proof, so he couldn't dismiss the incident, but his relief proved the stronger sensation. More than relief, he'd just defeated a real monster.

She dropped his hand to her lap, not yet finished working on it, and gave him a bland stare. Not too bland. A contest took place in her mind by the look in her eyes. A contest between doubt and hope perhaps, something close enough to what he juggled.

"Some elves are born with a magical ability or two," she said, going back to wrapping his hand. "It is conducted through a certain mineral in our blood, the mineral Wikshen had come here to obtain. Some *farhah* notice they have psychic abilities at a young age, and this leads to them joining the Desteer when they reach maturity. Some *saeghar* find out they can create a colored light orb. They're useful for keeping a village lit up at night. The lights ward off wolves and other threats. The rarest born elves find out they can heal wounded people. These are the sorts of magical abilities that are positive. They're useful too."

Arson held up his other hand, its palm riddled with white and yellow bubbles of fluid; the fingertips and heel were singed black. "And making fire isn't useful?" he argued. "I can be your chef."

Her seriousness melted into a smile of suppressed laughter. She snatched his hand out of the air.

"Ow! Careful with that."

She moved to his other side and tended that hand, glazing the ointment tenderly over the hideously damaged surface. The contact stung, but he didn't want her to stop. "It's not useful when it does this to your body," she said.

"Why did it happen? And why did it not happen until tonight?" he had to ask as he watched her graceful hands move along his.

"I have a theory," she said. "You would've always had the ability, but it might've never awakened within you. And…" She took a deep breath. "My performing *milhanrajea* on you might be what activated the ability."

Arson believed her. The electric shock *milhanrajea* gave his head could've had any crazy effect on him.

"It's a common happening in villages," she explained. "When elves reach their teen years, they might get their first evaluation from the Desteer, and *milhanrajea* can sometimes activate their Bright One endowments by sending the electric charge into the mysterious blood mineral—which we actually call *raythite*. It happens consecutively, as in getting *milhanrajea* one night and then waking up the next morning able to perform some magical feat. It's not a rule, of course."

Arson nodded, although all those big words made his head spin. "I've spent my entire life practicing fighting. I never thought I could ever light someone's head on fire with my hands."

"Arson." She was studying his face quite like he'd been doing to her.

"Huh?"

"Your name. Doesn't it mean 'one who starts fires' in the common tongue?"

"Yeah."

"Your father named you?"

"Yeah. He wanted to give us all fierce warrior names."

"Here we have another mysterious theory. In Norr, naming children is considered a sacred undertaking. The children must receive their perfect name in order to achieve a good and balanced life."

"My father named me Arson, and then I find I can make fire magically," he mused.

"Indeed." She tied off his second hand and sat back with her knees together and her hands folded in her lap. She looked positively feminine in her light dress with its belt tie. It wasn't grand and shiny like her official princess robes, but it showed her pretty curves. She was a flower.

"I need to continue my study of you," she said yet again.

Hearing that irked him a bit, but Arson smirked and spread his hands. "Which part?"

She huffed, dropped her head, and her hair fell forward. Simultaneously she put her palm over his face like some kind of playful gesture to shut him up. Taking her hand down, her face remained lowered so he could only see the top of her head and her nose bridge below. "I am thinking something ludicrous right now."

"Well, don't leave me out of a good joke."

"It's not a joke." When she raised her head, a tear was rolling down her cheek, through the light grime on her skin.

"What's wrong?"

"Arson…" She huffed again. "You said I was your wife."

"I'm not trying to make you mad at me, but—" She put her hand up, and he stopped talking.

"After what you did tonight, I believe you deserve a reward. However, the threat against you from my people remains. If I agree to be your wife, will you go back to the palace with me—willingly—and endure whatever they put on you?"

He didn't know what those things meant, but one thing made his heart increase speed. "You'll be my wife?"

She bowed her head again. He reached out and tilted her chin back up with his bandaged hand.

"Hold on," he said and repeated, "you'll be my *wife*?"

"It's unorthodox and forbidden. I'm going to be the Grand Desteer. If I marry you though, I can't guarantee your protection. All I can do is try. I'm hoping my bonding to you will ease their treatment at your arrival. Also, I *must* study you. It will be a lifelong study if we're married."

It was ludicrous! For Arson as much as her. She was proposing a deal with him, to be his wife in exchange for his surrender to her and her people—to let her study him. But he'd have to leave his father and brothers…

Hanhelin waited patiently for his answer. He had to think fast. *Hanhelin* of all people, the bloody *princess* of the elves, had offered herself to him! He wouldn't have to kidnap her. He wouldn't have the heart to kidnap her anymore anyway.

"What do I have to do?" he found himself asking. The words from his true heart emerged before he could overthink it. He wanted this flower for himself. Today Hanhelin would be his.

"You'll do it?"

"How do we go about it?" His body quickly shifted to excitement from its exhaustion.

"Arson…" Her voice shook. "Will you protect me and die for me if needed?"

"That might've easily happened last night," he said.

She nodded. "Will you learn to be an honorable *saehgahn* and serve me for the rest of your days?"

She had been making him do that all along. Besides, it was a small price to pay. "Yes. Hanhelin, are you g—"

"Arson," she said over him. "Will you turn against your clan and kill for me if need be?"

He blinked. He didn't have a "clan," but he had already figured he'd have to leave his family. He said, "Sure, I—"

"Arson, will you agree to be my *daghen-saehgahn*?"

"What's that?"

"My guardian-servant. My husband, Arson. Will you be my husband?"

"Yes." His heart pounded. Hanhelin—of all people!—asked him to marry her. She was choosing him! "What do I have to do?"

She bowed her head yet again and wiped her tears with her hands. "Now we have to…" She shrugged, rose to her knees, and then swung one leg over to perch herself on his lap. So focused on her every movement, Arson rounded his lips to steady his breathing. Her hands shook as she reached for his collar to loosen it. "I've… I know what happens generally, but I've never done this before."

Watching her fiddle with his clothes, he put the pieces together. Now she wanted to do *that*? He let loose a laugh in a breath he'd been holding. "I might be of service to you." He took her face between his injured hands, forgetting how much it hurt to hold things. "It begins with a painless kiss…," he said in recital of her ancient fairy tale and treated her to a nice, long, tender one. In his hands she trembled harder than he. At least he'd done it once before, but this was definitely better.

Obviously she'd never kissed anyone, with the way she tested his lips, sometimes adding tongue and then pulling it back with uncertainty. She put her hands along his face as he did her, and he took the liberty to stroke his exposed fingertips down her soft, long hair. It hurt like hell, but he didn't care. He trailed his hands down her waist and squeezed. She jumped, not expecting such handling.

"Sorry," he said with a laugh against her mouth and went back in, taking the lead as he had one night more experience in this than she. She swiftly gained some confidence in her kissing, and her body melted down to his. How inconvenient that they were both fully dressed and he still had his sword belt on. He considered pausing to undress but couldn't bear the thought of interrupting this exhilarating contact.

"I have a confession to give you," she told him, and he let her speak but maintained the intimate touch by moving his lips down to her throat. She mewed like a kitten at the sensation but otherwise kept talking. "You said I was jealous of Yhulin. You were right. But you were wrong about how… Or, actually, you were right there too. I used to be jealous that she was born to have a choice for her destiny. More immediately I felt jealousy at what she did with you. I've been attracted to you since we first met. Back then, I had to ignore such feelings though. Yet when she did the deed…with you…it made me very unhappy."

He shushed her and went back to kissing her mouth but moved his hands to his own lapel to attempt to undress. It wouldn't work unless they paused. He couldn't bear it. What if she changed her mind during any pause?

Hanhelin couldn't begin to describe all the whirling feelings within, emotional and physical, this situation gave her. Fear was present but not the strongest of the sensations. She nestled her body against his, finding it easy to get comfortable on this perch. "Arson," she groaned. A name she'd recited many times in the past two weeks. She loved saying it. He made no expression at her confession, but she'd spoken the truth. Everything about this situation was forbidden, which made going through with all of it so much more exciting.

They were getting nowhere as they were though. They would have to undress like her Desteer teachers described to her long ago when she attended her schooling. Married couples joined their bodies together to enact the ritual. But they were exposed out here in the growing morning light, in the forest. They could be caught by anyone, particularly trolls. However, the brightness of the light and thinness of the mist could remedy that danger. Hopefully they were retreating back to the underground on this day. The troll raids were always as fleeting as the mists. It was urgent that Hanhelin go back home and let everyone know she had survived and then get an assessment of her country's damage, but first she had something else urgent to take care of.

She pulled her mouth away from Arson's and sat back on his lap.

He got straight to unlacing his lapel strings, and she grabbed his hand to stop him. "No."

His expression melted. "No?"

"Just leave your clothes on; we've no time to fiddle with clothing. Loosen your braies."

A hint of relief washed across his face, and he unbuckled his sword belt and put it aside. While he adjusted his clothing, she stood up awkwardly, reached up under her gown, and discreetly slid her braies down to her feet. The enamored stare he gave at her act was interesting enough to make her smile—despite her growing nervousness.

He did as she told him and loosened his braies to release his penis. She knelt down beside him again and leaned in to continue the kiss. She reached her hand out and let her palm run across the tip of it. It stood erect and ready and should need no coaxing from her, but that simple touch put him into a frenzy. He seized her head and kissed her more aggressively, and with his other hand he wrapped hers around it with a tight squeeze. He groaned.

She considered sitting on his lap again to see if she could initiate the bonding ritual, but he pushed her over, guiding her gently but firmly, and hovered over her with his sore hands against the ground. She laid her head back upon a patch of grass without much choice. He took on a fast and wild demeanor, delving his tongue into her mouth, abandoning all fear, hesitation, and reason. His long blond locks fell around her face. She carefully put her hands on his shoulders, maintaining her own caution though he'd thrown his away, and she slid them over his hard shapes. He was so strong and big compared to her, taller than the Norrian *saehgahn* she'd known all her life.

He disconnected his mouth and reared back, one side of his hair trapped behind his sculpted ear. A vacancy showed in his green eyes. He had exchanged his smile for a mien of business. What he did next shocked her to her core, so coldly she couldn't manage to move or speak to question it. He raised her dress, pushed her knees apart, and bowed down to put his face in her crotch.

She gasped out loud and arched her back, knees raised high. The world suddenly disappeared. It all went dark, and several minutes passed by before she realized her eyes had merely fallen closed. She made no effort to open them.

His tongue moved and explored in places she never would've guessed. Her Desteer life lessons didn't mention this. The bonding of two bodies, yes, but a tongue? Licking a place like that? The life lessons in her upbringing were kept technical and scientific, as a matter of fact. Diagrams were shown to her along with the cold-worded speeches on how it worked and what it meant for reproduction, but none of that could've delivered a clue for how miraculous it *felt* in real life.

It was so deliriously amazing her body felt light. She hovered above the ground, but not really. Opening her eyes confirmed she lay spread-eagle. The cold air went long forgotten. The trees swayed in the slight breeze, the breeze which pushed all the mist away to make way for the warm sun. Arson's blond head was still down there, moving with his licking motion. His pale green eyes suddenly turned up and connected with hers, and she might've spoken, she might've asked him what he was doing and why, but instead she moaned and dropped her head back down. She didn't want him to stop and didn't care why he performed this strange act on her. She raised her knees higher and pushed at his mouth. She raised her arms over her head and arched her back, so exposed but so naughtily uncaring.

Her legs were shaking, and her lower area was soaking wet by the time Arson pulled his tongue out. She lay there like a glob of jelly, unable to speak and barely able to move. She could, however reach her arms toward him in welcome.

He wiped his mouth across his arm and came over her. And they joined. She felt it. It hurt only a little and for an instant. Arson had made her so moist and ready that it was easy and delightful to take in for the first time. She embraced him hard and he embraced her back, laying kisses all over her face as he thrust into her, slowly at first, but increased his speed. If his eyes were vacant before, they were empty and spaced now. He grunted in delight and panted beside her ear.

Hanhelin had learned in her schooling that *faerhain* must keep quiet during this rite, but it was damn hard! She moved with his motion, feeling the exciting new sensation of being a married *faerhain*, finally joined to a *saehgahn*. She loved it. She loved him. She loved doing this with him and looked forward to it again tonight and tomorrow night.

"Arson," she breathed into his ear, barely able to do it as she took his fast and hard thrusts. She smiled, despite the fact that he didn't share it. Arson the fire starter, the one who saved her life. He deserved this. He deserved her for as long as she could be with him.

He made her feel so good, pushing her sensations higher and higher. Sweat beaded on her temples, and her mind bounded farther and farther away from her body. She ceased to care about anything in this moment, what had happened in the past, what will happen in the future—nothing mattered!

But then his eyes focused back on her and took on a wide, worried appearance. He leaned back, as if he'd get off of her, but her body was beginning to erupt with a new passion, some unfathomable pleasure to top what she'd already been feeling. She couldn't let him leave yet! Desperately she reached up and hooked her arms around his neck. She wrapped her legs around him too and held him inside until she could be finished with him. She tightened her hold on him, and her squeeze made him gasp out loud before gnashing his teeth, and he fell back over her, giving in to her demand rather than entertain whatever hesitance he had.

She erupted but clamped her mouth hard against the need to scream. He seemed to experience something similar. He hit against her, holding her down for leverage and seized up tight, still clenching his teeth, slowing his motion to come to a complete stop, and then collapsed on her. He pulled himself out and rolled off, leaving Hanhelin panting and dazed.

She finally let her voice out, something blending a sigh, a gasp—a laugh or sob. It proved impossible to keep inside. Now she shook all over, cupping her face in her hands. That was it. They had done it. She let out another, softer sob but not for sadness. She was bewildered! That experience was what Hanhelin had been missing when she suffered such jealousy of Yhulin.

Arson lay on his back with his arm resting over his eyes, catching his breath. His erection hadn't calmed yet. "Hanhelin. I'm sorry."

Her eyebrows drew together at that. "Why?"

"I tried not to do it, but you gave me no choice."

"Do what?"

He swallowed, looking up at the leaves. "That thing you had scolded me for doing before."

She reared her head up and frowned. "You mean…"

"Coming. And not pulling it out first. I thought you wouldn't want me to 'spread my taint.'"

She blinked, looked down at herself, and pushed her skirt down. "Oh." She had completely forgotten to think about that factor, so wrapped up in the moment and experiencing her own delirium. It was tough to think logically during that activity. "Doing that means that I might get pregnant," she said, reality hitting hard.

He turned his eyes to her with a pout. "That's what I gathered from your confrontation. I'm sorry."

She patted his chest, and he turned his face upward again, still pouting. "It's all right," she said. "I didn't let you part from me. Let's consider this one time a special case. But you're right. We must try not to make a child yet."

"Yet?"

She gave him a warm smile, probably the warmest she'd ever given anyone, and leaned over him to cup his face. She smashed a kiss to his cheek. "We're married now," she proclaimed.

He dropped his pout for a look of confusion. "Really? That easily?"

She nodded with a smile. "That easily."

"Then how was I not married to Yhulin?"

Hanhelin's smile slackened at the name, but she couldn't be too irked at him for his honest puzzlement of Norrian custom. "That wasn't a marriage rite because she hadn't *chosen* you, and she'd made it quite clear."

Arson relaxed his head back to the ground and smiled. "Oh." He groaned up at the tree canopy. "I'm so tired now. We never got around to sleeping last night."

Hanhelin inched closer and wrapped her arm around his head to stroke his hair. He closed his eyes, and she nudged him to keep him awake. "We have to head home," she told him and followed up with another light kiss on his forehead.

"My hands hurt."

At his groaned statement she gave a little laugh. "I suppose they do." She had forgotten about his injury and to worry over how he used them to support himself or cling to her throughout their session. It might've been better for them if she had sat on his lap and completed the ritual that way. If she had, the experience might not have been quite so wondrous with her unsurety and lack of practice. There was always tonight.

"I like it when you do that," he said, smiling with his eyes closed.

"I know." She continued the caress, running her fingers from his hairline out to the ends of the strands. His locks shone brightly in the sunlight, more platinum than blond. They made her sad. When he opened his eyes to show her their spring green color peeking between his pale lashes, the picture assembled once again. He was a walking hallmark of the Overseas Taint, and life would only get harder from here. They could be facing a dreadful situation back at the palace, but their marriage would stand and Hanhelin would use it and live by it. She'd give up her position as Grand Desteer—whatever it took to keep this person, her hero, alive. She'd sit outside his prison cell to complete the domestic picture if she had to. Maybe they could camp together for one more night before arriving, sleeping wrapped in each other's arms.

"Arson." He had drifted off, and she nudged him awake. "We have to go."

Chapter 20
Reunion

A peaceful walk through Norr made for the perfect opposite to yesterday's atmosphere—more like Arson's entire trip through Norr. He didn't even have any strict *saehgahn* barking and grunting at him in broken common tongue today. He had Hanhelin's smiling face and her confident grip on his wrist as they traversed along the thick forest terrain. His wife, a hard thing to believe and harder considering his lack of sleep.

The troll threat really was over, thank the Great Sea, and they came upon living proof of it. Actually, stone proof. More than one huge troll statue showed along their path, frozen in time in either a panicked huddling pose or a frantic dive into the ground, ass in the air, pose. That one made Arson laugh loudly as Hanhelin stood back in pity. She expressed her gladness to see visible evidence of the trolls' demise too though. Arson insisted they eat lunch under the shade of one of these stone wonders.

"It must've been your killing Wikshen that did this to them," she said, feeding wild mushrooms into her mouth. "Wikshen often travels with trolls, and he has control of the mist, so the legend goes. It must be a true legend. The dawn arose too quickly with Wikshen's death, leaving the trolls stranded in the light. I'm sure many of them escaped to the underground though."

Watching her talk and licking his lips, he leaned over to wrap his arms around her and nip at her neck.

Hanhelin tensed up. "What an odd place for affection."

"It's an odd day," he replied and attempted to nudge her to the ground with a kiss planted over her mouth.

She pushed him away. "Please don't." She looked up warily at the comical troll they'd been picnicking beside. "I don't want to have to look at that thing while you do your *er* on me."

"*Er*," he recited. "You elves are funny." He laid kisses along her face and head since she wouldn't let him do more.

"Why's that funny?"

"I noticed you use the word '*er*' when it seems wrong or at the wrong time and the word '*rite*' when it's right." He laughed lightly.

Hanhelin twisted her face, seeming to think about his observation. "By the way," she said, "when we get back in the company of other elves, for the love of the Bright One, don't say the word *er*."

"I know. It's forbidden."

Hanhelin studied him. "How do you know?"

"Yhulin warned me the same. She introduced me to that word right before I—" He stopped himself, realizing what he said. His new wife didn't want to hear anything more about that incident. It showed clearly on her pallid face, as if she might puke. "Sorry," he said. He laid his head on the undamaged side of his hand, bracing his elbow on his knee. "That was my first time. My chance to learn about it firsthand, after hearing my brother talk about it."

He shrank under Hanhelin's scrutinizing stare. It began to feel like she was evaluating him again and would follow up with a string of personal questions.

"I feel like you don't, or won't, understand my position," he added.

She finally alleviated the phantom pressure she held over him. "I don't," she confirmed. "And I won't. And… There must be a lot I don't understand—about normal *saehgahn*, let alone tainted ones." She made a faint smile, but it wasn't happy. It put off no infectious vibration. "For instance, I don't understand your motivation to join with her when you had obviously chosen me long ago."

Arson had opened his mouth to defend his position but stopped. "Chose you? Besides that moment in your tent when I offered myself to you, it was actually you who chose me—this morning."

Hanhelin shook her head. "There's something deeper going on between us and has been going on for some time. In my culture, it's forbidden."

"What forbidden thing have I done now?"

"Remember how I told you how *faerhain* are the ones to choose *saehgahn*?"

He nodded.

"Well, it's a greater natural urge for things to go the other way around."

"*Saehgahn* choosing *faerhain*?"

"Yes. By raising males not to long for *faerhain* and…'sex,' to stay focused on their daily chores and discipline, and to wait to be called for marriage, we are doing our best to suppress their natural instinct to choose certain *faerhain*. When they do choose one, they experience a deep bond to her. This bond can bring odd side effects, like feeling sympathy pain for her."

Arson remembered the moment when she got a paper cut and he had felt a simultaneous sting on his own finger.

"And also sensing her emotions." She nodded to him, as they had already talked about that phenomenon. "And as you might guess, we have this rule in place because of the shortage of females. If we were to let the males choose and court the females, like they do in your country, we would have multiple *saehgahn* after the same *faerhain*, and this 'bond' they experience is so strong that the *saehgahn* would kill each other over her. It would happen all the time and everywhere. Our society would collapse."

Arson said, "So I had decided, internally, that I wanted you."

She nodded deeply. "Yes. You exhibited perfect signs for it."

He smiled. "You were nice to me. You were beautiful and mysterious, and you touched my hair and made me feel all tingly."

"I probably shouldn't have touched your hair. I might've told you about this sooner, perhaps to try to discourage you, but it wouldn't have worked. You were adamant about getting a wife, whether it be me or Yhulin. I tried to act as if nothing was going on, as I couldn't let myself be tempted to give in to you, but I had made a mistake, because it caused you to do what you did with her. You come from human society, which has easier attitudes about sex than we do."

"I was just horny," he said, trying to lighten the mood but cringed at his words instantly.

Hanhelin didn't appear to take offense. "Your values and understanding is a world different from ours, so what I saw in your mind disgusted me, but I couldn't blame you. I couldn't blame you for the Yhulin incident either, especially not when she lured you to her."

"She…manipulated me," Arson murmured absently.

Hanhelin nodded. "Yes." She dragged in a deep breath. "It's not totally unheard of among Norr elves. That's why I can forgive you, Arson. She was the one to be punished. I suppose if it were a normal situation, you would've been punished too, but I had to protect you."

Arson shook his head and told her in all honesty, "I never would have done that if I had known you liked me or that we'd be married in the future."

"You didn't know. And neither did I. I never realized how salacious Yhulin could be either. We lived pretty closely, especially out here on the road, but it was oddly hurtful to learn such a dark secret about her."

He wrapped his arms around her, and she laid her head on his shoulder. "Let's not talk about it anymore. It's over."

She nodded. "We have the future ahead of us."

Though Arson liked her words, he couldn't deny how flat and joylessly they rang. He knew what she implied. Their marriage would be fraught with hostility from her people and who knew what sort of discomforts. Imprisonment had been the best guess Hanhelin could offer him. She'd told him that she'd stick by him though, and he believed her.

"Hoooo!" A voice echoed far through the trees. A familiar voice doing a call Arson knew well. He dropped Hanhelin's hand and leaped forward on the path.

"What's that call?" she asked.

Arson answered the voice, calling through cupped hands, "Hooooo!" pumping his voice as hard and far as he could. He turned around with a smile. "It's Bludgeon, my brother."

Hanhelin stuttered as the rest unfolded. Up the path, Bludgeon sprinted, yelling, "There you are, runt!"

Arson put his hands out. "Bludgeon!" The two slapped their hands into a hard handshake.

"You got one!" Bludgeon said, looking over Arson's shoulder.

"I did!" Arson stepped back and took Hanhelin's hand back up. She looked about as confident as a frightened deer to meet her brother-in-law. He patted her hand for reassurance, saying, "This is Hanhelin. Hanhelin, this is my brother, Bludgeon."

"Great Sea," Bludgeon said, eyeballing his wife up and down. "She's a better strumpet than Linhala and the other one put together."

"Other one?"

Bludgeon nodded. "Bleed caught one yesterday. He made her scream good last night—we were all listening, not that we had a choice."

Arson wanted to give a faint smile to try to mirror his brother's amusement, but he cringed instead, blinking, quite aware of Hanhelin's presence and hoping this talk wouldn't upset her.

His discomfort went unnoticed to Bludgeon, who crossed his arms and did another visual sweep of the two of them. "You both look awful. What the hell are you wearing, Arson?"

Arson was still wearing the white Norrian leggings known to Hanhelin's White Owl guard. He held his sore, bandaged hands up. "I've got stories to tell."

"Well, come!" Bludgeon said. "Father'll want to know what happened to you. We were really worried, but thank the Great Sea you're mated already. That leaves lonely ol' me. As soon as I catch one, we can go home. C'mon."

Bludgeon started walking, and Hanhelin stepped in front of Arson, looking up at him like a hungry shark down in the water. Sensing trouble, Arson licked his lips. He took her hand and gingerly attempted to guide her along after Bludgeon, but she wouldn't budge.

"How will you fix this, Arson?"

"Fix what?"

"They've kidnapped *faerhain*."

Arson winced at her tone. "I can't *fix* it," he whispered. "You want me to get down on the ground and brawl with my three brothers, telling them they can't have wives? They'll kill me."

Hanhelin frowned deeply.

Already far down the path, Bludgeon paused to see what held them up.

Arson responded by taking Hanhelin's hand and jerking her along.

She hesitantly followed, giving him plenty of resistance, and it embarrassed him! So he added as much force as he needed and hauled her.

"Arson!" she hissed in cold anger behind him. "We can't go that way anyway; we must go back to the palace!"

He shushed her. "We will, but I should check in with my family and see if everyone is okay."

She went silent from there, and though he didn't like it, he didn't like the embarrassment in front of his brother she caused him either. He gave his wife no choice.

"I found our runt. He's back!" Bludgeon announced when he broke through the tree line to the meadow where Arson could see his father's caravan parked.

"There he is!" Bleed chimed in, and the rest of the company, save for the female captives, gave a cheer.

Haus came out from one of the small tents they'd erected. "Arson? Thank the Great Sea, welcome back, you scoundrel!"

Arson lowered his head at the attention. Hanhelin clung to his arm at that point, radiating a fury he could feel better than any of her other emotions.

Uncomfortable at her silent anger, Arson whispered, "I'll go back home with you, I promise. Just let me say goodbye."

"Look what he has!" Poison shouted merrily. "You brute of a runt! What are you wearing, man?"

"I have a lot to tell you," Arson said. As Bludgeon had mentioned, two female elves sat in one of the wagons much like he remembered Linhala before his capture. The moment Hanhelin spotted them, one roped tightly, she dropped his arm and ran to them, stealing the attention from Arson's welcome.

"Catch her, don't let her escape!" Haus ordered, and Poison approached brandishing a spare rope.

Hanhelin reached the side of the wagon and extended her hands to the captives as he drew near. Arson had to be the quicker; he stepped up behind her with his sword drawn to fend his brother off, ignoring the pain it caused his burned hand to grip a weapon.

"What's this?" Poison said, once again with Arson's blade against his throat.

"No one touches her; she's my wife!" he warned. "That goes for all of you!" Everyone froze—devils, Haus, Manfred, and what was left of House LinGor's guard.

"We know, Arson, that's why we can't let her get away," Poison said.

Arson shook his head, trembling with rage in this odd situation. "You don't understand. She's actually my wife—she won't run away. So don't tie her up. Don't touch her." Arson meant his words, but deep inside, his level of anger astonished him. Hurting his wife was the worst thing anyone could ever do to him since he'd joined with her this morning. It felt so right to have her against him, embracing her protectively with his free arm. She reached her hands over the wagon toward the other females, who managed to complete the contact. The one called Linhala no longer wore ropes on her wrists.

"*Ameiha* princess," Linhala said. "This is strange indeed; how did you come to be married to this devil, and will the royal army soon rescue us?"

"Shh, be patient," Hanhelin said and paused to look hard at Linhala's face. "You've been hurt."

Linhala nodded slowly. "I will be fine, *Ameiha*."

Poison dropped the rope and relaxed. Arson lowered his sword in turn.

Poison smiled. "We're married too, Linhala and I. We consummated it four nights ago. Isn't that right, darling?"

Linhala scowled in response.

"What?" Hanhelin shrieked.

Arson turned her away from the prisoners with an arm around her shoulders and silenced whatever she would protest.

"We're in a delicate situation," he whispered to her.

Hanhelin shook her head. "We can't let this abomination stand. This Desteer maiden is not married to him."

"How would you know?" Arson asked.

"I sensed sadness in her vibrations, as well it's clear on her face. She's putting up with him to spare an innocent, but in her heart she has not married him as I have married you. She didn't officially choose him. You can't let him molest her again."

Arson clenched his teeth and chose not to respond. He couldn't stop his brothers' campaign for wives, nor could he keep Hanhelin from returning to her people. He had to find an out somehow.

"Arson!" Haus barked, and he jumped as he was conditioned to do at that sound. "What are you doing? Put your wife in the wagon and let's go!"

He endured her angry glare, not wanting to let her be treated as a prisoner. "Will you ride in the wagon please?"

She lowered her eyebrows at him. "I'll be waiting for you to form a plan." She climbed up with Arson's help and took a seat as close to the other two as before.

Haus approached to throw his stubby arms around Arson's waist. "You had me scared, you know that? I don't think I'd take it very well if I lost one o' my boys." The attention made Arson feel odd. Haus had always been more of a rough kind of loving father. He must've realized the awkwardness in his warmness too because he followed up with, "Scare me like that again, and I'll chop off yer pinkies!"

Laughing it off, Arson reclaimed his old horse and once again rode beside the wagon, this time with the desperate instinct to protect it. Now he had a lot to think about. Maybe he shouldn't have returned at all even though the joy in his father's eyes at his appearance was nice. He'd wanted to let his family know he was alive, but now he didn't know how he could leave again in order to please Hanhelin. They could run away tonight, but he knew she wouldn't leave without freeing the other females. How could they free the women from Poison and Bleed, who would probably fight for them as fiercely as Arson would fight for Hanhelin?

Arson sighed and deflated a bit in his saddle, watching Hanhelin caress and whisper to the other two. She believed they were in her care. She was the princess, and they were her subjects. He wanted nothing more than to explain all he knew about the situation to his father, but he didn't think the old man could ever understand. Haus LinGor wanted what he wanted.

Arson stood on the deck of a boat, far out at sea. None of his brothers were with him out there. No Father either. He'd never really gone anywhere without his brothers before. The water heaved him up and down their nauseating waves, but he kept his feet, though unsurely. He made his way to the side of the vessel to cling to the taffrail.

The up-and-down motion from this spot only deepened his illness. The world around him was a calm, flat water stretching into eternity. Only a thick mist gliding here and there along the ocean's grey surface broke up the empty view. The sun illuminated the mist brightly but couldn't break through to warm him with its light. Only the spray of cold ocean water hit his face.

Finally he noticed the sound.

Looking down, a crate stood by his feet. A crate with crying within. He pried open the lid with his fingers, its wooden pegs swelled from the high moisture, but it came loose easily enough. Just as he suspected. Babies were in there, sleeping on a bed of straw. One, two, three… Where was the fourth one? That put a little bit of a panic in him, and the fact of seeing babies in a box was upsetting enough. He saw no other baby placed on the ship's deck nor heard any lonely crying coming from elsewhere. There were only three in this box.

Arson's heart ached. What to do with them? He couldn't help them, he was only a man, and he saw no women on board with him.

He resealed the crate, held it over the side of the boat. And let go.

The floating box quickly drifted into the distance.

He'd made the wrong choice. Arson immediately wanted them back! But he couldn't get them. If he left his boat, he might never get back to it. He watched the box disappear, somehow knowing he'd sent away something precious to him. He bowed his forehead to the taffrail, weeping in agony.

"Arson!"

Arson snapped awake and found himself on his horse. The swaying of his steed's body beneath him registered similar to the pitching boat in his dream. Only a dream, thank the Great Sea. Amazingly, he didn't fall off the horse while asleep.

From the nearest cart, Haus barked a laugh. "Sleepin' on a horse. You've been run ragged, I'll bet, boy."

Arson replied, "You've no idea, Father."

Behind his father, in the wagon bed, huddled the three *faerhain*, Hanhelin and the two who'd been kidnapped. All three of them drooped in a gloom. Hanhelin watched him with a blank stare, her eyes big and round, set in an oval-shaped face, framed by two heavy curtains of long black hair on each side of it. He longed to touch her after however many hours they'd spent riding apart, but he wasn't sure if she thought very highly of him at that point. She held her stare on him and let it intensify until he broke the eye contact and cantered his horse ahead.

"Whoosh!" Arson yelled later that night over the sparking campfire. He threw his hands out wide to animate what he said. "His whole body turned to ash and vanished on the wind!"

The identical faces of his brothers showed nearly the same gaping amusement at his fantastic story. Haus sat forward, rubbing his hands as if he were eating up the action to sate his thirst for bloody stories—a thing he'd always enjoyed.

"The monster was dead finally," Arson continued. "And there was Hanhelin." He motioned to her where she sat in the shadow with the two other females like a tight clutch of chicks. She hadn't even spoken to him since that morning. He wrapped up his story with, "And then she chose me and consummated our marriage." Arson sat down and let them all take it in. Oftentimes his brothers and Haus glanced back at his wife. She frowned deeply now, still very unamused.

"She's a beauty, she is," Haus declared loudly. "Manfred," he barked, startling the man out of his study of the star patterns. "Get us out some rum! We got to celebrate this great feat Arson has accomplished. Tonight he is officially a man!"

"Ah, my brother's not a virgin anymore!" Poison declared and lurched over to knuckle Arson's scalp.

Arson gave a brief laugh and shrugged out of the headlock, but something his father said made him start. "Hold on!"

Everyone froze. "What's the matter, me boy?"

"We can't drink alcohol, it's poison to elves."

Haus frowned and looked across the four of his sons. "Is it?"

Sitting next to him, Poison shrugged. "We've been drinking it since the night Bleed found you and reported your good progress."

Arson lowered his brow. "And it didn't make you ill?"

They all shook their heads. "It's good," Poison confirmed. "It doesn't make us tipsy like it does Father either. We didn't drink much, regardless."

"Oh." Arson checked Hanhelin in her shadow across the way and couldn't read her blankness. He refused the cup of alcohol Bleed offered him anyway, and Poison, holding his own cup, nudged his shoulder.

"Tell me all about it, and describe what her body looks like."

Swallowing, Arson tore his gaze away from that somber corner of the camp and said, "Um. We didn't have time to undress."

"Pity!"

"Yeah." Arson opened his story, a bit more quietly than the one about defeating Wikshen, yet Hanhelin still should've heard him. He didn't really want to talk about it, but Poison asked and they were all having such a good time. The other two leaned in as well to hear all the details about when Arson gave her oral sex based on Poison's older story about Lady Lexion. He earned hundreds of credit points from him for this reason. He'd always wanted to make Poison proud, but in this case, it brought him awkwardness and he couldn't guess what to do about it.

"Leave me alone!" Hanhelin hissed in his face when Arson tried to catch her in the shadow hours later when she prepared for bed. Arson didn't know how to handle her right now. She was obviously mad that he'd told his brothers about their consummation, but Arson couldn't have shut them out and shrugged off precious bonding time with them. Now it was time to bond again with Hanhelin, and she was having none of it.

Linhala and the other kidnapped *faerhain* were off with their new husbands at the moment, leaving Hanhelin free to take care of Arson, and Arson ached for another release at the thought of what his brothers were getting in this moment.

There wasn't much privacy at the camp, but he at least knew everyone else should have enough sense to back off for long enough. He embraced Hanhelin from behind and nuzzled his nose into the back of her neck. He grazed his injured hands over her bust. It would be nice to get her naked so he could experience his wife's beautiful body in full.

"Arson," she said coldly, locked in his arms. He tightened them up when she tried to push out of them. "Linhala is a Desteer maiden and had capitulated to marrying your brother, but Enrha, the other one, is already married. Your nasty brother snatched her right out of her family's grove and raped her. She needs to be returned to her home."

Arson maintained his hold on her. "Have you ever thought of maybe going back to Kell's Key with me? You can take care of your friends there, and we won't have to live in imprisonment under your people."

She scoffed. "Take your question back, because I will *never* abandon my people! Besides, do you really want the whole country of Norr hunting you down through the rock forest?"

That's what had dissuaded Arson from the thought of stealing Hanhelin. It's why he had considered Yhulin to be a more viable candidate for his wife. "There's not much I can do, okay?" he said. "Especially in this hour. We can talk about it in the morning. Now lie down please." He attempted to walk her over to the skimpy bedding she had assembled out of a tarp and cloaks found among Haus's goods.

"Enrha's husband will hunt you all down and kill you all the same, don't you understand?"

"We'll be long gone soon enough." He squeezed her breast and noticed its large size, larger than Yhulin's, a detail he hadn't made note of when they performed the marriage rite. It excited his lust to the point of no return.

She lowered her voice to a soft whisper. "Listen to me. How would *you* feel if some stranger showed up and snatched me away from you?"

Arson paused because the question brought up heat in his stomach at the dreadful thought. "I'd hate it," he said honestly. "I'd hunt them down and—"

"Kill them," Hanhelin said, nodding. "Which is what I said this *faerhain*'s husband would do. He's probably out there right now, hunting for your brother's head."

Arson sighed and shrugged. "But I'm in a difficult place, Hanhelin."

She faced him squarely, hands stiff at her sides. "I understand, but you better wise up." She motioned to the bedding. "If I join with you again tonight, will you promise to free the other *faerhain* in the morning and then go home with me?"

"Sure." She'd made a good point, but he loved his brothers and would also gladly support their cause, so they could experience happiness like what Hanhelin already gave him. "It's not an easy thing to consider—or accomplish though."

She reached up and touched his face. He put his hand on hers to prolong the touch; he loved it! "I understand that too," she said. "We'll have to make some difficult decisions."

He huffed, unsure whether his neediness bothered him or her heavy demand.

The wind had picked up speed this evening, oddly seeming to change its direction. She took her hand away and slogged over to the bed, against the breeze, to pull back the top cloak.

"Come," she said to him. "I'm doing this because of your promise, but you're also my husband and this is my duty. And we're keeping it covered up."

Arson shed all of his clothing and got in the bed with her, though she stayed fully dressed. He tucked the two of them in snugly so the wind couldn't take their covering away. Regardless of her clothing and the darkness preventing him from seeing her lovely features, he took it upon himself to discover those fine round breasts she kept so secret by sliding his hand up her dress to feel her if not see her. Throughout, she managed not to make eye contact and she certainly didn't make noise. He lost himself in her though and never really noticed when he fell asleep.

Chapter 21

Fire

"The woods are on fire! Arson!" Bludgeon called, startling Arson awake.

Indeed, a large wall of smoke rushed into the sky over the trees.

One of Haus's men ran in from the woods. "It's blocking our path; we'll have to change course!"

Haus stood amid the stirred crowd, tossing out orders about packing up, leaving items behind, and gathering up the elf women lest they escape. "We'll have to go back the way we came," he yelled to anyone who could hear.

Arson stood up, remembering he was naked, and searched around for wherever he'd thrown his leggings. Hanhelin met him as he turned, shoving a neatly folded stack of clothes at his chest with a silent demand in her eyes. He threw the clothes on, enduring her stare.

"Do you think this has anything to do with that fire we started while fighting Wikshen?" he asked her at his horse. She surprised him with her knowledge about putting the bridle on.

"Probably," she answered. "I'm not worried about the forest."

"But it's your home."

She pointed to the sky where a dark cloud hovered in the west. "Rain is coming. Nonetheless, this makes for a good distraction to get away."

Arson sucked in a breath. He now stood at a crossroads he had wished he'd never come to: fulfill Hanhelin's request or stay with his beloved family.

Bleed emerged from the forest next. "It's bad," he said. "We're almost totally surrounded."

"Shit!" Haus replied. "Is there a path to get out of here?"

Bleed pointed. "I found one, but it goes along the rough terrain. The one with the pits and trenches made by trolls."

Haus gritted his teeth and surveyed his wagons full of goods and riches. "We'll go as far as we can. Put the women on that wagon."

Arson guided Hanhelin, who made a faint effort to resist, to the designated wagon. "Just get on," he told her. "No telling if we'll find our chance…" He left her at that. She gave only a yelp of protest as he lifted her up by her waist and then pushed her rear end to make her move to the front of it. Right now it was more important to escape the forest fire than his brothers and father.

It took some effort, but they managed to turn the wagon around and roll it in the direction of Bleed's recommendation, away from the ominous black smoke. Haus's man drove the wagon hastily while the others ran beside it. The devils rode their horses, Arson staying as close as he could to its precious cargo.

Heavy smoke and the sight of flames met them in the woods, but Bleed directed the way through the trees, over rough dips and bumps. Just like he'd said, the ground rose up along the path with freshly churned earth and exposed roots where the trolls had messed things up days before.

They moved forward on faith when the wind blew the smoke over them all, coughing their way through. The forest was dark inside the smoke, as if the morning never came, and Arson half expected Wikshen to appear in his path with blades and barbed wires shooting from his hands to snatch and destroy everyone he loved.

The horses struggled over the terrain, and they soon found themselves off-road. The wagon carrying Haus and the females hit a dip and halted with a rough jolt, its wheels jamming fast. One of its two horses caught an unseen tree stump and released a beastly scream of agony. The wagon fared poorly too; the front axle cracked and gave out, and the rest of the wagon cracked with loud wooden sounds.

Arson dismounted to help his father and wife out of the wreckage. He used his elven dagger to cut the rope that bound the third *faerhain* to the wagon. Her wrist appeared broken after the turbulence, and she whimpered and wept through the pain. Arson couldn't help but notice that Bleed didn't come running at her sounds of pain. Arson certainly would've done so for Hanhelin.

The group reassembled, Haus now limping, and together they found the road again but had to weave between patches of flaming grass, pillars of toxic smoke, and spooked deer bounding erratically. They formed a human chain and moved as fast as they could along the road until a mass of rattling and footfalls sounded up ahead.

Elves! was Arson's only thought. They were in trouble considering they'd kidnapped three *faerhain*, one of them the damned princess!

"A company!" Haus said. "Everyone shut up; let me do the talking." They stood blind in the smoldering forest, waiting to see who approached. When the company marched into view, Haus's party paused. It wasn't an elven company. They were wearing House LinGor uniform. "Oh, bless you all, my men!" Haus roared. "And just when I need ya."

A rapid patter of horse hooves sounded within the fog, and the cluster of armored men parted for the rider. Tobas, Haus's oldest son, his original son, sat atop Haus's prized horse. "Bless ya, Tobas!" Haus said. "When we get back, you're getting a promotion."

"Promotion indeed!" Tobas spat. He was dressed in Haus's finest clothing. The golden circlet, holding down his wavy red hair, happened to be one Haus wore often.

The four devils regarded each other warily.

"I'm your real son, and today I will inherit House LinGor—in honor of my poor mother's death."

Haus gawked up at him, face quirked up tighter than Arson had ever seen. "Tobas. You're a good kid—"

"Silence!" Tobas barked. "My mother was a good woman, and I'm your true son, and today I'll have no more of your nonsense." He sneered down at them all in turn. Arson's stomach ached like he'd swallowed a handful of the forest fire. "I see you're all worse for wear," Tobas continued, "but you still have your monsters with you."

Haus looked back at his quadruplets, his jaw working up and down, but no voice came out.

"You're all going to die now!" Tobas unsheathed his sword and held it high. "I said *now!*" And the company of armed soldiers advanced.

Arson pushed Hanhelin away from him and nodded to her. They shared a hard and serious stare. He flicked his eyes to the other women and she noticed. She received his silent order to take them back to the elves. "I'll find you again," she promised him and then pulled Linhala's sleeve for the other two females to run with her from the violence.

The quadruplets fought hard. The remaining soldiers they had with them were torn at first but quickly opted to keep their loyalty to their original LinGor master and fought their own house members. Arson fought closest to Haus, defending his father faithfully. The enemy showed as much desire to kill Haus as Arson. Arson's training had been quite a bit heavier than theirs, and it showed, although he struggled to grip his sword with his severely burned hands. He dared not try to summon the fire to his hands again for fear of incinerating them clean off his arms.

Poison had stayed on his horse and now used it to his favor, plowing through the throng, laughing as he slashed the helmets off the soldiers. The devil sons' gear was finer than theirs. Many lost their heads when they were caught unguarded. Bleed managed to keep a distance from the fight and used his crossbow effectively while Bludgeon, keeping to his namesake, bashed the enemy with his war hammer. The ones who weren't smashed to bone shards at least suffered armor damage or lost helmets, opening up victims for Bleed and Poison to cut down.

Arson performed well in thinning the crowd around Haus, despite his blisters and all the many scrapes and bruises he'd picked up recently.

Tobas, also fighting from horseback, taunted, "My so-called father! If only you had not forsaken me and my mother! Choosing monsters instead of your own flesh and blood." Spittle flew with every word. His angry face already wore a stippling of blood.

"At least these 'monsters' kept their loyalty without question," Haus responded from behind Arson's guard.

Tobas shook his decorated head amid the noise and fighting around him. Clearly he'd taken over Haus's wardrobe before leaving the manor. "You are a madman! I stayed loyal all those years even after you demoted me from your very bloodline, choosing these creatures instead. Your madness and paranoia prevented you from seeing things as they were. That my mother was good—that I was loyal. You were delusional."

Arson paused to listen to what Tobas said before moving on to his next violent engagement. He glanced back at Haus after Tobas's statement, and the man's old face, a face usually rallied with fire and determination, now appeared droopy and lost. Arson did recall their Desteer captive foretelling his "other son" heading toward Haus and how violence loomed. Is this what she'd meant? That would make it true that Tobas was Haus's biological son. Arson couldn't help but see Tobas differently now. Unlike the devils, Tobas had a mother. Tobas had enjoyed his mother's love and tenderness growing up—a thing Arson now envied. A thing Haus did not respect. Maybe Tobas wasn't evil for this attack. He was very hurt. Haus had treated him so coldly for all these years!

"Tobas!" Arson lowered his sword and stepped forward. "Call off your men!"

Tobas frowned tightly down at him and raised one eyebrow.

"We, the devils of House LinGor, are content as we are—with our loyalty and simplicity. We don't ask for status and inheritance—only the love of our father and wives to call our own. Let's go back home together! You will have your inheritance. When you get it, we, the devils, will serve you as the next patron to House LinGor! Our families will serve yours!"

For a long moment, Tobas kept silent. Arson stole another glance at Haus to find tears streaming into his beard.

Tobas burst out a pithy laugh. "You think I'm a fool, monster? I grew up in House LinGor, and I know better!" A great shudder happened under their feet in the ground recently ravaged by burrowing trolls. Tobas ignored it and charged forward on his horse, sword poised.

"Father!" Arson called and threw Haus aside. Tobas's sword pierced Arson's ribs as the earth gave way, and Arson, Tobas, and the horse tumbled together down the massive landslide. The sight of Haus disappeared behind the kicked-up dust and swirling smoke.

"Tobas, my son!" was the last thing Arson heard his father cry.

Chapter 22

The Grand Desteer

Hanhelin stopped cold as the other two faerhain pulled on her hand and robes. She turned back. "Arson."

Standing in the path behind her was a tall blond elf. Or maybe... not quite as tall as she'd expect. The elf put one hand up, telling her not to approach. The other hand appeared to be holding a box, which hung from a strap on his shoulder.

"Go home, *Ameiha.*"

Hanhelin blinked. One of her hands was shaking in the direction of the strange elf. "Arson?" she called, but the black smoke engulfed him. She suddenly felt sick.

"What's the matter?" Linhala asked, tugging her forward. Hanhelin didn't want to move.

She pointed behind her. The others hadn't seen him? Didn't they hear him?

They couldn't discuss it now because a new voice ripped through the mist. *"Faerhain!"* A Norrian voice. It came with a large company of others—*saehgahn* roving the forest.

"It's the royal army!" Enrha yelled, favoring her broken wrist. "We're saved!"

The battle had died soon after Tobas fell. Haus, Poison, Bludgeon, and

Bleed all frantically but cautiously climbed down the new landslide to search for Arson and Tobas. Both lay dead. Arson's body bled from the side, and falling with a horse couldn't have been kind to him or Tobas, whose body lay beneath the dead horse. Haus fell to his knees and ripped and mangled his own clothing in grief. His remaining three sons collected their fallen brother's body and covered it over respectfully with a cloak. They had a long, hushed discussion with each other, and then Poison led them back to face Haus sternly.

"Farewell," Poison said.

Haus paused his weeping at the shock of his offered word. "What?"

"You heard me. Farewell."

"But, Poison, why?" Haus said. "You'd abandon your old dad at a time like this?"

"Your neglect of Tobas caused this mess. He stabbed our brother, and then you shouted Tobas's name as Arson fell, bleeding, to his death—trying to save *you*. Shame on you."

Haus shook his head and rose to stand on shaky legs. "No, no, please!" Haus whined. "Now Tobas is gone—he's out of the way, and it's just us! Me and my last three boys! Let's go home. When we get there, you don't have to wear masks anymore." At the idea, Haus licked his lips and nodded. "No more pleasure box either; you can have run of the manor! Food! Women! You are my jewels. Let's go home, my sons." Haus fell to his knees, but the remaining three devils kept their arms crossed. Haus walked forward on his knees toward them. They all stepped backward to avoid his grasping.

"We're broken now," Poison said. "Our brotherhood of four. It hasn't been long, but it has already set in: an emptiness I'm sure will burden us for the rest of our days. And it's *your* fault."

Haus shook his head and tried again. "Let's go home and be comforted for our loss. I lost a son today—"

"Which one?" Poison said and turned his back. The other two followed his lead. He paused to say, "We'll leave his body with you. Take him home and give him the hero's burial he deserves."

Poison, Bludgeon, and Bleed all turned their backs on Haus's groveling and crying. The broken quadruplets didn't look back. In fact, they walked off in different directions, having earlier decided not to speak to one another again. If they were each alone, perhaps they could forget one was missing. So they departed, each with a plan to settle in a far corner of the continent.

The small company of the royal army put Hanhelin, Linhala, and Enrha on horses and took them about an hour's distance to a base camp they had erected as the trolls had ravaged the land. It served as a discharge point to send help to all surrounding clans who'd been struck by the fiends—not to mention deal with the fire. Entering this settlement full of her own people, Hanhelin oddly felt more alone than ever. What had become of Arson? Was he all right?

Once there, Linhala and Enrha were taken off to be cared for, and a tent was cleared to house the princess—the king's general's own tent. Gentle *saehgahn* doctors had been in and out for the past hour, offering Hanhelin everything from headache remedies to sleep-inducing tea, and also a tray of lunch. She took the lunch but refused to sleep. She also refused to tell anyone about what she'd been through in the past forty-eight hours besides her own company's troll raid. Though she longed to ask about any sightings of blond elves to try to get an update on Arson's well-being, she couldn't risk alerting anyone to the presence of the Overseas Taint, for the *saehgahn* may decide on their own to kill him.

As she took the last few bites of her mushroom-and-potato soup, the tent flap flew open again and she didn't bother to look up. "I only have a few scrapes," she said to whichever doctor had entered this time. "I need no more ointments." If only the person coming in were Arson. Their separation weighed her down. She knew somehow that she'd never see him again and blamed her ancient *faerhain's* intuition for that lack of hope. If only she hadn't been so harsh with him in those last hours. He had needed her faith that he'd eventually do the right thing. The fire and the confusion of those humans who'd shown up turned out to be the perfect cover for getting the captive *faerhain* away from the devils, and Arson himself had signaled her to act. In the end, he had proved to her enough that he would choose her side. She knew he loved her; it's what made her decision to marry him such an easy one.

"Apologies, *Ameiha*, I have no ointments to offer."

She gasped and raised her eyes. "Cav…" She couldn't finish the name. She leaped up and sprang across the space to throw her arms around him. He grunted, and then she noticed his injury. She leaped backward to give him space. Cavlihen wore a bandage on his upper arm, but that's all he wore on it, the lower part below the elbow was missing.

He chuckled despite the pain she knew he must be in. "Troll bit it off," he said.

She covered her mouth. "I'm so sorry!"

He waved his remaining hand. "What's an unmarried *saehgahn* for, if not troll food?"

"That must've been quite a battle you won." She gaped at him and absently took her seat. She motioned for him to do the same.

"I'm just glad you're alive," he said in all honesty. "What happened? Where's Yhulin?"

"Arson," she said. "He took me away. He…protected me."

Cavlihen raised an eyebrow as she struggled through her story. She didn't want to spill everything yet, not even the part about Wikshen. Maybe she'll tell him after she sorted it out with her great-aunt.

"He did, huh?"

She nodded. "It's absolutely thanks to him that I'm alive."

"Where is he now?"

Hanhelin searched her mind for the explanation. He was dead, but she didn't know how. She couldn't share her story. Not yet. Emotion mounted within her, forming as a pout on her face until she couldn't hold it in any longer. She burst out crying, and for the next second Cavlihen froze on the edge of his seat, as if unsure whether it was acceptable to comfort the princess or not. She extended her arms, and that's when he got up and approached. She embraced him around his waist and sobbed into his stale shirt.

"What about Yhulin?" he pressed.

"Dead," she said between sobs, half-thankful the conversation had moved from Arson.

Cavlihen swayed as if he'd faint. "Dear Bright One."

After a few wordless moments, Hanhelin weeping openly, Cavlihen placed his hand atop her head. He didn't move it; he left it there. Hanhelin didn't mind. She welcomed any bit of comfort he felt he was allowed to offer.

After a sufficient amount of rest, Hanhelin received a sensible *hanbohik*, courtesy of the nearest clan, and then a large entourage assembled for a hasty trip back to the palace. Cavlihen, with his sore new injury, insisted on accompanying her despite her protests. At the very least, he rode beside her in the carriage for company. Before they left, Hanhelin was given another surprise in the appearance of Ari, her young page, who had also survived the chaos.

"As soon as we get home, I'm declaring you *saehgahn* and excusing you from having to do Caunsaehgahn, my sweet lad," she told him, and at that he fell on his face in humility, thanking her profusely—to the point of tears—for the honor. Caunsaehgahn was a coming-of-age journey all males took after their *saehgahn* naming ceremony. Usually a daunting thing to undertake, most young *saehgahn* were eager to return from it and be picked for marriage. He'd probably be the youngest *saehgahn* in Norr at only fourteen. Cavlihen vouched for his bravery in the face of danger.

Just like Hanhelin had predicted to Arson, the rain fell, hopefully enough to douse the rest of the fire. From under the carriage's canopy, Hanhelin watched it fall. Cavlihen sat beside her, but they barely said a word for the whole trip. Hanhelin couldn't speak. She kept it inside her what she had done and what had happened to her. She couldn't guess how well it could go when she arrived to greet her parents and her aunt. She no longer had Yhulin to confide in for the sake of unburdening her feelings. Even if she did, Yhulin would be the wrong person to talk to about Arson. Hanhelin had been wrong to talk of him to Yhulin long before their incident. Maybe Yhulin's folly with Arson was partly her fault. She cursed her own voice, echoing in her head the words she'd said to the young *faerhain* about Arson being "preoccupied with the business of married couples." Yhulin was too young to be involved in Hanhelin's business with Arson. She was probably too young to even be named *faerhain*—that would be the mistake of the Desteer chapter to raise her to the status.

She let out what must've been the hundredth sigh before finally becoming aware of them. She looked to Cavlihen briefly, and he was checking her also. They shared gazes for a long moment. She squeezed her jaw teeth together, knowing he suspected something. She chose to say nothing. Instead of talk, she laid her head on his broad shoulder.

The musical howl of the palace horns startled Hanhelin awake. They were announcing her arrival, as her company would've been spotted a distance away. At the sound, Cavlihen closed the carriage's hatch. It didn't take long for many voices to sound outside as her carriage passed through the gate, voices carrying various tones, particularly cheerful.

"Ahhhh-mei-haaaa. Ahhh-mei-haaaa," people chanted. The shadows of hands grazed along the outside of her silken canopy. She wasn't Grand Desteer yet, but her clan knew well who she would soon become.

Hanhelin took a deep breath and straightened her spine. She didn't have any of her fine arraignments but intended to enter the palace with an air of dignity and strength.

"The White Owls should meet us at the plaza," Cavlihen said. "They'll escort us to a meeting with your father."

Hanhelin nodded. She'd left and returned to the palace many times but had never experienced something so traumatic in between.

"Stand down!" The carriage came to a jolting halt, causing Cavlihen to lurch and fall on his raw stump. He hissed but otherwise kept his statement of pain confined to his clenched expression.

"What's going on?" Hanhelin asked him, and he had no answer.

"I know we're not at the plaza yet," he said. The hand and body shapes pushing against the sides of her carriage intensified. The shouting did too.

The hatch flew open. "Princess!" A deep, commanding voice barked with the unsettling appearance of a member of the White Moths, an awe-inspiring person wearing eerie white face paint, similar to the Desteer they served. He wore a cloak, fitted over his shoulders, with slits for his arms to go through. Hanhelin knew that underneath they wore fine leather armor with flexible metal scales, also white, and would be hiding sleek, curved knives on each hip under the cloak. Everyone in the palace feared the White Moths. They were the personal guard of the Grand Desteer, and up until now, Hanhelin had no reason to face them.

Hanhelin sat back with her mouth agape. "Where are the Owls?"

she asked.

Several other Moths pushed in to flank the first one, who extended his hand. Cavlihen bristled beside her at the intimidating person. He wore his face paint so thick he didn't look alive, and unlike his Desteer counterparts, the insides of his eye sockets were painted dark grey to make his brow look pronounced and his eyes shaded. Over tightly plaited hair, he wore a bunch of feathers arranged like a sort of crown, despite being a mere guard. The Moths certainly walked around as if they outranked the king's guard.

"We were sent to protect and escort you to the Grand Desteer's chapel," the lead Moth said. The crowd quieted down, and the silhouette shapes disappeared from her carriage walls. The Moths could clear a space effortlessly.

Hanhelin blinked and regarded Cavlihen. "I have to go."

"Princess," Cavlihen whispered.

"I have to go," she said again, whispering back, knowing this was the end. She was being transferred to the care of the Grand Desteer. Her aunt had the power to do such a thing since Hanhelin was dedicated to that office at age ten and turned over to her tutelage. Her ultimate road to becoming Grand Desteer would start with the simple action of letting these Moths escort her into the palace, leaving Cavlihen behind.

Standing bent forward in the carriage between the two different sects of guard. She reached out and squeezed Cavlihen's hand. As she let go and switched her reach toward the Moth, Cavlihen called out to her, voice trembling.

"Princess!"

She didn't look back.

The White Moths were all tall and formed an impenetrable human wall around her, allowing her to walk easily through the crowd. Because of this, she couldn't exactly see where she headed, mostly straight toward the Grand Chapel instead of the main palace. The chapel, capped with a plump, onion-shaped dome, rose up over the crowd and the Moths' heads the closer they ventured. It wasn't the tallest structure on palace grounds, but it was definitely the most beautiful. Its sculpted, gold-plated arches and tips pointed straight into the sky where the Bright

One walked across the earth every day. The lavender-colored lanterns, already lit in anticipation of the evening, accentuated the mysterious spirit of the Desteer. That beautiful dome on top of the building, bulging as if pregnant, was also colored purple, unlike anything found on the main part of the palace since the Tinharri clan's livery colors were dark blue and silver.

The crowd on this side of the palace grounds quieted themselves and watched speechlessly as the third Tinharri princess made her way into the chapel. Her life would never be the same. Her aunt must've received her letter about the "tainted elf," which explained this treatment. She probably wouldn't even get a foot in the door before her aunt would be asking after the whereabouts of the tainted one. Or maybe she knew. The Grand Desteer boasted a stronger psychic sense than Hanhelin. In the near future, Hanhelin would be learning how to use her own senses more thoroughly.

The Moths took her through one of the side entrances into a private corridor and up a long flight of stairs. The Grand Desteer's apartment lay above the main chapel. It would be her apartment someday. For now, Hanhelin easily guessed that her aunt had set up a room for her somewhere close.

A White Moth stood in every corner, not a new sight for her. Though it wasn't their job to interact with her, she'd always been terrified of their heavily painted faces and frowning mouths as a child. They were an enigma quite unlike the normal sect of White Owls, who would be found in the other section of the palace where the royal family lived. The Moths still put her a little on edge to revisit this space, but she would have to get over it fast. Maybe once her aunt introduced her to them personally, it wouldn't be so awkward anymore.

The Moth in the lead opened one more door and held it. "The Grand Desteer is inside," he said without making eye contact. He did nothing more but waited for her to enter, motionless. He'd probably wait all day long if Hanhelin wanted to delay her entry.

She went right in and found Jinlah, her aunt, sitting in a huge room of polished slate walls, a fireplace, a brown oxskin rug, doors leading off to other rooms of the apartment, and one big window showing the greater part of the palace grounds. Jinlah sat casually, no face paint but veiled for a slight formal appearance. She'd never seen her aunt in total casual posture, in fact. It didn't matter though. Hanhelin ran forward and let herself fall on the older *faerhain*'s lap where she wept openly, ready to spill everything that had happened.

Jinlah absently stroked her hair, not bothering to share a word yet. When Hanhelin made an effort to leash up her flood of tears, the other *faerhain* said, "I received your letter."

Hanhelin met her eyes through the veil, feeling like a child, but nodded. It was a formal letter, as formal as she could express, but she knew someone like the Grand Desteer would've read extensively between the lines.

"What has changed since you wrote the letter?"

What has changed? Everything! And now Hanhelin had to fess up. She wanted to unburden herself, but her next bunch of words would be awkward to wade through.

She started at the beginning. One day, her *saehgahn* captured a strange elf… Resting her arms on her aunt's lap, she carefully recounted everything. Her concerns about studying the Overseas Taint, the way Arson spoke and acted. How he'd been raised by humans and therefore exhibited their crude speech and mannerisms. His reason for coming to Norr. Her impression of him. How she had felt about him secretly. Her discomfort about his joining with Yhulin. Arson's interactions and his stated feelings about her. She detailed very carefully all of these subtleties, just needing her intuitive aunt to understand the specifics of everything leading up to Hanhelin's most rash act of her life.

"I married him."

She waited for a response, holding her eyes to the floor. When she got nothing, Hanhelin looked up to find Jinlah displaying the same blankness she'd held throughout the story. The wise elder *faerhain* had no surprise or emotion to show at hearing about Arson's pairing with Hanhelin *or* Yhulin.

Hanhelin played Arson's heroic acts through her mind. Was it wrong to reward him in that way? Was it also wrong that she had *wanted* to enact those rites with him? On that one morning, she'd lived the most thrilling moment of her life. Not only how pleasurable but how scandalous!

Waiting for the Grand Desteer's response, her gut boiled up. It was done and all over, but she couldn't figure out if things would be all right from here. Would the Grand Desteer punish her?

"Your marriage was fruitful."

Hanhelin regarded Jinlah through the veil. She leaned forward, and Hanhelin removed her arms from her lap. She raised her veil to show her smooth face with expressionless blue eyes and high cheekbones. This Grand Desteer was also her father's aunt. She'd known and counseled so many others before Hanhelin.

"Fruitful?" Hanhelin asked. What did that mean? It sounded like a loaded word. "Fruitful…" She pondered it until the Grand Desteer laid a hand on her shoulder.

"Your run-in with Wikshen wasn't the hardest trial you will face in your life, young one," she said, and it sent a chill up Hanhelin's spine. "It's good that Wikshen was burned. He won't be back for another century or more. We can talk about and plan for any future threat from him, especially now that we know he covets raythite. For now, everyone will want to know what became of your husband. His brothers will have to be eradicated from Norr, and…"

Hanhelin waited. "And what?"

Jinlah sat back, watching her in her humble seat on the floor.

Hanhelin swallowed.

"Something will have to be done about your offspring."

"My what!" Hanhelin stood up, heart instantly racing—to the point that she worried for her health. She swayed, and the Grand Desteer leaped up to steady her. She helped Hanhelin walk weakly to the nearby settee. She guided her to lie across it rather than sit. From Hanhelin's horizontal position she watched Jinlah pace.

"Fruitful," the woman repeated in a voice stronger than she'd been using. "I would conduct *milhanrajea* on you to gather more details, but it could harm the child in you."

"I didn't know," Hanhelin said.

"Of course you didn't; it's too early for you to know."

"But you know psychically." Desteer maidens, and the Grand Desteer, all possessed various talents and levels at which they could use those talents.

Jinlah sighed. "I also know that your husband is dead."

Still so emotionally raw about Arson, Hanhelin erupted with a new sob, burying her face in her hands. Couldn't her aunt at least have said it a little less matter-of-factly?

It didn't matter because she kept talking. "That's good for him, you, and all of us."

Hanhelin rubbed her stomach. She was pregnant. Jinlah was exceedingly talented in being able to tell things like this psychically, and Hanhelin knew she'd never reach that level. Hanhelin had a mind mostly for learning. Caressing her stomach to try to send love to Arson's son, she sat up and vowed, "I will protect this child!"

Jinlah paused and raised her eyebrows. "A quick resolve. Would you not prefer to remove it from your womb and carry on as you were before? Life will be simpler that way."

Hanhelin took a step back, and her calf hit the couch; she had already forgotten it was back there. "Remove?" she shrieked. "Elves do not *remove* children from their wombs!"

"The witches in the Darklands can do it," the Grand Desteer informed her. "I could make a case for you, considering your dangerous situation. You will have the Bright One's pardon."

This conversation pushed Hanhelin closer to her first pregnancy vomit. "No!" She stepped forward, a bit wobbly, but she'd never been so serious in her life. "Don't you hear me?" She reached out and grabbed the Grand Desteer's sleeve. "I will have my child, and he will be mine, and I will love him until I die!"

Silence.

Over the Grand Desteer's shoulder, Hanhelin could see through an open door into the lavatory, a decently spacious room with mirrors for dressing, grand enough for the highest seat of the Desteer. Someone stood in the doorframe.

"Arson?" Hanhelin called. She released Jinlah's shoulders. Far across the wide floor of the sitting room, Hanhelin swore she spotted blond hair—a bit messy, as if the person had just risen from bed. "Who do you have in here, Aunt?" she demanded. In the split second it took her to storm across the space, the person had turned his back and casually disappeared into the room, vanishing quickly, but in no apparent rush to do so.

"I have no one in here, my dear," she answered.

False, Hanhelin knew it. She'd seen a *saehgahn* in there! A blond one. Possibly one of those Moths wearing an extra heavy dusting of powder to lighten his hair. They did that to continue the pale tone from their white face paint. By the Bright One though, he looked like Arson!

Hanhelin whirled around the doorframe... There was the bathtub. The basin. The toilet bench. Mirrors. But no person, not even a White Moth.

"I'm going insane," Hanhelin whispered. She spun back around, ready to faint again, yet also embarrassed at her mistake.

"You had said the word 'him.' You're expecting a son?"

Hanhelin twisted her face. Was she not confused at what just happened? "Yes, I... Um..." She stuttered, too flustered at the moment. She searched for her words, striding carefully back across the space. "It's most likely to be a...him, isn't it?" she said and glanced back at the lavatory's open door with the soft lighting through its windows. How could she have made that mistake? "You know it's three times more likely to be a male."

The Grand Desteer eyed her, clearly choosing to shrug off Hanhelin's odd behavior but certainly calculating it. "We must pray for a 'her,'" she replied. "The Bright One has told us long ago that a female spawned from the Overseas Taint would be harmless to our people and even a marriageable blessing. The taint ends in a female birth. Males always carry it forward."

Hanhelin nodded and eased herself back onto the settee. It wasn't a girl; somehow she knew it. "You're right. I remember reading about it once." She regarded the large bookshelf along the back wall. The Grand Desteer harbored a collection of deeper knowledge in them Hanhelin had always salivated to dive into. Soon those books would be hers. She'd use them better than Jinlah had. She gave a reassuring nod to the older *faerhain*. "We'll beg the Bright One for a *farhah*," she said.

"But yes," Jinlah conceded, "it is likely to be a *saeghar*. And it's very possible, if you insist on keeping this child, that you can't be Grand Desteer."

"I don't care." Hanhelin stared toward the window. She knew exactly what she wanted. "Sell me to some rich lord in the Lightlands. Banish me to the Darklands. I don't care. There are hundreds of *saehgahn* outside who would marry me if I wanted company in my banishment… You're not touching my child. Nor will the Sa-Destrai, the Fa-Destrah…"

"So you've made up your mind."

"Yes."

"Do you realize we could force you to abort it?"

"Go ahead. I'll kill myself. If I can't have him, you won't have me."

"We could send your child away after it's born."

"I'll go with him. You're not sending my child away."

"Why do you insist on keeping a child with the Overseas Taint?"

Hanhelin knew the Grand Desteer was evaluating her—without the use of *milhanrajea*. She'd analyzed every answer since Hanhelin's arrival and would try to form her own conclusion as to what to do with a pregnant future Grand Desteer. She had brought a messy situation back with her—Hanhelin could never deny that—but it would've been worse if she'd brought Arson.

She fixed her eyes hard on Jinlah's. Frowning. "I want my child. I'm entitled to him. I never chose to be Grand Desteer. I had always wanted a family, and now an unlikely stranger to this country has given me one. Is it a dangerous situation? Yes. But will I do everything I can to defuse the danger and perhaps mold him, as he grows, into a fine Norrian citizen? Yes." Hanhelin pointed a stiff finger at the window. "Out there in the wilderness, I got a taste of love—*real* love—from a *saehgahn* who chose me. One who touched me. I've never known and will never know such intimacy with another person again. Now that I've known love, I will not go back. I will have the love of my child. I will never give up on him."

The older *faerhain* stared at her without a speck of emotion showing on her face. This was a previous "third Tinharri princess," one who was also born to be Grand Desteer and has never known love like Hanhelin had discovered out there. "You're using the common word version of *er*."

"This is not *er*! This is different! It's better. It's pure and beautiful."

The Grand Desteer sighed through her nose. "How would you propose to solve this issue?"

"I'll be Grand Desteer if I must, but I will keep my child. I'll raise him well and teach him."

Jinlah dipped her head and did a circle pace around the oxskin rug. "Hanhelin." She drew her gaze back. Hanhelin knew she must look atrocious and had dried tear stains all down her cheeks, not to mention her snotty nose, but she now acted as if she were the Grand Desteer's perfect equal. "You speak with conviction. There is something about this child that moves you, whether you realize it or not. It's a movement I can't feel, for I am a third party, but you are the future Grand Desteer. One who has her thumb on all of Norr. One with immense spiritual power. I don't know what this could lead us to ultimately…but I choose to take your side in this."

Hanhelin nodded confidently and returned her stare to the dying light outside the window.

"I will hold a conference with the Sa-Destrai," she continued as Hanhelin listened. "I will keep you under my protection. You won't go anywhere without a Moth at your side. In fact, you'll be assigned a few of them. You'll have one standing in your room while you sleep."

That drew Hanhelin's attention to the door where she knew they waited outside, guarding the Grand Desteer with their lives.

"You will deliver the child and more conferences will follow. Evaluations will be given—of you and of…him."

"I'll study him." Hanhelin stood up again. Her blood now moved more normally as her heart had returned to its normal pace.

Jinlah waited.

"I'll study my son like I studied Arson," she said. "Except better. I'll be able to study him from birth. I'll see his every movement and hear every word and ask him about every dream that enters his head."

"An interesting prospect, Hanhelin."

"I know," she said. "We'll learn all about how the Overseas Taint acts in a second generation. We'll see what it does and how it changes him—*if* it changes him. I'll also raise him well, perfectly, with discipline and education. I'll make sure *he* understands his tainted blood. If he understands it, he should be able to fight it."

Jinlah licked her lips and inhaled deeply again through her nose. "This study idea might make a good case for allowing him to grow up in Norr. If we can uncover the mystery of the Overseas Taint and eliminate its curse, we may save Norr forever. We might perhaps— dare I say—solve the dilemma of the *faerhain* imbalance."

Hanhelin stepped forward and reached out her hand. The Grand Desteer received it. "Please help me do this."

The other *faerhain*'s facial expression finally softened to one closer resembling a warm family member, but it shifted back to cold, or maybe determined. "Your best defense in this situation… Your greatest power won't lie in your status as third Tinharri princess."

Hanhelin cocked her head.

"You must become the Grand Desteer. And soon."

Chapter 23
The Tinharries

hanhelin and the current Grand Desteer shared an embrace
to seal their agreement, but a sudden tremor in the whole building cut
it short.

Hanhelin jumped in fright, her heart setting off. "Trolls," she hissed.

Jinlah lowered her brow and shook her head. "No," she said and
then hurried over to the big window overlooking the palace's main
plaza. "They're pounding on my door."

Hanhelin liked those words less than her own. Following behind
her aunt, she only needed to glance out to notice a sea of white filling
the street, and a large flow of red was already expanding across the
glaze of light rain running between the plaza's interlocking stone
pavers.

"It appears the Owls want their princess back," Jinlah informed her,
somehow managing to keep her expression cold. Hanhelin couldn't
hope to mask her horror. Right below her, the White Owls were
trying to break in and the White Moths had barred the door and had
already started spilling blood to prevent their entry.

"Oh dear Bright One!" Hanhelin sobbed into her hands. She didn't
want this! "Why?" she asked.

"They don't know our situation yet," Jinlah said. "We should tell
them." She pulled Hanhelin away from the window, telling her, "It's
not safe," and went into her lavatory where Hanhelin guessed she'd

put on some vestments for making an appearance.

The door to the hall slammed open in her absence, and Hanhelin stood stiffly, finding herself staring at an extra tall, scary Moth with his weapon drawn and his face as cold as a venomous snake. It looked more like he wanted to ravage the place than protect them.

A few things rolled through her head in that moment, the most bizarre of which was a strange parallel she finally noticed between the way the Moths were trained and that of the "devils." Those two groups were from two different worlds, but it appeared Arson's father might've had *this* in mind when he raised those quadruplets.

Before Hanhelin could bother to speak, three more Moths entered behind the first. "We are to protect the Grand Desteer and her heir," he finally said.

Hanhelin threw a shaking hand toward the room Jinlah occupied to tell him where he could find the Grand Desteer, but it didn't matter because he took off in that direction and the other three crowded around Hanhelin, locking her inside their tall cage of hot bodies. It became clear to her that the Moths were chosen for their size as much as their ability and discipline.

They held her in so close she could hardly see the room beyond them, only their white cloaks and leggings, similar to the Owls' livery but with clear distinction in the cut of their outfits and the weave of their armor. The moths wore woven white leather cuirasses and extra wide pauldrons under their cloaks, as if in contest with the Owls' shoulder width.

The powder they wore in their hair soon became apparent; it's earthiness went right up her nose, and she pinched it to keep from sneezing and embarrassing herself. Maybe this powder helped the reason they were so closely associated with moths, besides the symbolism that moths flew toward light.

One other thing struck her from this new vantage, enough for her to forget all about having to sneeze. Behind one's cloak, swept aside and caught on his empty scabbard, the *sarakren* brand showed on the visible portion of his buttock between his *sa-garhik* leggings and braies. The Moths were all *sarakren*. It must be a part of their initiation to take the dreaded "unmarriageable" brand.

The Grand Desteer came out of the lavatory with her face painted white and the purple stripe running across her eyes. She could paint herself so quickly after four hundred and twenty-five years. Watching her hurry toward the group, Hanhelin marveled, and it started to sink in: her life would be like this eventually. Except… She glanced around her, unable to see much of the room for the alert guards around her. Where would her child fit into this?

Jinlah bickered with her Moth all the way to Hanhelin's side to be locked into the formation as well. "We're going to go about it formally and with complete and utter stern authority," she told Hanhelin and then grasped her chin. "Can you keep your emotions in check? Stay quiet? I'll tell you when to speak."

Hanhelin stuttered and blinked. How would she keep from weeping when she saw her mother and father?

The fourth Moth closed in the formation, and they moved ahead as a unit. The door opened via a Moth outside of it, as did all the rest of the doors. They made the building seem haunted, and the shivery feeling the guards gave Hanhelin completed the effect.

Jinlah sent word ahead to the Owls outside that the princess was well and to stand down for her emergence. This calmed the violence. In the chapel's private courtyard, Hanhelin and the Grand Desteer boarded a basket cage sedan, over which the Moths drew a purple drape to hide them, and from there, they carried them into the main palace where her closest family members lived.

Even as early as today, Hanhelin no longer lived here. She would visit it often but as a separate entity. As Grand Desteer. The sad thought pinched her stomach, and she suddenly remembered the child within it.

"No more sad thoughts," she whispered, rubbing her midsection. She noticed Jinlah watching her, who turned her face forward a beat later.

"Do you think it will be okay?" she asked her aunt over the sounds of upset echoing all around them in the palace halls. The Owls, in their devotion to protecting the royal family, didn't like seeing their princess being carried around by the Moths. Shouldn't they have known this day would come eventually? It just so happened to be sooner instead of later. Normally she'd have to wait for the current Grand Desteer to die before making this drastic change of housing, guard, and office.

However, Jinlah was already twenty-five years over the average age expectancy for elves, so it shouldn't have taken too long otherwise.

"No," Jinlah answered her question. "But you will survive." Her aunt's honesty didn't help her nerves at all.

The basket sedan finally stopped, and the shouting only intensified.

"Silence for the Grand Desteer!" boomed the voice of one the higher-ranking Moths.

"Silence for Sa-Destrai!" countered the Owls' equivalent.

This sort of pageantry Hanhelin knew well. Whether it was the Sa-Destrai or the Grand Desteer entering the room, silence would be called for, but never had she witnessed them shouting as if to each other like that. Hanhelin herself couldn't hope to make a peep in her tension.

Everyone else in the room also must've felt the same oddity, for the voices stopped immediately, almost at once.

The next shouting voice made Hanhelin pout. "Where is my daughter, Grand Desteer?"

Jinlah shot Hanhelin a look and whispered, "Remain in here." She rang a bell she'd stowed in her sleeve, and her side of the curtain flipped up. The Moth outside opened her door. She stepped out, leaving Hanhelin under the covering to wait, twisting her skirt nervously in both hands.

In the next long hush, she imagined the Grand Desteer gliding up to the center of the room to meet her father. "The princess is back safe and well, *Sahbentrei*." She'd just called the Sa-Destrai "father" in the least formal way to address the king; it must be an attempt to calm him down.

"Then let me see her!" he demanded, full of the emotion Hanhelin would expect. "Can't you see her mother is—" He cut himself off, more emotional than Hanhelin guessed.

The whole purple sheet slid off her basket, and Hanhelin gawked at all the faces staring back at her. She suddenly remembered her disarrayed appearance, the plain *hanbohik* donated to her at the base camp, and she hadn't had the chance to comb her hair yet.

Everyone else noticed her pitiful state too, at the low number of breaths registering throughout the large room full of people.

There stood her poor father at its center, facing the Grand Desteer as if in a standoff. Behind him her mother stood, locked arm in arm with her two sisters, and her five brothers stood to the sides, poised as if they'd charge toward her if not for the heavy guard of Moths brandishing naked blades. Seeing them all now, she wished more than ever to run over to their side of the room and embrace them all.

"As you all know," the Grand Desteer began, "Hanhelin was born into the office of Grand Desteer."

Her father stood blinking as he listened. Today's transfer of the third princess must be more unorthodox than Hanhelin assumed.

"And on this day, I have deemed it necessary take her into my care until a quick and formal transfer of power can take place."

"No!" the Sa-Destrai barked. "This is not how it's done!"

His outburst caused the Moths and Owls alike to tighten their stances and Hanhelin to cringe.

"My senses have determined a need for such a change in this generation," Jinlah told him. "And I will obey this sensation." She prolonged the next instant, and no one else bothered to talk. Everyone hung as caught up in the anticipation as Hanhelin. "In this age, I will step down and swiftly promote Hanhelin to Grand Desteer."

Her proclamation didn't cause another outburst but a chorus of murmuring instead. The Sa-Destrai stood there with his head slightly cocked. "Why, *Ameiha*?" he asked.

The Grand Desteer twisted slightly, to spy Hanhelin in her wicker cage. "The princess has returned from a long campaign. The clans favor her. She is adored."

Her father shook his head. "This makes no sense. That's not a reason to expedite her inauguration."

"There's more," Jinlah replied. "She has returned holding a destiny different from when she left. Inside of her she carries a new prince of Norr. Or princess perhaps, but this prince of Norr is a blessing to us all because he will aid in our new movement to know and conquer the Overseas Taint."

Another hesitance followed the news, and Hanhelin sympathized with everyone for the complexity of the statement.

The king began with a stutter. "D-did you just say my daughter is pregnant?"

The room erupted.

The Sa-Destrah, her mother, swayed and collapsed. Her two sisters eased her to the floor as they had been holding her arms to begin with, and three of her brothers swooped in to check on her. She had fainted cold.

The Moths tightened around Hanhelin's basket with their swords drawn, and over all the noise another voice shouted, "Silence for the Grand Desteer!"

"Where's Captain Cavlihen?" her father shouted before the room finished quieting down. "Bring him in here!"

Jinlah twisted around again, and Hanhelin caught a glimmer of panic in her eye, panic which her cold face paint couldn't mask. Cavlihen would have to tell the truth of what he knew, not that the Grand Desteer would lie, but Jinlah would have every intention to unfold all of this news in a slower, calmer way than dragging the poor injured *saehgahn* in here to tell the story.

Drag him, they did, and without much of a wait; perhaps they found Cavlihen in the plaza, listening to the disturbing echoes. His fellow Owls hauled him in as if under arrest, and he stumbled and fell before the king, adjacent to the Grand Desteer.

"They tell me my daughter is pregnant and under *your* watch, what have you to say?"

Cavlihen took the news as horrified as everyone else. He jerked his head to look from his place on the floor to find Hanhelin's basket. From his vantage, he probably couldn't see much of her through its tight weaving. She leaned forward and put both hands on its front wall.

"I did not know, Sa-Destrai!" Cavlihen declared and attempted to rise, but her father pushed him back down with his booted foot.

"Stay on the floor where you belong!"

Now Hanhelin shouted, but the noise of the dramatic new spectacle drowned her voice out.

Jinlah attempted to step in front of Cavlihen so she could continue with her telling of the story, but the king wouldn't have it.

"Was it you?" he demanded to the astonishment of all.

"No!"

"No!" Hanhelin shouted. The Grand Desteer shot her a warning look not to butt in.

"Then who? Tell me what happened along her campaign."

Cavlihen struggled to swallow, and he took a deep breath. Braced on the floor like a frog, he had but one arm to hold him up. His stump's bandage was reddening with a new leakage of blood in need of care.

"We," he began. "We found a foreigner—a blond elf with the Overseas Taint."

More noise. More disruption. And a few more *faerhain* fainted. Her mother had slowly awoken by now but remained on the floor, lying against one of her middle sons, a favorite of hers, for support. Her other two daughters were petting her hand and patting her shoulder in comfort.

Hanhelin was ready to faint now too. She sat back on the bench inside the basket sedan.

Even the king swayed on his feet but widened his stance. "Bring out my daughter. I must speak with her!"

The Moths shoved in to cover her again.

"I'm afraid I can't do that, *Sahbentrei*," the Grand Desteer said. "She's in my care now, and I won't allow it. All this drama will be harmful to her child, so if you don't take control of the hysteria—"

"Wait!" the king shouted before Jinlah could motion for the Moths to take Hanhelin away. He ordered the room and its two hundred or more Tinharri family members, guards, and council members to maintain utter silence.

Her father squared himself with the Grand Desteer. "You're my aunt," he reminded her. "Tell me straight and in simple truth: did this foreign elf attack my daughter?"

The Grand Desteer took a second, and it felt longer than it should've. "No," she said, and it brought a whiff of relief to the crowd, all trying their best to leash up their reactions. Jinlah followed up with, "She joined into marriage with him and conceived this most important prince." And the crowd couldn't restrain themselves this time. Some of the Moths drew out whips to lash at the rowdy *saehgahn*. On the opposing side the Owls did similarly.

Hanhelin hated it for Cavlihen most of all, who sat forgotten and defeated on the floor in the chaos, shoulders shaking over his bowed head as he wept. On the day of Hanhelin's birth, Cavlihen had taken up the task of keeping her out of trouble, and because she had been so stubborn and willful—and childish—she'd caused his ultimate failure. Through all of that adventure she'd spent with Arson, she had never paused to worry about how it would reflect on Cavlihen. She'd failed *him*.

The king, glistening in his sweat, blew a breath out. "Jinlah. You're telling me that while Hanhelin, my daughter, was out on campaign to befriend the clans for her future office as Grand Desteer, she caught a tainted elf, married him, and then conceived a tainted child with him?"

"Yes," Jinlah said simply. "Though in reality, things were a bit more complicated."

Her father balled his fists and turned his new wave of rage back on Cavlihen. "And Captain Cavlihen allowed—"

Hanhelin kicked the wicker door open and leaped out of the sedan. "Enough!" She weaved through the Moths' guard, dodging their hands and pushed through the crowd until she reached Cavlihen to stand over him like she did for Arson when he lay unconscious. Cavlihen stared up at her in bewilderment, like everyone else. The Moths charged forward to prevent any potential attempt for the opposing side to snatch her. She ignored all possibility and instead fixed her focus on her father.

"Cavlihen has done nothing wrong," she pleaded, getting her words out quickly lest she lose the chance to do so. "We suffered a troll attack from which the tainted elf rescued me. He rescued me from more than trolls. Wikshen had come to our forest with his disturbing creatures. The tainted elf *killed* Wikshen—he defeated a living deity, and he did it for me! Cavlihen wasn't present when I made the choice to marry the foreigner. And I'm glad that I now have a child!" The Grand Desteer's hand landed on her shoulder at some point during her speech, and Hanhelin shrugged it off. "We have a plan, the Grand Desteer and I," she told her father. "I'm to take her place and keep my child for the good of our people."

"Why?" the Sa-Destrai asked. "What good can a dangerous elf do for us?"

"Education," Hanhelin said matter-of-factly. "Yesterday, the Overseas Taint was both mysterious and terrifying to us. Tomorrow it will be neither."

Her father had suddenly gone cold, leering at her and Jinlah as if they were deceitful Darklandic witches. Behind him, her mother rested on the floor where she'd fainted, her eyes and nose glowed red.

"Listen to me, Hanhelin," her father said. "You are proposing a dangerous liability. I will not have a carrier of the Overseas Taint walking among us."

Hanhelin shrugged. "You'll have to learn to love your grandson like any other of them."

He shook his head gravely. "I won't. Listen. We'll have to hold meetings on this. I don't want to see this child—ever."

Jinlah stepped forward. "You won't."

Hanhelin dropped her jaw at that. "I won't have my son ignored. He's a prince of Norr!"

The Grand Desteer raised her hand to silence her. "He will be raised in my realm, protected by the Grand Desteer and her Moths. He won't leave the Grand Chapel."

"No!" Hanhelin protested, but it did no good. At Jinlah's signal, the closest Moth standing by took Hanhelin by the arm and hauled her back to the sedan where they stood at either side to prevent her exit.

The crowd murmured, and under their loud hum, the Grand Desteer and the Sa-Destrai spoke more quietly to each other. Hanhelin strained her ear but picked nothing out of their exchange. It took several minutes for them to reach a conclusion.

"What did you say to him?" Hanhelin demanded when Jinlah boarded the sedan and the Moths lifted the structure to their shoulders.

"We are not concluded," she answered. "Your father talks of forced abortion, banishment of the infant, or death to him when he reaches *saehgahn* status."

Hanhelin choked up at that horrid news.

"For now, he's under Grand Desteer protection. You are not to leave the chapel while pregnant, and *he* must not leave it after he is born."

Hanhelin wept into a handkerchief borrowed from Jinlah as she listened. She couldn't imagine how all of this would've gone if Arson had survived and come home with her. She had been naive to think it would've worked out for them as a family.

"So that's it?" she said in return. "We'll rot in the apartments above the chapel, with Moths for family—both kinds of moths."

Jinlah shushed her rambling. "He might," she said. "But as long as you keep him secret, pretend he doesn't exist when you go outside and allow him to fade in your family's minds, he may survive well into adulthood."

"What a horrible plan!"

"You said you wanted to study your child. You will."

"But he's not just a test subject, he's a person. A *saeghar* and someday a fine *saehgahn*. I love him. I won't treat him only as an oddity, and I don't want others to forget about him."

The Grand Desteer sighed through her nose. "Today only begins a lifetime of grueling arguments and compromises with the Tinharri clan—and possibly all of Norr. If you insist on his participation in the family, it will be up to you to convince your father, and then possibly your brother after he becomes Sa-Destrai, that your son is harmless to our country."

So maybe there was hope. She would argue for her son. From this day forward she lived for him.

epilogue

Nine months later, hanhelin wallowed in agony on the bed.

"Isn't he all right?" she shouted, deliriously pained but too afraid to try to look at the dramatic happenings. The tall vaulted ceiling, painted dark blue with star patterns, spun above her. They had converted the attic, or the "onion" of the Grand Chapel, into a temporary hospital. She couldn't make sense of any of it with all the movement and the voices. Her aunt oversaw about a dozen subordinate Desteer maidens, all dressed in simple white *hanbohiks* with short sleeves, moving all about, some taking on huge bloodstains to their aprons.

White Moth guards stood about the room, their number heavily increased for this particular day. Over these past nine months, in her isolation, Hanhelin had gotten used to their constant eerie presence, including in her bedroom at night, as her aunt had told her, and right outside her garderobe where she did her business or vomited for her pregnancy.

They kept everyone not chosen by her aunt and who weren't a member of the Desteer cult out of the entire building. Today the chapel was closed to worship. All ceremony canceled. Not even her poor mother, the queen of Norr of all people, could come and check on or comfort Hanhelin in these desperate hours. She hadn't gotten the opportunity to speak with her mother since that very intense day of her return to the palace. She couldn't guess what her mother thought of her situation, but her unresponsiveness to Hanhelin's letters didn't bring much hope. Couldn't she at least have the heart to sympathize with her laboring daughter?

Her contractions kept coming, but she knew about the afterbirth which would follow the baby, so Hanhelin closed her eyes against her dizziness and focused on finishing her chore.

So much murmuring went on, filling the room and distracting her from trying to listen for the sound of her baby. Why wasn't he crying yet?

"Smack him!" Hanhelin told them. "I want to hear him!" Her concern blended into her next wail of pain. She writhed in her difficulty. How long did the pain last after a delivery? Something aligned to make its exit again, and it must have been bigger and harder than afterbirth. "Ahhhh!"

Her aunt told her nothing except, "Hold still, you're not finished yet."

"Isn't he out though?" She could've sworn she'd delivered already.

Jinlah didn't answer her question, and so far, Hanhelin heard nothing.

"Give us another push," she ordered, and Hanhelin wailed in sorrow and pain, unsure which sensation was the stronger.

There! She delivered. Still no crying though. "Am I done?" she asked, lying back in exhaustion. She knew she had lost a lot of blood at that point but made up her mind to refuse to die. Her son needed her protection.

The maidens didn't answer her. In fact, her contractions continued. A quick hush washed over everyone, and then the maidens regrouped, some breaking off to huddle around a table and others returning to their work between her legs, often reaching up to feel her womb with their deep-pressing fingers.

"Stay on the bed," the maiden warned her, and Hanhelin wailed again, having to tense up for more labor. Her tears streamed out.

"Don't cry, you'll dehydrate." Jinlah hurried to the other side table and poured water into a cup.

"This one's not breathing," she caught a voice saying among the commotion, and Jinlah froze to shoot a stare at that side of the space.

Hanhelin called out, "What? What do you mean he's not breathing?"

Jinlah stepped up to her bedside, placed the water cup on the table next to the bed, and pushed her back down by her forehead. "You have to relax, or you'll make it worse."

"Make what worse?"

"It's been two minutes; he could die!" a female voice shrieked at another in the background.

"I'm doing my best! Keep counting, sister," she answered.

"No!" Hanhelin screamed despite Jinlah's recommendation.

Jinlah said in answer to Hanhelin's question, "There's an ominous…"

Hanhelin didn't like that word. As Jinlah trailed off, a meek little squall erupted. Now Hanhelin could lie back and relax, except her contractions persisted.

"Put your knees back up," Jinlah ordered her, feeling around her belly with five poking fingers yet again. "We're not finished."

The Grand Desteer stepped down in order to expedite Hanhelin's inauguration. On the day of her ceremony, she couldn't stay away long. With both joy and a great new level of confidence in her elevated position, Hanhelin rushed away from the banquet, which followed the sober rites of passage, to the spacious apartment she had inherited from the previous Grand Desteer. Jinlah moved to a more modest apartment in the Grand Chapel, meaning to be present to assist Hanhelin in her study as well as to provide guidance for how to handle the shaky political situation she juggled with the Tinharri clan. None of the Tinharri members attended her banquet, only Desteer members and a select few clan elders and their wives from across Norr, Lehomis Lockheirhen included.

Hanhelin had everything she needed in these days.

She strode past the two Moths who practically lived beside her door, guarding her home, and into the big main hall with the fireplace and huge window. She'd never forget the day she came home from her long campaign and entered this place to see her great-aunt sitting in the cold setting, waiting to hear her wild news but already half knowing it.

Tonight the space was warm with the fireplace well fed and the cradle placed close enough to provide the right amount of comfort. The other major difference was the huge, beautiful harp she had ordered brought in to play music for the ones she loved. She hurried past it.

"*Ameiha*," the attending Desteer maiden said. "You've returned so soon. Go back and enjoy your banquet."

Hanhelin couldn't hold her smile down. She bypassed the maiden and looked into the cradle. It had to be built big enough to hold three babies at once.

Three had come out on her day of labor, not one.

They were all sleeping. They hardly ever spent their time differently from each other. Either they were all sleeping or none were sleeping. Never one awake or one asleep. She tucked their shared blanket around the two babes on the outsides. Little Rem snoozed warmly in the middle. He was thought to be stillborn on their day of birth, the one who had struggled to take his first breath.

"I'm the Grand Desteer now," she whispered to them, brushing a finger over their silky yellow hair in turn. Three cute and tiny infants, the most beautiful people in the world to her. "I swear to you, on this day, I will use my office to protect you, my little princes. My sons: Adrayeth, Remenaxice, and Hathrohjilh."

The End... for now.

Thank you so much for choosing *A Basket of Devils*!
This story is very special to me and I've been dying
to release it for the past several years. I want to let you
know that though this book can be read as a standalone,
it actually opens the door for a whole series with a
generational progression theme. So buckle up!

If you like the kind of stories I write and would like to join
my mailing list of elite fans, scan this QR:

And PLEASE don't forget to leave a review on Amazon,
Goodreads, or whichever retailer you found this book
on. Reviews are crucial for hardworking authors like me,
who chose power and freedom over the constraints of
traditional publishing. Our books really can't stand without
YOUR support, so please help us out!
Thanks again, and see you in the next one!

www.jchartcarver.com

Glossary

Characters

Ari: Hanhelin's page.

Arson: One of Haus Lingor's devil sons; thought to be the "runt" of the quadruplets.

Bleed: One of Haus Lingor's devils sons.

Bludgeon: One of Haus Lingor's devil sons.

Cavlihen: The captain of Hanhelin's sect of White Owl guard, and also her personal bodyguard.

Deveghen: A member of Ferry Clan in Norr.

Enrha: An elven woman.

Gilqured: One of Haus LinGor's men.

Hanhelin: The third princess of Norr, destined to become Grand Desteer.

Haus LinGor: A rich and powerful man from Kell's Key.

Jiminick: One of Haus LinGor's men.

Jinlah: The current Grand Desteer. Hanhelin's great aunt.

Lehomis Lockheirhen: The elder of Clan Lockheirhen who wrote the book *The Questionable Tales of Lehomis Lockheirhen*, a famous series in Kaihals.

Lexion, Lady: A rich and powerful woman in the Darklands.

Linhala: A common Desteer maiden in Norr.

Manfred: Haus LinGor's hired scholar.

Nanelle: A servant in House LinGor.

Poison: One of Haus LinGor's devil sons; the unofficial leader of the quadruplets, thought to be firstborn.

Tobas: Haus LinGor's biological son.

Wikshen: A man possessed by a dark pixie who roams the Darklands to spread violence and fear for his own entertainment.

Yhulin: Hanhelin's handmaiden.

Places & Things

Banalweed: an illegal drug in Kell's Key.

Battleshift: A supernatural garment worn by Wikshen.

Braies: Underwear which covers the pelvic region.

Bright One, The: The god of the Norr elves.

Darklands, The: The northern side of the continent of Kaihals.

Dreadwitch: A supernatural sort of witch created by Wikshen.

Geomelding: A type of magic which allows the user to reshape the earth.

Great Sea, The: A god of the sea typically worshipped by common people along the coasts of Kaihals.

Ilbith: A very powerful city in the Darklands.

Jestmages: Street performers who use real magic to entertain.

Kaihals: The name of the continent.

Kell's Key: A city in the Darklands.

Ko Hanilka: The name of the palace in Norr where the Tinhiarri clan lives.

Kullixaxuss: The underworld, a.k.a. Hell.

Lightlands, The: The southern side of the continent of Kaihals.

Mastaren: A form of address to Wikshen used by his worshippers.

Morkblades: A magical practice only accessibly to Wikshen which creates temporary flying blades.

Neitherban: The most powerful house in the Darklands.

Norr: The country of the elves within a huge forest located between the Lightlands and Darklands.

Norrian: The language of the elves.

Raythite: A glittering mineral found only in elven blood.

Swine, The: The most powerful evil force in the netherworld. The king of Kullixaxuss.

Tinharri: The ruling clan of Norr.

White Owls: An order of guard who protect the Norrian royal family.

White Moths: An order of guard who protect the Grand Desteer.

Wik: A famously dark pixie.

Wikshonism/Wikshonite: The religion that follows Wikshen.

Worshippers are referred to as Wikshonites.

Wormsbury: A city in the Darklands and unofficial haven for witches.

Norrian Words

Aahmei: informal "mama."

Ah: "Yes."

Ameiha: "Mother." Formal. Often used to address a Desteer Maiden.

Amonimori: "Good morning."

Caunsaehgahn: "Coming into service" coming-of-age trial for males.

Cha!: A sound Norrians make in annoyance.

Daghen-saehgahn: "Guardian-servant:" a husband.

Desteer: "Whisperer" The religious leaders in elven culture.

Enherahp: "Conclude."

Er: "Desire." One of the "filthiest" words in the Norrian language and forbidden for elves to say.

Fa: "She"

Fa-Destrah: The queen of Norr.

Faerhain: "life carrier" an adult female.

Farenkin: "sister."

Farhah: "soon to be life carrier" a young female.

Gaulaerhainha: "Choosing her fate" a female's coming-of-age ceremony.

Guenhighar: pet name for a young boy.

Guenhihah: pet name for a young girl.

Hanbohik: The traditional dress for females.

Harran-henn-hi: "Thank you."

Hik-hik: Informal "sorry."

Kowhahere yuten: "Welcome."

Krons: A measurement about the length of a hand.

Lau-gaul-en-trei: "the lake of the dead tree," the final resting place of elves who have passed on.

Milhanrajea: "Mind Viewing." The practice in which a Desteer maiden uses her psychic ability to delve her sight into the mind of an elf to see their thoughts, intents, problems, and desires.

Pahkahen: "father" a more informal version.

Pawbhen: "papa" informal for father.

Sa: "he"

Sa-Destrai: The king of Norr.

Saeghar: "too young to serve" a young male.

Saehgahn: "servant" an adult male.

Sa-garhik: Traditional leggings worn by males, consisting of two separate pieces for the legs fastened to the braies, a garment that covers the pelvic area.

Sahbentrei: The most formal "Father," often used to address the king of Norr.

Sarakren: "He is forbidden." *Sarakren* is a status given to *saehgahn* who are forbidden to marry. This status comes with a brand on his left buttock (always visible between his braies and leggings) to warn *faerhain* away.

Sarenkin: "brother."

Tok: "No."

About the Author

J.C. Hartcarver is an artist. She can't write without painting or paint without writing. She lives in Tennessee with her husband and two birds.

Milton Keynes UK
Ingram Content Group UK Ltd.
UKHW042201031123
431935UK00019B/214/J